I0689201

Danny's Boy

LAURIE ROSSIN

Published by
HIGHVIEW CREATIVE
Eagan, Minnesota

This is a work of fiction. Names, characters, places and incidents either are the product of the author's imagination or are used fictitiously. Any resemblance to actual persons, living or dead, business establishments, events or locales is entirely coincidental.

Published by HIGHVIEW CREATIVE
Eagan, Minnesota 55121

Copyright © 2016 Laurie Rossin

ISBN 978-0-9978518-3-0

DEDICATION

This book is dedicated to all who have loved, lost and have had the courage to follow their hearts and love again.

ACKNOWLEDGMENTS

Special thanks to Cyndy for her insightful and honest feedback and editing of the first draft.

With loving gratitude to my first readers, Tom, Kathie and Bob, who couldn't wait to finish reading the book so we could talk about it on our beach vacation.

I so appreciate my dear Oak Cliff Ponds book club friends, Dot, Kit, Sue and Susie, for their encouragement, support and lively book club review and discussion.

And thank you to my husband Tom, for his steadfast love and his promise to carry my luggage when I become famous.

Danny Boy

Oh Danny boy, the pipes, the pipes are calling.
From glen to glen, and down the mountain side.
The summer's gone, and all the flowers are dying.
'Tis you, 'tis you must go and I must bide.

But come ye back when summer's in the meadow,
or when the valley's hushed and white with snow.
'Tis I'll be there in sunshine or in shadow.
Oh Danny boy, oh Danny boy, I love you so.

And if you come when all the flowers are dying,
and I am dead, as dead I well may be.
You'll come and find the place where I am lying,
and kneel and say an "Ave" there for me.

And I shall hear, tho' soft you tread above me,
and all my dreams will warm and sweeter be.
If you'll not fail to tell me that you love me
I'll simply sleep in peace until you come to me.

Frederic Edward Weatherly (1848-1929)

Danny's
Boy

CHAPTER 1

Danielle made the transition from small town schoolgirl to university coed without missing a beat. With her sights set on becoming a writer and intent on experiencing life beyond Sioux City, Iowa she had stood firm against her parents' desire to keep her close to home. Her best friend Ginny was going to live at home and attend the local community college and Danielle's parents strongly urged her to do likewise.

Her dad Richard O'Neil was an officer at the American National Bank and he took his fiscal responsibilities at home as seriously as he did at work. He tried to reason with Danielle based upon the economic advantages of attending the community college first. After all, he rationalized, credits toward a liberal arts degree could be earned close to home and at a lower cost.

Danielle's mom Nicole hated the idea that her baby girl, her only child, wanted to go away to college in the big city of Minneapolis. Danielle had always been a rather quiet girl, introspective and content to spend time socializing with her parents' close circle of friends. Nicole couldn't picture her daughter being happy in the chaos of a huge university in a big city without any friends or family nearby. She tried to convince Danielle to attend the local college for two years and then transfer. Secretly, she hoped that the transfer part of the plan would never happen.

After many discussions, Richard and Nicole finally

agreed to send her to the University of Minnesota where she would live in Territorial Hall, her dad's choice and the lowest cost dormitory for freshman students. Nicole insisted on a single room hoping it would make the transition to dormitory life a little easier.

Now that Danielle was here, actually living on the U of M campus, she was glad her parents finally acquiesced. She was thankful for the security of the dormitory and her private room. With over forty-five thousand students on the Twin Cities' campus, the U of M was absolutely enormous. Six months ago, she couldn't have imagined living among the three million people in the Twin Cities of Minneapolis and St. Paul, the crowded sidewalks and soaring skyscrapers. She was both intimidated and enthralled by the maze of streets and constant traffic congestion and, at the end of the day, she was eternally grateful for the quiet respite of her dorm room surrounded by the little comforts she brought from home.

Once she became acquainted with the students on her floor and dozens of others she met in class and at ZIPS, the Coffman Student Union's coffeehouse, classmates sought her out. She was a good listener, mature beyond her age of seventeen and a captivating storyteller. These attributes, along with her open friendly demeanor, quickly endeared her to new friends of both genders. By the time she got back to her room each night her head was bursting with the newness of it all, her classes, the massive campus, the interesting students she met from all around the world, and she needed the solitude of her own space.

She set up a strict regimen of study, exercise, socializing and of course, writing. After giving up on keeping a journal of everything that was on her mind, she had to be satisfied with writing about only the most remarkable experiences of each day. Likewise, she had so many stories to tell her parents and Ginny in her weekly letter, she couldn't possibly convey them all. At thirty cents a minute, long-distance calls were reserved for special occasions and even then they had to be kept short. Danielle quickly adapted to her new environment and loved being at the U as much as Ginny loved her classes in home economics and early childhood development back home.

Ginny Myers and Danielle had been best friends since first grade. The oldest in her family of six brothers and sisters, Ginny loved taking care of her younger siblings and helping her mom with the many household chores while her dad managed the farm. Her goal was to get married, have lots of kids and be the best wife and mother she could possibly be. She planned to home school her children so they would grow up immersed in the same strong Christian values that had been central to her own upbringing. But instead of convincing Danielle that being a wife and mother was a woman's primary purpose, she had been influenced to see the value in continuing her education albeit in the areas that supported her view of a woman's role.

Danielle's class schedule was craziest on Tuesday afternoons. Her Journalism and Mass Communication class, or Journalism 101 as she fondly referred to it, was in Murphy Hall at one o'clock followed by Speech in Ford Hall at two fifteen and Biology at three thirty in the Science Building. As always, she was late leaving her Speech class and was rushing to Biology when she heard a familiar call. Instinctively she stopped dead in her tracks and turned around but no one was behind her. Then she heard it again coming from the tree across the sidewalk – the call of the black-capped chickadee. "Fee-fee-bee-bee." In an instant, an unexpected wave of homesickness came over her as she thought of her dad and how he could imitate the call so well that during mating season, the chickadees would fly right up to him. The four-note whistle became their private signal and whenever her dad wanted Danielle's attention, or if they were separated in a store or crowded room, they would whistle back and forth until they found each other. Once at an Iowa State gymnastics meet, Richard had been out of town and Danielle wasn't expecting him to be at the meet.

Just before her balance beam routine she heard her dad's distinctive whistle and followed it until she saw him smiling and waving from the bleachers. She gave him a little wave and got the best score ever on her beam routine – nine point one two five.

She tried to whistle back to the chickadee but her throat was dry as she choked back the tears and lost sight of it behind the bright autumn leaves of the big oak tree.

"Now I am going to be late," Danielle said aloud. As she spun around to hurry off to class she saw a blur of blue and the next thing she knew she was sprawled out on the sidewalk.

"Oh my gosh! Are you all right? Let me help you up."

Danielle looked up as the man in the blue lab coat reached out for her hand. Being in a rather precarious position, she had no choice but to scoop up her books and her pride and take the hand that had been offered. As quickly as she went down the remarkably strong and handsome man pulled her to her feet.

"I am so sorry. Are you okay?" said the man with the most incredibly blue eyes Danielle had ever seen.

"Yes, I think so...not feeling too graceful, but otherwise not mortally wounded. It was my fault. I was following a chickadee and...well...not important...late for class. Nice bumping into you," Danielle said as she rushed off.

"Nice bumping into you? What a stupid thing to say!" Danielle wrote that night in her letter to Ginny. "I was so overcome by his amazing blue eyes that I was totally flustered – speechless actually. Can you imagine? And after just finishing my Speech class. That's where we learn to communicate with people. Ha! Ha! Wow! Was he ever cute! Blond hair, dimples – a real doll. I did take one glance back and noticed him walking into Lyons Lab in the medical research center. Maybe he's a doctor or something. I hope I run into him again – literally – and all because of the call of a chickadee. Well, I'd best hit the books. Say Hi to all. Love, Danny."

Danielle didn't mention the tears brought on by missing her dad's chickadee whistle nor how much she missed being outside raking autumn leaves with her mom. As much as she wished she could share everything with her best friend, she didn't want to admit to her that she missed home terribly. Ginny might mention it to Danielle's parents and cause her mom to worry. As she drifted off to sleep she softly whispered, "I miss you Mom and Dad."

In the morning she decided to stop for coffee at ZIPS before class. Not that the coffee tasted good to her, but with enough cream and sugar she tolerated the adult beverage of her parents' generation. And, the caffeine helped.

"Good morning, Jake," Danielle said as she reached the front of the line. "Busy in here today."

"Hi, Danielle. It's crazy! Want a job? Free coffee. Speaking of which, you look beat. Need a large cup today?"

"Yeah, I must not have slept well last night and I have to sit through one of those boring video lectures this morning."

"Okay, extra strength regular with three creams and four sugars." Jake had learned how to make the bitter brew palatable to his favorite customer. "Hey, I've been here since five and am ready for a break. Can I join you?"

"Sure but I'm not promising a stimulating conversation."

"No pun intended? After you drink this, you'll be singing like a bird," Jake said as he handed her the steaming mug.

Danielle's eyes fell at the reference to the bird, the gesture didn't go unnoticed by Jake as he rounded the counter and followed Danielle to a small table by the window.

"Up late studying?" Jake asked.

"Not really."

"Hot date?" Jake tried again.

"Very funny."

"Okay. How about I talk while you drink your coffee and wake up? Just nod once in a while so I know you're still conscious," Jake said. "Is everything okay? You seem a little down."

Danielle nodded. "I'm a little tired today...and honestly, a little homesick."

"Yeah, I get that. For as annoying as my sister can be, I really miss the little bugger. My folks, not so much but that's a story for another day. Hey, do you know Sarah Spengler? I think she lives in Territorial on your floor."

Danielle nodded.

"She's in my photography class and has been asking a lot of questions lately about taking pictures indoors in a dark room. That's dark room – two words. Get it? Never mind. Anyway, yesterday she asked me if I would be interested in earning a little extra cash and I said, 'Duh'. Then she launched into this long exposé on A.R.M.S. some student group she's in and how they need publicity. So I'm thinking, photographs, publicity, sounds like a no brainer. Then I thought, maybe Miss O'Neil would like to write a story for the Minnesota Daily. You know, see your name in print. You're a writer aren't you?"

"You know I am, you moron," Danielle was starting to wake up. "You're in my Speech class. Remember the first week when we had to do a speech on our career aspirations?"

"Yeah, I know. That's my point. You want to be a writer, you should do some writing."

"I do miss it. In Sioux City I wrote all the time for our school newspaper and even had some articles published in the Sioux City Star. I just haven't had time since..."

"You had articles published? Wow! What were they about?"

"Oh, just small town stuff. Anyway, back to Sarah. She's in my Mass Communications class and goes on and on about the media and how the press won't publish negative commentary against their big advertising clients, especially the medical community, blah, blah, blah. She's kind of a soap boxer."

"Yeah I guess she is, but I need the experience and it would be cool to have my photographs published, so I'm going to do it. They are planning an event, I'm not sure exactly when, but I think it's in a few weeks. Why don't you give me your phone number, and I'll call you when I get the details?"

"Oh, so that's it!" Danielle laughed. "This was all a ploy to get my phone number."

"Don't flatter yourself," Jake huffed. "If I wanted to ask you out I've had plenty of opportunity. We live in the same dorm, sit next to each other in Speech and I make your damn coffee just the way you like it!"

The truth was, Jake liked Danielle a lot. She was smart, strong and had a great sense of humor, not to mention her beautiful brown eyes. He looked forward to her visits to ZIPS and had a deal with the other servers that when she came in, he got to take her order.

"Okay. Okay. You don't have to get hostile," Danielle teased. She scribbled her number on the back of her coffee stained napkin and tossed it at Jake. "Just make sure I don't see this on the Coffman Union bulletin boards!"

"I'll see Sarah this afternoon and find out what's happening. Better get back to work; look at the line. See ya' later." Jake pushed back his chair. "Oh, and do think about working here. It's not a bad job and we sure could use the help."

"I'll think about it. Talk to you later, Jake. Thanks! Have a nice day!" she added sarcastically. That was one thing about Minnesotans that drove her nuts. No matter what was going on, people said, "Thanks, have a nice day!" *I bet these goofy people say it when they get a speeding ticket,* she thought. *Thanks, officer, have a nice day! Insane.* She drained her coffee and left for class.

Danielle thought about Jake as she waited to cross Washington Avenue, the busiest street on campus. *He is a nice guy, I just can't imagine dating him. His curly red hair and freckles and his plaid shirts don't exactly make him a candidate for the GQ best-dressed list. He is easy to talk to though – after I've had some coffee - and he does know how to make my coffee.* Danielle's friendship with Jake had happened almost without her being aware of it. Since she wasn't attracted to him romantically, she felt free to be herself around him and enjoyed their playful banter. She now realized that sometimes she told him more of what was on her mind than she shared with Ginny. She didn't mention her collision with the guy in blue though. It was either that thought or the effects of the coffee that brought a warm flush to her face.

One afternoon when Danielle returned to her dorm room there was a message from Jake taped to her door, "You won't be able to reach me. I'm out and about. Meet us at Jackson Hall at ten o'clock tonight for the 'event.' It sounds like there will be lots of people – bound to be a story for you somewhere. Hope I see you there."

Danielle hadn't heard anything about A.R.M.S. since Jake mentioned it weeks ago but assumed that his cryptic note was somehow related. Since most of her homework was done and the rest could wait until tomorrow, she decided to go down to the lounge to see if anyone knew what was going on. There was a group of students gathered around Sarah Spengler, clearly the organizer of whatever it was that was taking place. Danielle edged her way to the front of the group.

"The U of M tortures helpless animals in the name of science. They purposely give those poor creatures cancer and then cut them up to examine the tumors. Some of the monkeys have their brains exposed with wires and probes sticking out of their heads. It's cruel and we must protest!" Sarah said to the gathering crowd. "Join A.R.M.S! March with us tonight and send a signal. We will not tolerate inhumane treatment of any of God's creatures on our campus," she shouted. "We will meet at Jackson Hall and march to the Medical Center complex. At ten o'clock we will pass out flyers to the medical students and doctors as they leave the research building. Join our protest against cruelty to animals!" Sarah shouted.

Maybe Jake was right. She needed to get her nose out of her books and write a story. Danielle ran back to her room, grabbed a notebook and her favorite red sweatshirt, the one her dad brought back from his trip to Oklahoma, her *Little Red Riding Hoodie*, and headed out into the crisp November air. There were students already gathering on Oak Street making the turn onto Delaware and she could see others up ahead between Ford Hall and the Medical Center. As she met the oncoming crowd she took the flyer that was thrust at her, stuck it in her pocket and fell into pace with the group. As they approached the courtyard outside of Lyons Lab, she saw Sarah standing on a park bench with a megaphone in her hand. She wondered where Jake was and made her way to the front of the crowd. Sarah started the chant, "Stop the torture! Stop the torture! Stop the torture!"

The protesters joined in and pressed toward the entrance to Lyons Lab. Danielle was pushed along in the fray. At ten o'clock the light in each window turned dark and as expected, a stream of people in white and blue lab coats exited the building. As the crowd of students surged forward, flyers waving, Danielle lost her balance and toppled into the entryway of the building hitting her head on the concrete floor. Just as the interior door was opening out and about to crash into her, she was picked up and carried into the safety of the building.

"Are you hurt? I don't believe it! We meet again!"

Danielle, stunned from her fall looked up and saw, once again the handsome man with the incredibly blue eyes.

"Can you walk?" he said as he gently lowered her legs to the floor.

"I, I...my head...don't think I can," Danielle said as the room went black.

When she regained consciousness she was in what

appeared to be a small medical examination room. Next to her stood her rescuer. As she tried to sit up the pain in her head immediately forced her to lie down. "Ohhhh," she moaned.

"Hey there, can you tell me your name?"

"Danielle O'Neil."

"Danielle. Good. I'm Dr. Goodman. You have a nasty bump on your head – a possible concussion. Let's see those eyes. Mmm, brown with very large pupils. Can you try to sit up for me?" Dr. Goodman said as he gently helped Danielle.

"Whoa, everything is spinning," Danielle said.

"Okay, let's put you back down. Here, squeeze my finger. Good. Now, can you tell me what happened?"

"I was coming back from the coffee shop. No, I was going to class, I, I don't know how I got here."

"Do you remember marching in a protest?"

"Why would I do that?" Danielle answered, confused.

"I found this in your pocket," Dr. Goodman said holding up the A.R.M.S. flyer. "You were unconscious for a couple of minutes and I was looking for your identification. You really should carry I.D. you know and emergency contact information."

Danielle strained to see the paper the doctor was holding in front of her. "Everything is blurry. What does that paper say?"

"It's, ahem, information about A.R.M.S.," Dr. Goodman said choosing his words carefully not knowing the girl's involvement with the radical group – Animal Rights Militant Students. "But that's not important now. What is important is getting you up to the hospital to be checked out. You may have suffered a concussion and they will want to run some tests to make sure you're okay."

"Hospital? No way! I just have a little headache," Danielle said as she tried to get up off the examination table. She immediately fell back, dizzy and in pain. "Doctor, what's going on?"

"Like I said. I think you have had a concussion."

"Yeah, you said that," Danielle said as she closed her eyes.

"Your brain is composed of soft, delicate structures cushioned by blood and spinal fluid within the rigid skull. Surrounding the brain is a tough, leathery outer covering called the dura. Within the brain are cranial nerves that carry and receive messages that allow you to think and function normally. An injury to the head causes the brain to bounce against the rigid bone of the skull. This force may cause a tearing or twisting of the structures and blood vessels of the brain, which results in a breakdown of the normal flow of messages within the brain. Because of this damage, the normal function of the brain signals are interrupted which is why you are having trouble remembering what happened."

Danielle opened her eyes. "But I don't want to go to the hospital. Do I have to?"

"Well, I work down here in genetic research but in my professional opinion, yes. They should do a CT scan and keep you under observation at least until tomorrow. I'm going to call for someone to bring you up to admitting."

"Okay. My head is killing me and everything is blurry." Danielle said. "Doctor – what did you say your name is?"

"Goodman. Nick Goodman."

"Dr. Goodman, do I know you? Something about you seems familiar but I don't know why."

Nick answered, "You've probably seen me around campus. I teach a few classes here and do research." He didn't want to get into the details of their last meeting. No point in confusing her further. "Now, just lie still. I need to make some arrangements to have you brought up to the hospital. Do you want me to call your parents?"

"No," Danielle said. "I don't want them to worry."

"All right then. Lie still and try to stay awake. Count to one hundred. I'll be right back." Nick left Danielle and walked down the laboratory corridor to his office. All was quiet – no sign of any further trouble. After making a few phone calls he quickly walked back and found Danielle as he left her.

"Hi there. I'm glad to see you are still awake."

"Yes, but I don't want to be awake. My head still hurts and I feel..." Danielle turned her head just in time to prevent the vomit from spraying him in the face. Mortified, she burst into tears.

Nick grabbed some paper towels, wet them in the sink and dabbed Danielle's forehead. "Here. Does that feel better?"

Danielle nodded, not able to look up at his amazing blue eyes and afraid to move her head.

"Your head will hurt for a while. You may also have some dizziness and trouble remembering things. You might feel anxious or more emotional than normal. These are all a result of the bump on your head. I'll make sure they check you out to make sure there aren't other more serious injuries and hopefully you'll be able to go home tomorrow. I think I hear the orderly coming," Nick said as he backed toward the door.

As Nick looked down the hallway, a dark shape emerged from one of the doorways and walked toward him.

Nick called out, "Hey! Who's there? This building is closed for the night!"

A young man dressed in jeans, a plaid shirt and brown leather jacket emerged. There was a camera hanging around his neck.

"Who are you and what are you doing in here?" demanded Nick.

"My name is Jake and I...," Jake paused not knowing what to say.

"Jake?" Danielle moaned.

Jake looked past the doctor in the doorway and immediately recognized the pale face in the red sweatshirt. "Danielle?"

"Do you know this young lady?" Nick asked.

"Yes. She's a friend of mine. Danielle, are you okay? I've

been looking everywhere for you," Jake said, thinking quickly and covering his reason for being in the lab. "Is she all right Doctor…?"

"Goodman. Nicholas Goodman. Yes, I think so," answered Nick, "although she has a nasty bump on her head and likely has suffered a concussion. I predict she'll be spending the night in the hospital. Are you a member of A.R.M.S.?" he asked without covering his disdain toward the organization.

"No way!" said Jake. "I'm just a photographer and Danielle is a writer. We heard about the, ah, gathering and came down to see if there was a story in it for the Minnesota Daily. We both want to be published and I thought this story might be interesting to the student news editor.

"I was toward the back of the crowd, making my way toward the girl with the megaphone – you know, to try to get an action shot - and had just spotted Danielle in my viewfinder when they started pushing and shoving toward the door. After asking around, someone said they saw a girl wearing a red hoodie fall and thought she had been taken inside.

"Danielle, I've been looking all over for you!" Jake said to Danielle. This wasn't a total lie. He did wonder what happened to her but, in all the commotion, he took the opportunity to sneak into the building and make his way through the dark corridors to the testing labs. He found the caged animals, just as Sarah said, and while Danielle was unconscious, he had been taking pictures. It was pretty creepy down there in the dark with only sick, tortured animals for company. He was pretty much shooting in the blind using low light film and a low level flash. If there was anyone still in the building, he didn't want to alert them to his presence, especially after the pamphlet distribution had gotten a little out of hand. He hoped he had some great shots for the paper, but wouldn't know for sure until they were developed. Now he felt incredibly guilty. He had heard about the girl getting hurt and should have known it was Danielle. If he hadn't talked her into coming, she wouldn't even be here.

"Can I go with you to the hospital?" Jake asked Danielle and then explained to Dr. Goodman, "She doesn't have any family in town."

"Miss O'Neil, is it okay if your friend Jake accompanies us over to the hospital?"

"Sure," she said. "I don't care. I just want to sleep."

The orderly arrived and Danielle was wheeled through the tunnel, into an elevator and taken to the emergency admissions desk. Once there, Dr. Goodman made a few notes, handed them to the nurse and said to Danielle, "You'll be well taken care of here. I will stop in and see how you are doing tomorrow. Good night." He looked at Jake and said, "Keep talking to her. Try to keep her awake and, you may want to help her get a hold of her family. She said she didn't want to worry her parents but someone will be worried if she's not home tonight. Maybe a roommate?" He saw the concern in Jake's eyes and patted him on the arm, "Don't worry, she'll be fine." Dr. Goodman left the hospital admissions area, his steps echoing as his well-polished shoes clicked on the hard hallway tile.

It was a good thing Jake was there because Danielle had difficulty answering the admissions nurse's simplest questions about where she lived, her telephone number and the like. Once the nurse was able to get the basic information, she located Danielle's records in the U of M student database and completed the remaining paperwork. Jake waited with her until they came to wheel her into the CT scan room. It had been a long day and after the excitement of the demonstration, the covert photographic excursion and the shock of running into an injured Danielle, he was exhausted. He groaned to himself as he looked at the clock, he had to be at ZIPS in four short hours. He would have to start his shift by chugging the awful black brew himself. Luckily the coffee was free. *One of the perks of the job,* he thought and groaned again at his unintended pun.

Jake leaned over Danielle's bed. "Danielle. I have to leave now."

"Dad? Why are you going? Can't you stay for my gymnastics meet?"

"Danielle, it's Jake. Remember? Your favorite coffee guy?" He tried to sound casual but was worried about her. She looked so frail, her brown wavy hair and dark eyes the only color on the sterile white hospital bed and her mind definitely scrambled. "You are in the hospital and they are going to take good care of you. You'll feel better tomorrow. I promise." He reached over the bedrail and gave her a hand a gentle squeeze. "Catch ya' later."

Even if she had had the energy, Danielle had no time to respond. The X-Ray technician was ready for her and for the next few hours she was scanned, tested, poked, prodded, asked a million questions, wheeled from room to room and finally allowed to sleep.

She dreamt she was in the forest following the black-capped chickadee from tree to tree. She could hear the familiar "fee-fee-bee-bee" echoing, seeming to come from all directions. Her dad was calling her, first with the whistle, "fee-fee-bee-bee" and then, softly by name, "Danielle, Danielle." But when she went to him it wasn't her dad, it was a much younger man with red curly hair and freckles. For some reason, this didn't startle her. The man was wearing blue jeans and a plaid shirt and winked as he asked her to stand by the tree and smile while he focused his camera to take her picture. As the light flashed, she blinked her eyes to try to get rid of the white circles in front of them and as she did so she noticed the man was now wearing a blue lab coat. A lock of blond hair fell onto his forehead framing his incredibly blue eyes.

"Danielle? Good morning, Danielle," she heard and as she opened her eyes a bright light shone into them - first the left, then the right.

"I'm just checking your pupils. Good. They look much better this morning!" said Nick Goodman as he looked into her eyes. "Danielle, it's Dr. Goodman. How does your head feel today?"

"Is it morning?" she said as her eyes adjusted to the light. "That's weird," she said. "I was just dreaming about you."

"I'm flattered but what will your boyfriend say?" Dr. Goodman smiled.

"Boyfriend? What boyfriend?" Danielle asked as she looked up into the doctor's eyes. She could not believe how blue they were and how familiar; something about those eyes was very familiar.

Based on her tone of voice and the puzzled expression on her face, Dr. Goodman didn't think Danielle was teasing him and assumed she was still suffering the effects of the concussion. "Don't worry. Your memory and thought processes will return in time. Your pupils are back to normal and, it sounds like your vitals have been good all night. The CT scan shows an area in the left frontal lobe that was damaged by your fall corresponding to the bump on your head here," he said as he gently touched her head.

"Ouch!" Danielle said. "Didn't I see you in a park once? I remember something about a chickadee and some trees, but I think I was just dreaming and now I'm a little confused." Danielle's voice trailed off as she scrunched together her eyebrows, struggling to remember.

"Try to relax. You should be able to remember everything in time. Let me try and help you. A few weeks ago, on the walkway between Ford Hall and the Science Building, you were looking up into the trees and we bumped into each other. You and your books went sprawling. I helped you up; you said something about a chickadee and being late for class then rushed off. I didn't even get to introduce myself. Then last night, I was locking up the lab building and as I was leaving there was a large crowd of students pressing toward the entryway. You were pushed into the doorway, stumbled, fell, and hit your head on the concrete floor. Luckily I saw you before I opened the door into you. I carried you to the lab."

Danielle looked puzzled.

"You were unconscious for just a couple of minutes and then I brought you here to the University Medical Center for tests and observation. I thought you had a concussion and Dr. Ackerson confirmed it. Your boyfriend met up with us in the hallway and he stayed with you after I left. Do you remember any of this?"

"Sort of," said Danielle, "but it seems like a dream. So, you are my doctor and that's why you look familiar to me?"

"I am a doctor but I don't often work directly with patients anymore, not human ones anyway. Your doctor is Dr. Ackerson. He has been checking on you since you were brought in and I'm sure he'll be back again later. I specialize in genetic research here at the University and I just happened to be there when you got hurt. I took care of you until I realized you needed to go to the hospital and I wanted to check in on you today. I hope you don't mind."

"Not at all," said Danielle. "I'm glad to have someone to talk to who knows what the heck happened. Thanks for rescuing me."

"No problem."

"I'm still confused by this boyfriend thing though. You'd think if I had a boyfriend, I'd remember that!"

"Like I said, don't worry about it and try not to think so hard. You'll only get frustrated. Your brain needs time to heal so your brain signals can be transmitted normally again. This may take some time so try to be patient."

"I'm not a very patient patient, Dr. Goodman," Danielle said with a small smile.

"Very clever and a good sign that your brain is working," Dr. Goodman hesitated for a moment, "and since I'm not your treating physician, how about you call me Nick? My full name is Nicholas but please, just call me Nick."

"Okay Doctor, I mean, Nick. Will you come and visit me again?"

"That depends on how quickly they release you. Hopefully by the time I'm done at the lab tonight, you'll be out of here. So, you take it easy. Don't try to push yourself for a few days and keep Dr. Ackerson informed of everything, even if it doesn't seem important," Nick said.

"I will and thanks," Danielle said as she looked up one more time into those incredibly blue eyes. As Nick left the room she closed her eyes and wondered if she would have any more dreams about the handsome man in the blue lab coat with the matching eyes. She sincerely hoped so.

CHAPTER 2

He had made up his mind and it was now or never. Jake was determined to get into Danielle O'Neil's head this weekend even if it meant risking their friendship. He had convinced her in December, while her heart was still soft from the beautiful handmade journal he had given her for Christmas, to reserve the first weekend in March for a trip to Winona, Minnesota. Each year the U of M's Photography Club sponsored an eagle watching trip consisting of a coach bus tour from the University campus down Highway 61 about ninety miles to the Wabasha/Reads Landing area located on the Mississippi River where the Chippewa River flows into it. The migrating eagles are drawn to the area every year because of the ice-free conditions caused by the Chippewa. And because they stay close to this open portion of the river to feed on fish and perch along the banks, one can easily see dozens of bald eagles on a single day. It was a nature photographer's dream and Jake hoped he could get some prize shots.

He smiled as he remembered using the brief stop in Pepin, birthplace of author Laura Ingalls Wilder, as bait to get Danielle to agree to go. He wasn't surprised that she had read all of her books. *Little House in the Big Woods* and *On the Banks of Plum Creek* were her favorites and she had watched the television show "Little House on the Prairie" whenever she could even though, as she told Jake, "the books were much better." As a girl, Danielle had been impressed by the strength of the American pioneer women portrayed in Laura Ingalls Wilder's books and when Danielle was faced with a challenge, she would think about Laura grinding wheat in a coffee grinder to make bread during the terrible blizzard of 1880. Now, serious about becoming a writer, Danielle admired the author and particularly the story of Laura's real daughter, Rose Wilder Lane. Rose was a reporter for the American Red Cross and assigned to write about the conditions in war-torn countries following World War I. She published several novels of her own before helping her mother, Laura Ingalls Wilder, write the stories of her childhood – the *Little House* books.

After Jake mentioned the stop in Pepin, he was in! Danielle didn't pay much attention to Jake's explanation about the rest of the tour that would continue another thirty miles down river to the small town of Winona where they would meet up with specialists from the Minnesota Department of Natural Resources and U.S. Fish and Wildlife Service. On Sunday morning they would be guided to several prime bald eagle viewing locations in the Mississippi River Valley and study the wintering eagles at the nearby Whitewater Management Area. She also didn't bat an eye when he told her the group would be spending Saturday night at the Winona Quality Inn and if she wanted to, they could save some money by sharing a room – separate beds of course. Ever since that mix-up at the hospital when *Dr. Blue Eyes*, as Jake called him, mistook Jake for Danielle's boyfriend, she had made it clear to absolutely everyone that they were *just friends.* That was why this trip was so important to him. He wanted to be more than friends. He was nervous about the weekend but he was ready.

The weather forecast included snow flurries mixed with freezing rain and northeasterly winds from ten to twenty miles per hour so Jake was surprised but happy to see clear blue skies when he looked out of his window at seven twenty a.m. Saturday morning. It was only thirty-five degrees and it did look breezy, but as long as the sun was shining it would warm up nicely and the blue sky would make a nice backdrop for the majestic eagles in flight. He had carefully packed his bags and checked his equipment last night, but he couldn't leave without double-checking one more time. He quickly made sure he had his toothbrush and clean underwear. Other than that, he didn't concern himself with the clothes he had hurriedly tossed into his duffel bag. However, he did spend every second of the remaining five minutes checking his film, batteries, tripod, lenses and filters before he threw on his leather jacket and dashed out the door.

He spotted Danielle as he entered the student center and made his way through the Photography Club crowd greeting a few of his friends as he passed through. She was easy to spot in her khaki jacket with her favorite red hoodie underneath. He liked to tease her that she wore the red hood so that she wouldn't be mistaken for a deer in the woods. He was quite taken with her huge brown eyes, dark eyelashes and wavy brown hair and often thought her eyes had an innocence to them – like Bambi's.

"Mornin', Danielle," he said brightly as he put his arm over her shoulder and gave her a little hug. "I see you have your morning fix from ZIPS. I hope Dougie didn't make it for you. When I'm not there to watch out for you, who knows what he puts into your coffee."

"Morning, Jake. Actually this isn't too bad although not nearly as good as you make it."

"Well, are you ready? It looks like a great day. Let's get up toward the front of the pack. I want to get a good seat on the bus," Jake said as he steered Danielle through the crowd. He wanted to sit behind the equipment seat so there wouldn't be anyone in front of them. He was planning on some serious conversations and didn't want to worry about anyone overhearing them. Jake took the seat by the window and Danielle slid in next to him on the aisle.

As the bus pulled out of the parking lot, Danielle handed her coffee to Jake. "Would you hold this for a minute, please?" She reached for her backpack in the overhead storage area and pulled out several books. "Thanks," she said as she sat down and took her coffee cup.

"A little light reading for the trip?" Jake asked.

"I wish. I have a Sociology midterm on Monday and a paper due Friday for Environmental Issues. Listen to this assignment for the paper. 'The student will choose a current environmental issue and provide insight and analysis of an environmentally stressed situation. Include in your analysis modes of avoiding and redressing pollution in the context of cultural and social systems and customs."

"So what is your topic?"

"Actually, you gave me the idea. I decided to look at the environmental causes for the severe decline in the American bald eagle population. I have most of my research done and thought I'd incorporate this trip into the final portion of my report which discusses efforts made by the government and environmental groups to save the bald eagle from extinction."

"Cool," Jake said. "Hey, if you want, I can give you some pictures to include in your report – that is, assuming I get some shots this weekend."

"That would be great and I'm sure you'll get some fabulous pictures. You are one of the best photographers I know."

"I'm the only photographer you know."

"That's not true," Danielle said. "Look around you. This bus is full of them!"

"Well, I'm glad you are going on this trip for more than just Laura Ingalls Wilder. I was afraid you were going to read *Little House on the Prairie* books all the way and I was going to have to listen to that all weekend."

"Not to worry. I can't read on the bus for very long before I get nauseous. I did bring them along, however. I thought you could read them out loud to me," Danielle teased.

"Very funny! I had enough of that with my little sister. Luckily by the time she got interested in the *Little House* books, she was reading them on her own. It was kind of fun reading *The Cat in the Hat* and *Green Eggs and Ham* to her. I swear, I knew them all by heart. Sometimes out of boredom I would change up the words – I will not eat them with a pickle; I will not eat them with a tickle and then I would tickle Stephanie until she begged me to stop. I will not eat them on the bus; I will not eat them with a fuss. I will not eat them with a beagle; I will not eat them with an eagle. See, once I get going I can't help myself!"

"Okay, Dr. Seuss, I give up!" Danielle laughed. "I always wished I had a big brother and a little sister."

"Yeah, even though my little sister can be a pest, I wouldn't trade her for anything."

"So how old is Stephanie?"

"She's four years younger than me which makes her fifteen. It's so weird to think of her going out on dates. She's a knockout so she'll have plenty of boyfriends. So Danielle, I bet you had lots of dates in high school, didn't you?" Jake asked.

"No, not really. With gymnastics practice three nights a week and Journalism Club I was too busy to do much dating. How about you? Tell me about your first date."

Jake was aware that Danielle shifted the topic back to him but this time he had a strategy. He would be very open and honest about himself but also relentless in getting her to reciprocate. In the past, he hadn't even realized until later that she had totally avoided all of his questions. She was so smooth!

"My first date? It was with a girl named Laurie and we went to the Minnesota State Fair. I was fifteen at the time and didn't have my driver's license so my dad had to drive us. Not too romantic. We picked her up at her house on a Saturday afternoon and Laurie and I rode in the back seat while my dad drove us to the fairgrounds. It was hard enough trying to keep the conversation going without saying something weird in front of my dad. Once we got there we had fun though. We went through the arts and crafts building, her choice, the animal barns, my choice, and ate everything in sight as long as it was on a stick."

"What do you mean, on a stick?" Danielle asked.

"It's unbelievable how many foods are made at the concession stands and served on a stick: corn on the cob, pork chops, pronto pups, caramel apples, pickles. They even have deep fried candy bars on a stick."

"Num! Would you eat them with a lick; would you eat them on a stick?"

Jake laughed at Danielle's quick wit. "I think you've got it. Although I don't think they have green eggs and ham on a stick, yet. After feeding our faces, we went over to the Midway and rode the Screaming Eagle and a bunch of other rides that made me feel like puking my guts out."

"Are you serious? Did you get sick?"

"No but I sure felt like it. Laurie loved rides that twirl and spin you upside down and I didn't want her to think I was chicken so, of course, I went on them. In between rides I tried like heck to win a panda bear for her. Those carnie games are such a rip off! I spent a fortune before I 'won' a stuffed green frog for her. What a mistake! From then on my nickname was Kermit! It probably was appropriate at the time given my greenish complexion."

"So did you kiss her?"

"I don't think that is any of your business," Jake answered with a teasing smile, "but, I'll make you a deal. I'll tell you about my first kiss if you tell me about yours."

"What makes you think I've had mine yet?" Danielle shot back.

"Do you think I'm dense? So, is it a deal?"

"Just tell me. Was your first kiss with Laurie?"

"Maybe, maybe not. I'm not telling until we have a deal," Jake said.

"Okay. Okay. Deal."

"Our last ride at the fair that night was on Ye Old Mill. It's an ancient building with water flowing through it, dark and musty smelling with boats that float through a series of tunnels. It's really lame but it's the only place at the fair you can be alone and in the dark with your girl. Not that I was Don Juan or anything but I did like Laurie and we had a really good time together."

"So did you kiss her in the tunnel?"

"Sort of. I had my arm around her and it was really dark. Just as I leaned over to kiss her the boat bumped and startled Laurie. She was holding a stick of cotton candy that got in between my lips and hers. I can honestly say it was the sweetest kiss I've ever had!"

"Did you guys continue to date after that?" Danielle asked.

"That's another story. First you have to tell me about your first kiss."

"Do you mean my first kiss by a boy or my first romantic kiss, because my first kiss by a boy was in first grade. This boy named Timmy Zalinski told everyone I was his girlfriend and he chased me around the playground at recess. I was usually faster but one day he caught me off guard and planted a big one right on the lips. Yuck! I prided myself on being the fastest runner in the class and after that he never caught me again!"

"I knew the boys had to be after you with those big brown eyes but I had no idea it started that young! Now, tell me about your first *real* kiss."

"All right. It was in ninth grade at a school dance. There was a boy named Bill Nelson. He was in tenth grade, a sophomore, on the East High gymnastics team. He was a small guy, not too much taller than me but really strong. His sister was on my team – that's how I met him and since we both were totally into gymnastics we had a lot to talk about. I had a crush on him but I didn't think he liked me until the night of the dance when he came over to talk to me. We danced a few fast songs, he made them into athletic events, and then the band played "Colour My World" by Chicago. The bands all played that song to slow dance. Remember?"

"Yeah. That was one of the squeeze songs they played at our dances too."

"Bill was a pretty smooth slow dancer and at the end of the song, he kissed me."

"Did you kiss him back?" Jake asked.

"What kind of a question is that? But, if you must know, yes! It was my first real kiss."

"You know, I don't think I've ever seen you blush before. It's cute."

"Thanks a lot for embarrassing me," Danielle said. But even as she said it she was glad for reliving the memory. It had been a long time since she thought about that night and even longer since she had told anyone about it. She and Bill went out a few times but she was only fifteen so her parents didn't let her go out very often. Then both their schedules got busy and usually conflicted. Eventually her crush fell by the wayside.

"Did you date him after that?" Jake asked.

"That's another chapter. First you have to tell me about your second kiss."

"Very funny. If you want to hear about every time I kissed a girl in my life we are going to be on this bus for a very, very long time!"

"Jake! I didn't realize you were a poet *and* a lover!" Danielle said.

"Oh yeah! First I woo them with my Dr. Seuss lines, and then while they are laughing hysterically and off guard, I grab them and kiss them. Kind of like your Timmy what's his name. I don't care how liberal society is about roles and equality of the sexes, there is still a double standard. Guys are supposed to be out there putting notches on their belts and women are supposed to save themselves for marriage. When you were a teenager, did your parents talk to you about the birds and the bees?"

"My mom had a girl talk with me when I was at that age and by the time I was in high school my dad was working a lot at the bank so I didn't get into very many heavy conversations with him. I remember when I was in grade school we had pet hamsters in our room and one had babies. I was always very curious about everything that was happening around me so I think I had it pretty well figured out before my mom told me *the facts*. What I didn't know until just a few years ago was that Mom had complications when she was pregnant with me that prevented her from having more children. When I begged Mom and Dad for a baby brother or sister, they always just said that they were saving all their love for me. Until I got to know Ginny Myers and her family, I always felt sorry for kids in big families because I figured their parents didn't have enough love for all the children. Isn't it funny how things your parents tell you to protect you from the truth shape your entire way of thinking?"

"So do you want to have kids?" Jake asked.

"Yes and no. It's complicated," Danielle said. She was enjoying her conversation with Jake and didn't want to squelch it with her views on modern women.

"What do you mean?" Jake asked.

"Let's not talk about it now. How about we talk about something fun like," Danielle paused, "your first camera? Have you always wanted to be a photographer? I've wanted to be a writer for a long time – that is after I figured out I wasn't going to be an Olympic gymnast."

Jake had hoped Danielle would open up and wasn't surprised when she changed the subject. He did notice something different, however. She asked him about himself, as she always did with people. But wonder of wonders, she added a statement about herself. That was very unusual and a promising sign. He was happy to talk about his passion, photography and was still on the subject when the bus made its first brief stop in Red Wing. The students had about thirty minutes to take pictures so Jake grabbed his gear and they piled off the bus.

While Jake took pictures, Danielle made notes and described what she saw in her journal. Though Jake was concentrating on composition, light meter readings and f-stops, he couldn't help but notice Danielle as she worked. She seemed to take in the sights with as much focus and concentration as he, but instead of clicking the shutter, she would make notes in her journal. As they walked down Old West Main Street, Danielle asked Jake if he would be willing to take a picture of an old church from a particular angle. When he looked through his viewfinder he was impressed and praised her for noticing the great setting, the church steeple framed by the rocky cliffs with the river flowing beneath it. By eliminating the foreground with his zoom, the church appeared to be suspended in the water. He encouraged her to point out things of interest to her and by the end of their brief visit to Red Wing they were working extremely well together. Neither of them knew it but this was the first of many assignments that Jake and Danielle would capture as a team.

As Jake and Danielle boarded the bus they were talking excitedly, faces flushed from the still cold morning air, and anxious for their next stop, Wabasha. By the end of the day, the photographer and the writer were working as an inseparable team, a point that did not go unnoticed by Jake's friends on the trip.

While they were all having dinner at the Eagle's Nest, Danielle excused herself to go to the lady's room. Jake's friend, Curt seized the opportunity and said, "So Jake, you and Danielle make quite the couple! I didn't know you guys were dating."

"Who said we are dating?" Jake answered evasively but clearly pleased by the thought.

"Well, isn't it obvious? I mean, like, the two of you have been glued together all day."

"Danielle and I are just friends and we discovered today that we work well together. She has a great eye."

"She has more than great eyes. Go for it, man," Curt teased as he jabbed Jake in the ribs. The rest of the guys at the table joined in and were still whooping it up when Danielle came back.

"What's so funny?" she asked Jake as she slid into the chair next to him. "I could hear you guys laughing from across the restaurant."

"Nothing's funny," Jake mumbled, attempting to look busy with his salad. Each time he tried to stab the large crouton with his fork, it broke apart and pieces shot across the plate.

"I hate to miss out on a good joke. Tell me," Danielle pressed. But before Jake had to make another excuse, the waiter arrived with their dinners and everyone was busy making sure their order was correct, passing around the ketchup and then digging in. The fresh air had made everyone ravenously hungry and a hush fell over the room as they devoured their meals. Danielle had ordered a grilled chicken breast served with rice pilaf and fresh vegetables the odd, healthy meal amidst a sea of burgers, French fries and onion rings. She was content to eat in silence as the rest of the students ate and talked about the day.

Jake's friend Curt was the most talkative of the bunch and told stories of the perfect shots he almost had – the mating pair of eagles soaring overhead coming into range and then turning back toward the cliffs just as he was ready to take the picture. It reminded Danielle of a bunch of guys telling fishing stories about "the one that got away." Jake was not the bragging type and, having seen his work and watching him throughout the day, she was sure he had some beautiful photographs. He had coaxed her into posing for a few and although she feigned reluctance, she was anxious to see how they turned out. Danielle's dorm room was cluttered with many snapshots of her parents taken in the various places they had traveled and a few of Ginny and her family but aside from a picture of Danielle at a gymnastics meet, she didn't have many pictures of herself. When her senior yearbook picture was taken, she had the stomach flu and was fighting nausea. The photographer kept making lame jokes trying to get her to cheer up. The result was a series of poses in which Danielle looked extremely pale wearing a fake smile. She had reluctantly picked the best of the worst for the yearbook and deflected all attempts by the portrait studio to sell her hundreds of pictures for her family and friends. Her mom insisted that they buy at least one eight by ten to put on the hallway wall with the rest of the family portraits and that was the end of it.

She looked up and noticed Curt staring at her. "I'm sorry. What? Did you say something?" she asked.

"I said, a penny for your thoughts, Brown Eyes," replied Curt with a flashing white smile.

"Oh, nothing, really. I was just thinking about photographs and, of course the eagles. They are so powerful and free and yet, we almost caused their extinction. Wouldn't that have been tragic?"

"Yeah, but not as tragic as not seeing a smile on that beautiful face of yours. Jake, can't you do something to cheer your girl up?"

"His girl?" Danielle shot back with a look to kill. "Number one, I'm not a *girl*. Number two, I'm not *Jake's girl*. And number three, I don't need a *man* to cheer me up. So, if you'll excuse me, I'm going to take my tragic face back to my room so you don't have to look at it anymore. Good night!"

Danielle was still fuming as she fumbled to get the key into the lock of her motel room door. "What a jerk", she said aloud as she switched on the dim light and threw her purse on the lime green floral bedspread. Within a few seconds she heard a key in the door and Jake came in after her.

"Danielle, are you all right?" Jake asked. "Why are you so upset?"

"Why am I upset? I'll tell you why. I'm tired of guys who think women aren't complete unless they are on a man's arm. It's so typical. 'Smile, Danielle. You'd be such a pretty girl if you would just smile.' I could have killed the guy who was taking my senior picture. I suppose I could have told him I had reasons for not being Miss Congeniality - like I was ready to puke my guts out at any moment - but all he could say was inane stuff like, 'a pretty girl like you shouldn't be so serious,' and 'did you just have a fight with your boyfriend?'" She faced Jake and practically screamed, "Why can't you men take women seriously?"

"Danielle, please don't lump me in with Curt. I hope you don't feel like I treat you that way. I was so glad to be working with you today, not just because you are beautiful and I enjoy being with you, but because you are bright and thoughtful and you have a brilliant ability to take in the environment around you and see things that others are blind to. That is a gift few have and I am proud to be working with you."

"Thanks, Jake," Danielle said. "I'm sorry I flew off the handle. Guys like Curt really get under my skin. I shouldn't let them. Maybe I'd be better off just smiling sweetly and letting them think they're Joe Cool."

"No way. I admire you for standing up and calling him on it. I just don't like it when you put me in the same category. I'm sure your dad's not a male chauvinist – not possible knowing you."

"No, my dad's great. Since there were no boys in the family, just me, my dad showed me everything. He'd let me hang out with him in his workroom and show me how to use the screwdriver and electric drill. One time we made a little flatbed truck out of scraps of wood and some old plastic wheels. I was so proud, I ran up to show my mom and she acted like it was the finest vehicle on the face of the earth! She put a can of Campbell's soup on it and I drove it all around the kitchen delivering soup to my mom over and over again. 'Delivery for Mrs. O'Neil,' I would say. And she would say, 'Oh thank you. I really need tomato soup,' and hand me a penny. She never got tired of playing along with me," Danielle said as she smiled at Jake. "I wonder whatever happened to that little truck."

"You must miss your parents. They sound cool."

"Yeah. Even though my mom gave up her career to stay home with me, she and Dad always encouraged me to stretch and reach for the stars. I grew up believing that I could be a bank president, an Olympic gymnast, a nurse, a mother, a famous author or all of the above. Maybe it was because I am an only child but I never felt that my only purpose on earth was to get married and have kids." She glanced up to gauge Jake's reaction. Seeing only acceptance and a slight nod, she continued.

"My best friend, you know, Ginny, is so different from me. She's smart and talented but she has no career aspirations at all. Sometimes it's hard to relate to her. I remember when we were in our church youth group. We were discussing relationships, sort of a dating and marriage series of topics. Our pastor referred to a verse, I think it was in Ephesians, where the Bible says that wives should submit to their husbands and that the man is the head of the house. One of the boys in my class chimed in that women should be silent and take care of the house. I tried to interject that God wants us to use the gifts he has given us and that women can be leaders too."

"How did that go over?" Jake asked.

"Not very well. I got the nickname *Libber* – you know, like women's lib. Word got around school and the boys started teasing me about wanting to wear the pants in the family. I tried not to let it bother me but when it came time to choose a college, I knew I had to get away."

"I don't blame you, Danielle. If you ask me, people who believe that every word in the Bible is literal are kind of feeble minded. I mean really. With all of the scientific evidence on evolution, people still believe that the world was created in seven days? I believe in God, you know, but I got turned off to church a long time ago. It just seems out of touch with the times."

"I still go to church – I mean, I did until I moved up here. My mom asks me every week if I have found a church yet and I feel guilty for not going. It's hard for me to walk in, not knowing anyone, and then be swooped down upon to join. It's like I want to be an observer first. I don't know. I'm probably just making excuses."

Jake smiled. "I think you are like the rest of us just trying to figure out what we stand for and why. It's easier to just follow along with what our parents believe and not question anything. But eventually, you have to press the shutter and take the picture yourself. You know?"

"I do and I guess I overreacted to Curt's comments. I'm sorry if I embarrassed you in front of your friends."

"Don't worry about it. Like I said, some guys can be jerks. I'm glad you trusted me enough to explain."

"I do trust you. I've told you more today than I've shared with anyone for a long time. In case you haven't noticed I don't like to talk about myself and have found it easier to focus on other people's stories. Less conflict you know?"

"I think I understand why you do it. But you may find that your views aren't as radical as you think. I'm proud to be your friend and don't forget, friends are there to hold on to and watch out for when one gets too close to the edge of the cliff." Jake gently brushed the back of his hand across Danielle's cheek and smiled into her beautiful brown eyes. As he did so, she turned and gave him a hug.

"Thank you, Jake. Thank you for being my friend and for not thinking I'm weird." Danielle kissed Jake on the cheek and said, "Good night."

From that point on, Jake was her best male friend and she relied on him for advice on matters of the heart. Ginny was already serious with a guy at home and talked non-stop about marriage and babies. If Danielle so much as hinted about being involved with a guy from school, Ginny would start talking about having a double wedding. And her mom's dating advice always started and ended with, "Pray about it, honey. God will tell you if he is the one God has chosen for you."

For some reason praying didn't seem to make her relationships any easier. She struggled to remain faithful to her Christian values - *sex outside of marriage is a sin* - while maintaining her strength and independence. When she was in a quandary, Jake was the one with whom she could talk it through without having to be careful with her choice of words.

"So if I don't sleep with him now, how do I know if this thing we have is going anywhere? What if he's bad in bed? I don't want to marry a guy and find that out after the fact!" Danielle said.

"Exactly," Jake replied. "You know sex gets worse after you've been married for a while. If it's not good before you tie the knot you are doomed for sure. I think you should screw every guy on your first date. Just get it over with. Then decide if he has a chance of being a good husband and father."

"Jake, you are incorrigible!" Danielle laughed. "You know that's not what I mean!"

"I know. But if you believe that sex is a sin unless you are married, what choice do you have?"

"None really. Remember Jeff?"

"How can I forget? He was your first lover and I was so damn jealous I could hardly look at you."

"The chemistry was so hot right from the start. I thought he was the one. Then, after we had sex, which was great by the way..."

"Yeah, yeah. Don't remind me."

"I felt obligated to stay with him. I reasoned that God wouldn't mind if we had sex before marriage as long as we eventually got married. What a mistake!"

"You didn't even seem like the same person when you were with him. He made all of the decisions and you just followed along like a little puppy. He got insane when you and I worked together. Out of town? Holy crap! I thought he would explode. I never figured out what you saw in him."

"He was a jealous maniac wasn't he? At first I felt special that such a cool guy wanted me. He wanted to know everything I did, who I talked to, what I was thinking. I thought he really cared about me. Turned out he wanted to own me. I probably would have married him if he hadn't dumped me."

"Thank God he did! I know it broke your heart but I would have had to stop the wedding if you tried to marry him."

"Like in *The Graduate*?"

Jake set the phone down and pounded on the door. "Elaine! Elaine!"

They fell into a fit of laughter.

"Hey! Want to rent the movie? It's a classic," Jake said.

"Sure. You get the movie and I'll bring over the popcorn and a bottle of wine."

"You mean popcorn and beer?"

"Okay, okay. Beer for you, wine for me. See you in an hour."

So it was Jake she called after running into *Dr. Blue Eyes* the third time. Unlike the first two collisions, this was a classier encounter. Danielle was working on an independent study paper titled "The Effect of Social Roles on Individual Happiness and the Media's Impact". After completing her spring term finals, Danielle had arranged to spend a week in June at the Guthrie Theatre in Minneapolis interviewing the director and cast of *The Taming of the Shrew*. She was using the main character Katherine as an example of a woman who wanted nothing to do with her social role. Her shrewishness resulted directly from her frustration with her position. Because Kate did not live up to the expectations of how her society believed she should behave, she faced overwhelming disapproval and became miserably unhappy. In her paper, Danielle compared and contrasted the social roles of women in the sixteenth century depicted by William

Shakespeare to the roles of modern women in the twentieth century and how the media influences change in society.

Danielle was well-liked by the Guthrie's cast and crew and as she was leaving after her final interview, the day of the final dress rehearsal, she was given a complimentary ticket for opening night.

As she dressed for the evening, she tried to look the part of a patron of the arts instead of her usual *student journalist* attire and borrowed a little black dress and shawl from a friend on her floor. With her open-toed black strappy sandals and her hair in an updo, Danielle was quite striking and caught the eye of many as she made her way to the best seats in the house. She was surrounded by what she determined was the *upper crust* and enjoyed watching them sashay to their seats as she tried to figure out their stories - doctor, lawyer, old family money? She was thinking of how she could include this twentieth century societal impression in her project when the house lights dimmed and the play was about to begin. Just then, one last well-dressed man excused himself as he passed in front of several seated patrons and slid into the seat next to Danielle. She looked over at her neighbor and was stunned to see *Dr. Blue Eyes* sitting next to her. Before she figured out what to say, the first act began.

She tried to concentrate on the play but her mind kept wandering to the fabulously handsome man seated next to her. *Gosh, it's been almost two years since our first encounter and then the second when he treated my concussion.* She and Ginny and Jake had talked about him often, mostly in a teasing way about her crush, but they always referred to him by the nickname, *Dr. Blue Eyes.* His real name hadn't been important as she fantasized about him and now, here he was sitting next to her. *Dang... What is his name?* Danielle doubted that he would recognize her and imagined fifteen scenarios of what she would say or he would say during intermission. She couldn't very well say, "Dr. Blue Eyes. Long time no see!"

Well, he's probably married anyway. Then she glanced down and saw no wedding ring on his hand. *That doesn't mean anything. A lot of married men don't wear rings,* one of her pet peeves. Not that she was looking for a relationship, but she was often approached by men who were obviously hitting on her. It really annoyed her when she found out that one of her admirers, the owner of Mama Rosa's, her favorite Italian restaurant on the West Bank, was married and had four kids. Or when she learned through a friendly conversation with a teller at the bank that he was a happily married family man but noticeably wore no ring. *What's up with that anyway? It's like false advertising or something - you look available but you're not. Like the guy at the bank, not that he was on the move or anything, it just seems like a dis on his wife that he doesn't wear the symbol for all to see. If I ever get married, which I probably won't, but if I do, you can be sure my husband will wear a ring and be proud of it. In fact...*

The audience's laughter broke into her thoughts and she kicked herself for not paying attention to the play. She had seen most of the scenes rehearsed several times over in the past weeks, but this was opening night and the least she could do was give her new theatre friends her undivided attention.

The smell of his cologne surrounded her and seeing him again brought back the vivid memories of their chance meetings. Ginny still tried to convince her that those physical encounters were signs from God that he was the one. She remembered waking up with a nasty bump on her head looking into the most incredibly blue eyes she had ever seen. *Had he been wearing the same cologne that night? Gosh Danielle, get a grip! How could you remember that and what difference does it make anyway? If he's not married, he's probably involved with someone. But then, why is he here alone? Maybe his significant other got sick. No, there is no empty seat so that can't be it. Well, maybe she doesn't like the theatre and he, who obviously is fully engaged in the play and seems to be enjoying it immensely, goes to the Guthrie alone while she works out at the club. She felt a pang of jealously thinking about Dr. Blue Eyes with his beautifully trimmed and toned wife walking into the country club arm in arm...*

Again the audience erupted and Danielle realized with a pang of guilt and slight panic that it was almost time for intermission. She managed to stay focused on the scenes in front of her instead of the fantasies in her head for the next ten minutes and clapped enthusiastically at the appropriate times. At last the house lights went up and the VIPs around her got up and greeted one another – many already acquainted from the donor fundraising gala dinner or the recent wine-tasting party at the country club. Danielle suddenly felt awkward and out of place and tried to escape to the restroom, excusing herself as she began to leave her seat. As the object of her infatuation turned toward her to let her pass they came face to face and he recognized her immediately. "Danielle? It is *Danielle*, isn't it? Of course! You had a nasty bump on your head." Nick put his hand to his forehead as if pulling the memory from his mind. "It was...yes, the night of the animal rights protest. You wrote an article about it for the Minnesota Daily. My God! What are you doing here? You look fabulous. How are you? I can't believe we meet again!"

Another awkward moment passed as Nick's compatriots stood looking at Nick, looking at the beautiful woman next to him, looking at Nick...waiting. Danielle didn't know what to say. She was shocked that he remembered her and was utterly tongue-tied. Finally, Nick caught hold and introduced Danielle to the group around him. "I'm sorry. Everyone, this is Danielle – I'm sorry. I don't remember your last name."

"O'Neil," Danielle said. "Danielle O'Neil. Hello," she said to the group around her. "It's good to see you again, Doctor ... ?" She was embarrassed that she still hadn't come up with his real name.

"Goodman. Nick. Remember? Just call me Nick. So what brings you here tonight?"

"I'm working on an independent study and spent this past week here at the Guthrie. Yesterday, as I was leaving, they were kind enough to give me a ticket for tonight's performance."

"What a coincidence!" Nick exclaimed. "Yesterday, when I realized I couldn't use my other seat tonight, I called and released it to the theatre. I'm glad they found such a good use for it rather than having it sit empty."

Danielle couldn't resist the opening and blurted out, "Your wife couldn't make it?"

The man sitting in the seat directly in front of Nick's said, "Not his wife, his mother! Nick brings Liz to opening night of all the season performances at the Guthrie. Isn't he a good son?"

"Not for long," the man's wife chimed in. "I think Mrs. Goodman might be losing her seat."

Danielle blushed deeply but was quick to respond, "I know better than to try to come between a man and his mother."

With that remark the awkwardness passed and Danielle chatted comfortably with Nick and the rest of the group until the chime rang signaling it was time to settle in for the rest of the play. If she found it difficult to concentrate before intermission, it was nearly impossible now. Periodically, Nick would look over and smile or check Danielle's reaction to what was happening on stage. She was flattered and thrilled that he remembered her from their chance encounters and was giving her so much attention.

After the performance, Nick asked hesitantly if Danielle would be interested in going out for coffee and dessert – a tradition he and his mother shared on opening night. She graciously accepted and accompanied him to Piazzo's, an elegant restaurant on the fiftieth floor of the IDS building, where they had coffee and tiramisu and talked until well after midnight. It was the most exciting night of Danielle's life and she couldn't wait until morning to share the news. Ginny wasn't her best at night so she called Jake. There was a good chance that he was still up. She sensed an edge of jealousy in his voice or perhaps it was just sleepiness – after all, it was two in the morning and her call did wake him up.

"Danielle, he's got to be in his forties. Don't you think that's a little old?"

"He's only thirty-nine and besides, what difference does age make? We had the most wonderful conversation. We talked about the play and my report and his work. Did you know he works with Dr. Marino on the stem cell research team?"

"Stem cells, huh? Sounds like one of those mad scientist types," Jake said, not trying to hide his jealously.

"No, not at all! Nick is the most empathetic, well-grounded doctor I've ever met. He told me all about his work and how he wants to help restore health to people who have serious diseases – like repairing the pancreas for diabetics and restoring function to quadriplegics. He really believes that their research is on the verge of breaking through to some astounding results. You should have seen his face when he was telling me about helping children that have damaged kidneys. A life without dialysis!"

Jake couldn't help being critical. "All I know is that a lot of doctors in research are all about the fame and power that come with major discoveries. You know, name recognition – like Louis Pasteur – pasteurization."

"Nick is not at all like that. He is brilliant but humble. We talked a long time about God and the synergy between religion and science. We even shared our thoughts about having kids. The whole night was unreal! It was a little uncomfortable for me though when he talked about fertility treatment, artificial insemination and *in vitro* fertilization. I mean, when do we stop trying and accept infertility as God's plan and when do we use science to help us along? Or does God provide alternatives through medicine and desire us to make use of it?"

Danielle chattered on and on, and, much as he wanted to, Jake did not interrupt. He felt himself nodding off periodically but, for the most part, he stayed with her. He had never seen Danielle take such a serious interest in a man and since he had figured out long ago that there was no romantic interest on her part in him, Jake had resigned himself to the fact that one day she would fall in love with someone else and get married. She had dated several men since Jeff but no one had captured her heart the way Nick Goodman seemed to in just one night. He wished that Danielle would love him the way he loved her but if that wasn't to be, he pledged to Danielle and to himself that they would remain friends no matter what. Tonight was the first time that commitment was truly tested and Jake struggled to keep his jealousy in check. At last she seemed to be winding down. "Danielle, it sounds like you had a really good time and I'm happy for you. What a coincidence that you ran into *Dr. Blue Eyes* again after all these years. Maybe Ginny's right. Maybe it *is* destiny."

"Thanks, Jake. I knew you'd understand and I just couldn't wait to tell you. I'm sorry I woke you. Do you have to work in the morning?"

"Yeah, in about three hours so I'm going to try to catch some sleep and you should too. Pleasant dreams, Danielle."

"Good night, Jake. I'll talk to ya' later," Danielle said as she hung up the phone. Telling Jake about her incredible night helped make it real. She wasn't sleepy but as she lay in bed, reliving every word, every gesture, the smell of his cologne, she drifted between sleeping dreams and waking dreams and when she awoke the next morning, the two were undeniably intertwined.

After a long hot shower and a hot cup of coffee, Danielle dialed Ginny's number.

"Ginny? Hi! It's me!"

"Danny? What a surprise!"

"I know. I can't talk long but I just had to call you. You'll never believe who I ran into last night!"

This time when Ginny mentioned a double wedding, Danielle just smiled and said, "You never know."

"I'll be home on Wednesday – that's July nineteenth right? My parents are coming back from Spain on Thursday and I want to surprise them, you know, be there to welcome them home and hear about their trip. It's the first time they have been out of the country so it's a big deal. Are you going to be around?"

"Of course! I'm working at the day care center until noon. I could see if someone else can work for me."

"No. That's okay. If I leave here by eight, I won't get there until around one. How about I meet you at your house?"

"Okay, Danny. See you Wednesday!"

Danielle had barely hung up when the phone rang.

"Ginny?"

"Ah, no. This is Nick."

Danielle felt a surge of warmth when she heard his voice. "Oh, hi! I was just talking to my friend Ginny and I thought she was calling me back."

"I hope you are not disappointed."

"Are you kidding? No! I'm glad you called. I had such a good time last night."

"Me too," Nick said. "I still can't believe we ran into each other again. Luckily you weren't injured this time!"

Danielle laughed. "I agree! If I had ended up on the ground again for a third time, I think I would have to take the hint and stay clear of you."

"This time it was you who knocked me off my feet. I hope I am not being too bold but I can't wait to see you again. Are you by chance free tonight?"

Danielle thought a moment before responding. Her first instinct was to say yes but she had already made plans with Jake and a group of their friends. After her disastrous relationship with Jeff, she had promised to not ditch her friends in favor of what seemed to be a better offer for a date.

"Unfortunately, I already have plans. Do you remember Jake from my night in the hospital?"

"I do. Wasn't he your boyfriend?"

"No, just a really good friend of mine. I promised him I would play hostess and help him with a party he is having at his place tonight. He and a few of his photography friends are taking off next week on a camping and photo expedition in the Boundary Waters and others are heading home for the summer. It's kind of a *bon voyage* party."

"Well I'm disappointed but I thought it was worth a try. I should have known you would already be booked on a Friday night. Any plans for the rest of the weekend?"

"Nothing too exciting. I have to finish my paper and planned to work on it tomorrow. Why? What do you have in mind?"

"I have work to do at the lab tomorrow too. Maybe we could both take a break and meet for lunch? If you have time, we could come back to Lyons afterward and I could show you around. That is, if coming back here wouldn't be too traumatic."

Danielle laughed. "No, as long as it's not dark and I don't have a concussion, I should be fine!"

"It's a deal. Want to meet at Annie's Parlor at noon?"

"Works for me, Nick. I look forward to it!"

"Me too. See you tomorrow, Danielle."

Danielle's heart skipped as she hung up the phone. *How am I supposed to think about my paper with Dr. Blue Eyes waiting for me at Annie's? I guess I'll just have to figure it out!*

With Jake's party preparations and helping him get his place in some sort of order, the day flew by. Being with him and so many friends was good for her soul. She felt grounded and loved and happy. Of course, there was also the underlying anticipation for her lunch date with Nick. After warm hugs and prolonged goodbyes to Jake and his entourage, the night ended as the day had begun with warm, tingly thoughts of seeing Nick again.

Her alarm rang at seven and Danielle was up like a shot. She forced herself to spend three hours deeply entrenched with her coffee and the *Shrew*. Luckily she had spent so many days with the cast and crew in rehearsal that the blurriness of last night's performance didn't impede her writing. She reviewed and edited her earlier comparison of the profoundly different nature of the two sisters, Katherine and Bianca. As she reread the section of her paper that dealt with the social aspects of marriage and the impact the institution has on not just the couple but their family and friends, she felt her mind wandering. As a doctor, does Nick have a different set of expectations than Jake would have of her in a relationship as a couple? Would her being significantly younger and still a student influence her acceptance into his social circle? Since he is affluent, his wife would not have to work. Would Nick expect her to stay home and plan garden parties? She never worried about equality issues with Jake. They were in the same boat and both worked hard to make ends meet. Jake was supportive of her desires to have a career and encouraged her to pursue her ambitions. There were so many unknowns with Nick!

Well, he will just have to accept me as I am and either take the whole package or nothing. I learned my lesson kowtowing to Jeff to the point of losing my own identity. I won't do that again!

In this frame of mind she dressed for her date in her normal unglamorous style – a brown peasant skirt, white blouse and sandals. She debated whether or not she should put her hair up and opted to leave it down as she normally wore it in loose curls falling over her shoulders. She looked admittedly younger than she did last night but felt comfortable and determined to be true to herself. She just hoped she wasn't underdressed.

Nick stood as soon as he saw her enter the café and gave her a warm smile as she approached his table. He gently placed his hand on the small of her back as he guided her into her chair. She was relieved to see him dressed casually in jeans and a polo shirt and blushed at his obvious delight in seeing her.

The waitress quickly appeared to explain the specials of the day and after taking their beverage orders left them to peruse the menus.

"I usually have a burger and a malt here," Danielle said, "unless you have another suggestion."

"Me too. I think they are the best on campus," Nick said as he closed the menu. "So how are you doing on your paper?"

"It's coming along. Most of it is drafted so I'm now in the editing stage. I have a tendency to strive for perfection so my writing is never really done until I have to turn it in. Sometimes I think that if I didn't have deadlines, I would never finish."

Nick smiled. "It's like an artist. A painting or a musical performance can always be improved. In the artist's eye, it is never really done."

"I never really thought of writing as an art but I see the connection. Do you feel that way about your work?"

"Yes and no. In the broadest sense, there is always more to be learned, new discoveries to be made. In that way, research is never done. But when I'm working on a particular project, there is great satisfaction in solving the puzzle. It's kind of like electricity. If you make the right connections, the light bulb will come on and once it does you know that your work is done."

"Dr. Goodman, are you ready to order?"

"We are having hamburgers and malts. Danielle?"

"Yes. I'd like mine with just lettuce and tomato and a dark chocolate malt, please."

"Ditto. Thanks, Gloria," Nick said as he handed her the menus. "Looks like we have something else in common."

"Hamburgers, dark chocolate malts and what else?" she said with a smile.

"Great taste in theatre, of course," he said as he picked up his water glass. "Here's to another great performance at the Guthrie."

"I'll drink to that even though it's the only performance I have been to. My student budget doesn't leave much room for culture!"

"Well. I am committed to attending opening nights at the Guthrie with my mother but I would be honored to escort you to other events in the Twin Cities. Did you know we rank second only to New York in the number of theatre and arts events per capita? That and golf seem to be our claims to fame and I enjoy both immensely."

"I would love to take you up on that," Danielle said. "Ah, the arts that is. I don't know beans about golf."

"It's kind of a silly game. Grown men in knickers whacking away at a little ball. My dad is an avid golfer so I grew up with the sport. We play together every week – weather permitting of course. It's one thing we have in common and enjoy doing together. How about other sports?"

"Through high school I was in gymnastics but that's not really an activity one does as an adult with friends."

"Wow. I'm impressed. Did your family get you into it?"

"Sort of. My mom and dad weren't gymnasts but from little on I was jumping and tumbling around the yard so they decided to try to channel my energy. Based on our past experience you wouldn't know it but I can be rather graceful."

"I have no doubt," Nick said. "I was thinking last night of how we have literally run into each other and now, here we are. Do you believe in destiny?"

Just then the food was delivered and Danielle said, "That sounds like a question that shouldn't be answered on an empty stomach. Can I get back to you on that?"

"Yes. Let's eat. We can save that topic for later."

Between bites and slurps of their malts, Danielle and Nick chatted easily sharing details about their families, childhood experiences and interests. Building on his theory about liking the same foods, she put him to the test.

"Do you like vegetables?" she asked.

"Of course. I love vegetables!"

"All vegetables?" she teased.

"Yep. I like them all," he asserted.

"Brussel sprouts?"

"Yep."

"Broccoli?"

"Yes, raw and cooked."

"Cauliflower?"

"Yep."

"Asparagus?"

Nick's frowned. "Oh. Is asparagus a vegetable?"

"Indeed it is."

"I guess I lied. I detest asparagus. When I was a kid my mom served it out of the can. It was so stringy and tough that it never really broke down. It reminded me of a cow chewing its cud. Can't stand it to this day. Sorry!"

"Good to know!" Danielle laughed. "I'm glad we got that out of the way. I don't know if I can be serious about a man that doesn't like asparagus!"

"Now it's up to me to discover your fatal flaw. But first, let me get the check and let's head over to the lab. Maybe seeing some blood and test tubes will gross you out."

Nick helped Danielle up from her chair and guided her through the crowed café. Once outside, he took her hand as they walked in the warm springtime air the five blocks to the Lyons Lab building. They both stopped at the precise spot where they first met. Danielle hearing the call of the chickadee whistled to it in response. "Fee fee bee bee."

Nick seeing her whistling lips pursed as if to kiss, leaned down and brushed his lips against hers. It was the lightest kiss but one that Danielle felt to her very core.

CHAPTER 3

When Danielle arrived home on July 19, 1989, it was a normal hot summer day in Sioux City Iowa. The temperature on the American National Bank sign read eighty-one degrees and there was not a cloud in the sky or a hint of breeze. The humid air caused Danielle's naturally wavy hair to lie in damp ringlets on her bare neck and the hot vinyl seats stuck to the back of her thighs. Her dad's old pick-up truck didn't have air conditioning, other than what he referred to as nature's air conditioning - windows wide open. She didn't complain though. She was thankful that her parents gave her the old truck when she went away to college and since she didn't drive it much in the city, it felt good to be tooling down the familiar country roads to her best friend's family farm.

Ginny Myers got home just as Danielle drove in and after a few minutes of hot sticky hugs, they took off to give Ginny's brother Max a ride to his job at the gas station and convenience store near the airport. As they turned onto County Road 42, Max remarked on the height of the corn this season and insisted they pull to the side of the road to admire the head-high crop.

As they scanned the horizon Max suddenly yelled, "Oh my God, look! That airplane...the wings...it's tipping over!"

They jumped out of the truck and watched in terror as the plane passed them, too low, much too fast and obviously in serious trouble. First the right wing dipped and it looked like the plane was going to flip over. They heard a loud roar of the engines as the plane lurched, leveled off again for a short time before the left wing dipped.

"How far are we from the airport?" shouted Danielle.

"About three miles," said Max. "I don't think it's going to make it!"

"That plane is out of control," Ginny shrieked. "It's going to crash!"

The three watched until the plane was out of sight then stood horrified as a cloud of black smoke appeared followed by the sound of an explosion.

They piled back into the truck, all three dripping with sweat. As Danielle started the engine they heard sirens behind them. Waiting until the patrol car passed, Danielle pulled out onto the road and headed toward the Sioux City airport. The airport road was closed and the convenience store parking lot was already jam-packed with vehicles still streaming in. Max spotted a friend of his and rushed over to find out what was happening. They learned that United Airlines flight 232 with approximately three hundred passengers aboard came in without hydraulics and crash-landed just moments ago. Emergency vehicles and rescue personnel had been waiting for the plane to land and all non-emergency vehicles were advised to stay out of the area. The parking lot was chaotic as open car windows broadcast police scanner and CB radio announcements. Danielle, Ginny and Max were speechless as they tried to take in the flood of information coming from all directions.

The Red Cross was now appealing for blood donors and all off-duty medical staff were called to report to St. Luke's Regional Medical Center. One CB announcer shouted over and over, "This is *not* a drill! I repeat. This is *not* a drill! All emergency personnel and volunteers should report to their appointed stations." Instructions were given to police, medical personnel, volunteer firefighters, clergy and the general public.

Danielle remembered the air disaster drills her high

school Civics class participated in. The entire community was involved as they simulated the crash of a Boeing 747 with one hundred and fifty survivors. She had wondered at the time if anyone could survive a large airliner crash, but if there were survivors, Sioux City would be ready to respond. She had led the team of high school students that met in the East High gymnasium to discuss how they could help if such a disaster occurred. Danielle couldn't believe it was actually happening and she was both terrified and excited, her stomach lurched and rolled, and had her thighs not been stuck to the vinyl seat of the truck, she would not have been able to sit still.

"It's a DC-10 – that's a huge plane," said Max.

"Oh my God, those poor people!" Ginny burst into tears. "They're all going to die!"

"Ginny, take a deep breath," Danielle said as she took command. "Max, you'd better get to work. Looks like you will be super busy today. I'm going to go to St. Luke's to see how I can help. Ginny, you can drop me off then drive my truck back home to be with your brothers and sisters."

It took fifteen minutes to get to the hospital taking the back roads. As they neared St. Luke's they met a stream of emergency vehicles heading back to the airport. The latest news on the radio gave little encouragement as reporters and eyewitnesses described what they saw as the plane neared the airport and attempted to land.

"The right wing was tilted down!" a man recounted. "I was afraid the tip would hit the ground and sure enough, it did! I saw the plane cart wheeling across the runway right into Josephson's cornfield on the south end of the airport."

"It was awful," a shaky woman's voice said. "The plane broke apart and burst into flames. There was a huge explosion and so much smoke. I don't know how anyone could have survived!"

The reporter conveyed that the scene was still chaotic as emergency crews and firefighters fought through the flames and smoke desperately working to locate survivors amid the burning debris though it was doubtful anyone had survived the horrific crash.

As they pulled into the hospital parking lot Ginny lost control. "I can't do this. Those people burning! There will be blood. What if there were kids on the plane? Oh my God, Danny! Oh my God!" Ginny was hysterical.

Danielle reached over, put her hand firmly on Ginny's shoulder and tried to calm her. "It's going to be okay," she said. "I'm going to go in now. Take a minute to calm yourself and then drive straight home. Your family should be together and your mom is going to be worried. You know where I will be." She handed Ginny the keys, grabbed her backpack and jumped out of the truck. "I'll call you later!" she shouted over her shoulder as she raced to the hospital's ER entrance.

Just inside, as she knew there would be, was a command center bustling with activity. She hurried to the desk. "Hi, I'm Danielle O'Neil, a former East High student. I want to help."

Mrs. Jensen jotted down the girl's first name then stopped and asked, "Do you have any medical training?" She looked up at this slight young woman with intense brown eyes and wondered if she could handle the gory scene converging on the hospital.

"No," Danielle answered, "but I want to help. I'll do anything."

"Okay. There are shuttle buses loading right now at the East entrance. They are headed for the community college buildings and schools where emergency centers are being set up. The critically injured people will be coming here; those not needing immediate treatment will be taken to the centers. If you run you can catch one." Mrs. Jensen didn't think there was much chance that any of the passengers or crew from flight 232 would be taken to the centers and she even doubted many would be coming to the hospital – not alive anyway. She crossed Danielle's name off her pad. Just then, the doors burst open and for the next four hours Mrs.

Jensen thought of nothing other than trying to save the lives of the victims of the crash as their broken and burned bodies were rushed past her station. She directed the gruesome flow of patients, medical personnel, and volunteers, shouting out instructions and maintaining what order she could in the chaos. The phone rang incessantly, inquiries about passengers and crew. "Do you know if my wife was brought to the hospital? Have you seen my husband? I'm looking for my niece." She kindly but briskly transferred these calls to the passenger information desk where trained staff were on hand trying to connect families and answer questions from callers across the nation desperate to get word of the fate of their loved ones.

Mrs. Jensen did not think about Danielle again until eight o'clock that evening. A woman came to the desk - she thought she recognized her from church. Like so many others that day, the woman was distraught with a panicked look on her tear-stained face.

"Hello, please help me. I'm looking for my daughter's best friend, Danny."

Mrs. Jensen began to direct her to the passenger information desk.

"No, not a passenger, She came here to..." The woman broke down.

Mrs. Jensen went around the desk and led the weeping woman to a chair. "Here is some water. There, there. Drink this. Better now? Tell me your name. What can I do to help?"

"Thank you." The woman took a sip of water and dabbed her eyes. "My name is Marie Myers and I can't find Danny, my daughter Ginny's friend. She came here this afternoon after the crash – she wanted to help. I've been calling the hospital all afternoon and with the...it's just awful...the crash... so many dead. We've been watching the news and...got the call...I don't know where Danny is! I couldn't get anyone on the phone who could help me. I had to come here." Marie broke down again.

"Mrs. Myers is it?"

"Yes. Marie."

"Marie. As you can imagine, we've all been very busy and of course our first priority has been the injured. Terrible tragedy. Terrible. I've been here all day – it's all a blur, so many people, but I will try to help you if I can. Now, tell me what happened."

"Danny was with my son and daughter out by Nelson's place, when the plane was coming in. They..."

Mrs. Jensen broke in. "Oh my gosh! Did they get hurt? I thought they had all the roads blocked. There's no way she..."

"No she didn't get hurt. She and Max and Ginny saw the plane coming in. It was tipping and lurching. Danny heard about the emergency on the radio and came here to help. But I've been through the entire hospital asking about her. No one remembers seeing her."

"Okay. Sit tight and drink the rest of that water while I look at my list. I have a record of all of the volunteers who checked in here at St. Luke's. It's part of the disaster plan. Let's see. Do you know about what time she was here? There were people coming and going all day and it might help me locate her."

Marie looked at her watch. "I just don't know. This day has been so awful - I haven't even looked at the time."

"It's all right," Mrs. Jensen said as she tried to calm Marie. "We'll find her. Okay, you said they saw the plane coming in and then came right to the hospital so she would have been here early this afternoon, not later. We had about thirty minutes notice before the plane, um ... So, she is probably on the first page. Let's see, Jack Peterson, Mary and Ted Brown, Gladys Reinhart. I don't see a Danny. Wait! Yes, now I remember. There was a young woman. What was her name again? Here it is, Danielle! Is that her? I crossed her name out because she didn't stay at the hospital. Yes, I remember her now. Small, pretty young thing. I sent her over to the remote emergency centers to help. That's where any victims that were not seriously injured were taken. I never thought there would be any, but quite a few passengers were transported there. Also some of the friends and families, reporters and so on that have come from out of the area are staying at the schools. If she is there she's had a busy afternoon too."

Marie grabbed her purse. "Do you know which school she might be at?" she said as she stood up to leave.

"No, but I'd try either Morningside or Briar Cliff first. Being closest to the airport, they probably received the first groups. I'm sure she's just fine. Try not to worry," Mrs. Jensen said as Marie rushed to leave.

Marie stopped and turned, tears streaming down her face. "You don't understand. Danny's parents were on that plane!"

As Marie Myers left the desk a man carrying a medical bag arrived.

"Hello. I'm Doctor Nicholas Goodman. I work at the University of Minnesota's medical research facility," he said as he showed her his campus photo identification. A friend of mine is from Sioux City so when I heard about the crash, I hopped in my car. I'm not licensed to treat patients in your hospital but I'd like to help in any way I can."

Thinking quickly, Mrs. Jensen pointed toward the door behind him. "See the woman exiting through the revolving doors? She is headed to one of the emergency centers where the less critical patients are being taken. I'm sure they could use your help."

"Thank you," Nick said as he dashed out to catch her. After a brief explanation, Nick got into his car and followed Mrs. Myers as she sped to Morningside Middle School.

By the time Nick reached the command center's reception desk, the distraught Mrs. Myers was being directed to the school's gymnasium. He gleaned that she was looking for her son, Danny.

After another brief introduction Nick too was sent to the gym to help tend to the injured. There was a lot of noisy activity in the room but things appeared to be well organized and under control. He walked up and down the rows of cots and chairs checking vitals and bandages that had been hastily applied earlier in the day. He was astounded that so many had escaped and with just minor injuries. As he rounded the corner, he saw Mrs. Myers's back as she held a young woman close. As he approached he could see the brown hair of a girl whose face was buried in Mrs. Myers's bosom. Just then the girl lifted her face and Nick was stunned to be looking directly into Danielle's red swollen eyes.

"Nick? What are you doing here?" she gasped.

"Danielle. My God! Are you all right?" he said as she left Mrs. Myers's embrace and fell into Nick's. He saw Mrs. Myers sadly shaking her head no. "Are you hurt?"

As Danielle tried to compose herself, Nick held her shoulders firmly and looked into her face. "It's okay. I'm here. Tell me what happened."

"My...my parents," Danielle stuttered. "They weren't supposed to be home until tomorrow...from...from Spain." Danielle was sobbing. "They were...were on the plane."

Nick saw tears streaming down Mrs. Myers's face and reached out to her. The three huddled together forever bonded by Danielle's profound grief.

CHAPTER 4

Being alone in her childhood home for the first time since the accident was both terrifying and comforting. After spending three full weeks living with Ginny's family, Danielle was looking forward to the much-needed solitude and felt ready to face her grief in private.

Nick had stayed by her side for the first four awful days. He had an amazing ability to help her clarify her thoughts and feelings while allowing her to make the decisions about her parents' funeral and burial. He held her close as she cried and didn't try to answer her agonizing question to God, "Why?" He allowed her to stand strong on her own or crumble into his arms as a child. And when she pushed him away, needing to be alone, he retreated without malice. The tragic experience had not only endeared him to Danielle but to Ginny and the Myers' family as well. He roughhoused with the boys, had long conversations with Hal about the science of agriculture and graciously accepted the healing power of comfort food prepared by Marie, Ginny and the girls. After the funeral he had to go back to work but while in Minneapolis he called Danielle every day. He even drove down twice to visit, much to the delight of the entire Myers family and, of course, Danielle.

She now understood the comfort of a large family and knew that without Ginny, Marie and Hal and the kids, she would not have made it. When she needed to talk, Ginny and Marie were there for her. But mostly, just being surrounded by the normal, everyday activities of the busy farm family helped her cope. She felt most vulnerable in the quiet of the night but she often fell asleep to the soothing sound of Nick's voice on the phone. They talked about everything from world events, politics, sitcoms and sports to God, life and death.

One night when she was once again questioning why God would take her parents when one hundred and eleven other lives were miraculously spared, Nick asked her a question. "Danny," for he had since adopted her childhood nickname, "if medical science made it possible to bring your parents back, would you do it?"

"Of course! I desperately wish that they were still alive. And I don't believe it when people say it was God's plan to take them to heaven now. God didn't micromanage their travel arrangements or cause them to change their flight. And I certainly don't think God is so cruel as to want me to suffer this way!"

"I don't believe that either," Nick said. "I believe in a loving God that cries with us when we suffer and holds us up when we are too weak to make it on our own. But I believe He does that through people. If in some way my physical touch comforted you, that was God using me to show His love for you. I think about that a lot in my work."

"What do you mean?"

"Well, you know that we are working on a process to rebuild damaged bodily systems through the use of stem cells. The potential benefits to humankind are enormous but critics accuse us of playing God."

"Do they think that if a child has diabetes, it's God's will and you shouldn't try to cure her?"

"I suppose some feel that way. The main objection though is that we are using human stem cells from embryos that were created through *in vitro* fertilization. So, not only are we creating new life outside of the way God designed it to be created, we are also destroying that same life in order to save another."

"Hmmmm. I guess since babies are a result of the merging of an egg and a sperm, it shouldn't really matter if that union happens naturally or with help. I'm not sure how I feel about *in vitro* though. I don't know if I would go that route myself. My mom always said that if God wants me to be a parent, He will make it happen!"

"Yes but doesn't God work through man – in this case both literally and figuratively?"

"Dr. Goodman, you are making me blush!"

"Sorry. But I do want to explore that topic further the next time we are together."

"Uh huh. Me too."

"Anyway, when I am at work, I feel like I am just working with biological material in a tube or under a microscope. But, if I really think about it, we can't precisely answer the question of when life begins. And if we can't answer that, don't we have the same dilemma surrounding when life ends?"

"I know what you mean. In a way, I am glad Mom and Dad died instantly so I didn't have to make the decision some of the other families did - whether or not to remove life support. As awful as it was, my parents were gone and there was no chance for survival. But what if they had somehow been kept alive by machines? I think you are asking if I would want medical science to use extraordinary means to essentially bring them back to life?"

"Exactly. At what point are we mere humans providing our hands and minds to God and when are we stepping over the line to fulfill our own will over God's?"

"My mom would say, *pray about it.* I don't know how God answers our prayers but I do believe that he listens and somehow provides the answers and the guidance we need," Danielle said.

"Good advice," Nick said. "I should let you go. It's almost midnight and I have an early start tomorrow. I'm playing golf with Dad in the morning and he booked a six thirty tee time."

"Arggg. That's way too early for me! Enjoy!"

"Good night, Danny. Sweet dreams."

"Night, Nick."

In the morning, Danielle pondered the task in front of her. It was enormous so she started by making a list. She had already met once with her parents' attorney regarding their estate but wanted to talk with him again after reading through their Last Will and Testament documents. Jim Oliver had assured her that everything was in order but it would take some time for the estate to be settled through probate. She didn't really understand what that meant and wanted to meet with him again soon. The whole thing overwhelmed her, so in a way, she was glad that she didn't have to decide what to do with the property just yet. She did wonder about money for school though.

As she sipped her morning coffee she looked out at her mother's beautiful gardens. The recent rain and hot weather had nourished not only the perennials but also the weeds. Abandoning her list, she found a pair of gloves and headed outside. The years spent with her mom in the garden flashed through her mind as she attacked the weeds and tended the flowers. A few times she yanked on what she thought was a weed but when it didn't yield, she decided it must be a flower. She closed her eyes and could almost hear her mom's voice naming the flowers and bordering shrubs. When the silence was interrupted by the sound of two chickadees calling back and forth across the yard she felt the hot tears on her cheeks. Wiping her sweaty face on her shirtsleeve, she attacked the job in front of her with vehemence until her muscles ached and her mind was clear. After dumping the weeds in the woods and cleaning the tools, she went inside for a cool drink and a warm shower.

Dressed only in a T-shirt, she walked from room to room. Everything was exactly as her parents had left it before their trip and yet nothing was the same. The furniture seemed to cry out in its emptiness, the kitchen begged to be used. Her mind tricked her into thinking that Mom and Dad would walk in at any moment and then jerked her back to the harsh reality that they were dead. The phone rang.

"Mrs. O'Neil?"

"No, she is not here. This is Danielle, her daughter."

"I am calling from the Lupus Foundation. When do you expect her?"

Unable to answer, Danielle hung up the phone.

She heard the mail drop through the slot in the front door. She flipped through the stack of bills, credit card offers and advertisements addressed to Richard and Nicole O'Neil before spotting a plain white envelope with her name on it. Inside was a beautiful photograph of a pileated woodpecker and a handwritten note that said:

"Dear Danielle,

We arrived home on Tuesday and when I couldn't reach you, I got concerned. I hope you don't mind but I went to the lab and Nick told me what happened. I am so very sorry especially that I wasn't there for you. He said the funeral was beautiful and that you are holding up as good as can be expected. Please call me when you get this.

Love, Jake"

Danielle had thought about Jake but in the blur of the past weeks, lost track of time and forgot when he said he would be returning from the Boundary Waters. She immediately picked up the phone and dialed his number.

After a long conversation and promises to talk again soon, Danielle hung up emotionally exhausted. Telling Jake about everything that had happened in the past weeks was like ripping a bandage off a fresh wound. She retreated to her girlish bedroom and curled up on the pink flowery bedspread. When she woke up, the sun was already low in the sky streaming in through the west windows. Groggy but ravenous, Danielle headed down to the kitchen in search of something to eat. Ignoring the questionable food in the refrigerator, she popped a frozen pizza in the oven and went back to her list. At the top she wrote, "Finish Shrew paper. Register for fall classes."

With school back at the top of the list, the other items seemed to fall into place. She wasn't emotionally ready to go through the house or her parent's belongings and since probate would take time, there wasn't a rush to do anything now. She decided that she would spend some time here during the summer but maintain her campus apartment as planned. She would talk to Marie and Hal and ask if they could keep an eye on the house. Maybe the boys could mow the yard. Since most of the mail was for her parents, she would have it forwarded to the attorney's office.

Glancing at the clock, she reached for the phone but before she could pick it up, it rang.

"Hello?"

"Hi, it's Ginny."

"Too weird! I was just going to call you. How are you?"

"I am so excited! You are the first to hear the news."

"What news?"

"Paul asked me to marry him!"

"No way! Really?" Danielle said. "Oh my gosh! And you said yes, right?"

"Of course! We have been talking about it for a while and I actually thought he might propose on the Fourth of July. We were watching the fireworks and it was so romantic. I thought it would have been the perfect night. Well, anyway. He just got promoted at the grain elevator and we went out to celebrate and he popped the question. He bought an engagement ring and everything. I am so happy!" Ginny gushed.

"Oh, Ginny. I am so happy for you! Have you set a date?"

"Not yet but we are talking about a December wedding. It's a slow time for him at work and the church will be all decorated for Christmas. Danny, will you be my maid of honor?"

"Are you kidding? We have been talking about this since fifth grade!"

"I know and now it's finally happening! Will you help me pick a wedding dress? And what about your dress? I think it should be red."

"I think you and your mom should plan a trip to Minneapolis. You can stay at my place and we can all go shopping together."

"Oh yes! That sounds great. Sioux City doesn't have that much selection and I want everything to be perfect."

"It will be," Danielle said. "Hey, before you called I was sitting here thinking about what to do with the house."

"Oh dear, I'm sorry," Ginny said. "That must be hard."

"It was until I made my list. Nothing can be done until after it goes through probate and I have one more year of school anyway. Now with your news, I wonder if maybe you and Paul would like to live here at least temporarily. That is, unless you already have other plans."

"This is an answer to my prayers! We want to work and save up for a house but that's not going to happen before the wedding. Of course I'll want to talk it over with my *fiancé'* but I can't imagine him not loving the idea."

"Oh my gosh! You have a *fiancé'*. I can't believe it!"

"Me either! I have a feeling you will have one soon too. Nick is amazing. I have to admit. I pictured him a little stuffy being a big city doctor and all. But he is so down-to-earth. Have you noticed how he plays with the kids? My entire family loves him and in case you haven't admitted it yet, you do too," Ginny said.

"There you go again. Planning a double wedding. Let's just focus on yours for now. Ginny, I am so happy for you. I love you like a sister!"

"Me too! Danny? I think my mom and dad are home. Time to share the news!"

"Talk to you later. 'Bye."

Later that night, Nick sounded happy when Danielle told him the news. He patiently listened as she chattered about shopping trips for dresses, a bridal shower over Thanksgiving and the romance of a Christmas Season wedding. Of course he was happy for Ginny and Paul, but even more grateful to hear the smile in Danielle's voice.

"Oh, and I forgot to tell you," Danielle said. "I told Ginny she and Paul can live here. I will be busy finishing my degree and the lawyer said probate will take a long time. This way there will be someone taking care of the house until I'm ready to decide what to do with everything. I can't tell you what a relief it is to not have that on my mind. Of course I'll have to pack some things away to make room for the newlyweds. Ginny can help and maybe she can move in sooner to get things set up. It all happened so fast! What do you think?"

"I think it's a good idea. I'm proud of you for figuring it out and relieved to hear that you will be coming back to Minneapolis."

"Was there ever any doubt?"

"It did cross my mind. You have been dealing with a huge loss. I've seen how life can twist and turn in unexpected directions."

Danielle was silent for a moment. "Nick? May I ask you a personal question?"

"Of course. You know you can talk to me about anything."

"How come you have never been married? You haven't been, have you?"

Nick smiled at her innocence. "No, my dear one. I have never been married. I've been close a couple of times but, as I said, sometimes life doesn't follow the course we have mapped out in our minds."

"Would you mind telling me about it? I mean, about the women in your life?"

"Hmmm. Where to start."

"That many, huh?"

"No, not really. Like most guys, I guess, I dated a few girls in high school and college. Nothing too serious until I met Nancy. I was pre-med and she was the younger sister of one of my close classmates, Matt. There was a group of guys that studied and partied together. For me, mostly the former,"

"Yeah. Right."

"No, really! The classes were intense. Matt and I would quiz each other on stuff, like anatomy, and end up making kind of a game of it. At the end of the night, we'd have a beer and I'd crash on his couch. A couple times, his sister Nancy came over with a friend of hers and the four of us would hang out together. She and I hit it off and things got serious."

"So, what happened?"

"I guess the timing wasn't right. My course load was crushing and I had a long road ahead. She started to complain that school was more important than she was and that I didn't spend enough time with her. I loved her, but she was right. She wanted to get married and I wasn't ready to make that commitment. I guess you could summarize it by saying that my education took priority and our relationship fell apart as a result."

"That's too bad."

"Yeah. She was a great girl but looking back on it now, I don't think it would have worked. She was really needy and dependent on me. True, I didn't have the time to devote to her but I knew even then that I wanted an equal partner as a mate. After that, I didn't have a serious relationship for a long time. School kept me busy and I purposely stayed detached. Then I met Robin."

"Robin? That's a nice name," Danielle said. "How did you meet?"

"We met during our surgical rotation. Robin was a brilliant student and shared my passion for medicine. She had a surgeon's hands and nerves of steel – a natural talent for surgery. She was hooked! I was more interested in genetics and research but I was very interested in her so I found my time in surgery both daunting and rewarding. We connected and essentially lived together for two years. Our life was a flurry of weird schedules, exhausting shifts and medical speak. She was not only my equal but in some ways, her drive and skills surpassed my own."

"Was that hard for you?"

"Not really. Our interests were in different areas so there never was a feeling of competition. We supported each other's ambitions and celebrated the victories, small and large. The turning point came when she was accepted into Harvard's surgical residency program. It's incredibly competitive and there was no doubt that she would accept it but we struggled to figure out how to manage our relationship. I had been offered a research residency here at the U and was excited to work with Doctor Marino. That's Sonny, my current boss."

"Oh yes. I met him that day you took me to the lab."

"The U had just received a major grant and I had the opportunity to get in on the ground floor of the molecular genetics project which led us into the area of stem cell research."

"So you both had amazing opportunities but in cities a thousand miles apart."

"Exactly. We decided to support each other's careers, thinking that once our residency was complete we would look for work in the same city. Other couples survived long distance relationships and we were committed to doing the same."

"I gather it didn't work?"

"We made it work for a while. But then the excitement of passionate weekends together wore thin for me. I was ready to settle down and missed the daily companionship she and I had shared. I started making inquiries about programs in the Boston area and flew out to pursue one. When she met me at the airport I could tell something was wrong. To make a long story short, she had been seeing someone else and had fallen in love with him. It was the most painful experience of my life."

"Oh, Nick. I am so sorry. How awful for you!"

"Yes. It was pretty tough. I poured myself into my work and numbed the pain with exhausting fourteen-hour days at the lab. I know we haven't known each other long, but when I felt you were being drawn back to Sioux City I had a profound feeling of déjà vu. Danny, I am falling in love with you and don't want to lose what we have begun together."

Danielle felt the sting of tears in her eyes. "Oh Nick. I have strong feelings for you too. My emotions have been on a roller coaster these past weeks and I want to be sure before I say those words to you."

"I understand and am willing to take it as slowly as you need. Just know that I am anxious to continue this beautiful thing between us. I can't wait to see you."

"Me too. Can you wait until Friday?"

"Are you serious? You'll be home on Friday?" Nick was ecstatic.

"That's my plan. I need to meet with the attorney again before I leave town and make arrangements with Ginny about the house. If all goes well, I should be on my way back Friday morning. Besides, I have a paper to write."

"Yes. *The Taming of the Shrew*. God bless William Shakespeare! Good night, Danny! Have a restful sleep."

"Night, Nick."

CHAPTER 5

Back in Minneapolis, Danielle was so busy that if not for the regular legal correspondence in her mailbox from Jim Oliver, there were days when she didn't dwell on the death of her parents. Finishing her paper was top priority and she dug into it with a frenzied drive. Next on her list was registering for her senior year classes. Check. Along with that was the task of lining up an internship. She made a note to talk to Nick to see if he knew anyone in the industry. Set a date to shop for dresses with Ginny and Mrs. Myers. Check. Schedule a bridal shower. Check. Help Ginny send invitations. Buy new underwear. New dress? Clean the apartment. Pay bills. Talk to Jim Oliver about renting the house to Ginny and Paul. Money for tuition. Call Jake. Plan dinner for Nick. Buy a journal. Check. Check. Check.

In their quiet moments together, Nick could feel her pain and learned that if Danielle wanted to talk about it, she would bring it up. Otherwise, it was best to let her work through her grief in her own way. Ginny thought Danielle should go to a grief support group but after several failed attempts to convince her, she gave up and was happy to spend their time together planning her wedding. Jake landed somewhere in the middle. Being an artist himself and knowing Danielle's passion for writing, he persuaded her to journal her thoughts.

Jake didn't realize that at his suggestion, Danielle's budding romance with Nick Goodman would become stronger and clearer through her journaling. For Danielle, there was a certain orderliness and logic that allowed her to chronicle the facts of her life's circumstances while gradually letting her emotions come to the surface. At times, the scale tipped wildly between profound grief and loss to the elation of new love. By November, Jake was relegated to a quick cup of coffee between classes now and then and occasional late night phone calls when Danielle couldn't sleep. She was careful not to gush about Nick to him but it didn't take a clairvoyant to see what was happening. She was falling in love with Nick and there wasn't a damn thing he could do about it.

"So," Jake said during a late-night call, "it looks like you have totally fallen for *Dr. Blue Eyes*."

Danielle smiled and silently shook her head yes. "Why do you say that?"

"For one thing, you never have time to hang out with me anymore. You're either studying or 'at the lab'. You'd think you were a Biology major or something!"

"I'm just really interested in what's going on over there. I don't know if I should tell you this but they do use monkey eggs in their research. Remember when we went to that A.R.M.S. protest? Sarah told us the monkey's brains were exposed and wired to computers. That was a lie!"

"Don't I know it. The only shots I got that night were of a bunch of ugly sleeping monkeys."

"Yeah. And all I got was a big bump on the head," Danielle laughed. "Anyway, after scientists figured out how to reprogram human skin cells to their embryonic state, they inserted the cell into an egg. The idea was that these donor cells could be used instead of embryonic stem cells to grow into specialized cells to repair or treat disease. Then they got stuck. The cells in the eggs wouldn't multiply. So our researchers used monkey eggs to try to figure out how to stimulate the eggs to start dividing. Can you guess what the secret formula was?"

Jake yawned. "Gee, I can hardly stay awake with anticipation."

"That's right!" Danielle said. "Caffeine!"

"Are you kidding me?"

"No, I am serious. They did hundreds of experiments and discovered that there were certain time frames when the egg was most likely to accept the donor cell and with the right timing and a little bit of caffeine for stimulation, the cells reproduced."

"I'd love to know how that was discovered," Jake said. "Some guy in the middle of the night sloshes a little coffee into his Petri dish?"

"I know. Weird isn't it? I'm so proud of the work that is being done right here on our own campus."

"Yeah. And I bet you're proud of the guy in the blue lab coat too. Right?"

"I can't deny it, Jake. Nick is pretty amazing."

"I know he's impressive but Danielle, he's old enough to be your father!" As soon as the words were out of his mouth, Jake regretted it.

"He is not!" Danielle shot back. "He's not that old! I've thought about the age difference and it doesn't make any difference. Maybe when I'm seventy it will matter more but I learned a valuable lesson from losing my parents. Life is fragile, Jake, and every day is precious."

"I'm sorry, Danielle. I shouldn't have said that. I guess I'm a little jealous and seriously, I don't want you to get hurt. But you are so strong. I'm amazed at how you have handled everything and, my ego aside, I am really glad that Nick makes you happy."

"He really does. Last summer I felt like I would never smile again – but I do. And, Jake, you make me smile too."

"Yeah, yeah, but funny looks aren't everything. Speaking of which, I'd better get some shuteye. Talk to you soon?"

"For sure. Talk to you later, Jake."

The next morning, Danielle's phone rang before her alarm. "Hello?" she mumbled.

"Hi sleepyhead. It sounds like I woke you!" Nick's cheerful voice was usually a delight but after too few hours of sleep, Danielle struggled to awaken.

"Mmmm, yeah."

"I'm Sorry, Danny. Want to call me back?"

"No, it's okay."

"I wanted to catch you before you left for class. You remember Roger Anderson?"

Silence.

"You met him a couple of months ago when you were in the lab. He is one of the docs on our team and I've become friends with him outside of work."

"Oh yeah," Danielle said.

"Well, his daughter sings in a group called Exultate. It's a professional chamber choir and orchestra here in the Twin Cities."

"I haven't heard of them."

"Me either but Roger says they are really good. Anyway, there is a concert tonight and he gave me two tickets. Want to go?"

"Tonight? Gosh, Nick. I am so busy today. You know my Friday class schedule and Ginny, her mom and the other bridesmaids are coming tomorrow to pick up the dresses. Final fittings and all that. I just don't think I can."

"I know you're busy, honey and I hate to add more to your plate but it's a Christmas concert and I think you would really enjoy it. I won't keep you out late. I promise."

"Okay. You know I can't turn you down! Don't blame me though if I fall asleep on you."

"No worries. I'll carry you up to your bed if necessary."

Danielle's heart skipped a beat at the thought. Now fully awake her body responded to his suggestion. She imagined him carrying her to her room but instead of tucking her in for sleep he...

"Danny? You still there?"

"Yeah. Just thinking. What time?"

"I'll pick you up at six. We can grab a quick bite at the club. The concert is at a church not too far from there."

"Okay. See you then. I'm a little stressed out so just be prepared."

"I will take you any way I can have you. See you tonight."

"Bye." There it was again. Was Nick being suggestive or was it just her hormones? With all of Nick's talk about fertility and human reproduction, she had become more aware of her monthly cycle. She quickly checked her journal and confirmed that her last period was two weeks ago. That could explain it. Or maybe she was just utterly attracted to the incredibly sexy Nick Goodman. She closed her eyes and thought about their last kiss. More than a kiss - it was a full make-out session and her body trembled at the memory. She could feel his hands on her as he touched her in ways that made her want him so intensely she couldn't hold back the passion. She imagined him slowly bringing her to...

"Beep, beep, beep, beep." The alarm jolted her from her fantasy.

"Okay, okay. I'm up already," she scowled at the clock.

On the bus ride to her first class, Danielle peered out the frosty window. Homes and businesses were decorated for Christmas and she smiled at the twinkling lights and decorated tress visible in the store windows. She wished now she had brought some decorations back when she was home for Thanksgiving. Mrs. Myers and Ginny insisted she join them for the long Thanksgiving weekend and she had made a quick stop at her house with Ginny. She and Paul had painted most of the rooms and added their personal touch to the place. It felt warm and cozy. It was still her home yet slightly different – a gradual transition from her life with her parents in that house into a new beginning. Ginny showed her where she was going to put the Christmas tree, right in front of the picture window facing the street. Danielle offered to let them use her family decorations this year not wanting to experience the pain of going through them just yet.

Once off the bus, Danielle had no more time for reflection. Her mind was spinning as she hurried to get ready for her date with Nick. Dressed in a cream colored fisherman's knit sweater, a brown corduroy skirt and leather boots, she checked her hair in the bathroom mirror. Luckily she had worn earmuffs and a scarf all day instead of her usual stocking cap so she didn't have *hat hair*. With a little cream to keep down the static she quickly finger combed her long curls and brushed a little mascara on her lashes.

"That's all I can do," she said to the mirror as the apartment buzzer sounded. "Be right down," she said into the speaker as she grabbed her coat and purse.

"Hi beautiful!" Nick beamed. He gave her a quick kiss then took her arm to lead her through the fresh snow to his car parked around the corner. "I lucked out! Someone was just leaving as I drove around the block the second time. Restricting parking to just one side of the street sure is a pain! Looks like we are going to get another inch or two tonight."

"Really? I hope Ginny and the girls make it up okay tomorrow."

"It's supposed to stop this evening. That should give them plenty of time to clear the roads before they head out tomorrow morning. I'm glad you're not driving though."

"And why is that?" Danielle smiled. "I'm an excellent driver."

"It's the other guy I worry about. These yahoos in their four-wheel drive trucks think ice and snow doesn't require them to slow down. I saw two of them spin out on the way to the lab this morning. Luckily it was early and not much traffic so no one crashed."

"Speaking of early, what time was it when you called anyway?"

"About six. Sorry about that," Nick replied. "I tried calling last night but your line was busy. For a long time, I might add. I had an early morning meeting so I couldn't wait up."

"Oh so you needed your beauty sleep, huh? What about me?" Danielle laughed.

"Danny, my love, there is no way you could be more beautiful than you are tonight. I am sorry for interrupting your sleep though."

"That's okay. I didn't get up until the alarm rang so I guess that counts as rest."

They were still chatting happily about the events of their day as they walked into the country club's dining room. Before the maître d' could seat them, Nick noticed a hand waving them in. He steered Danielle through the crowded room to a table next to the fireplace. The elegant grey-haired couple rose and gave Nick a warm hug.

"Nick! What a surprise! And who is this lovely lady?"

"Mom, Dad, this is Danielle O'Neil."

"Danielle. It's so nice to finally meet you," Liz said. "Nick has told us so much about you."

"Thank you, Mrs. Goodman. It's nice to meet you too!"

"Oh please, dear, call me Liz."

"And I'm Frank," Nick's father said as he gave her a firm handshake. "What a pleasure!" he said to Danielle. "Nick, why don't you join us? We haven't ordered yet," Frank said as he waived the waiter over.

"James, my son and his friend will be joining us for dinner."

"Yes of course Mr. Goodman," he said. "Dr. Goodman?" he said to Nick. "What can I get you and your guest from the bar?"

"I'll have a hot brandy. Danielle? What would you like?"

"Something hot does sound good. Any ideas?"

"How about hot chocolate with Baileys?" Nick suggested. "That and the fireplace should warm you up in no time."

"Thank you. That sounds good," Danielle said as she sat in the chair Frank was holding for her.

"So what brings you two out on this snowy night?" Liz asked.

"We have tickets to hear Exultate and have just enough time to grab a quick bite before the concert," Nick replied.

"Exul what?" Frank asked.

"Exultate. It's a professional chamber choir and orchestra. Roger Anderson's daughter sings in the group so we are going to check it out."

"How is Roger?" asked Frank. "I haven't seen him around lately."

"He's good. Busy like the rest of us. Without golf to get him here, he doesn't make much use of the club during the off season."

"A choral concert. Sounds nice. Are you a singer, Danielle?" Liz asked.

"Only with the radio when no one can hear me. I sang a solo in church when I was six years old. My dad told me that I sang flat but loud and enthusiastically so my Sunday school teacher picked me! I don't think I've improved much," Danielle said.

Liz reached over and patted her hand. "Don't worry. I can't carry a tune but I do love to go to the opera."

The waiter arrived with their drinks saving Danielle the need to reply. She was already nervous to be unexpectedly dining with the Goodmans and talking about opera was way beyond her comfort zone.

"Mmmmm. This is really good," Danielle said as she sipped her chocolaty drink. "And this room is really stunning! It feels so homey."

"Thank you, dear," Liz said. "I am on the decorating committee and this year we decided on a country Christmas theme. Bachman's does a fabulous job with the greenery and my interior decorator combed her inventory for antiques and pieces with country motifs."

"That must be why I like it," Danielle said. "I didn't grow up on a farm but my best friend did."

"Yes. Danny's friend Ginny is getting married in two

weeks and Danny is the maid of honor," Nick said. "I told you about the Myers' family. Great people! I'll be driving her down to Sioux City and spending the weekend."

Liz and Frank exchanged a knowing glance. It was clear that their son was taken by this lovely young woman and Liz could barely contain her excitement. She was anxious for grandchildren and couldn't understand why Nick wasn't married by now. He was smart, handsome, successful and kind. What more could a woman want? Her attention was drawn back to the table as the waiter reappeared to take their orders.

Danielle became more at ease throughout dinner but was grateful that they couldn't linger afterwards. After saying their goodbyes she and Nick got into the car - warmed up and windows scraped by the valet.

"I like your parents."

"I'm glad," Nick said. "I have been anxious for them to meet you but I have been waiting for just the right time."

"It was a surprise for sure. In a way I'm glad I didn't know in advance. I would have been even more nervous."

"You did fine and I know they loved you. My parents each have a tendency to take over the conversation but you held your own! I noticed Mom actually stopped to listen to you. That's rare! Dad is Dad. It's all about business and golf. Hope you weren't too bored."

"Not at all. I can see some of each of them in you. You obviously have your mom's beautiful blue eyes and charm and love of the arts. I know from your work at the lab that you have your dad's analytical mind. You've mentioned his work with investments but I didn't know he also runs a foundation."

"Yes. You can thank my boss for that."

"What do you mean?"

"Well, Dad has lots of connections and Sonny convinced him to start a foundation and encourage some of his high net worth friends to make donations."

"What is the purpose?"

"I feel a little embarrassed about it."

"Really? Why?"

"The purpose of the foundation is to support biomedical research. And you'll never guess who the primary recipient is."

"The U of M?"

"You got it," Nick replied.

"I thought that your work relied on federal funding."

"It does. But federal grants come with many strings attached. Our work is tightly regulated and closely monitored and Sonny has an independent streak. He claims he needs the freedom to push science beyond what the bureaucrats in Washington deem important. Private funding gives him that freedom."

"Makes sense. But why would you feel embarrassed about that?" Danielle asked.

"In a way, I feel like my dad is paying my salary – kind of like he is still supporting me."

"Well, I've only just met your father but it seems to me that he is incredibly proud of you. He probably wants to support some worthy cause and the one he has chosen shows his support for the important work that you do. I think it's great that your family is dedicated to advancing medical science in order to help those in need."

"You're right and there is a back story to your observation. But, that will have to wait for another time. Here we are. I'll drop you off at the door and park the car."

"You don't have to do that. I can walk."

"No. I insist," Nick said as he got out of the car and opened Danielle's door. He gave her a soft kiss on the lips and said, "I'll be back in a minute."

Danielle followed the crowd through the entryway into the church narthex where she stood quietly taking in the beauty of the sanctuary visible through the floor to ceiling windows. There were two huge trees in the front covered in white lights. A large Advent wreath with five candles hung over the center aisle and the altar cloths were blue for the season of Advent. In its simplicity, Danielle felt at home. She wandered to the welcome desk, picked up information about the church and tucked it into her purse. *It's time*, she thought. *I need a church home.*

Nick came in stomping the snow off his shoes. It was snowing harder now and the big wet flakes were beautiful. Nick playfully shook the snow from his head onto Danielle's face and took her coat. They found seats near the front and talked quietly while the Exultate orchestra warmed up and tuned their instruments. At exactly seven thirty the choir filed in and the program began. From the first notes of J.S. Bach's "Magnificat" Danielle was mesmerized. Her soul was filled with the music and there was no room for worry or stress. Nick held her hand - only letting go to applaud at the appropriate times. Being so close to the choir she could hear them breathe and felt the vibration of the bows on the strings. She had never experienced a concert like this and was beyond glad that she had accepted Nick's invitation. The first half concluded with a rousing arrangement of "O Come All Ye Faithful." She giggled when the tuba blasted his three important notes and sang vigorously with the audience on the last stanza. Clapping in appreciation the audience stood to acknowledge the wonderful music and Danielle and Nick stayed standing to stretch their legs.

The second half of the program was more circumspect and Danielle found herself missing her parents terribly. This was her first Christmas alone and the sweet Christmas melodies brought back wonderful yet painful memories. She was particularly moved by "Love Came Down at Christmas." The notes in the program explained that the Christmas poem was written by Christina Rossetti in 1885 and later set to music by several composers including Joseph Running. Exultate's conductor had arranged the simple carol for this performance. Only the women's voices sang the sweet, poignant text accompanied by soft, melodious strings.

Love came down at Christmas,
love all lovely, love divine.
Love was born at Christmas
star and angels gave the sign...
Love shall be our token,
love shall be yours and love be mine.

In that moment, as tears slowly trickled down her cheeks, she knew without question that she loved Nick and squeezed his hand tightly. And Nick knew too.

Relaxed and content, Danielle was quiet and sleepy as Nick navigated the icy streets on the drive home. Nick helped her from the car and guided her to her apartment. Barely able to keep her eyes open she went directly to her room, pulled off her skirt and sweater and tumbled into bed. Nick leaned over to kiss her good night. "I love you, Danny," he said.

"I love you too, Nick. I really do."

"I know, honey. I know."

CHAPTER 6

Two weeks later Nick entered another church and was ushered to his seat as the organist played. It had snowed overnight so his drive to Sioux City had taken longer than expected. Danielle was on break and had driven down on Tuesday but he needed to finish a report for Sonny and didn't want to intrude on the pre-wedding activities. Now that he was here, he had to agree that despite the hassles of the snow and the icy cold weather, Christmas was a beautiful time to have a wedding. In addition to the lighted trees and almost life-sized crèche in the front, each pew was decorated with fresh pine boughs tied with large gold ribbons. The center aisle was lined with candelabras and just before the bridal party processed, a white satin runner was rolled out. The music stopped for a moment and the room fell silent. The processional began and everyone turned to see the first bridesmaid appear. It was Ginny's thirteen-year-old sister, Laura, nervously carrying her lighted lantern, eyes fixed on the flame, as she slowly walked up the aisle. Nick waited patiently as the others made their way to the front of the church knowing that as maid of honor, Danielle would be the last one in before the flower girl and ring bearer. At last it was her turn and Nick turned his body to watch the love of his life walk up the aisle.

Danielle looked stunning in the fitted red satin gown, her hair piled loosely on top of her head with soft curls framing her face. She carried herself with such grace and ease it was hard not to compare her to the others – visibly nervous and slightly awkward. He caught her eye as she walked by his row and gave her a quick wink and a loving smile. He felt more nervous than she appeared to be as he fidgeted with the ring in his pocket. It had only been two weeks since she told him she loved him but those simple words had dramatically changed their relationship. He smiled as he thought of what was now their song, "Love Came Down at Christmas." He had purchased two Exultate CDs after the concert. *Joy to the World* had the beautiful carol on it and he gave this one to her as soon as she returned from the ladies room. When she saw that the *love carol* was on it, she teared up and gave him a huge hug. Together they had listened to it dozens of times since and he often heard it playing in the background as they talked on the phone. At the concert he also bought *A German Requiem* which he had tucked into his coat pocket. The Brahms *Requiem* was one of his favorite choral pieces and he had listened to the recording alone. He appreciated that Exultate sang it in English rather than the original German. The message of comfort, consolation and peace in the face of death seemed to be written for Danielle but he didn't want her to have it just yet. He didn't want to dampen the joy of the Christmas season and Ginny's upcoming wedding. He would wait for just the right time to share it with her. But he was not willing to wait too long before asking for her hand in marriage. He realized that the engagement would seem sudden to some, particularly to his parents who had only just met her, but in his heart he knew that she was the one he was meant to love.

As the pastor recounted how Ginny and Paul met and told a few stories of their young love, Nick reflected on his relationship with Danielle since their first meeting three years ago. Who knew that the call of a chickadee would cause his life to literally collide with Danielle's for all time? As Ginny and Paul said their vows, he was anxious for the day when he would publically make promises of love and devotion to her and to begin their life together as husband and wife.

"I now pronounce you husband and wife," the pastor echoed his thoughts. "You may kiss the bride!"

The wedding guests erupted into applause and cheers as Ginny and Paul kissed and beamed at one another. Danielle arranged Ginny's train and the newlyweds practically danced down the isle to greet their family and friends. Danielle and Ginny's brother Max were next and Nick's throat caught as she passed his row mouthing an *I love you.*

Nick had a front row seat at the bridal party's table when Ginny tossed her bouquet. He had worked it out with her to make sure Danielle caught it and the plan worked like a charm, much to the disappointment of the other single women and girls. When Danielle brought the bouquet back to the head table she noticed the small envelope tied to the white rose in the center. Inside was a note consisting of only four words and a ring.

At this point, Mr. Myers started to clink his glass. The bridal couple kissed, Nick leaned in close as Danielle read his handwritten note. "Will you marry me?"

His lips touched her ear as he whispered, "Well?"

She responded with a long and very public kiss followed by, one word. "Yes!"

Nick took the ring and slipped it onto her finger.

Ginny grabbed the microphone and asked for everyone's attention. "I have an announcement to make! Not only has the tradition of catching the bouquet come true - the woman that caught it will be the next to get married. But Danielle and Nick have set the record for the quickest engagement after catching the bouquet. Congratulations and love to my best friend, Danny O'Neil and her fiancé, Nick Goodman."

Finally Danielle's duties as maid of honor were complete for the day. Ginny and Paul sprinted through the snow to the Town Car and driver waiting to take them to an undisclosed location. Instead of throwing the birdseed that had been handed out, some of Paul's friends threw snow and before the all-out snowball fight erupted, the couple dove into the back seat and waved as they drove off.

Back at the Myers', Hal and Marie gave their heartfelt congratulations and best wishes to Nick and Danielle before going upstairs to bed. It had been a long and exciting day and the rest of the family was already sleeping. Danielle collapsed on the sofa and moaned, "My feet are killing me!"

"It's no wonder," Nick said, "with all the dancing you did tonight! You were really shaking it up! Want a foot massage?"

"Are you kidding? I have just enough energy to hobble to the bathroom for the lotion." Danielle returned barefooted and in her red plush bathrobe carrying the lotion and a towel. "I had to get out of that dress! The wedding really was fun, wasn't it? Everything was perfect."

"Yes. Especially the tossing of the bouquet," Nick teased as he squeezed lotion into his hands and rubbed them together. "Lie back and let me take care of those poor barking dogs."

"Barking dogs?"

"Yeah. Haven't you ever heard the expression 'my dogs are barking?'"

"Uh, no."

"I don't know how it started but the saying did lead to the Hush Puppies shoe brand. Apparently the owner of a shoe company was eating with a friend and hush puppies were on the menu. The friend said they were called hush puppies because he gave them to dogs to stop them from barking. The owner figured his shoes would soothe sore feet - *barking dogs* - so he trademarked the brand."

"Weird story but don't stop the massage. My *barking dogs* are beginning to *purr like a kitten.* Oops! Mixed idiom."

"I still love you," Nick said. "Hey! Did you know you have a little freckle on the bottom of your left foot?"

"Really? I had no idea."

"It's cute. You know, I thought you were cute the very

first time I saw you. Sprawled out on the sidewalk! I smile every time I think of it. I am eternally grateful that fate brought us together."

"That wasn't fate. That was God," Danielle said as she took a hold of Nick's arms and pulled him toward her. "I really believe that."

"And I believe that tonight you made me the happiest man on earth." Crushed together on the small sofa, Nick could feel her heartbeat as they kissed. Her robe had shifted exposing her breast and she gasped as he touched her.

"I love you Nick," she whispered, "and the ring is amazing. I want to hear the whole story someday."

"And all I want is you." It took all of his strength to pull away and tug her robe over her beautiful skin. "Danny, I have something I have wanted to ask you. Your answer won't change anything but, have you ever been with a man?"

"You mean, am I a virgin? No, but I've never been in love like this before," she said watching Nick's face carefully for his reaction. "Being with you is so different from my past relationships. It may sound silly, but I want to wait until we are married."

"I cherish everything about you especially your silliness," he said with a smile. "I've waited a lifetime for you and can wait until we are married. I think. As long as it's soon!" he added. "Let's set a date. How about tomorrow?"

"Mmmm. Let's see. Sorry, tomorrow I'm busy. Remember? We are all meeting over at my house – I mean, Ginny and Paul's house – to open gifts. I have to record everything."

"Ah, the maid of honor's work is never done. I should go so you can go to bed."

"I don't want you to go. Ever."

"We both need some sleep and my bed at the Sioux City Inn is calling for me. Good night my love, my wife to be."

"Night, fiancé. Sleep well."

Sunday was another whirlwind of activity and after the gift opening and one more enormous country meal, Nick reluctantly said goodbye and headed home. The roads were clear and dry so he allowed his thoughts to wander back through the past two days – the excitement of the proposal, the beaming smile on Danielle's face, the beautiful wedding and the warm and happy chaos among the Myers' family. As an only child he had never really considered having a large family. Nick made a mental note to talk to Danielle about this. She was an only child too and he had no idea how many children she wanted.

When it came right down to it, there were a lot of things they hadn't talked about yet. His career was well established but Danielle's was just beginning. He knew she wanted a career but Nick was anxious to have a child. Would she consider having a baby soon and put her journalism aspirations on hold or would she try to do it all? Selfishly, he hoped not – at least, not right away. He wanted all of her time and attention and didn't want to share her with anything or anyone. And, where would they live? Obviously not in either of their apartments. Nick had some savings but hadn't had to manage the financial burden of a mortgage not to mention the work involved with home ownership. But now he was ready. He wanted to provide the kind of safe, secure and warm home that he had as a boy even if it meant getting a different job.

Wait a minute. A different job? Would I really consider leaving the lab? My work? Sonny?

Dr. Sonny Marino was not just his boss but also his mentor and his friend. Sonny didn't play golf but at Nick's insistence he and his wife, Lauren, had joined the Southpoint Country Club as social members. Being new to the area and with Sonny's obsession for his work, the Marinos hadn't met many friends and the club seemed to be the perfect solution. It was located in the prestigious area near the Minneapolis city lakes and home to many of the Twin Cities' doctors, lawyers, politicians and business executives. The Marinos gained quick acceptance and soon developed relationships with the elite club members including Nick's parents. In the early years, they frequently dined together as a congenial fivesome or sometimes six when Nick made the effort to find a date. Sonny often met Nick and Frank at the club for lunch after a round of golf. Then there was a scandal involving Sonny and one of the club's attractive waitresses. After that, Lauren was less willing to join them unless it was a special occasion – a birthday or anniversary or special club event – so they had fallen into a new rhythm of socializing. Being closer in age and not constrained by the boss-subordinate relationship, Frank and Sonny were often seen having drinks together deeply engrossed in serious conversation. Frank had mentioned his involvement with Sonny on the foundation but that was a topic Nick shied away from and he didn't want to know the details.

None of this bothered him. It was the change in atmosphere at the lab that was concerning. Nick and Sonny had been like-minded from the very beginning. They both were dedicated to and bound by a common goal. They believed that by exploring human DNA and pushing the boundaries of stem cell research, one day they would make a major breakthrough that would restore health and vitality to millions of suffering people. They had shared their daily successes and disappointments openly with personal support and professional respect.

But over the past few months, things had changed. Nick had blamed himself for the periodic flare-ups with Sonny. Since he and Danielle began dating, his workaholic tendencies had softened. So when he felt like he was out of the loop with Sonny's work, he rationalized it as just a function of not being there every minute Sonny was at the lab.

Is that all it is?

Nick recalled his most recent argument with Sonny. Over the years they had disagreed on process but not on principle. Last week they had had a heated argument about the moral issues around human cloning. Sonny was adamant that the research should continue.

"Develop the science to make it a possibility. That's our job! Let the others figure out how and when to apply it," Sonny had insisted.

In Nick's view, advancing medical science to generate new organs or heal damaged ones was dramatically different from creating a human life that has viability independent of the original human donor. In Sonny's mind it was a fine line but one that he was willing to cross if the process could be improved and demonstrate positive outcomes for both the woman and the child she carried. Since the risks were still too high, the medical community was in agreement that based on the scientific evidence alone, human cloning was out of the question. It was only recently that the President's Council on Bioethics issued a paper delving into the ethical issues. It was based on the assumption that the eventual cloning of humans was considered a serious possibility. Sonny agreed with their assumption that it was possible and after reading the report, Nick realized that his arguments with Sonny were largely based on his own moral compass, not on the science. No wonder he was losing the argument over and over again. For the first time in their long work history, he wondered if he and Sonny had fundamental, irreconcilable differences.

Man! How did I go from thinking about Ginny's beautiful wedding and my future with Danny to that trite phrase used in divorce – irreconcilable differences? Maybe that's the key to any relationship. As long as you agree in principle, the rest of the details can be worked out. It doesn't matter where we live, how many children we have, or whether or not Danny is a working mom, as long as we share the same guiding principles in life.

As for Sonny, as long as we are just arguing theoretically, it shouldn't be that big of a deal. I wish we didn't disagree so passionately on the subject of cloning but as long as we can continue to work together on our common goals, I can live with it.

With that resolved and only thirty miles to go, Nick turned on the radio and caught up on the national and international news on Minnesota Public Radio.

As soon as Danielle got back to Minneapolis, the whirlwind of her own wedding planning hit her full force. After their initial surprise of Nick's engagement to the young woman of such modest roots, the Goodmans were ecstatic and Liz went into high gear. She had been dreaming of this event for a long, long time and she wanted it to be perfect for her son and his bride. After checking the schedules, she reported that the fifteenth of June was the only Saturday available for the ceremony at Como Park and reception at Southpoint. One of Liz's friends at the club told her about another friend's daughter's broken engagement and Liz swooped in and grabbed the reservations.

From that point on, Danielle's thoughts of a small church wedding were overtaken by her soon to be mother-in-law's enthusiasm and Nick's desire to please her beyond her wildest dreams. With classes to finish, finals to take and graduation details to attend to, Danielle acquiesced and accepted Liz's offer to handle everything. Well, almost everything. She and Nick would plan the ceremony and Ginny and Mrs. Myers would help her choose the dresses.

Unlike most of Danielle's college acquaintances, Danielle didn't have a large group of close friends from which to choose her bridesmaids. Sure, she had many friends at school but no one with which she had felt close enough to share her innermost self. After her parents' death, she found it even more difficult to relate to the carefree co-eds that shared her classes and campus life. Sure, they had things in common now but other than Ginny and Jake, there wasn't anyone else she felt certain would still be in her life on her first anniversary much less in the years to come.

Her mom had been an only child and all of her grandparents were deceased. She did have some cousins on her dad's side in Nebraska. The families had visited each other sometimes in the summer but she hadn't seen them since high school graduation and unless her dad reached out to them, there was no communication at all. Her cousins didn't even come to the funeral and other than the condolences offered over the phone and promises to stay in touch, there was no rekindling of family relationships. She hadn't received a Christmas card from any of them. In going over the guest list with Liz, she was embarrassed that she had so few to add to the list. Of course her aunts and uncles and cousins would receive invitations, but she didn't expect any of them would make the trip up for the wedding. She was overwhelmed by the extent of her husband-to-be's extensive guest list – hundreds of names that Nick insisted had to be whittled down to two hundred. He had promised Danielle he would not let the size get out of hand and had prevailed with his mother that no matter how important the people might be in his parents' circle, if he had never met them, they were definitely not on the list! There were a few exceptions, of course, but in the end, everyone was satisfied with the guest list and invitations were ordered.

There was no question that Ginny would be her matron of honor. The only other person she called a true friend was Jake, and Danielle had convinced him to be the photographer. Jake had hesitated at first. Weddings weren't his normal gig and even though Danielle had been completely up front that she and Jake would never be more than "just friends," he did love her and still held onto a glimmer of hope that someday she would change her mind. That is, until she told him of her engagement to Nick. In the end, she convinced him that not only was he the best photographer she knew, she would feel so much more comfortable with him behind the lens than some stranger of Liz's choosing.

Most of Nick's friends were either colleagues or guys he played golf with at the club. Roger Anderson was the one friend that crossed over into both circles so he was the logical choice for best man. Liz thought having only one attendant each was entirely too small so they all agreed to have the youngest Myers' children, Melissa and Grant, as flower girl and ring bearer.

The most painful part of the planning was not having her parents by her side. Who would walk her down the isle? Who would fill the irreplaceable role of mother as Danielle prepared for this the most important day of her life? She missed her parents tremendously and found her emotions bouncing erratically between sorrow, resentment and pure joy. Nick took her mood swings in stride and assured her that nothing could change the way he felt about her. He would love her forever.

Before the Christmas holiday season was over, most of the major decisions had been made. The ceremony would take place on Saturday, June 15, 1991 at the Como Park Conservatory where the bridal couple, their attendants and two hundred guests would be surrounded by lush greenery and a fabulous display of spring flowers. The outdoor wedding was, of course, contingent on the weather and Danielle had had her doubts about planning an outdoor affair. But Liz persuaded her that after the long, cold, colorless winter, spring in Minnesota was in and of itself worthy of celebration and an outdoor wedding provided a marvelous reason to get out, dress up and celebrate "without crushing your dress clothes under heavy coats and ruining your good shoes in the snow and slush." Looking out the window over the frozen river and snow-covered rooftops, it was hard to imagine an outdoor wedding and Danielle had countered, "Good shoes can get ruined in the rain too, you know." Nick had intervened with the statistic that more Minnesota weddings are held in the month of June than any other month of the year and since the reception would be at Southpoint, under Liz's strict management, the ceremony could be held there in case of bad weather. So it was decided.

Ginny and her mom trekked up to the Cities on a cold January morning to shop for dresses. The day brought back the warm, happy memories of doing the same for Ginny and since they already had a short list of shops to check out, they were confident that their mission would be quickly accomplished.

On their third stop, Danielle's eyes were drawn toward the back of the store by a beautiful blue gown.

"That's it!" she exclaimed as she dragged Ginny right past the sales clerk without so much as a hello. "That is the color I want for your dress!"

"Don't you just love it? It's the same color as Nick's eyes and will look great on you!"

By the time Mrs. Myers introduced herself to the clerk and was properly escorted to the bridesmaid section of the store, Danielle and Ginny had already decided that this was the one.

"Danielle?" Mrs. Myers said as she tapped her on the shoulder. "This is Miss Clark. She will be helping us today."

"Oh, hi!" Danielle said as she smiled and stuck out her hand. "I saw the blue from the front door and it's just perfect. Oh! Sorry! This is my matron of honor, Ginny. Can she try it on?"

"Of course. Let me take your coats and hang them up for you. Would you like some coffee or tea?" She led them toward the large leather sectional in the center of the room. "Let's get you settled here."

"Thank you," said Mrs. Myers. "I would love some tea to warm up. Girls?"

"No thanks," Ginny said.

"I'd like some water, please," Danielle said. "Shopping always makes me thirsty."

"Very well. Please make yourselves comfortable and I'll be right back with your beverages."

Ginny smiled and held out a plastic shopping bag to Danielle. "Here, Danny," she said. "I think now is a good time to give you this."

"What is it?"

"When Paul and I were moving around some boxes in your basement, I came across one marked SAVE. I didn't mean to be nosy but I wondered if it was something you might want."

Danielle reached in and pulled out a small bundle wrapped in yellowed tissue paper. Inside were a wedding invitation, a dried rose and a blue pocket handkerchief. "This is from my parents' wedding. Look! Here is the invitation bordered in roses, my mom's favorite flower. And this must have been my dad's boutonnière," she said as she carefully examined the dried flower.

Ginny couldn't contain her excitement. "And the hanky. It's the exact color of this dress!!"

"It is! Oh my gosh! It's the same blue!" Danielle was overwhelmed. "Thank you, Ginny! This was all meant to be," she said as she gave her best friend a huge hug.

"There's something else in the bag," Ginny said. "I think it's your mom's veil."

Danielle removed the carefully folded veil and held it up. Tears ran down her cheeks. She was speechless.

Just then the clerk returned with a tray of beverages and small cookies. "Here we are. Are we ready to try on some lovely gowns?"

Intended to save her friend any embarrassment, Ginny popped up from her seat. "I am. Do you have this in a size ten?"

"We do have several samples for fitting purposes. Of course, your dresses will be made to order. How many bridesmaid dresses will you need?"

Mrs. Myers jumped in quickly. "Just the one."

"Of course. Let me take this back to the fitting room for you. Right this way," she said to Ginny and led her off to the area behind the enormous mirrors.

Alone with Danielle, Mrs. Myers put her arm around Danielle. "The veil is lovely. So delicate. I can imagine how beautiful your mother must have looked on her wedding day."

"I've seen the pictures but to actually hold in my hands the precious mementos of their marriage. I guess I kind of lost it," Danielle said as she dabbed at her eyes.

"Don't worry. I'm sure Miss Clark didn't even notice. She has probably seen so many teary-eyed brides over the years that it doesn't faze her anymore.

"She's quite efficient, isn't she?" Danielle giggled.

Mrs. Myers nodded as they watched Miss Clark flitting about. At last Ginny came out wearing the blue gown Danielle had spotted from the front door.

"Turn around Gin," Danielle said. "The most important view is from the back."

"Thanks a lot Danny," Ginny laughed as she carefully pivoted to give them the full view.

Miss Clark fussed with the pins. "I think this size is the best. The waistline fits her nicely and we can make a few alterations to the bodice when it comes in."

"Gin, I love it on you. What do you think?" asked Danielle.

"I like it a lot but—"

"But what?" Danielle asked.

"I dragged you guys around to dozens of stores before I made up my mind. Don't you want to look around a little more?"

"Nope!" Danielle said. "This dress called to me when I walked in and when you brought out Dad's blue handkerchief, I knew it was a sign from heaven that this was the one. I mean, I hadn't even settled on the color theme for the wedding party and kaboom, there it was."

Miss Clark beamed. It was a small order and she was glad it had taken so little of her time. "Let me make a few notes and then we'll write this up."

"Yes, we'll take it," Danielle said. "Is it possible to have a sash made to match? My flower girl will be wearing a white dress and I'd like her sash to match Ginny's dress."

"Of course, no problem at all. In fact, this is one of our spring season's new colors so we have ties and pocket squares to match."

"I already have one for the groom but I'll need others. How many?" She looked at Mrs. Myers.

"I count four. The best man, the ring bearer and two ushers. Unless you want one for Jake too?"

Danielle laughed. "Not on your life! I'll be lucky if I can get him to wear anything other than his favorite plaid shirt and zip off cargo pants."

Miss Clark gasped.

"Don't worry," Danielle said. "He's the photographer so it's not likely he will be in any of the pictures. So, let's order two ties and four pocket kerchief thingies."

"Very well. Did you want bow ties?"

Danielle nodded. "Oh, and a little set for the ring bearer."

"I've got it down. Now, what did you have in mind for your dress? And for the flower girl? If I may make a suggestion. In a smaller bridal party the style of her dress can either follow the matron of honor or the bride. Perhaps we should focus on your dress next."

Ginny reappeared. "Yes!"

Danielle held out the veil. "This was my mother's veil and I was wondering if you have something that maybe would go with it?"

Miss Clark looked at Mrs. Myers who gave her a subtle

nod. "Let's take a look. The headpiece has some beautiful beading. Were you thinking of wearing ivory?"

Danielle blushed. "No. White."

"Why do you ask?" said Mrs. Myers.

"Well I'm afraid the lace and the tulle have yellowed over the years and it would be quite noticeable against a pure white gown. Would you consider just using the headpiece along with a new white veil? It really is quite lovely. In fact, we have several gowns with similar beading to what we have here."

Miss Clark returned in a few minutes with an armful of wedding gowns. Danielle tried them all. Incorporating her mother's veil made the selection more difficult but with Miss Clark's help and Ginny's and Mrs. Myers's encouragement, at last her dress was chosen. By the time they decided on the flower girl's dress, they were tired and hungry. Ginny and her mom were staying the night at the Comfort Inn just off 35W. Neither of them liked driving in the Cities so they preferred to stay close to the freeway. There was a steakhouse connected to the hotel and Danielle insisted on treating them to dinner. After their long goodbyes, Danielle drove back to her apartment. Cold and tired, all she wanted to do was take a long hot bath and fall into bed.

Just as she was about to step into the tub, her phone rang. Checking the caller ID she saw that it was Nick and picked up the phone.

"Hi Nick," she said.

"Hey. How's my beautiful bride to be?"

"I'm beat and not feeling too beautiful right now."

"Did you have a good day?"

"Yes. I just got home and was about to step into the tub."

"I wish I were there."

"No you don't. I'd be too tired to properly greet you."

"I doubt that. So how did the shopping go?"

"Wouldn't you like to know?" Danielle teased.

"Did you pick a dress?"

"I did. Believe it or not, we found everything in one shop.

I'd love to tell you more but I'm standing here naked and freezing my buns off."

"Now I really wish I were there!"

"Me too. I need someone to wash my back."

"Is that all?"

"Hmmm. I'd love to think about that but I really have to go. See you at brunch tomorrow."

"Can't wait. Good night Danny. I love you."

"And I love you. See you tomorrow."

The next morning, Danielle woke early and refreshed. It was ten degrees below zero and she worried that her car might not start. She was excited to see Nick so instead of waiting until brunch she got ready, warmed up her car and headed over to the Goodmans' house. Nick was house sitting while Frank and Liz were in Palm Springs. She was shivering on the doorstep when the front door finally opened.

"Here is your Sunday paper, sir," she said.

"Danny! It's freezing! Get in here!"

Nick's impulse was to hug her to warm her up but the cold air coming off of her drove him back. "God, you're cold!"

"Not really. I am nice and warm. It's my coat that's cold. How about a little hug?" She pressed her cold face against his and felt the warmth of his skin on hers. "Happy to see me?"

"Of course! Just surprised, that's all."

"I went to bed early and got a good night's sleep. Now that the dresses are all ordered, I feel so much better."

"Let's make some coffee. Come. Take your coat off. I want to hear all about your day."

Danielle laughed as she did her best impression of Miss Clark and then told him of the surprise Ginny had for her. The impact of the moment was not lost on Nick and he reached for her hand as she told him about the mementos from her parents' wedding.

"I hope you like blue," she said as she looked into his blue eyes. "It has become my favorite color."

"I will wear a gunny sack if you ask me to," Nick replied.

"How about a plaid shirt and cargo pants?"

"No, I'll leave that for Jake," Nick said as he kissed her.

"I should shower and shave. Make yourself at home. It will be yours soon, you know." Nick gave her another kiss before heading upstairs.

Mine? It's hard to believe that in five months I will be Mrs. Nicholas Goodman and this will be my home. She liked the house but with its traditional and elegant furnishings and décor, she was worried it would always feel like Frank and Liz's. She wandered through the kitchen to the formal dining room, living room, family room and study. She tried to imagine a mixture of her parents' furniture, Nick's newer furnishings from his apartment and the Goodmans' pieces that were not being moved to their new condo. With a vision of new carpet, freshly painted walls and colorful art, her new home began to come to life.

A new life, a new beginning, a new Goodman family.

CHAPTER 7

Jake was nervous about being the wedding photographer. He had done a few weddings for college friends but the Goodmans' social circle was intimidating so he resisted Danielle's pleas. In the end Danielle prevailed, as she always did, and he decided to put his insecurities aside and focus on his precious friend. She was a stunning bride; Jake had never seen her look more beautiful. Since she normally didn't fuss much with her appearance, the results of her day at the salon were truly extraordinary. Her long brown hair, usually worn in loose curls past her shoulders had been softly tapered and pulled back at the crown to set off her beautiful brown eyes and highlight her mother's bridal headpiece. Her lips and cheeks blushed a soft pink and her nails were French manicured. Danielle's gown was very fitted and the beaded bodice accented her tiny waist and long graceful neck. The V neckline was just low enough to give a hint of her breasts without taking away from her beautiful innocence. The skirt was full with a lavish train that Jake gathered around her – as if she were floating on a cloud. Jake posed her and created a soft filtered light. He thought she looked truly angelic and so incredibly happy. He couldn't help but think back to their field trip to Winona where he was alone with her in her motel room. *If only…*

"Huh?" Jake's responded to Danielle's voice.

"You said, try to look dreamy but I didn't expect *you* to go into a trance!"

"Oh, sorry. I was just thinking back to the first time we worked together. Remember Winona? I have to admit this isn't how I envisioned your wedding day back then."

"I know, Jake. You can't believe how much your friendship means to me. You know I love you like a brother."

"Hold that innocent thought and give me a nice smile," Jake said as he adjusted his lens for the shot. "Good. That was beautiful. Yeah, I know. You and Nick have something magical between you. It's almost spooky when you're together. It's like, you start to say something, I have no idea what you're even talking about and he jumps in and finishes the sentence. I've heard of couples doing that after fifty years of marriage but you two have been doing it since day one! I am glad you found each other and hope you guys are happy forever. Danielle, you deserve it. Just don't forget me, okay?"

"I won't, Jake. I promise."

"Now, let's get these pictures finished and get on with this wedding!"

Jake was not quite as comfortable taking pictures of Nick and his best man, Roger, but it did give him the chance to talk to Nick alone, one last time, before Danielle became his wife.

"Congratulations, Nick," Jake began and shook his hand warmly. "You know you are the luckiest man alive today."

"Yes, I know, Jake," Nick replied. "I knew from the first time I talked to Danny that she was special. She was only a freshman but even then she had a mystery and a maturity about her well beyond her years."

"Yeah, I felt it too. Most of the girls I met back then at ZIPS and whatever were still stuck in high school. They seemed shallow and boring to me. But Danielle was different. She seemed mature, but then in other ways, she had...ah...has an innocence of the ways of the world ...ahem," Jake nervously cleared his throat, "if you know what I mean."

"I know, Jake. She and I have talked at length about this.

After the death of her parents, she was forced to grow up quickly. I assure you, I love Danny with all my heart and will never do anything to hurt her. I know how people say that you need to have numerous relationships with a variety of people so that when the right one comes along you know it. I guess you could put me in that category. But I also believe that when you meet your soul mate you know it no matter what your past has been. Jake, you have helped Danny more than you may realize. She told me how helpful you were when she came back after the crash. It was important that she could open up and talk about it with you. I am glad that you guys are friends and want you to know that you will always be welcome in our home."

"Thanks, Nick. I know that you will be a good husband to her. That's important. But Danielle has amazing potential as a writer. It's like, writing is a part of her that she can't live without. Hard to explain."

"Don't worry, Jake," Nick interrupted. "Danny and I have talked about this too and I fully support her professional goals. It's one of the things that attracted me to her and is clearly a big part of who she is. I hope she doesn't have to travel too much to research her stories but I have my work too and I fully support her ambitions."

"That's great," Jake said. "I feel kind of funny talking to you like this – I'm not trying to act like her dad or anything but I really care about her and, selfishly, I hope to continue working with her for a long, long time. I'll have to admit, I was pretty apprehensive when the two of you announced your engagement after being together such a short time and now, getting married so soon. But I've had time to catch up and to realize that the two of you were destined to be together. Enough of that! Let's get a shot of you with Roger and then we'll bring in the little guy. You're a pretty good looking trio of goons in monkey suits."

The rest of the day for Danielle, Nick and Jake was a blur. Jake busied himself trying to capture every moment on film while Nick and Danielle simply enjoyed every moment together. At last, the ceremony and reception were over, the last goodbyes were said and the happy couple left their well-wishing friends and family. They climbed into the white stretch limousine waiting to take them to their honeymoon suite at the Whitney Hotel where they would spend their first night before leaving the next afternoon for ten days in Hawaii. Nick hesitated to be so conventional and honeymoon in Hawaii, but Danielle had never been to the islands and there were so many good reasons why Hawaii was such a popular honeymoon destination. When Danielle told Nick that she had chosen Hawaii for her fifth grade report on her favorite state, the decision was final. Like the blue scarf in his tux pocket, some things were just meant to be.

As meticulously as his mother had planned the reception, Nick tended to every detail for their wedding night. From the champagne and roses surrounding the whirlpool tub, to the soft candlelight illuminating the lush king-sized bed. He wanted everything to be perfect for the first night of the rest of their lives together.

And it was perfect in every way. The fatigue of the long day was soaked away in the tub as they sipped champagne and talked about the wedding, all of the new people she met, the reception and the music. Nick had surprised her by having the DJ play "Love Came Down at Christmas" for their first dance. Nick was embarrassed that Liz had a bit too much to drink and kept calling him Nicky, his childhood nickname.

"I thought it was cute, Nicky," Danielle teased.

"Not funny, Danny. I felt like I was five years old."

Danielle got a serious look on her face. "My dad used to call me punkin'. I'd give anything to have him embarrass me by calling me that again."

"I know, honey. I know."

Then Nick took the bar of handmade vanilla soap and gently washed Danielle's body starting with her arms, neck and back gently stroking and rubbing away the tension. She drew in a long breath as his hands moved over her breasts and when the two of them could wait no longer they moved to the candlelit bed and made love, slowly, passionately and completely, until at last they slept in each other's arms.

CHAPTER 8

All too soon Nick was back at work checking his voice messages and scanning through the mail on his desk. It was a good thing Nick loved his work and was dedicated to the project because going to the lab while his beautifully tanned, sexy wife was at home in his bed was no easy task. He took the snapshot he had of her wearing a strapless black dress with a beautiful purple and yellow orchid lei draped across her shoulders, and tacked it up on the corkboard next to his desk. He would have it enlarged and framed later but for now this would do. He quickly perused the printed reports left on his desk and scanned the updates on the team's research projects before heading down the hallway in search of Sonny.

"Hey, Nick. Welcome back! How was the honeymoon?" Sonny said as he pushed his chair back from the microscope. Dr. Sono Marino, *Sonny* to his friends, was a heavyset man in his late fifties. What was left of his once full head of hair was a tangled mass of black and grey always in a state of disarray. His dark bushy eyebrows were as unruly as his hair framing his dark, piercing eyes, which, when he was irritated, burned like hot coals from behind his thick glasses now dangling around his neck from a black cord.

"Hello, Sonny. How is it going?" Nick said warmly as he shook Sonny's hand. "Hawaii was great, as Hawaii always is, and our honeymoon was perfect. Danny and I had a wonderful time. Usually I do some island hopping but this time we stayed the entire time on Maui. Gave us plenty of time to see the sights without feeling like we were on the go all the time. I loved the pace – so relaxing. It was hard to get on the plane and come back," Nick sighed.

"Did you fly Northwest?"

"Right, the direct flight. We had seats in the first class upper deck of a 747 – only twelve people up there with our own flight attendant. Even with our seats reclined flat, there was room to walk between the rows. It's the only way to fly!"

"Well you look rested and well-tanned. You must have actually left the hotel room now and again," Sonny chided.

"Not that it's any of your business but, yes, we spent a lot of time on the water. Whale watching, sailing, sunning. I've always liked Hawaii but this time it was extraordinary. Like I always say, it's not paradise, but you can see it from there!"

"Well, being there with Danielle must have been paradise. You're a lucky man! Nick, I'm glad you're back. After you get settled, come back to the lab so I can bring you up-to-date. There have been some exciting developments while you were gone."

"Why don't we meet right now? I hope I didn't miss out on the discovery of the century."

"No, you didn't. But I think we're getting close to a major breakthrough," Sonny said as his eyes darted around the room. "The others haven't come in yet. Will you shut the door? I want this kept between the two of us for now."

Nick closed the door to the lab and sat on the stool next to Sonny.

"Forgive me for insulting you with the basics, but my mind works best when I can describe my research in logical progression," Sonny said.

"That's okay. After spending two weeks in paradise, I'll need a little time to get back in the groove. Go ahead, I'm listening."

"Okay. Let's start with what we know. Some stem cells can replicate themselves over and over without becoming specialized. Look at this analysis from the EMB030933 test we began four months ago. From that single cell, we now have thousands of cells each exhibiting the same traits of the parent stem cell. Each replicated cell has the ability to replicate itself and, more importantly, each replicated cell does not have any tissue-specific structure. In its current structure it is not a red blood cell, a nerve cell or a heart muscle cell. Yet, we know that each is capable of becoming any one of these specialized cells.

"Although all cells in the body contain the same set of genes, most cells are *differentiated,* that is, specialized for a particular function. For instance, a cell in the lens of the eye uses a different subset of genes than a bone cell or a brain cell. Right? But a few cells, the *stem cells*, can differentiate into virtually any kind of cell, under the right conditions. That's of course what we have been working on - creating the right conditions. We still don't understand why a stem cell differentiates into a particular kind of cell but by exposing them to certain controllable external factors such as chemicals secreted by other cells, physical contact with neighboring cells and certain molecules in the micro-environment we have now discovered how to direct stem cell differentiation. Your team identified the *pluripotent* stem cells that can generate *endoderm* cells for the formation of lungs and digestive organs, *mesoderm*, for bone, muscle and connective tissue, and *ectoderm*, giving rise to skin nerves and the brain. Great work, by the way.

"Now, look at the results from ADU350667. We see that while these stem cells also proliferate, they primarily generate the cell types of the tissue in which they reside. The best example of this is a blood-forming adult stem cell in the bone marrow that normally gives rise to red blood cells, white blood cells and platelets.

"So, what is the difference between the two and what is the significance?" Sonny asked.

Nick looked at the EMB030933 slide under the microscope. "These cells are healthy and undifferentiated and capable of long-term self-renewal. They come from the inner cell mass of a four or five-day-old human embryo and are capable of directed differentiation. The ADU350667 cells are adult stem cells and while their use is valuable in the maintenance and repair of the tissue in which they are found, they are rare in mature tissues and we don't yet have methods to replicate them in the lab. Obviously, that's why embryonic stem cells are so much more valuable in our quest to treat diseases such as Parkinson's, diabetes, heart disease and spinal cord injuries."

"Exactly!" said Sonny. "And, what has been our problem in obtaining embryonic stem cells? They are derived from embryos that develop from eggs that have been fertilized in an *in vitro* fertilization clinic. And now, because of pressure from the right wing and the damn governmental funding restrictions we don't have access to what we need to do extensive study!"

"I understand why couples are hesitant to donate their unused embryos for research purposes," Nick replied. "I can't say I blame them. When they go to extraordinary lengths to conceive a child and have experienced successful *in vitro* fertilization, many parents form a personal and moral attachment to the embryos. They know that this tiny group of cells is capable of growing into a child – similar to the one they see playing in the sandbox. Isn't the embryo a precious life?"

"Yes. That is their thinking and we're not here to debate the moral issues," said Sonny. "The point is, there is a very limited supply and our research is hampered as a result. Nick, take a look at this," Sonny said as he carefully removed a slide from a small black case and slipped it under the microscope. "This is sample CLO678612. Tell me what you see."

"Sorry, Sonny. I don't see anything unique here. Looks like the thousand other embryonic stem cell samples we've been working with."

"Exactly!" Sonny exclaimed. It was getting harder and

harder for him to contain his excitement. "But with one monumental difference! These cells were derived from a scientifically generated five-day-old blastocyst! It took over six hundred tries but I finally did it!"

"What? You actually cloned human cells? We have always agreed that we wouldn't take our research in that direction," Nick said.

"You are dedicated to curing diabetes and making it possible for paraplegics to walk again aren't you? Our work has shown time and time again that by leaving in the egg's DNA, the embryo has an extra set of chromosomes rendering it incompatible with the patient's tissue. I now know that the only way to truly create replicate tissue or organs is through cloning."

Nick could feel his heart accelerate and a fine bead of perspiration was forming on his forehead. He didn't want to jump to conclusions, but if Sonny had done what it appeared he had done, the ramifications went far beyond scientific. Trying to keep an even tone to his voice Nick said, "So Sonny, tell me more about this blastocyst."

"Well, it wasn't easy and it certainly wasn't cheap. The key was using young, healthy eggs. I started with seven hundred human egg cells harvested from female university students. An overseas colleague of mine paid for half the donations, the rest came from your father's foundation."

"Dad's? Really? Is he aware of what you are doing?"

"Well, in general terms, yes. It doesn't really matter, what's important are the advancements I've made! I removed each cell's DNA and replaced it with DNA from various human body cells. My initial test results yielded twenty-four embryos that stopped dividing at the four-cell stage. Only five made it to the six-cell stage. I kept after it and, as with the monkey research, I found that skin cells produced the most consistent results. I used the same electrical impulse and caffeine method to get them to reproduce until, by god, one progressed to a full-blown blastocyst! I couldn't believe it! I then extracted the inner cell mass, the stem cells, and replicated the exact process we've been using for the past eighteen months. And, by god, you're looking at the results. Undifferentiated embryonic stem cells, self-renewing and capable of directed differentiation! Nick, we've done it!" Sonny shouted as he pushed back his chair from the lab table and clapped his stunned colleague on the back.

Nick stared at the exuberant Dr. Marino in complete amazement. His temples pounded as his brain fired in a million directions at once. *Sonny has created a human clone? This is amazing. But we had agreed. No cloning! Who else knows? Has anyone at the lab been involved? Does Dad know? Who is this overseas colleague? This is wrong on so many levels. I thought I was his right hand. How could he risk the reputation of the University? Screw the U! He's putting all of our careers at risk!*

Sonny's smile faded as he studied Nick's expression. "Why Nick, my friend. I've never seen you at such a loss for words."

"Loss for words?" Nick said. "I have so many things to say to you, I don't know where to begin! Let's start with completely irresponsible. Cloning a sheep is one thing but a human being? There is no way this will be acceptable to the scientific community not to mention the social and moral outcry if this is made public. You will ruin our years of research and take down the University of Minnesota medical school with you."

"Nick, Nick, take it easy! You should be grateful. Even with my Italian roots I have too much pride in American science to let the rest of the world pass us by. Besides, I didn't actually create a human clone. No one in his right mind would try to make that accusation based on a five-day old blastocyst. It's not illegal you know and you are the only one here who knows about this breakthrough. I'm sure I can trust you to hold the confidence until we decide how to proceed, can't I? I've been so damned excited I couldn't wait for you to get back. Think of the possibilities!"

"So no one else at the lab knows what you have been up to?"

"No. I've worked alone on this," Sonny said.

"What about this *overseas colleague* of yours?"

"He provided the eggs, that's all."

"Oh, so you used the University's federal grant funds to procure samples under false pretenses?"

"Not exactly. The samples are being used for our other projects too and the rest of the funds came from the foundation."

"I feel much better now," Nick snapped. "And, thanks for dragging my father into this!"

"Get off your high horse Nick. When did you become the beacon of moral ethics? I thought you would be as excited as I am. Think, man! Think of the possibilities."

"I have thought of the possibilities and it scares the hell out of me! You may think you can control science but you can't – it will control you. And I don't think you will stop here. You will keep going *in the name of science* until we have an actual Frankenstein baby in our lab and I will tell you right now, I want no part of it!"

"You want no part? You already have a part of this," Sonny shot back. "You're the one that refined the process. What's the difference between recreating a body part from a stem cell and cells that have been cloned from the patient? The end result is the same and we'll have better success! Damn it Nick, get off your pedestal!"

Sonny turned toward the window and waited a moment. He was caught off guard by Nick's reaction and now he needed to bring him around. Nick knew too much and if he wasn't on board, Sonny had a serious problem. There was too much at stake to let Nick stand in the way now and he would have to find a way to convince him. Sonny toned down his anger, turned back to Nick and said in a softer but firm tone, "Nick, we've worked together too long to let this come between us. I'd like you to take some time to think about the benefits that can be derived from this discovery –

life changing benefits for sick and disabled people around the world. I really want you to be my partner in this. We are a team and I need your expertise to continue to explore the process. You and I have the opportunity of a lifetime to navigate uncharted waters and make a name for ourselves. Please, just read my full report and think about it before you jump to conclusions. I know once you fully understand the progress you will see the merits. I have a few updates to make and will leave a copy on your desk. I'm headed to Europe tomorrow and will drop it off on my way to the airport. You can review it first thing Friday morning."

As Nick's emotions and anger subsided, his rational, scientific mind kicked in. What if Sonny's technique could be used to cure cancer, provide a new heart to a dying child, new spinal cord cells for a paraplegic, and cure a host of other maladies? Wouldn't there be huge benefits for humankind around the world? Yet he couldn't let go of the baby Frankenstein image, deformed and grotesque or worse. But what would happen to his career, his future, if he didn't support Sonny, the prominent and powerful Dr. Marino? But what if he *did* and they were found out? His mind started to spin again as the conflicting thoughts fought each other, each position trying to get a foothold, the foundation upon which to base a life-changing, world-changing decision.

At last he turned to Sonny and with his best attempt at a smile said, "I'm sorry I reacted so negatively. You really caught me off guard and you know, the whole cloning thing triggers such powerful emotions. Give me some time to review and digest your research and I will keep an open mind to the potential for great things to come out of it." He tried to sound convincing as he said, "Congratulations."

"Thanks, Nick. I'm sure you'll see the benefits after reading my report. I'll compile the most recent findings and leave a copy of everything on your desk tomorrow. I'll lock your office door so make sure you take your key. Oh, and Nick. The team all donated skin samples while you were gone. Would you mind having Ted take care of that before you leave today?" As soon as Sonny turned away, his smile vanished and with a scowl he left the room.

"Sure, Sonny. No problem."

Nick retreated to the solitude of his office but was unable to concentrate on anything. He picked up reports, scanned them for salient points and then put them down on the desk as his mind drifted back to his conversation with Sonny. The backlog of research reports to review and responses to be written lay piled up around him in disarray instead of neatly organized and filed. By late afternoon, other than donating a slice of skin for science, he hadn't accomplished anything. He finally gave up, told the team he was suffering from jet lag, and left for the day.

"Danny? Honey, I'm home," Nick called out as he removed his shoes inside the door and walked through the kitchen into the family room.

He hadn't protested when Danielle suggested the main level of the house be re-carpeted and painted while they were on their honeymoon. The soft, off-white pile carpet and colorful walls gave the house a fresh new look, removed some of the dark masculine feel and provided, as Danielle said, "a new palette for the future." He wiggled his toes in the new carpet for a moment and was reminded that just two days ago he was wiggling his toes in the warm white sand. Nick willed himself to recapture the relaxed, carefree mood of their honeymoon and tried to forget Sonny's shocking news. The last thing he wanted was to break the blissful mood with Danny and upset her with his dilemma. "Danny, where are you?"

"Hi," Danielle said as she ran to greet him. "You're home early and I'm so glad! I've missed you terribly," she said as she stood on her tiptoes and gave him a warm, passionate kiss.

Nick let his worries wash away as his tongue met hers,

first playfully then with a profound sense of urgency. Danielle moaned softly as he guided her to the floor and once again discovered the depth of her passion.

"Now that's what I call breaking in the new carpet," Danielle whispered as they lay naked from the waist down on the family room floor. "Which room are we going to christen tomorrow night?"

Nick opened his eyes and smiled, "Who said anything about waiting until tomorrow?"

Danielle shrieked as he grabbed her and smothered her with kisses. "Hey, how about a shower and some dinner? Let's go upstairs and I want to hear all about your day," she said.

"Shower and dinner sound great but let's forget about my day. As far as I am concerned, we are still on our honeymoon and I want to focus all of my energy on you – and I mean all of my energy!" Nick said as he pulled her to her feet.

"Well then, let me tell you what I did today between unpacking, doing laundry and getting groceries. Did you know there was absolutely nothing in this house to eat or drink? No fresh pineapple, no Kona coffee, no macadamia nut ice cream. I looked out the window and couldn't see any palm trees, no white puffy clouds against the deep blue sky, no mountains in the distance. I couldn't hear the sound of the surf or smell the plumeria and I missed you immensely. So I took my camera to the student center with hopes that my feeble attempts to capture the beauty of Maui were successful. Guess who I ran into?"

"Who?"

"Jake!"

"What a coincidence. I hope you told him what a fantastic lover I am. I wouldn't want him to think he still has a chance with you."

"Nick, you know Jake and I are just friends."

"That's what you always say, but don't tell me he didn't want to be more than that. I saw the way he looked at you. I knew from the first time I met him – the night of the student protest - that he was in love with you. Wasn't he?"

"Dr. Goodman! I've told you a million times, you are the one and only love of my life," Danielle laughed. "Now drop the fake jealously bit okay? Anyway, Jake has a lead on an assignment to do a photo essay and asked if I would work with him. You may have heard about the Catholic priest right here in Minneapolis accused of sexual abuse."

"Did he do it?"

"I don't know, but in light of all the cases coming out these days, he probably is guilty. I can't imagine men coming forward with this accusation if it weren't true."

"What's the angle?" Nick asked.

"Well, it appears that Father Flynn was transferred from parish to parish over the years so it's possible that the church leadership knew about the abuse. Of course the Archdiocese denies this allegation."

"So do you want to do the story?"

"I'm not sure. Being abused as a child is bad enough but to have it happen within the church and be condoned by those in power. It's unimaginable! I don't think it's just a cover-up but a systemic issue. Anyway, there is certainly a story here. The topic is so sensitive and I doubt the church will be very cooperative. It will have to done very carefully."

"I know you can be objective. I think you should do it! Speaking of sensitive topics, there is something I want to talk to you about," Nick said as he stepped into the shower, "but that can be our dinner conversation. For now, come in here with me and let me wash your un-tan lines."

After their shower, Nick and Danielle worked together in the kitchen. Nick poured the wine while Danielle tossed the salad and cut the fresh green beans. Nick skillfully removed the skin from the salmon fillet, rubbed it with virgin olive oil and sprinkled it with lemon pepper. "Fifteen minutes on the grill and we'll be ready to eat."

"I'm bummed we can't have Mahi Mahi tonight, but your salmon on the grill is the next best thing," Danielle said.

"I'm anxious to use the beautiful china and crystal we received as wedding gifts but I haven't had a chance to wash everything yet. Let's eat in the dining room anyway. I'll set the table while you do your grilling thing."

As Nick went out and started the gas grill on the back patio, Danielle wanted to pinch herself to make sure she wasn't dreaming. Her life with Nick was just beginning and yet it was already more than she had ever hoped for. Being somewhat of a feminist, Danielle hadn't imagined a white-night romance and didn't aspire to Ginny's entire life goal consisting of marriage and family. But now that she found herself in this state of unexpected wedded bliss, she intended to savor every moment. That is, until she decided on her next project and immersed herself in its cause. Jake was wrong when he suggested today that if her head stayed up in the clouds too long, she might lose sight of the real world. *Wasn't he?*

"Danny, these will be ready in ten minutes," Nick called from the patio breaking her reverie.

Danielle steamed the beans, added papaya and mango dressing to the salad and carefully measured the freshly ground Kona coffee into their new coffeemaker. She was glad they brought back a few treasures from Hawaii to extend the pleasures of their honeymoon. As far as she was concerned, she wished it would last forever.

Nick and Danielle chatted lightly during dinner reliving the intimate and humorous experiences of the past weeks up to their romp on the living room floor. "If I had to be taken to the hospital tonight, how would I explain the rug burns on my buns?" Danielle demanded playfully. "You really should be more careful you know."

"Yes Miss Fragility. But you needn't worry. I am a doctor and fully trained to treat rug burns in the privacy of your own home." Nick tried to sound serious but didn't last long before bursting into laughter.

"Better Fragility than Frigidity!" Danielle joined in. "Let's take our coffee into the living room but you have to promise, no rug wrestling. I don't want coffee stains on the new carpet."

"Promise."

"So, what it is you wanted to talk about?" Danielle asked.

"Well, remember when we were on the beach watching the little Japanese boy and his dad building a sand castle?"

"Of course! He was so cute and the castle was very elaborate with the moat and turrets. So much work only to be washed away by the evening tide."

"But the joy was in the building; father and son working together. Danny," Nick said as he cradled her face in his hands, "I am overwhelmed by how much I love you and at the same time I am terrified of losing you. I am afraid that, now that we are home, we will each become engrossed in our work and the days and the years will slip by and we will never have the chance to play on the beach with our children."

"Oh, Nick," Danielle said as she pulled him close, "we have our whole lives ahead of us and after my parents' death, I learned not to take for granted the wonder of each day. You know I want to have children too, but first I want to savor the beauty of just the two of us."

"I do too. But what if once we decide to have a baby, we can't? That happens to a lot of career-minded couples that wait to start their families. I read some new research today by Dr. David Palmershein, he's a recognized and respected doctor of Reproductive Endocrinology & Infertility at Berkeley. His study supports what we've known for a long time that a woman is born with all of the eggs she will ever have. These eggs begin to diminish throughout childhood and into adulthood. By the fifth or sixth decade of life, women will have depleted the egg supply they were born with."

Danielle nodded.

"There is also the cessation of the production of the female sex hormones, estrogen and progesterone, which are necessary for pregnancy. In some women, there is an acceleration of this process, with egg depletion occurring before age forty. The scary part about his research is that there are forty percent more cases of infertility among thirty-five-year-old women today than there were ten years ago. There is no conclusive evidence as to why but the odds are getting worse, not better."

Danielle could no longer contain herself. Before bursting into laughter she managed to squeak out a serious, "Thank you for your report, Dr. Goodman!"

Nick joined her laughter. "I was getting a little deep wasn't I? But this is important and I want you to understand the risks of waiting too long."

"I do understand the risks and I'm really glad you are an expert on the subject, but we've only been married two weeks and I'm barely twenty-three!" Danielle smiled and squeezed his hand.

"Yes, but I'm an old man of forty-one."

"The report is about women your age, not men! Besides, judging from the past two weeks, I don't think we need to worry about you! I promise, we won't wait too long."

"Okay," Nick said.

"Speaking of babies, Jake was telling me today about Sondra Williams, a photographer we knew in school. She was an associate professor but we got to know her pretty well through the Photography Club trips. Anyway, she had the chance of a lifetime to go to South Africa to photograph a story on the release of Nelson Mandela. She was three months pregnant and unfortunately the long flight and the pace of the trip were just too much. She got really sick and there was no choice but to get her home as quickly as possible. Thank God the baby is okay but she told Jake that it could be the end of her career. Not that she can't go back to work after the baby is born, she just doesn't want to. She told Jake that if something happened to the baby while she was overseas, she couldn't forgive herself. My dad traveled some but Mom was always home with me. There is still an assumption that moms take care of the kids and dads work to support the family."

"I know, Danny," Nick said gently, "it doesn't seem fair but at least women now have choices. You are on your way to becoming a well-known writer and I am going to do everything I can to help you achieve your career dreams. Let's just promise each other not to let the time slip by before starting our family, okay?"

"I agree and I have to tell you, I'm kind of old fashioned when it comes to parenthood. I know infertile couples have options, but for me, I can't imagine going through the pain, frustration and expense of extensive fertility treatment. I mean *in vitro* fertilization and all of that. If I couldn't get pregnant, I think I would want to adopt. There are so many children in the world that need loving homes. I'm not saying it's wrong or anything, I just can't justify using all those resources just to have a genetic link to the future. It's kind of an egocentric view of oneself, don't you think?"

"Oh, I don't know," Nick answered cautiously. "It's such a personal thing. Many couples marry with the specific dream of having children together. It's such a central part of life that when it doesn't happen, they feel incomplete. Now that we have the ability to treat infertility, people have choices that weren't available in the past. It's one more reason I love my work – not just to save lives but also to improve the quality of life. Now, not to change the subject but how about a walk before the mosquitoes come out?"

"Sounds good," Danielle said. "That's another thing I loved about Hawaii, walking outside after dark and not being eaten alive."

"Except by your husband," Nick said as he leaned over and nibbled at Danielle's neck. "I'm going to throw on some shorts. Do you know where my tennis shoes are?"

"They are in the walk-in closet on the left side toward the front next to your brown loafers. I hope you don't mind that I put your things away. I hate to disrupt your organization."

"As long as you can tell me where I can find what I need, I'm a happy man."

Nick and Danielle left the house and walked hand-in-hand down the sidewalk out onto Mount Curve Avenue. Danielle stopped to look back at the beautiful brick mansion that was now her home. Nick and Danielle's engagement coincided with his parents' desire to move into a new penthouse condo in downtown Minneapolis overlooking the Mississippi River. Since Liz and Frank were spending winters in Palm Springs and summers at their lake home on Round Lake, they were happy to give the mortgage-free Kenwood house to Nick and Danielle. All they would have to worry about were utilities, taxes, insurance and maintenance - a manageable budget for the newlywed couple. Nick loved his research work at the U of M and wanted Danielle to be free from financial worries so he was glad he didn't have to trade their passions for the higher pay of private practice.

Danielle was more interested in the beauty and history of the area than the prestige associated with their Kenwood address and was anxious to explore her new surroundings. The Kenwood area was a fascinating historic neighborhood, so close to downtown Minneapolis and the Walker Art Center yet connected to the city's chain of lakes with miles of bike trails and acres of nature areas to explore. Nick had grown up here and was familiar not only with every house and alley in the neighborhood but he knew most of the old-timers names and their kids. As they walked, Danielle was excited to tell Nick about every detail of her day and he was more than happy to listen, adeptly avoiding any inquiry about his day at the lab by remarking about a home they were passing by.

"Not to interrupt you Danny," Nick said, "but look at how beautiful this lawn is. Bob Brinkman spends most of his free time working on his grass. He's a retired surgeon; he used to implant medical devices. He's one of the few in the neighborhood who does his own yard work. I guess he still likes working with his hands. In the spring it's dethatching and raking, seeding and fertilizing. He always mows in perfectly straight diagonal rows and bags the clippings. Look, not a weed in sight or a blade of grass out of place. Isn't his lawn beautiful? As it gets hotter and drier he waters and I swear, moves his sprinklers into exact position after precisely the same amount of time. He must set a timer in the house and no matter what is happening, by gosh, when the buzzer rings, he moves the sprinklers!"

"His poor wife!"

"Yeah, can you imagine? They are having the best sex of their lives and the sprinkler buzzer goes off. Hold that thought, honey, I'll be right back!"

Danielle looked up and down the block. "So do you think you can tell the quality of a neighbor's sex life by the condition of their lawn?"

"If so, our lawn is destined to be a complete disaster this summer!"

"Ya' think?" Danielle smiled mischievously. "Well I don't know much about grass but when I was a little girl, I spent a lot of time with my mom in her garden. There was always something blooming from spring until fall. Some of my best memories are of summers in the garden. Not that I was much help when I was little but it was fun just looking at the flowers, watching the butterflies and being with Mom. When I was older, I'd bring a notebook and sit out in the garden and write. Too bad I didn't write down tips on gardening. Mom knew everything and it would come in handy now. I remember keeping her company, tumbling in the grass practicing my handsprings, back tucks and round offs. One time when I was working on my aerial walkover I thought I had it and I called to Mom to watch. She stood up just in time to see me flying into her favorite rose bush. I don't know what she felt worse about, my scratched up bleeding body or the broken bush."

"Ouch! Somehow I can picture you doing that," Nick said. "I've never had time to do much more than cut the grass and now even that is done by a lawn service. I think it would be great if you restored our gardens. We could probably find some old photos of how the grounds looked back at the turn of the century. It would be kind of cool to recreate the look - of course with the modern benefit of a sprinkling system. We'd have to dig up some of the sod."

"We? You mean you'll hire someone to do it, right?" Danielle teased. "I'd love to do the research and create a nice blend of past and present. Maybe I could bring some plants from home. I really like the idea. Let's walk through the neighborhood tonight and get some garden ideas although, after the exotic flowers in Hawaii, it will be hard to settle for geraniums and pansies."

As they walked from house to house, Danielle stopped to point out the various annuals, perennials, shrubs and groundcover. Nick was impressed by how much she knew and was grateful for the diversion. They had made their way back home without a word about his day at the lab.

"Would you mind if we go to bed early tonight?" Nick asked as he unlocked the door and held it as Danielle went in. "I can't believe how tired I am."

"Am I wearing you out?" Danielle playfully tugged at his belt buckle.

"Not a chance!" Nick lifted her off her feet. "It happens every time I travel. My inner clock gets all goofed up. Maybe if we watch TV for a while I'll be able to go to sleep at a reasonable hour and get back on schedule."

"I know. It seemed like I had just fallen asleep when your alarm rang," Danielle said.

"It was so hard getting up especially leaving you so beautifully asleep in my bed. That will take some getting used to," Nick said as he gave Danielle a gentle kiss.

"I'm glad you can ease back into the real world. Work one day, off tomorrow for the Fourth of July, work one day, off for the weekend. Think you can handle it?"

"With you by my side I can handle anything!"

Nick had actually enjoyed their Fourth of July celebration at his parents' condo. Their tenth floor balcony overlooking the river was a perfect spot for viewing the fireworks. Danielle baked a cake, frosted it with whipped cream and decorated it with strawberries and blueberries like an American flag. But now that the festivities were over and Danielle was fast asleep beside him, his mind churned with worry about work.

Nick flipped between channels unable to stay interested in anything for long. He turned back to CNN. "The President has made it clear that he is one hundred percent opposed to any type of cloning of human cells," said spokeswoman Jennifer Millerwise.

The camera shifted back to the reporter standing in front of the U.S. Capitol "While the UK has recently passed the Human Fertilization and Embryology Act which bans the cloning of humans to create babies or embryos for research, the U.S. has no legislation prohibiting or controlling human cloning. Congress has been reluctant to consider the controversial topic leaving the issue up to the states. In light of tonight's news from Rome, we are left to wonder how far American scientists have taken this amazing, controversial technology. From Washington D.C., Pat Dickenson, CNN News."

"What? What news?" Nick whispered not wanting to wake Danielle. CNN had moved on to other news, none of which interested him. He flipped from station to station trying to find some other report but with no luck. *Well, it couldn't have been that monumental or Sonny would have called me. It will have to wait until morning.* Nick turned off the television and tried to sleep. He considered counting sheep but that got him thinking about the public outcry around the first cloned sheep. His mind whirled as he thought about the implications of human cloning. Not only was it immoral but he was outraged at the thought that anyone would go that far – especially without knowing what the outcome might be. *It's not a like an animal that can be euthanized if the outcome is bad. You can't just kill a person if your experiment becomes Frankensteinian. And now, what has Sonny done?*

With heart pounding and thoughts racing, sleep would not come. Nick finally forced himself to change his mental picture to the beach in Hawaii. He imagined lying face down on his towel next to Danielle, the sun hot on his back and the sound of the ocean waves rolling into shore. He could hear the roar of the waves crashing against the rocks, the sound coming from the right, moving past him and fading off to his left. The surf was constant, one wave after the next and the next and the next. It took a long time but at last he could no longer hear the waves slowly and steadily rolling toward him.

CHAPTER 9

Nick woke up just before the alarm rang at six thirty and reached over to turn if off before it could awaken Danielle. She was beautiful and when sleeping looked so small and innocent snuggled up in the soft cotton comforter. "I love you," Nick whispered as he softly kissed her and got out of bed.

Showered and shaved, he quietly dressed, gave Danielle another kiss and slipped downstairs to get the morning paper. He appreciated Danielle's thoughtfulness as he caught the aroma of freshly brewed coffee. She must have prepared it last night using the automatic timer to be ready for him when he got up. With only a few hours of sleep he desperately needed the large cup he poured. Nick sat down in the breakfast nook pulling the newspaper from its protective yellow plastic bag. The small article on the front page immediately caught his eye.

Italian scientist announces plan for human clone!
Italian professor Antonio Salvatori announced plans to begin transferring DNA from the nuclei of living cells into human eggs to create a human embryo that could potentially be viable if implanted into a woman's uterus. Salvatori and his unnamed American partner said that because of the genetic screening of the embryos, their methodology could produce a healthy human clone. The Italian medical association

is considering disciplinary action against Salvatori for his stated plans, although without express legislation prohibiting human cloning, sanctions will likely be unsuccessful. Italy's medical code stipulates that medical experimentation is allowed only for the prevention and correction of medical problems. But Salvatori, Director of the International Associated Research Institute, told Reuters news agency: "You can't put up arbitrary barriers on therapeutic cloning. Cloning will help us put an end to so many diseases, restore function to injured organs and give infertile men and women the chance to have children. We can't pass up this opportunity." Harsh public outcry is expected against Professor Salvatori and anyone who supports his efforts.

Nick knew that this was the report he missed on the news the night before. He took a long draw from his coffee and steeled his resolve to stop Sonny from going forward with his experimentation. He would not allow his name in the headlines! He shoved the newspaper into his briefcase and left the house.

He noticed traffic was light for a Friday as he merged onto I-94 headed east into the early morning sunshine. During the all too short summer months, Twin Citians headed up north "to the lake" on Fridays but since Thursday was the Fourth of July, many had left town on Wednesday. He took the University Exit and automatically maneuvered through the side streets to the medical complex. The beauty of the cloudless morning sky and the sound of the singing birds were lost on Nick as he made his way to his reserved spot in the ramp, right next to the vacant one marked Dr. Marino. His jaw clenched when he saw Sonny's name. *At least he is out of the country so I won't have to confront him today.*

Nick dashed up the stairs and out of the ramp. As he hurried across the park toward the lab, he was too preoccupied to stop, as he often did, at the spot he first ran into Danielle. Today was a day like the one four years ago. He had been thinking so intently about his work he was oblivious to the world around him and that propelled him smack dab into Danielle O'Neil. Without realizing it then, it was one of the most important days of his life. And with no more awareness of his surroundings than on that day, today would be as significant for both of them.

The lab was dark and the outside doors locked. Nick searched for his key and unlocked both sets of doors. The alarm chirped as he struggled to remember the code. It had been a while since he had been the first one there in the morning. On the second try the code he punched in registered and turned the control light to green. There was just enough light coming in for Nick to see; he was too impatient to turn on the hallway lights. As expected, his office door was locked but he had his key ready and the door opened easily. He turned on his office lights and walked immediately to his desk – anxious to read Sonny's report and review his findings. But, instead of a thick file, there was only a note which read, "Sorry. Didn't have time to make a copy of my report. My flight was changed – have to run. See you on Wednesday. S.M."

Nick crumpled up the note and threw it against the wall. "Shit!" he said as he flopped down in his chair. As he did so he heard steps approaching and a moment later Sonny walked into his office.

Confused, Nick said, "Sonny. What are you doing here? I thought you were in Europe."

"Well, I did take a cab to the airport last night and all indications lead to the conclusion that I left yesterday. However, I couldn't leave before you and I had a chance to talk. I'm sure by now you've heard the news."

"You mean about the Italian, Salvatori?"

"Yes. The damned fool went public with our plan and has created an international uproar."

"What do you mean *our* plan? What's your involvement in this?"

"Antonio and I met two years ago at a convention in Tokyo. We had similar ideas and interests in stem cell research and have been working together since. Ah, the power of the Internet! As you probably gleaned from our conversation yesterday, we are working toward a human clone – but, as I said, solely for laudable purposes. After seeing your reaction yesterday and then Antonio's blundering announcement, I was afraid you would put two and two together and do something to jeopardize the project. That would be both foolish and futile."

"Sonny, how can I just sit back and do nothing? My reputation is at stake here too!"

"Well I can't allow you to interfere!" Sonny shouted. "There's no way I can be linked to Salvatori - I've been very careful." Sonny saw that Nick's hands were trembling and there was no mistaking the look of anger and betrayal on his face. "I trusted that you would support me on this. If it's revealed that I am working with Salvatori on human cloning, our research will be shut down immediately. Everything we've built, everything we've worked for! That can't happen now. We are so close!" Sonny slammed his fist on the desk.

"Sonny you are only thinking about your own glory. You know any association with cloning will destroy my work!"

Sonny stepped closer. "What I care about is *my* work and I won't allow anyone to stand in my way, not Salvatori, not you, not the goddamned President of the United States, not God himself!"

Suddenly Nick's emotions changed from anger to fear. Sonny had always displayed a passionate zeal for his work, but the man towering over him now had crossed over. His flushed face and dilated eyes burned with an insane resolve. "Sonny hold on!" Nick said. "What are you saying? You know I support you and I have always stood by you. Don't forget the incident with the girl in your molecular genetics class. I was the one who went before the board on your behalf and got them to drop the sexual harassment claim."

"Yes, Nick," Sonny snarled. "I have relied on you as my partner. But now, my friend, I am afraid our paths are going in different directions. I've seen it before but I didn't think it would happen to you. American men fall in love and lose their balls! Greatness requires taking risks and now that you have Danielle, you just want to play it safe."

Nick tried to backpedal and said with as much humility as he could feign, "I know I reacted badly but I do respect your work and see that the benefits of cloning can be monumental. I want to read your report. I still want to be part of your team."

"Nice try, Nick. I know you better than that. We've had this intrinsic difference for years and now you've changed your mind? I don't think so. Even if I did believe you, surely you don't think I can trust you now to keep such a controversial discovery secret. Even my *real* partner Antonio has betrayed me!" Sonny slammed his fist on the desk as he leaned over, his face just inches from Nick's. "For Christ's sake, Nick, you're a newlywed. Do you think you can keep this from Danielle? Do you? Do you?"

Nick was unable to respond. The room was unbearably hot, sweat dripped from his forehead. Sonny was clearly out of control and unable to listen to reason. He rubbed his temples and closed his eyes for a moment to gather his thoughts but all he could think of was of Danielle lying peacefully asleep in their bed. He wished he were back at home out of this nightmare.

Sonny took the opportunity. He pulled the syringe from his jacket pocket and stabbed Nick in the back of the neck being careful to stay within the hairline. Nick had no time to react as the serum took hold immediately. As Sonny emptied the syringe, paralysis enveloped Nick. He slumped forward in his chair until his head rested on his desk.

"You've been given a lethal injection of mortacuratine," Sonny said. "You are probably aware of your surroundings but obviously unable to move or speak. The drug creates instant paralysis and within two minutes, your heart will simply stop beating. It is painless and leaves no trace in the bloodstream, tissue or organs. Don't worry about your family, Nick. They will likely be told by the coroner that you died of instantaneous total heart failure."

Nick could hear Sonny's voice but was helpless against the effects of the drug. For a brief moment, his brain commanded him to fight, to struggle, then a complete calm came over him. He no longer felt angry or afraid. His only vision was of Danielle, his love.

"See, my friend? Even now I imagine you are thinking of your beautiful wife and sadly she has cost you your life! Ah, the power of love. Why now? Why did you have to fall in love now? We were so close to success and she ruined everything for you – as wives usually do. I'm really sorry it had to end this way but I had no choice," Sonny said softly. "Nick, you were like a son to me. All these years working together, I always hoped you would be with me to share the spotlight. I promised that to your father. He supported our work more than you'll ever know. If only you could have seen it my way,"

Sonny took a second syringe, drew a small amount of Nick's blood and dropped it into his pocket. "For posterity, my boy." Sonny put his fingers on Nick's neck and feeling no pulse he was satisfied that Nick was dead. "So long, Nick. I have a plane to catch."

Sonny quickly walked out of Nick's office closing the door behind him but leaving it unlocked. He walked quickly down the hallway to the back entrance where he paused to put on the blue baseball cap and khaki windbreaker he had picked up at the thrift store. The lab was closed today because of the Fourth of July Holiday, a fact he had conveniently forgotten to mention to Nick, and it was still early in the morning. With summer session classes suspended for the holiday, most students would either be gone or still in bed. Yet, he couldn't afford to be recognized leaving the lab. After checking to make sure no one was in sight, he left the building and casually crossed the park to the street behind the ramp where he had left the rental car. He looked around again and seeing no one, slipped into the nondescript vehicle. Perfect! Five stoplights and five minutes later he was on the freeway headed toward the airport.

CHAPTER 10

Danielle awoke at seven thirty and hopped out of bed. She pulled open the drapes to confirm her euphoric feeling and it was indeed *a beautiful day in the neighborhood*. She was excited about the idea of restoring the gardens and wanted to follow up with Jake about the priest abuse story. All in all, it was great to be alive and it was absolutely fantastic to be Mrs. Nicholas Goodman. Professionally, Danielle intended to keep her byline, Danielle O'Neil, but legally she had taken Nick's name. She had considered keeping her maiden name but hyphenating it would have been weird with the apostrophe and the dash and Ginny, now *Mrs. Severson*, had pleaded with her to take her husband's name as she had done. Ginny said, "How would you have felt as a little girl if your name was Danielle O'Neil, and your mom was Nicole Boisette? Course a lot of the women who keep their names are career women and probably will never have kids but you want a family, don't you Danny?"

"Oh, yes," Danielle said as she turned on the shower. "I definitely want to have Nick Goodman's baby! Just not right away," she added just to hear herself say it. Nick's lecture about waiting too long hadn't fallen on deaf ears and she was utterly in love with him! But she had dreamed of being a writer since she was a little girl and was just now getting exposure in the field. She had the opportunity now to show her stuff and make significant strides in her career. A baby just wasn't in the picture right now. "But, someday," she said dreamily as she turned her back to the showerhead and let the hot water stream over her neck and shoulders. "Someday."

Danielle took her coffee and notepad out to the backyard, sat at the small iron patio table and made notes about the landscaping. The back of the house was oriented south so there was enough morning sunlight for a flower garden in the area not shaded by the massive oak tree. The concrete sidewalk that led from the back door to the row of bedraggled arborvitaes at the back of the lot was uneven, cracked and lined with overgrown hostas. Danielle wondered why there was a sidewalk leading to a hedge and made a note of its approximate location on her pad. She quickly sketched the existing trees, shrubs and perennials making note of where the sunny spots were in the morning sun. She would have to do the same in the afternoon and evening to get a feel for how many hours of direct sunlight various areas of the front and back yards would get throughout the day. She remembered her mom showing her the sunny garden full of Black-Eyed Susans, Coneflowers, Daisies, Sweet Williams, Marigolds, and Butterfly Bush. The sunny garden was Danielle's favorite because she was sure to see beautiful butterflies fluttering from flower to flower. Sometimes if she held her hand out, very still, they would land on her. She would get so excited and try to run to show her mom but as soon as she moved, they would flutter off. Of course roses needed lots of sun but she didn't think she wanted to tackle a rose garden just yet. It was hard enough keeping them from freezing in Sioux City so she wondered if they could survive the harsh winters in Minnesota. Danielle made a mental note to check into hardy perennials.

A grey squirrel scampered down the oak tree and across the sidewalk. *Why is that sidewalk there?* Danielle decided to see what she could find out about the history of the house and discover the reason for the path leading seemingly nowhere. The University library had an extensive Minnesota History section and she knew her way around that place like the back of her hand. After all the hours spent doing research while she lived on campus, she decided to start there.

Danielle had an idea. She could bring the cooler and a blanket, spend a couple of hours at the library, pick up some sandwiches at the Global Market Deli and surprise Nick at the lab. They could have a picnic in the park outside of the lab – the park where they first met. *When did I become such a hopeless romantic?* For the first time since her parents died, Danielle felt loved, safe and secure and she was happy to share her deepest thoughts and dreams of the future with Nick. She couldn't wait to see him!

As she backed out of the driveway, she opened the sunroof, turned up the radio and sang along. It was a great day! She was still humming as she left the library and drove over to the deli. With the cooler stocked with corned beef sandwiches, potato salad, kosher dill pickles and two bottles of water, she drove to the medical center complex and looked for a place to park. There were usually only a few summer school students around this time of year and with the Fourth of July holiday the campus was deserted. She found a spot on the street across from the park and plugged six quarters into the meter. Danielle piled the blanket on top of the cooler and pulled it across the lawn toward Lyon's Lab. Luckily Nick's cooler was fairly new, the kind with wheels and a long handle. She contemplated leaving it all under the tree but thought better of it. Just her luck she would lose the cooler and her lunch. *That's life in the big city.* So she pulled the load down the sidewalk and up to the doors leading into the research lab building.

I'm not dragging this thing downstairs though. Finding the outer doors unlocked, she left the cooler and blanket in the entryway. As she went through the second set of doors she noticed that there were no lights on in the hallway. *That's odd.* She found the set of switches and flipped them all up turning on the entryway lights and both rows of hallway lights. Danielle didn't see or hear anyone in the building as she quickly walked down the hall to Nick's office. The door was closed and Danielle shouted, "Surprise!" as she opened the door and popped into the office.

No response.

"Nick?" Seeing his head rested on the desk, she walked over to the chair and shook his shoulder. Her smile turned to horror as his head dropped to the side. His eyes were open but lifeless - mouth open - face grey. The room spun as Danielle's mind simultaneously tried to understand the scene and denied what she was seeing. "Oh my God!" she screamed. "Nick!" She stepped into the hall and screamed hoping someone would come to help him - to rescue her from this nightmare. "Help! Help me!" she screamed. But no one came. The building was quiet. Adrenaline kicking in, she ran to Nick and touched his face hoping beyond hope to feel some sign of life. Her hand jerked back from the cold feel of his skin. "This isn't happening! God, please! This isn't happening!"

By the time the 911 operator answered the phone, Danielle was hysterical. "Help me! Help me!" she screamed.

"Ma'am, what's wrong?"

"My husband! He's…"

As Danielle's brain tried to form the word *dead* the reality of it sickened her. In the roar of the huge wave, the sound of the operator's voice was lost. The darkness rescued her by removing the sight of her husband's dead body from her eyes - darkness and silence enveloped her.

The emergency response team entered the lab prepared for anything. The woman on the phone has given them few clues as to the reason for her distress and the phone number only directed them to the University's research lab building. The building appeared quiet and empty as they carefully walked down the hallway, guns drawn. Following the lighted hallway and seeing only one office door open with its lights on, the officers entered cautiously. One kept his gun drawn, alert for any movement in the room, as the other went to the man's body behind the desk and checked for a pulse. "Nothing," he said then leaned down to the woman on the floor. "She's breathing. Radio the paramedics. We need two stretchers."

The officer relayed as much information as he could about the victims and directed the paramedics, Stan and Jackson, to the office location. Jackson quickly tended to the woman and worked to revive her while Stan checked the man's vitals.

"Carotid pulses, negative," Stan called out after ten seconds. He quickly pulled up the man's shirt and attached leads to the chest. "Asystole – no cardiac electrical activity," he added for the benefit of the police officer standing in the doorway. "Slight rigor mortis in the face and livor mortis visible on the left hand. No need to resuscitate, he's been gone for a while."

"Ma'am. Ma'am, can you hear me?" Jackson said as he looked into Danielle's eyes then checked for injuries. She had a bump on her head where it touched the floor. As he felt it, Danielle winced. "Ma'am, my name is Jackson. Can you open your eyes?"

Danielle blinked.

"That's a girl, nice and easy. Can you tell me your name?"

"Danielle."

"Good. Don't try to move. Are you in any pain?"

"My head."

"Danielle, do you know where you are?"

"The library?"

"You are in Lyon's Lab, the University research lab."

"I have to go," she said as she struggled to sit up. "I'm surprising Nick for lunch."

"Okay," Jackson said as he applied gentle pressure to prevent her from sitting up. "We're going to keep you lying down until we're sure you are okay. Do you remember calling for help?"

Help me! Help me! She could hear her own voice

screaming it over and over. *This isn't happening. This isn't happening.* "This isn't happening," she said with a jolt as she once again became aware of her surroundings. There were voices in the room and the crackle of a radio – *sounds like a walkie-talkie.* She looked up and saw a bulletin board on the wall with a picture tacked to it. *Hawaii. That's me in Hawaii. I was there with – our honeymoon.* Her mind strained to remember. *Packed a picnic. Lunch in the park with...* "It's a surprise," she said aloud.

"Danielle, what's a surprise?" Jackson asked gently as he braced her neck and checked for broken bones and lacerations. To Stan he said, "Let's get her over to the ER."

"The picnic. Going to surprise him at the lab." *The lab. Why are the lights out? No one is around. Going to surprise him. Surprise!* Danielle's eyes grew wide as she remembered. "Oh my God! Nick! What's wrong with Nick?"

Stan nodded as Jackson asked the question with his eyes. Stan had checked the man's wallet for identification and quietly confirmed, "Dr. Nicholas Goodman."

"Danielle, try to stay calm. My buddy Stan is taking care of Nick. We're going to take you over to the hospital and check you out. Just try to relax while we move you onto the stretcher. Let me know if anything hurts, okay?"

"No! No!" Danielle shrieked. "He's dead. My God! Nick is dead!" she screamed. Her entire body shook as the enormity of what had happened invaded her consciousness and threatened her sanity.

Jackson and Stan carefully lifted her to the stretcher and covered her with a blanket. She shuddered violently and struggled against the safety restraints crying, screaming, shivering.

"Let's go," Jackson said as he put up the sidebars and wheeled the stretcher out into the hallway.

The ER admissions nurse was shocked when the paramedic standing in front of her said, "This is Danielle O'Neil. She has a bump on her head, possible concussion.

Pulse and respiration strong, no signs of other injury. We found her in Dr. Nicholas Goodman's office. Not sure of the relationship."

The ER admitting nurse knew Dr. Goodman quite well and had been invited to his wedding. "Danielle O'Neil? You mean Mrs. Goodman. She is Dr. Goodman's wife."

"You know him?"

"Yes, I've known him for years – just met his wife a couple weeks ago at their wedding. What happened to her? Where is Dr. Goodman?"

Jackson considered for a moment before answering not wanting to further upset the distraught young woman he had brought in. "Dr. Goodman is dead," he said softly. "Can you help find a family member – a friend – someone to help? And, she needs to be checked out."

Jenna immediately made a phone call and then prepared the necessary paperwork to admit Danielle. "Here," she said as she handed a clipboard to the waiting paramedic. "There are a few spots for you to complete, then sign here," she said as she put a red X in the box at the bottom of the form. Jackson scribbled the required information on the form, signed and handed it back to her.

"Thanks, ah . . . Jackson," Jenna said after checking his nametag. "We'll take care of her from here," she said as the orderly arrived.

"Here, let me give you a hand," Jackson said as he helped the orderly transfer Danielle from his stretcher to the hospital's. "You take care kiddo," he said to Danielle as she was wheeled away.

The staff on duty at Fairview-University Medical Center quickly heard the news about Dr. Goodman's death and those called upon to test, examine and care for his young bride did so with extra care and concern. After it was determined that Danielle hadn't been seriously injured, just a minor bump on her head and bruises caused by her fall, she was placed in a private room and given a mild sedative to keep her calm and allow her to rest.

When she awoke the blinds had been pulled to block the summer sun and the lights in her room were dimmed. Someone was sitting on the edge of her bed holding her hand and softly stroking her hair. She heard a man's voice.

"Danielle, are you awake?"

"Nick?"

"No, Danielle. It's Jake."

"Jake? Where am I? Where's Nick?"

"You are in the hospital. You had a fall and were brought here to make sure you are okay. How do you feel?"

"Thirsty. Jake? Why are you here? Where's Nick? My mouth is so dry."

Jake poured a glass of water from the small green plastic pitcher on her bed table, put a straw in it and held it to her lips. "Here's some water."

"Jake?"

"Yes, Danielle. I'm here."

"Where's Nick?"

"Danielle, I'm so sorry."

Images of Nick slumped over his desk flooded her consciousness. "Nick's dead! But that's not possible! What happened? I'm so confused. I keep seeing these images of Nick in his office – cold and pale but then we're walking on the beach, talking, laughing. Am I dreaming? I can't keep my eyes open."

"They don't know what happened. Apparently you found him at his desk, called 911 and then passed out."

"Yes, I dreamt I was calling out for help. I was at the library and had a picnic basket and...what happened? I'm so tired."

"It's okay, Danielle. Close your eyes and try to rest."

A few minutes later Jake heard voices in the hallway and

went out to find Frank and Liz Goodman talking with the nurse.

"Jake. Hello," Frank said. "How is Danielle?"

"She is sleeping now. She woke up for a few minutes and talked some though it was all pretty jumbled." He looked directly into Mrs. Goodman's swollen eyes and then at Frank. "I'm so sorry about Nick. I just can't believe it."

"Yes, we're stunned. We just came up from the morgue – had to identify the body. There will be an autopsy of course. Absolutely no warning – just gone." Frank put his arm around his wife as she started to cry.

"And Danielle. Poor thing. She's in shock," Liz sobbed.

"It's so unreal," Jake said. "Any idea what happened? Did Nick have any heart problems or anything?"

"None that we know of," Frank said. "There's no family history and, my God, at his age, it shouldn't even be a consideration. I could see if he didn't take care of himself, was overweight, smoked. But, nothing. It's a complete mystery. Liz, let's stop in and see Danielle, then I want to take you home. We were up at the lake when the hospital called. I drove like a madman to get down here – two and a half hours fighting Fourth of July traffic. Come, Liz," Frank said as he led his wife into Danielle's room.

Danielle stirred when Liz took her hand. "Danielle, dear. Are you sleeping? It's Mom. Frank and I are here for you."

Danielle was conscious of voices and felt her mom holding her hand. But – *that can't be. Mom is gone. I must still be dreaming.* But there was no refuge as she dreamt of the day she learned that her parents were both dead. She saw the high school gym filled with injured passengers and family members gathered to greet the survivors and mourn the victims. *I'm sorry. Your parents died in the crash.* Danielle struggled to open her eyes.

"Danielle. Can you wake up?" Liz asked gently.

"Maybe we should let her sleep," Frank said.

"I'm awake," Danielle said softly. "I was having a bad dream."

"We got here as soon as we could," Liz said. "We talked to Jake out in the hall before we came in. He said you were sleeping."

"Jake's here? I'm so tired."

"I know, dear."

"Danielle, can you tell us what happened? Do you know what happened to Nick?" Frank asked.

Hearing Nick's name was like an electric shock ripping through her body. Images of his body slumped forward in his desk chair flashed in front of her eyes. Her beloved husband – cold – lifeless – dead. She shuddered and squeezed her eyes shut as it all came rushing back. When she opened them she saw the tears streaming from Liz's blue eyes, *so blue like Nick's.* Frank sat down on the edge of the bed, put his arm around Liz and took Danielle's hand in his. For a moment the three could do nothing but cry together sharing their unspeakable shock and grief.

At last, Danielle was able to speak. "May I have some water?"

After a long drink and a deep breath, Danielle tried to put the events in order. "This morning I went over to the library to do some research and then to the deli to pick up a picnic lunch for us. I wanted to surprise Nick. I remember pulling the cart across the park. When I got to the lab it was dark and quiet. I wondered why no one was around."

"We were told that the lab was closed today because of the Fourth of July weekend. Why did Nick go in?" Frank asked.

"I don't remember. I don't know why he went in."

"Maybe he had some catching up to do – being gone and all," Liz offered.

"I don't know. I wanted to surprise him so I didn't tell him I was coming...just went to his office and," Danielle choked out the words, "he was slumped over at his desk...not moving. I called for help but no one came. I couldn't save him!" Danielle sobbed.

Frank took her hand. "It's not your fault. We don't know

what happened. The hospital called us up at the lake and told us to come right away...that there had been an accident," Frank said. "When we got here, Dr. Peterson told us that Nick was gone. No visible cause of death – no injury, no trauma. Of course we'll have an autopsy. Nick was so healthy. This is all so..." Frank couldn't continue.

"My baby boy!" Liz cried out.

"Let's get you home, Liz," Frank said as he took his wife's arm and helped her up from the chair. "Jake will stay here with you tonight, Danielle. We'll come back to see you tomorrow."

"Frank...Dad, do you think I can go home now? I really don't want to stay in the hospital tonight."

Frank looked at Liz. She nodded. "If you are sure you're feeling up to it, maybe you can be released," Frank said. "Liz, why don't you sit with Danielle for a few minutes while I have the doctor paged? It would be good for all of us to be together tonight." Frank gave Danielle's hand a squeeze and left the room.

"I just can't understand it," Danielle said. "He was fine this morning. We did a lot of walking and swimming in Hawaii. I couldn't keep up with him. No sign of anything wrong. Do you think he had a heart attack?"

"I don't know, dear," Liz said. "We will have to wait for the autopsy." She took Danielle's hand as they sat silently each lost in her own thoughts.

Frank returned with the doctor and after checking her vitals one more time, he released Danielle to Frank and Liz's care.

"Be sure to call me if you have any dizziness, blurred vision or vomiting. You can take Tylenol for your headache and apply ice on the bump. You should feel better tomorrow," he said.

I doubt I will ever feel better again.

"Thank you doctor," Frank said. "Liz, can you help Danielle get ready? I'll get the car and pick you up at the front entrance."

Liz went to the small closet, collected Danielle's things and helped her put on her clothes. "From the first time we met you, you became a part of our lives. You are our daughter and we love you. We are a family now and we should be together," Liz said.

"I love you too," Danielle said as the tears started to flow again. "I want to go home. I want to be with Nick."

"I know, dear. I know."

CHAPTER 11

If Jake had been asked to take photographs at Nick's funeral, the one major event in a person's life that is rarely captured on film, the faces would have been the same as in the wedding photographs taken just two weeks ago - minus the smiles. The men, Nick's colleagues, students, family members and friends wore the same dark suits they wore to Nick and Danielle's wedding but without the bright ties. The women though were more subdued in their most conservative dresses and tailored apparel. He watched the long line of people slowly move toward Danielle and Liz and Frank Goodman to offer their condolences. From bride to widow in the blink of an eye, Danielle was holding up remarkably well - offering comfort to the comforters and sharing silent hugs with those too taken with grief and sympathy to find words to say. He watched her closely looking for the slightest sign that is was too much for her, but she stood strong the entire day.

After the graveside service, a few of the closest friends and relatives gathered at Nick and Danielle's home in Kenwood. The Goodmans had arranged for a caterer to provide a light supper and staff on hand to take care of all of the details. Jake found Danielle and led her to the sofa in the family room. "Danielle, come sit down and rest. I will bring you something to eat and a cup of hot coffee."

"Thanks Jake, but I'm really not hungry."

"I know, but you've had a very long day and need to eat.

Sit, please. I'll be right back," Jake said and went to the dining room where the massive oak table was laid out with silver trays of small sandwiches, several fresh salads and an assortment of cookies and bars. When he returned to the family room he saw Danielle standing surrounded by the Myers family - Marie and Hal, Ginny and her husband Paul, Max, Laura the flower girl, Grant the ring bearer, and the others – he couldn't quite match up all of the names and faces. She looked beat. He maneuvered through the room stopping to greet the people who had been Danielle's family since her parent's death as he made his way over to Danielle. "Excuse me. Hello Max. I know. It's unbelievable isn't it? So sad. Ginny, hi. How are you? Danielle, here's some coffee," he said as he set the plate on the coffee table next to the sofa and handed her the cup of hot coffee. Jake shook Hal's hand and gave Marie a brief hug. "She hasn't eaten anything," he whispered to Marie. "See what you can do."

Taking his cue, Marie said, "Danielle, please go ahead and eat. You need your strength. We'll get ourselves something in a little bit. Have you been sleeping?"

"Not too well," Danielle said after taking a sip of coffee. Even though it had been a warm day, the hot liquid felt good, comforting. "I stayed with Nick's parents the first night and then Saturday was the Fourth - lots of noise, fireworks and stuff. Last night I read myself to sleep but then woke up around two. Had a terrible dream and couldn't get back to sleep. Even though I spent a lot of time here with Nick before we were married, the house still feels a little strange especially at night, all alone."

"Of course. You poor thing," Marie said. "Here, try the potato salad. That was always your favorite in the summer. Kids, why don't you fix yourselves a plate and take it out to the sun porch? We don't want to spill on this beautiful white carpet. Jake, can I get you anything?" It was clear that Marie was used to taking care of others and loved her motherly role.

"That's okay," Jake said. "I'll eat later. Thanks."

"Are you sure?"

"Well, coffee sounds good."

After the Myers had left the room, Jake took advantage of having a minute alone with Danielle - a short time of privacy that he knew wouldn't last long.

"Danielle, you know there isn't anything I or anyone else can say to take away your pain. I just want you to know that you can call me day or night, any time - like you used to. I will do anything I can to help you. You don't have to go through this alone." His eyes teared up as he gave her a big hug. He quickly wiped his eyes with the back of his sleeve. "Now, eat. You need food. Try a strawberry, they look great."

When Marie and Hal Myers came back into the room Jake motioned for Marie to take his place on the sofa next to Danielle. Hal sat in the La-Z-Boy recliner in the corner. Jake took the coffee Marie brought him and excused himself. He knew Marie would take care of Danielle and make sure she ate something.

Jake wandered through the house stopping now and again to chat or listen to the snippets of conversation he caught as he moved from room to room.

A tight group of Nick's colleagues including Nick's best man Roger Anderson, and other men and women from the University, gathered in the Goodman living room trying to explain the inexplicable. "Such a tragedy. Can't understand how this could happen. He seemed so healthy. They were so happy. Just married. Poor thing. What will she do now?" Jake's ears perked up as he overheard a man's voice saying, "The cranial nerves and blood vessels were normal; no hemorrhage or abnormalities. His coronary arterial system was free of atherosclerosis, the atrial and ventricular septa intact. The pulmonary arteries contained no emboli..."

"I already know he was in good health. God dammit! I want to know why he died!"

"I do too, Frank," Dr. Peterson said. "You'll get a

complete copy of the autopsy when the report is finalized. I spoke to Dr. Johansen before I came over and, technically, I shouldn't have told you anything. Bottom line, there doesn't seem to be any visible reason why Nick died. His heart just stopped."

"But young, healthy men's hearts just don't stop. How can they call it death from *natural causes?* There's nothing natural about my son's death!" Frank Goodman's raised voice caused a few in the room to glance over in his direction. Dr. Sonny Marino said, "I can't understand it either, Frank. I saw Nick on Thursday. Just back from his honeymoon, tanned, happy, the picture of good health. Ben, did they run toxicology?"

"Of course. Negative. Everything negative. No sign of drugs, alcohol. Nothing out of the ordinary."

It took extraordinary effort for Sonny to keep from beaming. As he expected, the mortacuratine had gone undetected.

Jake walked through the arched doorway into the dining room and decided to take his own advice. Not that he had much of an appetite, but he hadn't eaten much either all day and maybe there would be some comfort in sharing food with those connected through the loss of a loved one. He fixed a plate and headed out to find Ginny.

The sun porch was a few degrees warmer than the rest of the house but not uncomfortable. The ceramic tile was cool on his stocking feet and the setting sunlight created an amber tone to the room. Ginny was sitting on the glider with her brother Max, gently gliding forward and back, forward and back.

"Hey, Jake," she said as Jake came into the room. "Have a seat."

Jake pulled up a cushioned lawn chair next to Ginny and Max. "How's it going out here?" he asked.

"Not too bad," Max answered. "How's Danny?"

"It's really hard to tell," Jake said. "She doesn't talk much about what's going on in her head. She seems so together yet, I don't know. I worry about her. I think that just beneath the surface she is barely holding on."

"Yep, that's Danny," said Max. "After her folks died she acted, well, sort of normal. I don't mean happy... it's just that, well, you know, she didn't break down or nothin'. Did she Gin?"

"No," said Ginny. "Whenever she talked about the accident it was very factual - like a reporter. Sometimes at night though I'd wake up and hear her crying. She slept in my room after the accident. I'd talk to her but she never answered so I'm pretty sure she was having bad dreams. I'd ask her the next morning if she was okay and she never let on that she had a bad night. Maybe she didn't remember after she woke up."

"Since she's been with Nick though, she's been different, don't you think?" Jake said. "Much more open about her feelings."

"Yeah, I guess so," Ginny said, "but it's much easier to share happy feelings. She was *finally* happy again. I just can't imagine what she will do now without Nick."

"Probably what she's always done," said Max. "Write."

"I hope so," said Jake. "She has so much talent. It might help if she got involved with a project to take her mind off of things. I have a lead that we talked about just last week. I don't know if I should bring it up again or if it's better to let her rest for a while."

Ginny smiled. "Knowing Danny, I don't think she will rest and nothing we say will make a hill of beans difference. She will decide for herself what she needs to do and then do it no matter what anyone else thinks is best for her."

"Ginny, I think you're right about that," said Jake.

Danielle stared absently at her plate as she slowly pushed a bright red strawberry from one side to the other.

"Danny, you really should try to eat something," said Marie.

"I'm just not hungry, Marie. I feel numb and empty." After a long pause she continued, "I can't believe he's gone.

Nick is amazing. I remember when we first met, it was comical really - we literally ran into each other on campus. Talk about fate. I was flat on my back on the grass looking up into his incredible blue eyes. I've never seen anyone with such beautiful eyes. He was so good to me. I could be myself with Nick and he loved me anyway. He was there for me after the crash and now..." Danielle's eyes could no longer hold back the tears that welled up in them and spilled onto her cheeks. Her shoulders shook but she made no sound.

Marie took Danielle's plate from her, set it on the table, and put her arms around the young woman whom she had known since she was a little girl. "It's okay, Danny," Marie whispered. "Just let it out. It's okay."

Danielle was aware of voices and struggled to regain her composure. "Thanks, Marie," she said. "I'm okay now." As she dried her eyes and softly blew her nose she looked up and saw the group of men entering the family room.

"Danielle, I'm Sam Gupta. I worked with Nick at the lab. I'm so sorry for your loss," he said as Danielle stood and shook his outstretched hand.

"Thank you. Thank you for coming," Danielle said softy.

"This is Dave Bennett our top lab assistant. He worked closely with Nick this past year. Dr. Ben Chadwick, Dr. William Proctor, Dr. Yakima and, of course, you know Sonny."

Danielle shook each man's hand as they offered their condolences. Danielle's loss of her husband was tremendous but these men had worked with Nick for years and they were also visibly shaken by his unexpected and untimely death. As Danielle shook Sonny's hand he gave her an emotional embrace.

"Danielle. I just can't believe it," he said with tears in his eyes. "Our Nick gone. Just like that."

Nick had spoken often of Sonny Marino over the past year and a half – Danielle felt as if she knew him very well even though they had actually only spoken at length a few times. She recalled the first time when she and Nick first started dating.

Sonny and his wife Lauren had invited Nick and Danielle to a six-course gourmet wine dinner at Southpoint. Absolutely exquisite food - a once in a lifetime meal she would never forget. *Lobster Bisque with julienne of vegetable au gratin accompanied by Sauvignon Blanc; Venison Roulades with roasted chestnuts and Minnesota wild rice served with a rich Merlot; Mushrooms stuffed with shrimp, crab, scallops and spinach served with Chardonnay and Roasted Breast of Pheasant and leg stuffed with pistachios served with sweet potato pancakes and Pinot Noir.*

A fine dining rookie, Danielle followed Nick's lead as to which fork or spoon to use and she was careful to only sample each of the wines. Even at that, not accustomed to drinking much, the wine caused her cheeks to flush – a fact that did not go unnoticed by Dr. Marino. *Sonny.* She still wasn't totally comfortable calling him Sonny – a throwback to her days on campus and her work as a writer where respect and proper use of titles were expected and required if you wanted to get the best possible interview for a story. Yes, Sonny had noticed the effect the wine was having on her and said, "Nick, your beautiful lady is positively glowing this evening. It's either true love or, perhaps the wine?" Even though Danielle was in love with Nick, she had not fully admitted it to herself and had not used the word *love* to express her feelings to Nick. Having Sonny lay it out at the dinner table like that as if it were the seventh course for them all to savor made her blush deepen. Nick took her hand and squeezed it and said, "True love, I hope."

"Danielle? Are you all right?" Sonny asked. "You seem a million miles away."

"Hmm? I was just thinking back to that wonderful gourmet dinner we had at the club."

"Ah. You and Nick were already in love – it was obvious to Lauren and me. I knew it was only a matter of time before you'd be married. Time," Sonny sighed. "You and Nick had so little time together and yet it seemed like you had been together forever. Nick talked about you constantly – he was so in love with you." Sonny dabbed at his eyes. "Danielle, Nick and I spent many years together – like family. I feel like I have just lost a son. If there is anything I can do for you, please ask me. I truly mean it. Anything."

"Thank you, I will," Danielle replied.

"Nick was a fine scientist and a wonderful, caring human being. Those combined qualities gave his work special meaning and his efforts to advance science for the betterment of all people were commendable. Sonny hesitated for a moment before continuing. "I'd like you to come to the lab. Not right away of course, but when you're ready, so I can show you some of the projects Nick was working on. Very exciting progress that wouldn't be where it is had it not been for Nick. And, there are some personal items that I'm sure you will want to have."

"Thank you. I appreciate it," Danielle said. She heard the words Sonny was saying but the reality of it was incomprehensible. And when the reality of what she saw at the lab got past her defenses, it shook her to her very core. Her stomach tightened and the room started to darken.

Sonny grabbed Danielle as she started to go down. "A cold towel!" he shouted. "Get me a cold towel and some water," he said as he helped Danielle over to the sofa.

Marie was alarmed when she saw how pale Danielle looked. "Is she alright?" she asked. "I've never seen her like this."

"Well, she's been through a terrible shock," Sonny answered as he placed the cold wet towel on the back of her neck. "Danielle? It's okay. Take some deep breaths." He held the glass of ice water to her lips. "Drink this. You need to stay hydrated."

Marie and Hal stood by while Sonny tended to Danielle who was feeling better and somewhat embarrassed by the attention. "I'm okay, Dr. Marino. I feel much better. Thank you. I guess Marie was right, I haven't been eating enough lately," she smiled weakly at Marie.

Marie nodded then turned her face away from Danielle and leaned in close Hal. "I've seen her go through some very bad times and she never reacted physically like this. Do you think she might be pregnant?"

Sonny stiffened as he overheard Marie's question. *Could she be? They've only been married two weeks but that's not to say she couldn't have gotten pregnant before the wedding. Having a baby would be good – help keep her mind off of Nick's tragic death. Yes, tragic wasn't it?*

Hal didn't have time to consider the possibility before Marie jumped in and took charge of the situation. "Danielle, you have had a very long day and I think it's time we left so you can get some rest," Marie said, as she looked kindly but directly into the eyes of Nick's many friends gathered. "We'll stop by tomorrow on our way out of town to see if there is anything you need and say our good-byes."

Danielle stood slowly. Marie and Hal gave her a big hug and left the room to gather the rest of the Myers family.

"Danielle," Sonny said as the Myers left the room, "I should be going too." He took her hands which felt cool to him and covered them with his own. "This has been a very difficult day. Make sure you take care of yourself and I will talk to you soon." He leaned over and kissed her right check, then her left in the European fashion.

On his way out he once again expressed his condolences to Frank. "Your son was a brilliant doctor. I shall miss him greatly," Sonny said.

"I don't know how we will be able to live without him. I would give anything to have my son back." Frank said softly. "Thanks for coming Sonny."

With that, the rest of Nick's colleagues expressed their sympathy one last time to the beautiful, young widow and to Nick's parents as they made their way to the front door. Marie had done a good job of starting the exit in motion and as other friends and family heard about Danielle's *spell,* they took the hint that it would be best to go so she could rest. The caterers were finishing up in the kitchen packaging the leftovers into small portions that would be easy for Danielle to fix over the next couple of days.

After making sure everything was clean and her instructions for the leftovers had been followed explicitly, Liz Goodman paid the catering staff and thanked them for their service. She found Frank and Jake in the study – the one room on the main level that had not been changed. It still had its burgundy and forest green striped wallpaper, dark oak bookcases and hardwood floors. The unlit fireplace had a red brick face and large oak mantel upon which various knick knacks were displayed: the golf trophy Nick and Frank won at the Southpoint Father-Son Tournament, a picture of the twenty-five pound sailfish Nick caught in the Florida Keys, the *Mountain Man* bronze Remington reproduction and the gold anniversary clock given to Frank's parents on their fiftieth wedding anniversary. The clock had been on the mantel since Frank's mother died at age 92 and still retained its prominence in the room. When Liz and Frank moved out of the Kenwood home into their condo, they left the clock on the mantel to carry on the Goodman tradition under Nick's care. As she watched the pendulum swing, the hour turned to seven o'clock and the Westminster chimes played as they had every hour on the hour year after year. *Nick. My baby boy. You can't be gone. You just can't be gone.* As the chimes rang their last tone Liz stood quietly shaking her head back and forth in disbelief, tears pouring from her eyes.

With some gentle coaxing, Danielle agreed to go upstairs and take a warm bath. She sat on the side of the tub as the bath filled with water. After a long day bent over his microscope, Nick enjoyed a relaxing soak and Danielle had been looking forward to joining him in the oversized Jacuzzi. She had teased him when she saw the CD player in the bathroom but tonight she was grateful for something to drown out the silence. She ejected the disc and saw that it was a recording of the *Brahms' Requiem* by Exultate. She didn't know Nick owned a second CD of theirs. She started the music and carefully stepped into the tub.

Eyes closed, enveloped in the comfort of the warm bath water, Danielle listened as the choir sang:

Blessed are they that mourn, for they shall have comfort. They that sow in tears shall reap in joy.

Behold, all flesh is as the grass and all the goodliness of man is as the flower of grass, for lo, the grass withers, and the flower decays.

Lord, make me to know the measure of my days on earth, to consider my frailty that I must perish. Now, Lord, oh what do I wait for? My hope is in Thee.

Danielle silently prayed. *So, God. You've made your point. You have shown me again that life is frail. Withers like the grass. I guess that means short-lived. Are you trying to tell me something? Am I too self-sufficient? I don't lean on you for everything? First you took my parents so I had to learn to be strong on my own. How can I rely on you? All you do is take the ones I truly love from me! What's the point?* God's apparent answer came to her in the chorus:

How lovely is Thy dwelling place, O Lord of hosts! For my soul, it longs and faints for the courts of the Lord. My soul and body cry out, yes, for the living God. O blest are they that dwell within Thy house; they praise Thy name evermore!

She had gone to church with her parents as a girl, but since the plane crash hadn't been able to reconcile the kind, loving God she had learned about at First Lutheran Church in Sioux City to the God that allowed hundreds of innocent people to die leaving behind mothers, fathers, and children to mourn. She thought back to the words spoken today by Pastor Gunderson so similar to the message given at her parents' funeral. *Nick is in heaven now where there is no pain, no sorrow. But Nick was young and happy and healthy. He didn't need rescue from an awful existence. That may be comforting to old people or those who suffer with terrible disease and pain – they slowly whither away. But Nick? No, there is no comfort for me that he is in a better place. His place was with me. God, why? Why bring him into my life only to snatch him away at the very start of our life together? I'm mad at you! Why God, why?*

Danielle squeezed her eyes tightly closed as if to prevent her pain and the intended comfort of the words of the *Requiem* from raging war within her. She breathed deeply and tried to calm herself with thoughts of the beach and the warmth of the sun and most of all she thought of Nick.

Blessed are the dead which die in the Lord – they rest from their labors. Lord, oh what do I wait for? My hope is in Thee. My hope is in Thee.

The sun shone down warmly from the blue sky adorned with the perfect number of white puffy clouds. Enough to provide brief respite from the heat of the sun but not so many as to cause a chill. Nick and Danielle lay side by side on large red raft gently rocking to the rhythm of the waves. Nick's skin was deeply tanned and smelled of coconut oil; his eyes the color of the blue sea beneath them. A sudden breeze blew Danielle's straw hat into the water. "I'll get it for you, honey," Nick said as he sat up and took off his sunglasses. "No, Nick. Just leave it. I'll get another one." But Nick, eager to please his new bride, rolled off the raft into the ocean water.

Danielle watched her hat bob in the waves and waited for Nick to surface. He was a strong swimmer but Danielle had heard too many stories of swimmers getting caught in currents – rip tides that carried them away from shore to their death. At last Nick came up, looked around and gave her a quick wave before swimming after the hat. The scene was comical. Just as the hat appeared to be in reach, a wave would carry it away. Danielle laughed and clapped as Nick got close again. But alas, the hat eluded him. Soon Nick and the hat were so far from her raft that Danielle had to squint to see him. She called for him to come back but he continued to pursue the hat – always elusive, always just out of reach. Danielle, alone on the raft, waited for Nick to return. She stared at the horizon always moving as the waves rolled in, straining to see Nick. A large cloud formed in the sky shading the sun. "Nick! Nick!" she called. "Come back!" The water lapped onto the raft. It was cold. Nick was nowhere in sight. "Nick!"

Danielle woke to the sound of knocking on the door. She shivered in the cold bath water. "Danielle? It's Jake! Are you okay?"

Fully awake and cognizant of her dream, Danielle got out of the tub and put on her thick terry robe. She opened the door a crack and saw Jake in the hallway, a panicked look on his face.

"Danielle? What's wrong? I heard you screaming."

"I must have fallen asleep. Had a bad dream. I'll get dressed and be out in a minute."

"Are you sure you're okay? Do you need anything?"

"I'm fine. Just give me a minute." She slipped out of her robe and into her terry lounge pants and tunic top. After running a comb through her hair she went downstairs and found Jake, Liz and Frank in the study with worried looks on their faces.

"Danielle, dear," said Liz, "are you all right?"

"Yes, Mom. I'll be okay."

Liz was an elegant woman accustomed to the finer things in life but not pretentious. She had hoped Nick would marry a woman with social stature and made an effort to introduce him to the daughters and nieces of her socialite friends. She always bought season tickets to the Guthrie –

about the only time she had alone with her extremely busy son – and took every opportunity to invite friends to join them for coffee and dessert afterward. Ironic that the one performance in the last two years Liz missed, brought Nick and Danielle together. Liz was skeptical when she first heard of Danielle's background – small town girl from Iowa – but was won over when she met her and saw how taken Nick was with her. She was a bright girl, pretty with her dark brown eyes and hair, slightly reserved with an obvious inner strength and Liz welcomed her new daughter-in-law to be into the family. Now that Nick was gone she couldn't help but wonder if their relationship would survive without Nick as the bond. She hoped so.

"Frank and I will stay the night if you want us to," Liz offered.

"That's okay. I'm so tired tonight. I'll be fine," said Danielle. "You need your rest too and I'm sure you'll be more comfortable in your own bed."

"She's right Liz," Frank said with concern for his wife. "You'll sleep better at home." He gave Danielle a hug and said, "We're only a few minutes away so please call if you need us."

"I will, Dad," Danielle said. It still felt strange to call Liz and Frank *Mom and Dad*. Nick had been so pleased that they got along so well and she needed them now more than ever.

"Good night, dear," Liz said as she kissed Danielle's cheek and embraced her. The two women were now bound together in their grief, gathering both strength and sadness from each other. Liz brushed the tears from her own eyes and then Danielle's. "I'll call you tomorrow."

As the Goodmans were leaving, Jake walked through the house making sure the doors and windows were locked and turned off most of the lights. He met Danielle in the front hallway. "Everything is locked up. You know how to alarm the security system, right?"

"Yes. Nick showed me how to use it. There is a special

setting for at night. Thanks, Jake. You are such a good friend," Danielle said as she hugged him.

"Are you sure you are okay, being alone tonight? I can stay, you know."

"I'll be fine. I just need some time alone to get my head around this. It's like part of my brain knows he's gone and the rest of me expects him to walk into the room at any moment. Oh God, I wish that were true! I'm struggling to believe this is happening at the same time not wanting to believe it. I need to be in this house where Nick's presence is still so strong. I need one more night alone with my husband."

"Okay. I hope you can get some sleep. Call if you need me. Good night, Danielle."

"Good night, Jake."

Danielle left the hallway lights on and went upstairs to the bedroom. As she went through the motions of putting on her nightgown, brushing her teeth, taking out her contact lenses, she was painfully aware of Nick's presence and absence. His toothbrush stood unused in its holder, electric razor fully charged and ready to go. On the nightstand next to the bed was the latest edition of *Newsweek* still open to the article Nick was reading. She turned off the light and climbed into bed on Nick's side. With her head on his pillow she was engulfed by his smell. Here, in this place, he was so close she could feel him. In the profound silence she could hear his voice, his laughter. In the warmth of their bed she could feel his love. And holding on to that feeling, she closed her eyes and prayed for rest. *Grant them rest eternal.*

CHAPTER 12

"Hello?"

"Danielle? This is Sonny Marino. Did I get you at a bad time?"

"No. I just came in from the garden. Digging in the dirt and working out in the sun has been good for my head." It had been exactly two years since her parent's death and it was all she could do to keep from crumbling under the horrible memories of that day without Nick. And now Nick was gone too.

"Yes, I know what you mean. Work has a way of keeping one's mind occupied. It's one of the reasons I called. First, of course, I wanted to see how you are doing."

"There are days when I don't think I can bear it. But I've been through this before and know that somehow life goes on. And those of us whose fate it is to be the survivor must do just that."

"I admire your courage, Danielle. I miss Nick terribly and can only imagine how difficult this is for you. I hope it's not too soon to ask but I wonder if you feel up to coming to the lab. Unfortunately we have to clear out Nick's office and I thought you might like to get his personal items – that is, if you don't think it would be too upsetting. I could always box them up and bring them by."

"No, that's okay. I can come," she said. "Seeing the lab busy with activity might help replace the picture I have in my mind of it the day Nick died. I suppose I could come this afternoon – if that works out for you."

"That will be fine. How about around three o'clock? I'll let the others know you're coming. They'll be happy to see you again."

"Okay then. I'll see you this afternoon." Danielle hung up the phone and as she put on her gardening gloves, realized her hands were trembling. Thinking about going to the lab brought back the vivid images of that horrific day in living color.

Well, I said I would go, so I'm going. It's a good thing I don't have too much time to think about it and change my mind.

Sonny made a point to meet Danielle in the hallway when she arrived and walked her through the lab skirting Nick's office. Nick's former colleagues greeted her warmly and without being too technical, updated her on some of the projects they were working on. It was easier for them to talk about their work than of their loss. Roger was the exception. Having been Nick's closest friend and best man at his wedding, his death had hit him the hardest. He gave Danielle a teary hug.

"Danielle, it's so good to see you," Roger said as he embraced her. "Please let me know if there is anything you need."

"Thanks, Roger. I will. Please tell your daughter that I have been listening to Exultate's recording of the *Brahms Requiem*. It is beautiful."

"I'll tell her. Take care, Danielle."

Sonny led her through the rest of the lab and into his office where he offered her a seat in the large leather chair across from his desk.

"I'm sorry Danielle. This must be very difficult for you."

"It is for sure, but seeing Nick's colleagues and the importance of his work reminds me that something of him lives on in this place. What beautiful pictures," Danielle remarked as she picked up the photo collage on Sonny's desk. "Is this your family?"

"Thank you. These were taken last summer in Italy where my family had a reunion of sorts. Most of these are of cousins on my father's side. This of course is my wife Lauren. These are my two sons, Robert and Jonathan. Robert is a surgeon in Maine – this is his wife, Sofia," Sonny said as he pointed to a beautiful dark-haired woman. "And Jonathan has a veterinary practice in Colorado. He and his wife Alicia are expecting their first baby in October. It will be our first grandchild. Lauren and I are very excited."

"Congratulations and send my best to Lauren. You are blessed to have such a beautiful family. It's so strange. Only weeks ago Nick and I were talking about having a family. Nick was adamant about having children soon and gave me this big lecture on what can happen if couples put it off too long. I thought we had all the time in the world. My response was to tell him how difficult it is for women to have a career and be a mother. I'm afraid I made it sound like being a journalist was more important than having his child. I wish I could take that conversation back! It's not like we had much time to discuss it and now...well, there's nothing I'd rather be right now than his wife and the mother of Nick's child." Danielle fell silent and steeled herself against her emotions as she thought about all of the things she and Nick didn't have a chance to share.

Sonny waited for a moment and said, "Nick talked often about having children and much more so after meeting you. One of the reasons he was so good at what he did is he really cared about the quality of human life. The fact that his work here had made it possible for infertile couples to have children and the potential to restore health to people with terminal medical conditions, especially kids, sparked a passion in him that drove him beyond what others have done in this field. I know that after you came into his life and having children of his own became a real possibility for him, Nick became more and more excited about becoming a dad."

Danielle sighed. "If only things were different."

"Danielle, I hope you don't think I am stepping out of bounds but Nick was like a son to me and, even though you don't know me that well, I feel a certain bond between us. I mean, because of Nick. If you're serious about having Nick's baby, I mean, well...there are means you know and...I could help."

"Sonny, I'm not sure what you mean. I'm pretty sure I'm not pregnant, if that's what you're suggesting."

"No. I'm sorry Danielle. I shouldn't have said anything."

"I've always believed in straight out communication – a quality that serves me well in my writing, not always so appreciated in my personal relationships," Danielle said, "so don't worry about offending me. Just tell me what's on your mind."

"Okay. But please remember that my life's work has revolved around reproductive science so I just naturally think in those terms. Anyway, as you were talking, I was thinking that if you are really serious about having Nick's baby, I could help make that happen. I hope you won't think this is out of line but..."

"Sonny, stop worrying. Just tell me."

"You know we do extensive experimentation with reproductive material to determine what affects various conditions have on the replication of cells in their earliest stages of human development. Well, at one time or another, most of the men in our lab have, shall we say, donated to the cause. Nick was among the donors and, as it happens, I'm sure we have viable sperm here in storage."

"You have Nick's sperm? Are you suggesting, artificial insemination?"

"All I'm saying, Danielle, is that if you are serious about having Nick's baby, it is possible."

Danielle's mind was flying in a hundred directions. *Didn't I just tell Nick a few weeks ago that I would never consider conceiving a baby under artificial circumstances? But I don't have a chance to have Nick's baby any other way. God cheated me out of a long life of happiness with my husband, why should I be cheated from having his baby? What will people think?* It was this thought that she got stuck on.

"What will people think?" she said. "I mean, now that Nick's gone, won't people wonder about my loyalty?"

"Well, if you get pregnant right away, most would think you conceived on your honeymoon and you always have the option of confiding in those you care about. Danielle, it is very common in today's society to use artificial insemination or other fertility treatments to have a baby. Single women, couples where one partner is infertile, gay couples and even women who otherwise would be considered past their childbearing time. There are so many reasons why people who want children need assistance. Can you imagine how much love awaits the baby who has come from deliberate and sometimes painful procedures, tests, medications and surgeries?"

"So, if I decide to do this, what is the process?"

"It's quite simple really. We perform a series of tests to determine when you are ovulating. When the time is right, we inject the sperm – a painless process, no worse than your annual exam. Then we wait. If you don't get pregnant on the first try, you can decide whether or not you want to try again."

"And how many people here will know what I'm doing?"

"Danielle, as head of the department I am in a position to keep the entire procedure entirely confidential. In fact, if you prefer, I can perform the insemination myself and absolutely no one else has to know." Sonny could not believe how quickly he'd won Danielle's confidence. Having such a willing participant was almost too good to be true and if it worked, Nick's beautiful widow would be forever indebted to him. And with a baby to think about and tend to, would Danielle have time and energy to question and further probe into Nick's untimely death? Highly unlikely.

"Dr. Marino, Sonny, this is all happening so fast. I mean, I've been thinking about having Nick's baby but not in terms of a reality. My thoughts are consumed by my loss and the grief is unbearable. Not only did I lose my husband but I lost the future too – a future where I am a mother, the mother of Nick's children and we grow old together. Some days I wake up in the morning thinking it was all a bad dream until I turn and see the empty pillow beside me. Then the horrific reality sets in again as if it just happened."

Sonny nodded.

"Now you offer the possibility of changing the empty future I have been trying to accept. The idea is very inviting. I just don't know if I'm ready to take that step. Being a single mom isn't easy."

"Of course, Danielle. I totally understand and there is absolutely no need for you to make this important decision today. Even if you decide to wait a while, it's still a medical possibility. You just have to reconcile the thought of having Nick's baby even though he is gone. Knowing the Goodmans, I'm sure they would be supportive."

"Nick's parents are great but I'd rather not have to explain how I got pregnant. No, if I'm going to do this, I want it to appear that my conception was natural. If I do decide to go forward, what's the next step?"

"First we determine when ovulation is most likely to occur. Do you have a regular cycle?"

"Like clockwork. In fact, I'm probably close to the time now. How can I tell?"

"I'll give you a special test kit to take with you. There is a new test developed by Dr. Gupta that we have used here in the research center with a very high rate of success. He's close to being ready to take it to the FDA for approval. All you have to do is take a urine sample first thing in the morning and add three ccs to the vial I give you. The test solution in the vial is a colorless liquid that reacts to the hormones found in your urine. Just prior to ovulation, the solution will turn light green. For three days during ovulation, the peak time for conception, the solution will turn dark blue. After ovulation, the solution will turn pink. It's pretty easy to use. You'll be our first in-home test user. Just keep the vials refrigerated until the morning you are going to use it. It's best if the solution is brought to room temperature before adding the urine sample. I do have to ask you Danielle to keep this procedure confidential. It's completely safe but I have to be sure Dr. Gupta's research is protected until we are ready to apply for FDA approval."

"Don't worry. This way we'll each have a confidence to keep. It will keep us both honest."

"Indeed. Well then, shall I prepare the solution for you to take with you today?"

"I still need some time to think it over but it won't hurt to have it on hand if I do decide to go ahead with it."

"Yes. Very good. I'll get it ready and while I'm doing so, you may wish to gather Nick's things."

Danielle had almost forgotten about the purpose of her visit. As she walked down the corridor toward Nick's office her stomach tightened and her palms started to sweat. As she opened the door she braced herself for the vision of Nick's lifeless body slumped in his chair. Taking a deep breath, she entered the office and turned on the light. It was pretty much as it had been the day Nick died – thankfully, minus the body. She could smell his cologne as she walked into the room and went behind his desk. As much out of relief as out of grief her eyes filled with tears and her heart's pace quickened. She gently lowered herself into Nick's large leather desk chair. As she leaned back she closed her eyes and was filled with Nick's presence all around her. She thought about her conversation with Sonny and said aloud, "Nick, what should I do?"

When she opened her eyes her attention was drawn to the bookcase on the opposite wall. On the shelves among the scientific journals and reference materials she saw a small pink and blue book cover, quite out of place among the large grey and black bindings. Danielle took the book from the shelf, *Your Baby, a New Life*. Inside the front cover was written, "Nick, It's about time you thought about making a baby the old fashioned way! Congratulations on your marriage to Danielle. She sounds wonderful! Best wishes. Pete."

Danielle turned the page to the Prologue and read, "There are many reasons why people have babies and there are many more reasons why, for some, it is difficult or impossible to conceive. The creation of a new life is not only a miraculous joining of two individual's genetics but the joining of two souls, for the two shall become one. This book is dedicated to Dr. Nicholas Goodman who helped me understand that God is present in the creation of every human life even those of us whose first days of life were lived in a test tube."

Danielle closed the book and slipped it into her purse. As she looked around the room she wondered how many lives had been touched by Nick and his dedicated work. She once again felt the terrible loss – now not only her own loss, but also the loss of all the life-saving advancements Nick was committed to. She began packing Nick's belongings. Other than the little book, she didn't spend time reading or thinking. There would be plenty of time for that at home. She was just about done when there was a soft knock on the door.

"Danielle, how are you doing?" Sonny said as he walked in.

"Fine. I'm just about finished here. I left some books on the shelf that look like they belong to the University. Would you please look at them?"

"Of course. I'll take care of everything and if there is anything else of Nick's here at the lab, I'll make sure you get it." Sonny paused and studied Danielle carefully before he continued.

"Danielle, Nick was a brilliant man and we will all miss

him tremendously. His contributions to medical science were countless and his commitment to helping people was never ending. I knew Nick like a son and while I won't presume to know exactly what he would want you to do, I do know this with certainty. Nick loved you as he had never loved anyone or anything before and he would want you to do what is best for you – whatever will make you happy. One of the things he loved about you is your determination to do what you think is right regardless of what others may say. Don't change now and don't let me or anyone else influence your decision. Here," Sonny said as he handed Danielle a small brown box. "There are written instructions and ten test vials. Just put the whole box in the refrigerator. Take as much time as you need to think things over and call me anytime."

CHAPTER 13

"Ginny? Hi, it's me, Danny," she said when her childhood friend answered the phone.

"Danny? How are you? I've been meaning to call you. I've had a cold since we got back from Minneapolis. Turned into an ear infection and now I have bad cough. I've been on antibiotics now since a week ago Monday and am finally feeling better. Summer colds are the worst! Oh, Danny. I'm sorry. I'm going on and on. How are *you*?"

"Well, considerably better that what you're describing. I have something to tell you. Is now a good time?"

"Yes. I'm just doing some laundry."

"Are you sitting down?" Danielle asked.

"No, do I need to? Danny, what is it? Are you okay?"

"Ginny, I'm pregnant!"

"Oh my God! Hold on!"

"Ginny?"

"Yeah. Okay, now I'm sitting down. You're pregnant?"

"Yes, the doctor just confirmed it yesterday," Danielle said and added before Ginny could ask, "it must have happened on our honeymoon. Can you believe it?"

"No, I'm shocked, although Mom won't be. She had a feeling when we were at the house after the funeral. You know, when you sort of fainted. I told her it was just the shock and all but, well, you know Mom. Danny, I don't know what to say. How do you feel about this? I mean, with Nick gone and now, a single mom. That's a lot to adjust to."

"I know. I haven't had much time to think about it. I've been pretty sure since last week – did one of those in-home tests – then saw my doctor yesterday. I really want this baby! It's as if God has given me back this little piece of Nick to hold onto and care for. And I've decided to take a job at the *Star Tribune* as a community news reporter. It won't involve travel and I can still freelance if I have the time and energy to."

"Wow! I'm stunned! I never thought you'd have a baby before me. I wish I could see you! You sound so happy and together. Are you?"

"Well, I don't know about happy. I am still struggling and some days I don't think I can bear the sadness. But now, I think of the baby – a brand new life waiting to come into this world. I only wish Nick were here to share it with me."

"Me too, Danny. You deserve to be happy and there is no higher calling for a woman than being a mother. Of course, you have to put up with the diapers and the crying and the sickness. How will you manage all that on your own?"

"I haven't told them yet but I'm sure Nick's parents will help. I know they wanted grandchildren. I plan on telling them tonight. And, if I have to hire someone to come in to help me, I can."

"So, you're okay financially?"

"Nick had a sizable retirement account built up through his years at the University and several life insurance policies both personal and through work. The insurance investigator approved the payout of his personal policy after receiving the final autopsy results. I guess they investigate all cases where the policy is substantial and taken out fewer than ninety days before the death of the policyholder. Nick bought the policy as soon as we were engaged and named me as the sole beneficiary. Thank God Nick's family believes in keeping things in order. His dad has been immensely helpful and a friend of the family is an attorney who is handling the estate and all of that."

"So, will you stay in the house?"

"At first I didn't want to. But now, with the baby, I think I will. Nick grew up in this house and I think it is sweet that his son will grow up here too."

"Son? So you think it's a boy?"

"I'm sure it's a boy!"

"Okay, I believe you," said Ginny. "But don't tell Mom that. When she was pregnant with me, she was so sure I was a boy they hadn't even talked about girl's names. The women at church didn't help. At the baby shower potluck they did the pencil on a string thing – just for fun."

"What's the pencil thing?"

"They tie a pencil to a piece of string and hold it above the expectant mother's wrist. If it swings up and down along the arm it's going to be a girl, if it goes back and forth across the wrist, it's a boy. Or is it the other way around? I don't know. Anyway, they did it to my mom and they were all sure I was going to be a boy."

"I haven't tried anything quite so scientific," Danielle laughed. "I just have a feeling, that's all."

"It could be your first maternal instinct. Who knows? Just don't be surprised if you're wrong."

"Okay. So what do you think your mom and dad will think?"

"Like I said. Mom won't be surprised. I think they'll have some concerns, like I did. Heck, they had a big family and survived so, once they get over the shock, I'm sure they'll be excited too. Do you want me to tell them?" Ginny asked.

"No, I should be the one to tell them. Do you know if they're going to be home tonight?"

"I think so. But if you don't get them tonight, try first thing tomorrow. I'm not going to be able to hold this news in for long!"

"Deal. Ginny, thanks for being such a good friend. I'll be counting on you for advice on being a mom."

"You know I will help in any way I can but learning about parenting in school and actually experiencing it are two different things. Mom has lots of experience with kids and even though there are times I don't want her telling me what to do, it will be nice to have her close by when I get pregnant. I know she will help you if you need it."

"Are you and Paul trying?"

"Let's just say we're not doing anything to prevent it."

"Well, I'm sorry I beat you to it."

"Are you kidding me? I am so happy for you," Ginny said. "After everything you have been through, you deserve this gift from God!"

"Thanks, Ginny. That means a lot to me. I'll let you go. I hope you feel better. Stay in touch okay?"

"Take care, Danny. I'll talk to you soon."

Danielle was relieved that her first announcement went so well. She had been expecting the questions about managing as a single mom and glad Ginny didn't press on the topic of how she got pregnant. It was her own paranoia that caused her to dread comments like, *I thought you were on the pill or I thought you wanted to wait to have kids until your career was firmly established*. Of course Ginny was the easiest one to tell. Danielle and Ginny had become even closer since her parents' death and ever since Danielle met Nick, the common bond of love, marriage and now having a child was all it took to close any gap in their relationship.

She expected the conversation with Hal and Marie Myers, to go as well so long as they believed that Danielle's pregnancy was natural. Based on what Ginny said, Marie would buy the story quite easily. She didn't think the Myers would be as supportive if they knew Danielle made the conscious choice to become a single parent using artificial methods. There was still a cultural difference between the Myers, rural, conservative, Missouri Synod Lutherans and the Goodmans, liberal, big city Episcopalians. She wasn't quite sure where she fit in, somewhere in between she supposed. As she thought about the process she used to get pregnant, she knew she wouldn't get into that discussion with the Myers. It really was a miracle that she got pregnant on the first try – no one would suspect the circumstances.

Because the time frame was short, she hadn't taken the medication commonly prescribed to increase egg production so Sonny suggested she improve her odds by using the intrauterine insemination – IUI – method. He explained that the newly developed procedure involved using a catheter to place Nick's sperm directly inside her uterus to facilitate fertilization. She was apprehensive at first; the process was even less natural than she thought. But when Sonny explained that her chances of conception increased from ten percent to fifty percent and that he would give her something to ensure the procedure was painless, she agreed.

She had crossed off the days on her calendar waiting and wondering. Each day was filled with questions and self-doubt as she considered whether or not she had done the right thing. *If God is really in control of everything, maybe Nick was taken from me for a reason. Maybe my higher purpose will be fulfilled through my work and having a baby might prevent that from happening. But God gave science to man and the intellect to discover amazing things. How could He be displeased with my desire to be a mother?* She reasoned and rationalized until she decided that either way, pregnant or not, she would accept whatever happened. God's will be done. If she didn't get pregnant the first time, it wasn't meant to be. In reality, she probably would have tried again but that was one decision she did not have to make.

The pregnancy happened so easily. Now it was easy to believe it was God's will. Sonny had told her to be prepared for failure but the insemination was successful on the first try for which she was grateful. She waited only two weeks after her period was expected – just to be sure – and then made an appointment with her doctor. Yesterday it was confirmed. She was pregnant!

She had known for only twenty-four hours but in that time her thoughts raced through the past to the future and back again – over and over. She wept tears of sorrow and joy intermingling in a wash of emotions. Sorrow for the loss of her parents, for losing Nick and at the same time, pure joy because of the miraculous new life inside her. And now it was time to go forward and not look back. Telling Ginny made it a reality. She was going to be a mother and there was no longer any doubt in her mind about her decision. Her doubts and fears were erased as she thanked God for the miracle of having Nick's baby!

She had thought carefully about how to break the news to Nick's parents. Danielle really believed that they would be thrilled by the news of having a grandchild – a possibility they thought was lost with Nick's death. The continuation of the family line and the family name would overshadow any initial questions of how and when. It had been easy to tell Ginny and tonight she would tell Liz and Frank.

Telling Jake, however, would be more difficult. He knew Danielle better than anyone and, while he was happy Danielle had found true love, he didn't have a vested interest in Nick's continuing legacy. They had had many conversations about career and family and Jake knew how important it was to Danielle that she make a name for herself as a writer. Jake had even talked to Nick about it on their wedding day. Danielle smiled as she remembered Nick telling her how Jake had taken a fatherly tone with her husband-to-be about the importance of her career.

She had no idea how she was going to tell Jake about the baby. Ever since the first time she opened up to him on that bus trip to Winona, she had been comfortable talking to Jake and she trusted him implicitly. She didn't want to keep the truth from him but wasn't quite prepared to handle a barrage of questions that might reveal any uncertainty she might still have about her decision. It would be bad enough telling him about her new job as a community news reporter. She could hear him say, "Now that's a lofty position! So filled with controversy and important social issues."

Let's see, she thought. *Should I cover the Edina Country Club's remodeling plans or Wayzata's decision not to have their annual Fourth of July fireworks display? What about the goose poop problem on the walking paths around Lake of the Isles?* In the end she rationalized that there are still important issues to cover such as the lack of affordable housing in the suburbs and Eagan's approval of a new women's shelter. Besides, it was too late to second-guess that decision. She had accepted the job and that was that. She would make the best of it and if Jake didn't think it was good enough, he could just…

"No, I'm not quite ready for Jake yet," she said aloud. Danielle picked up the phone and dialed her in-law's number. After four rings the answering machine picked up and Danielle left the message that she'd like to stop over later. Then she decided to busy herself by spending the day working on her decorating plan. It still felt strange being in the big house all alone, the house so steeped in the Goodman family traditions. She was glad she convinced Nick to paint and re-carpet most of the house but that's all the further they got. There was no master plan and now she felt the need to make the big house feel like home to her and her baby – their baby.

Danielle grabbed a notebook, measuring tape and pencil and headed upstairs. At the top of the stairs to the left, at the back of the house, there were two bedrooms with a walk-through bath. On the right was another bathroom and a third bedroom with a vaulted ceiling and shuttered window overlooking the foyer below. At the end of the hallway was a trap door with a pull down staircase leading to the small attic. The house had been remodeled by Nick's parents to convert the other two bedrooms and bath into a master bedroom suite that stretched from the front of the house to the back with its massive private bath, walk-in closets and sitting area with fireplace. Danielle couldn't bear the thought of changing their bedroom so she closed the door and focused on the rest of the upstairs.

The first back bedroom would be the guestroom, Danielle decided. It had direct access to the large walk-through bathroom that adjoined the second bedroom that would be the nursery. Danielle could envision Nick's parents spending the night in the guestroom while their grandson slept in the next room. Or, if she had to have a nanny or overnight care for the baby while she traveled, this arrangement would be perfect.

The guestroom currently held Danielle's old bedroom set in addition to some miscellaneous furniture leftovers from the Goodmans. The dark stained oak floors were in pretty good shape, what could be seen of them, and Danielle decided to tackle this room first. She carefully measured the walls and sketched the room marking windows and doors. Then she took measurements of the main pieces of furniture that she wanted to keep in the room. Her queen-sized bed with the iron headboard and footboard fit nicely in the Tudor styled home and the spare bedroom was certainly large enough to hold it. The bed had belonged to her great-grandparents and she was glad her dad had saved this piece of family history.

She walked into the large closet where her three memory boxes were safely stored. Before Ginny and Paul moved into her parents' house, Danielle had sorted many of their belongings. Not able to bear going through them at the time, the most personal items had gone into these three boxes. Most of them would remain untouched even now, but Danielle immediately unpacked her mother's bed quilt.

She pulled the quilt from its plastic bag and shook it out onto the bed. The quilt immediately brought a cheery lift to the room and became the focal point for the room's redecorating. Danielle's mom had appliquéd all of her favorite flowers onto white squares and quilted them together with a deep green border. The purple pansy, pink rose, yellow daffodil, lavender iris and all the others sprang to life on the beautiful quilt. Here and there her mother had stitched a ladybug, a bee, a butterfly – the little creatures Danielle loved to watch while playing in her mother's garden. Yes, there was no question that this quilt belonged on this bed in this room. She made a few notes – soft yellow paint, white chenille rugs – took a quick inventory of the other pieces of furniture and moved on to the next bedroom.

The second bedroom was a mirror image of what she now called the guestroom and its windows overlooked the backyard. Danielle made a note of the view so that she could incorporate it into her gardening plans. This room was also filled with a hodge podge of old furniture, boxes of toys, books and who knows what else. The room was easy to sketch because of its similarity to the one she had just measured. Danielle had never really paid much attention to its contents which now took on a whole new meaning. Tucked away in the corner was a small maple bed with matching dresser, student desk and nightstand.

She moved the boxes out of the way and made her way back to the little desk. The center drawer was filled with pencils, crayons, scraps of paper, rocks and a myriad of other little treasures. In the top drawer on the right was an envelope marked *Nick's school pictures*. She took the envelope and sat down on the bed to examine what appeared to be Nick's school pictures. Not all of them had dates on the back but there was one for each year, kindergarten through grade twelve. She recognized Nick's senior picture as a smaller version of the large framed one, hanging on the wall at Frank and Liz's condo. Danielle replaced the envelope and quickly scanned through the other drawers. She brushed away a tear as she looked at the mementos of her husband's childhood. It was clear that this was the furniture from his room when he was a child and she thought that this was most likely his bedroom. There was no doubt in her mind that this would be her child's room, Nick's son's room, and she set about the task of cataloging its contents.

That done, she sat back on the small bed and looked out of the window. She imagined the small boy, little Nick, lying in bed. What would he have seen? Would the oak tree in the backyard have been tall enough then to see from his bed or would he have had to stand on the little blue step stool next to the window in order to look down at it? She could see the neighbor's house from the south-facing window. Did Nick have a little friend next door whose bedroom window faced his? Did they signal each other with flashlights at night while their parents thought they were fast asleep?

"Oh, Nick," she said. "It's just not fair! There is so much about you I don't know and may never know. We should have had a lifetime together to share stories about the past. And what about our future? You will never know your child and he will not know you." Danielle couldn't think of her unborn child as anything other than a little boy especially with the power of being in Nick's room filled with the things of his boyhood influencing her thoughts.

Was it fair to bring a child into the world that would never know his father? Unfortunately, it happens all the time. Unwed mothers whose impregnator flees, babies born to mothers widowed by war or acts of violence. She had been asked to write a story about the women who lost their husbands in the crash of United Flight 232 but the subject had been too personal, too painful. *How did they get through it?* She wondered if the mothers felt comfort and purpose in making a home for their children – an enduring legacy to their husband's memory. Even now she yearned for her father, to ask his advice and to hear stories about her childhood. But an entire life without a father? In her own grief she began to understand what those wives and mothers went through that day and every day since the crash. She understood the precious gift of life.

"And now I have the opportunity to create a future," she said as she patted her tummy. "A future for me and my son filled with hope, love, and wonderful memories of the only man I've ever loved."

She decided she would wait to decide on a decorating theme for this room until she spoke with Nick's mother. Did little Nick like boats, cowboys and Indians, sports? She so desperately wanted her baby to know its father and if it had to be through pictures and stories and yes, even the décor of its bedroom, so be it.

Danielle went into the adjoining bathroom and as she contemplated the dark oak cabinetry, gold flocked wallpaper and amber sconces her stomach contracted and forced her over to the toilet. With nothing in her stomach she tasted the bitter acid causing her to retch again and again. The nausea finally subsided and as she splashed cool water on her pale face she felt a little better. "So little one, is it the wallpaper or are you trying to tell me I should have eaten breakfast?" She decided it was the latter and the thought of toast and a poached egg sounded palatable.

She sat at the counter to eat her breakfast with the morning paper spread out around her. It hadn't taken long for Danielle to resume her old habits: grab a snack here or there, one night's supper a piece of chicken and a roll, the next night all vegetables eaten in front of the TV. She used to tell Nick that she had eaten well-rounded meals, just not served simultaneously! As she was breezing through the headlines, a small article caught her attention. *Antonio Salvatori, Director of the International Associated Research Institute, announced successful pig clone. Members of World Voices Against Mass Reproduction have perpetuated speculation that Salvatori's research is linked to the University of Minnesota. A spokesperson for the organization which opposes any genetic manipulation as "an affront to God's role in creation" has stated that they strongly suspect that the University is using federal research funds to support efforts to create a human clone. Officials at the University could not be reached for comment.*

"Hmmm. Interesting. Wonder what Nick would have to say about that?"

Her thoughts were interrupted by the phone ringing.

"Hello dear. This is Liz. Is everything all right? I just got your message."

"Hi. Yes, everything is fine. I just wondered if you were going to be home tonight. Thought I'd stop by."

"Of course you know we'd love to see you! I have a hair appointment this afternoon and Frank is playing golf but he should be home late afternoon. Why don't you come for dinner? Say sevenish?"

"I don't want you to go to any trouble," Danielle said.

"Not at all, dear. I'll pick something up at Byerly's. It's right down the block from the salon. They have such lovely salads. With some fresh baked bread and lemonade... nothing fancy. We can eat out on the patio. It's supposed to be a beautiful evening."

"Yes, I heard the weather report – sounds fine. Do you want me to bring anything?"

"No, thank you. No trouble at all. We'll see you tonight then?"

"Okay. See you later," Danielle said.

She was relieved to hang up the phone. Mrs. Goodman still intimidated her a little. Luckily Liz had no idea this would be more than just a casual visit but Danielle was still nervous about breaking the news. From the first time she had met Nick's mother – she had Nick's beautiful blue eyes – Danielle had felt a little out of place. Growing up in rural Iowa and then life as student hadn't done much to prepare her for society's upper echelon. But Danielle's genuine interest in people and her quick wit had a way of cutting across social borders. Liz Goodman was no exception and while her role as daughter-in-law was short, they had grown quite close. Danielle took the newspaper, curled up on the lounge in the sunroom and rehearsed how she would deliver the news to the Goodmans.

She needn't have worried. Liz and Frank were thrilled that they were to become grandparents!

CHAPTER 14

"Dr. Marino. Please pick up line four. Dr. Marino, line four please."

Sonny cursed as he left his lab work and walked to the wall phone on the other side of the room. He hated to be interrupted while he worked and hated the new hand-held mobile phones even more. He did not plan to get one any time soon. He regularly complained to Lauren when his golf partners held up play because of a "god dammed phone call." He ranted, "Why do they think they are so important that they need to carry a phone around with them? If it's an emergency, they can send a caddy out here to fetch him." At home, Lauren answered the phone to shield him from unimportant calls (most of them) and at work, his staff knew better than to bother him in the lab unless it was extremely urgent.

"Marino here," he barked.

"Hi, Dr. Marino – Sonny. I'm sorry to bother you but I thought you would like to know that it worked. I'm pregnant!" In her excitement, Danielle forgot to identify herself.

Sonny knew right away who is was and immediately got over his aggravation of having been interrupted. "Danielle! What wonderful news! I had a feeling that the stars would align and we would have success on the first try. I take it you have seen Dr. Yakahma?"

"Yes. He confirmed that I am pregnant and, despite my morning sickness, said I am very healthy. I have to take a bunch of pre-natal vitamins and follow up with him in a month!"

Sonny had arranged Danielle's care with his colleague in the OB-GYN practice at the University of Minnesota Medical Center. Because of their relationship working on advancements in infertility treatment, they often collaborated on specific patients' care and Sonny therefore had online access to their medical records. Of course, the patients had to approve this disclosure and Danielle had readily signed the myriad of HIPAA authorizations and forms. He couldn't wait to get into her file and monitor every aspect of this life-changing event.

The fact that she was pregnant was only the first step. Would the baby be healthy, carried to term and normal in every way? The ramifications of what he had accomplished were staggering.

As the weight of the news started to sink in, his mind raced with thoughts of fame and glory, international recognition and wealth. If he couldn't promote himself publically through this advancement, how could he profit surreptitiously?

"Sonny? Dr. Marino? Are you there?"

"What? Oh, yes. I'm sorry. I'm just so happy for you I got lost in thought for a moment! Thank you for letting me know the good news. I'd love to check in with you from time to time. Would that be okay?"

"Of course! I'm still adjusting to the news myself. I'll be in touch soon. Doctor, um, Sonny? I am so grateful to you for all you have done. If not for your friendship with Nick and your frank counsel with me, this never would have happened! Thank you."

"Well, my part was quite small. The rest is up to you! Take care and I look forward to seeing you soon."

As Sonny hung up the phone he quickly glanced around to see if anyone in the lab seemed to observe his call. There were only a few in the lab and they were engrossed in conversation around his most senior lab technician's table. Undoubtedly they were discussing the results of the latest effort to create new beta cells from embryonic stem cells to treat diabetes. Their reports were due to him at the end of the week although, after the call from Danielle, he was only vaguely interested in their findings.

If it were true, if the baby went full-term and was delivered as a completely normal human infant, he would have achieved the impossible. As he rushed back to his office and passed the department's secretary, he could barely contain his excitement when she asked, "Is everything all right?" It was highly unusual for him to pick up an unexpected call in the lab and she hoped he was not angry with her for paging him.

"Yes, Aster. Everything is fine. Thank you for paging me. Please hold my calls now though. I'll be tied up until after you leave for the day. Have a good evening."

Aster was stunned. A *thank you* and a *have a good evening* both in one day? She couldn't imagine what prompted her bellicose boss to be so nice but she guessed it had something to do with the phone call.

In his office, safe from the scrutiny of his secretary and staff, Sonny allowed himself an extremely rare moment of complete jubilation. Not only did he deserve this triumph but for the moment, he refused to think about any downside. He poured a glass of Scotch from the bottle hidden in his drawer and offered a toast. "Nick, old buddy. Whether you wanted to or not, you made this moment possible. You and your lovely bride."

The brief celebration ended as Sonny's attention drifted to the locked file drawer next to his desk. This is where he kept the documentation of his most confidential research and results including the work he had done in collaboration with Antonio Salvatori to advance the process of human cloning for therapeutic purposes. His arrangement with Nick's father Frank was also kept safe here. Though he suspected at the end, Nick didn't know the full scope of Sonny's work. Frank did, though he questioned the legality of it citing Minnesota's 1973 Human Conceptus Statue 145.422 which prohibits "the use of a living human conceptus for any type of scientific, laboratory research or other experimentation."

Sonny had disagreed with the "outdated" opinion that cloning creates a human *conceptus* since the term includes both the embryo and the membranes and appendages that are part of the placenta. With no federal or state laws banning therapeutic or reproductive cloning, he convinced Frank that there was nothing to worry about. Not that it would have mattered. Sonny was determined to go forward in any event.

Why don't the nutcases that protest outside our lab check the facts? They ignore the laws and send hate mail to anyone they can find involved in the research including me! Brings me back to the days when students stormed the building and released the animals. Those snot-nosed kids were all 'holier than thou' and hell-bent on saving the rats. Wait until it's their child lying at death's door hoping for a miracle. Well folks, miracles don't just happen. It takes someone like me willing to take a risk to advance scientific knowledge.

When we found ways to help infertile couples have children through artificial insemination and in vitro fertilization, the wackos pounded on their Bibles and said we were the devil. "Only God can create life," they screamed. I'd love to know how many of them have been helped by the very science they protested against. Two-faced hypocrites!

"Damn!" Sonny said. "Why am I wasting my energy on those idiots? I should be celebrating! But what if I missed something?" Anxious to assuage his doubts, Sonny took the key hidden in his desk drawer and opened the locked file cabinet. There it was, SCNT – Somatic Cell Nuclear Transfer.

Sonny flipped through the file back to the beginning. Start with the human egg. The donor's name was Mary Smith – an alias of course. She and her husband came to the University five years ago for fertility treatments culminating with *in vitro* fertilization. They implanted two embryos that were successfully gestated and born – let's see – in the margin he had scribbled a four and a five. His notes were purposely cryptic but that meant the fifth of April.

Over the years, he had often bent the rules to gain access to the University's vast network of databases. He paused a moment and thought of Gabriella the beautiful and brilliant researcher he had taken as a lover. She was in the U.S. in collaboration with the Milan International Medical School's research on the correlation between homosexuality and identical twins. Her hypothesis was that homosexuality is environmental, not genetic since there are more incidences of one identical twin being gay and the other straight versus both being gay. She received a grant to work with the University of Minnesota's Twin Registry. The program began in 1983 and followed twins born in Minnesota from 1936 to 1955 and between 1961 and 1964 and had recently begun a new study of twins born in the past five years. Their records and findings were perfect for her research and even though Minnesota was a world away from her beloved Italy, she jumped at the opportunity.

Sonny met Gabriella in the staff cafeteria and after only a few words the attraction was palpable. His Italian heritage and good looks, not to mention his power and prestige in the University's high-profile medical research lab made him extremely attractive to her. She could stand on her own as an expert in her field but she missed Italy and yearned for someone with whom she could speak her native Italian and share as an intellectual and scientific equal. Sonny was both. They met often for lunch and discussed their work and news from Italy.

Soon, at his suggestion, they were meeting after work and continuing their discussions over wine and dinner. The attraction was mutual and soon their discussions moved into Gabriella's bedroom. One evening as Sonny started to undress her she smiled and said, *"Sono, il mio piccolo furfante."* She often called him "Sonny, my little villain". But she didn't think of him as evil and certainly not a villain because he was a married man. She had often slept with married men in Italy – it was not at all uncommon. It was Sonny's deliberate disregard for authority and pushing the boundaries in his research that captivated her. She teased him about being a *furfante*, a villain, but was thrilled by it.

"I do wanta you, yesa? But firsta, I have sucha exciting newsa!" Gabriella said.

Sonny was turned on by her sexy Italian accent but now extremely curious to hear her news.

She had completed the study of all of the identical twins in the database and had interviewed those for whom the data pertaining to sexual preference were incomplete. There were no cases of identical twins both being gay. In every situation, only one of the two was a homosexual.

"Yes, *il mio amore*, my love," replied Sonny as he tenderly stroked her beautiful hair. "But I'm not sure this proves your theory that genetics is not involved. What if both twins really are gay but one has not admitted it? There are many cases of gay men and women who are or were married with children. To the world, to the researchers, and maybe even to themselves, they are straight, yes, but in fact they are not. Perhaps if you showed me some of the data, I could help you prove your case."

While somewhat dejected, Gabriella was eager for Sonny's help and affirmation so as she left the room to get a bottle of wine from the kitchen, she told him how to login on the Twin's Registry database.

The beep of his computer brought Sonny back to the present breaking his reverie of Gabriella's passionate lovemaking and interrupted the growing bulge under his lab coat.

With a few quick keystrokes he was at the database's

login screen. "Now, *il mio amore*, what was that password?" After just two attempts, he was in!

The most recent study had the names of all twins born in Minnesota in the past five years and indicated whether or not their parents had agreed to participate in the research. Of course, not all agreed but it didn't matter. All he had to do was access the master records of twins born on the Fifth of April. He quickly searched for all twins born in Minnesota on that date in each year and then cross-referenced the results with the *in vitro* procedures at the University of Minnesota Medical Center over the past five years. *Yes. There it is! Twin boys born to Diane and Gregory Landermeier on April 5, 1988. Let's see. That would make them about three years old now.*

"Okay. So how are you boys doing?"

It was common for couples receiving fertility treatment through the University's medical system to continue coming to the Family Medicine Center for pediatric care. The U's pediatric specialists were among the top in the nation and after going through the arduous conception process, families were well acquainted with the massive facilities. The Landermeiers were no exception and Sonny quickly accessed the boys' pediatric medical records.

He learned that Timothy and Thomas were within normal ranges of physical and intellectual growth. After reviewing their earliest checkups, immunizations and several routine ear infection treatments, he was satisfied that there was no cause for concern over the viability of Diane's eggs. He supposed he could dig deeper to see if any other of her donated eggs resulted in successful pregnancies, but he was more intent on reviewing his own protocols that resulted in Danielle's pregnancy.

He quickly reviewed the steps taking Diane's donated egg to an enucleated egg. He had done this hundreds of times. Check.

Cell isolation. He used the blood he had taken from Nick on the day of his murder and following Japan's recent success in using granulocyte donor cells, he had extracted a single cell containing Nick's DNA. Check.

Synchronize the cell cycles. Sonny had studied both the Roslin and the Honolulu techniques and tried both. It was his triumph over the success using the Honolulu technique with human cells that had caused the blowup with Nick and necessitated his demise. Unfortunate. Check.

Fuse the enucleated egg with Nick's cell. The nucleus of the blood cell was inserted into Diane's enucleated egg and in exactly fifty-seven minutes the egg cell had accepted the new nucleus. Check.

Wait five hours. Check.

Place in A32566 chemical culture to accelerate the cell's growth. Check.

Confirm that Cytochalasin B was effective in preventing the formation of the polar body cell as in normal fertilization. Check.

Monitor cell development until 16 cells are present. Check.

After the three-day incubation period, insert embryo into the uterus by inserting a thin tube through the cervix. Check.

Sonny was satisfied that he followed the exact process he had used to successfully create the human embryos in his lab just a month ago. And now, his creation had taken hold and was growing in Danielle's body. He carefully returned the files to the cabinet, locked the drawer and hid the key.

"Oh hell! One more for the road." After downing another Scotch, he took off his lab coat, turned out the lights and went home.

CHAPTER 15

Frank was on the golf course when he got word that Danielle's contractions were three minutes apart. By the time he got to the hospital, the tiny infant was already in the nursery and he found Liz standing by the window.

"Oh he's beautiful! He looks just like Nicky doesn't he, Frank?" Liz Goodman gushed over her newborn grandson.

They were surprised to see Sonny approach them from the delivery room waiting area. He explained that Dr. Yakahma had delivered the healthy baby boy and was now tending to Danielle. As a trusted friend of the family, Sonny explained the situation to the Goodmans.

"The baby is absolutely fine but Danielle had complications after the delivery. The placenta did not separate from the uterus causing what's referred to as uterine inversion. Danielle suffered severe bleeding, has received a transfusion and is now on an oxytocin IV," Sonny said.

"Oh no! Will she be okay?" Liz had become quite close to Danielle these past months and felt less like her mother-in-law and more like her mother. "What else does that poor girl have to endure?"

"Her prognosis is very good but she will likely have to stay in the hospital for five or six days. She'll need help during her recovery at home."

Frank and Liz sighed with relief. "Of course", Frank said. "We will make sure she is well taken care of – and little Tyler too."

"Tyler? Is that his name?" Sonny asked.

"Yes. Tyler Nicholas Richard – Nicholas after his father of course and Richard was Danielle's father's name." Liz said. From the very beginning, Danielle was so certain the baby was a boy. She had already chosen his name by the time the ultrasound confirmed it."

"Tyler Nicholas." Sonny was not surprised that she named the boy after Nick but little did she know. "How appropriate."

"A name says a lot about a person, don't you agree?" Frank said. "Danielle did some research on boys' names and their meaning. Our last name is self-explanatory – the good man. Nicholas, from the Greek *nikolaos – victory of the people*. Of course, everyone knows Saint Nicholas, Santa Claus, the bishop from Anatolia who, according to legend, saved the daughters of a poor man from lives of prostitution. He is the patron saint and protector of children."

"Now Frank," Liz chided. "Don't make it sound like we knew all that when we named Nicky. Honestly Sonny, we just liked the name."

"Ah. And Tyler?"

"Well, Danielle liked the name Tyler and when she found out that it means 'doorkeeper' her mind was made up. She told me about the doors closed on her when Nick died and now the new doors opening through the birth of her miracle baby, it seemed so right," Liz said.

"Miracle baby?" Sonny was jolted. *Did Danielle change her mind and tell the Goodmans about the procedure?*

"Well don't you think it's a miracle that she got pregnant on their honeymoon? We were sure they were going to wait for a while. Danielle wanted to establish her career before starting a family. Last week, Danielle told me that God must have known that Nick would be taken and wanted her to have something to live for," Liz said, "and I believe it's true."

"And our hope is that he grows to be a *good man* – like our son." Frank's voice broke under the emotion of the past twelve months – the joy of seeing his son finally find love, the look on his face as he promised to love Danielle 'til death us do part', the incomprehensible horror of Nick's death and now, the birth of his one and only grandson.

Liz reached over and took Frank's hand. It was rare for her husband to show emotion but she knew only too well the toll the past months had taken on him. While she had obsessed over Danielle's pregnancy, doting on her, making sure she ate well, took her vitamins and kept her doctor's appointments, Frank was devastated by Nick's death and held back any hopes for the future. Perhaps today he was finally seeing a glimmer of happiness in his grandson. No one could ever replace Nick in his father's eyes, but a grandson? Yes, she believed Tyler could begin to heal the hole in his grandfather's heart just as Danielle had mended Liz's hurt of losing her own baby girl so many years ago.

"So when can we see Danielle?" Liz asked.

"It shouldn't be too much longer. Dr. Yakahma will come out and give you the full update." Sonny reached out to shake Frank's hand. "Congratulations, Frank, or should I say Grandpa?" He patted Liz's shoulder as he walked out of the waiting room.

"Grandpa? Oh Frank! I can hardly believe it's true. So many years of wondering if Nick would ever marry, and then..." Liz's voice trailed off for a moment. "But Grandpa?" she teased. "That sounds like some old geezer. How about you be Granddad and I'll be Grandmama?"

"Grandmama? That sounds a bit too uppity. How about just one *ma*? Grandma. That suits you much better," Frank said as he pulled his wife close and wrapped his arms around her.

They were still standing at the nursery window admiring their grandson when Dr. Yakahma greeted them.

"Mr. and Mrs. Goodman?" He smiled warmly as he shook their hands. "Danielle is doing fine. We had a bit of a complication after the delivery."

"Yes," Frank interrupted. "Dr. Marino filled us in."

"Is Danielle going to be ok?" Liz asked.

"Yes, I believe she will be fine. Uterine inversion is quite rare but since our facility is referred many of the high-risk pregnancies, my team has actually treated quite a few cases. If a woman has had a previous inversion, we need to be prepared for it to happen again."

"So it doesn't prevent a woman from having another baby?" Liz asked.

"No, it just makes the next delivery more complicated. At least we know what to expect. Luckily, with Danielle, we saw what was happening and started the IV immediately to control the pain and relax the uterus. The uterus was repositioned without the need for surgery. She did lose some blood and will need to be closely monitored for the next forty-eight hours. But barring any additional complications, she should be able to go home in a few days."

"Thank you, doctor," Frank said.

"You are more than welcome. Don't hesitate to call my office if you have any questions or concerns. And, congratulations on your new grandson!"

"Oh, thank God!" Liz said as she finally let her tears flow. "Frank, she's going to be okay! In a few days we can take them both home."

"Yes, Liz. Just like I did with you and little Nicholas forty some years ago. To the very same home."

CHAPTER 16

"Thank you, Mom. I don't know what I'd do without you!" This had to be the hundredth time Danielle said these words to her mother-in-law and they weren't just words. Liz and Frank had practically lived there since Danielle and baby Tyler came home from the hospital and she was eternally grateful.

"I know, dear. I'm just glad I can help." There were days when Liz wondered if she was spending too much time with Danielle and Tyler. She and Frank had talked about paying for a personal assistant to help at home while Danielle recovered. But when the time came for them to be released from the hospital, the happy grandparents jumped at the chance to help Danielle with the baby and even agreed to take turns getting up at night to bring Tyler to her for feeding. The guest room was comfortable and, truth be told, Frank hardly ever work up when Tyler cried, but he was a big help during the day allowing both Liz and Danielle to catch up with naps here and there.

When Liz was too tired to cook, Frank picked up freshly prepared meals from Byerly's gourmet delicatessen and heated them up. He learned which dishes were best, the meatloaf and wild rice chicken salad, and his selections were certainly much better than fast food takeout. He was also happy to shop for groceries and kept the pantry and freezer well stocked.

For the first couple of weeks it was difficult for Danielle

to go up and down the stairs so she mainly stayed up in the master bedroom suite. She was instructed to take it easy and get as much rest as she could while her body recovered. With Tyler waking up every couple of hours to nurse and her strength zapped from the delivery, it was all she could do to eat, bathe and feed Tyler. Once she was up and about she made a few meals but mostly just enjoyed the food that magically appeared on her plate.

Liz did bring in someone to help with the laundry and housecleaning. The washing machine and dryer were still in the basement although Frank was getting bids from a contractor to move them to the upper floor. Liz had never liked going down two flights of stairs to tend the laundry but at least then, when Nicky was little and she was washing clothes almost every day, she was young and strong. After she miscarried Nick's little sister and learned that she wouldn't be able to have another child, she had to give up her dream of a house filled with children. By that time Frank's business was flourishing so they could afford to have a housekeeper who made most of the trips downstairs to the laundry room.

"Danielle, I hope you don't think we are imposing on you too much. I like Frank's idea of moving the laundry upstairs but, it's your house dear. I was just thinking back to when Nicky was little and I was running up and down those stairs every day. So many of the new houses these days have the laundry near the bedrooms. We just thought..."

"Don't worry. I'll let you know if you go too far. Like, for instance, if you guys totally move in." Danielle smiled to put Liz at ease. "I like the idea of the upstairs laundry and appreciate your help figuring that out. Nick and I probably would have thought of it sooner or later. Maybe." Having experienced her small family's home, the organized chaos of the Myers' large farmhouse and single life in teeny campus dorms and apartments, Danielle hadn't really thought about managing her own household – and a mansion at that. She loved Frank and Liz but she also needed to honor her own past and not be totally taken over by their generosity. *There will be plenty of time for independence. For now, it's nice to be cared for.*

"Oh, by the way," Liz said. "Sonny called and wondered if he could stop by tomorrow evening. He just wants to check in on you and Tyler and I thought it might be nice to have a little company. Nothing fancy. Maybe for dessert and coffee?"

"Sure. That sounds good. Tyler doesn't have a schedule yet so it's hard to know when is a good time."

"How about around seven o'clock? He might get a few minutes with Tyler awake, but, if not, that's okay too. I'll call him and let him know."

"Okay. I know I'm not supposed to eat chocolate but a piece of chocolate cheesecake really sounds good to me right now. Maybe I could sneak a few bites since we're having a guest?"

"That sounds good to me too. I'll ask Frank to pick it up on the way home from Southpoint tomorrow. He is on the tournament planning committee and they have a meeting tomorrow afternoon to plan this summer's charity golf event."

"Summer? I have been so cooped up I feel like I'm missing spring. I wonder what is happening in the garden. Did I ever mention that I was thinking about restoring the grounds to what they may have looked like when the house was built at the turn of the century? I doubt I'll get to that project any time soon. Not that I'm complaining," she said beaming at Tyler.

Sonny arrived promptly at seven bearing gifts – a bottle of champagne for Frank and Liz to toast their grandson, a bouquet of pink roses for Danielle and a wrapped package for Tyler. Danielle had just finished feeding him and he was fast asleep in her arms.

"Hello Danielle. Please don't get up. You both look so comfortable," said Sonny as came into the living room.

Liz was right behind him. "Look at the beautiful roses

Sonny brought. I'll put them here on the table for you to enjoy. Sonny, please sit down. Frank will bring out the champagne and we'll all have a toast."

"So, Danielle. How are you feeling? You look wonderful," Sonny said.

"Every day I feel a little better. If not for getting only a couple of hours of sleep at a time, I'd be back to full power. Tyler is doing great and is eating much better now. Those first few weeks were hard on all of us but, as you can see, he is a beautiful, content baby."

"So I see. I brought this for him – well, it's really for you both," Sonny said as he handed her the package.

Liz hopped up. "Let me hold him for you while you open your gift, unless you would like to hold him, Sonny."

"Thanks, I'd like to. It's been a long time since my children were that small," Sonny said as Liz placed the tiny bundle into his arms. "Hey there little guy. How's the world treating you?"

Danielle carefully removed the pastel blue bow and wrapping paper. Inside the box was a beautiful white leather bound book with Tyler's name engraved on the front. The record of his birth weight, length and head circumference were neatly written on the first page along with his footprint and a snapshot of him wearing a tiny blue cotton beanie.

She was deeply moved. "Oh Sonny, thank you so much! How did you get these? Those first days of his life in the hospital are a complete blur to me."

Sonny and Liz exchanged glances and smiled. "Let's just say it was a group effort," Sonny said. "This baby is nothing short of a miracle and I thought you would like to have a special place to record his growth and the many important milestones you have to look forward to."

"I kept just such a journal of Nick's childhood," Liz said. "Frank, that reminds me. Have you seen Nicky's baby book? I didn't find it in any of our boxes after we moved. I wonder if it's still around here somewhere."

"I haven't seen it, Liz but I did notice some old boxes

marked 'NICKY' when I was showing the contractor the closet upstairs. Sonny, we are planning to move the laundry room to the bedroom level so it's more convenient for Danielle. She will have her hands full and running to the basement to do laundry is not the best situation. Would you like to come up and see the plans?"

"Thank you again for the thoughtful gift," Danielle said as she took the sleeping baby from Sonny's arms. "I'll go put Tyler down for the night while you guys look at the plans. Mom, I'll be down in a few minutes to help you serve the coffee."

"Okay, dear. Take your time. Night night baby boy," Liz said as she gave Tyler a gentle kiss.

Frank and Sonny went upstairs to check out the large walk-in closet between the guest room and the hallway bath. "The contractor said we could close off this end of the closet to create a small laundry room. We can use a bi-fold or sliding doors for access and the plumbing can easily be run from the bathroom. This room has another closet on the south wall so repurposing this one shouldn't be a problem. Here, let me show you the plans."

Frank spread out the drawings on top of a stack of boxes stored in the closet. Sonny noticed the box labeled "NICKY – BABY – SAVE" and wondered if the baby journal book was in it. It would be really interesting to see how closely Tyler's development mirrored his father's. More than interesting. Scientifically relevant!

"What do you think?" Frank asked.

"Hmmm? Oh! The plans. Yes. I think it will work though my expertise is with a microscope not with hammer and saw."

"I can relate to that. That's why we hired a contractor. Let's go down and pop that champagne open."

"Good idea. Mind if I use the restroom?"

"Of course. We'll be in the living room."

Sonny stepped into the bathroom and waited until he heard Frank's footsteps reach the bottom of the staircase.

Danielle was singing softly to Tyler in the nursery so the coast was clear. He quietly opened the closet door and opened Nick's baby box. Underneath a plastic bag holding what appeared to be a baptismal gown and a hand-knit blanket was a small blue book. Yes! He had found it. He tucked it in his suit coat pocket and neatly replaced the other items and the box top. He quietly slipped back into the bathroom and went through the motions of flushing the toilet and running the water. As he exited into the hallway, Danielle came out of the nursery.

"Is he sleeping?" Sonny asked.

"Like a baby," she said giving him a warm smile. "Let's go eat some chocolate."

CHAPTER 17

"Hello Mrs. Goodman. Please sit wherever you are most comfortable," said Dr. Olivia Dunham. She was a rather plain woman in her mid fifties with shoulder-length mousy brown hair streaked with gray. Her hazel eyes sparkled when she smiled, which she did easily, putting her patients at ease.

Danielle glanced around the room. A blue and yellow striped sofa with coordinating pillows, two floral armchairs and a white wicker glass topped coffee table appointed the room. With the morning sun filtering through the partially closed blinds, she almost felt like she was on the porch of a lovely country cottage. On the coffee table were hot water, an assortment of herbal teas, a delicate pitcher of ice water, white mugs, a box of tissue and a crystal bowl containing wrapped hard candies.

On the wall opposite the window was a desk with a computer monitor and a small floral arrangement. Above the desk hung several framed photographs and the doctor's certifications.

Danielle chose the sofa and nervously waited for the doctor to take her place in the adjacent armchair.

"I have read the notes and information you provided to our intake specialist and I am really glad you are here," said Olivia. "Everything we discuss is completely confidential although if you share information that leads me to believe that you pose a physical danger to yourself or others, I am bound to report such danger to law enforcement. Are you okay with this?"

Danielle nodded. She had never had therapy before and wasn't at all convinced it would help but felt she had to do something. There wasn't anyone on earth she could talk to and feared she was losing her mind. Dr. Olivia Dunham had come highly recommended and her entire practice was devoted to helping women with mental health issues.

"Good. If you are comfortable, please call me Olivia. And how would you like to be addressed?" Olivia smiled warmly. Though she had to start with these formalities she knew from experience that the first few sessions were critical to establishing the doctor-patient relationship and her methods had proven to be quite effective.

"Danielle is fine."

"Okay, Danielle. Why don't we begin by telling me why you are here?"

Danielle took a deep breath and began. "I am having difficultly in my relationship with my son Tyler."

"How old is he?" Olivia found that asking easy, factual questions helped start the dialogue. It took time to get into the deep issues that troubled her patients.

"He is thirteen."

"Ah. Is he going through puberty?"

"Yes. I've had to buy him bigger shoes and longer jeans three times in the past six months. He eats like a horse, has started to grow facial hair and his voice cracks."

Olivia smiled. "Classic signs of puberty for a boy his age. Have you noticed any change in his moods or behavior?"

"Yes but," Danielle hesitated, "it's my feelings that worry me. He reminds me so much of my late husband and, well, he knows things that make me feel like I'm losing my mind."

Olivia saw that her patient was fighting to stay in control. "How long ago did your husband die?"

"That's just it. Nick died before Tyler was even born and we had so little time together. Sometimes my marriage feels like just a dream."

"Perhaps if we start at the beginning?"

Danielle quickly recounted her courtship and marriage to Nick. Indeed, they hadn't had much time together. Olivia was impressed by the courage it took to go forward with artificial insemination to bear her late husband's child. She had heard of other women taking such steps but hadn't as yet treated a patient in these circumstances. She understood the human need to hold on to a loved one that had been lost.

Olivia wondered if Danielle's struggle could be related to a legal issue. Recently the Supreme Court considered a case brought by the wife of a member of the military who was killed in Afghanistan. They were both concerned for his safety when he was deployed so he left a frozen sperm sample in the event he was injured or rendered infertile. After his death, his widow used the sperm to bear another child – they already had a daughter – she had twins. She then filed for Social Security survivor benefits on behalf of the twins. The Supreme Court ruled that since the children had not been dependent upon the deceased father at the time of his death, they were not eligible for survivor benefits. However, the ruling had effectively skirted the broader issue of the legal status of children conceived through artificial means after the death of a parent.

"The first few weeks of Tyler's life are a blur," Danielle continued. "I had complications during the delivery so I needed more help than I'd planned after we came home from the hospital. Liz and Frank, my late-husband's parents, practically lived with us. I don't know how we would have made it without their help."

Danielle hesitated before she went on. "I love my mother-in-law but, sometimes I felt like Tyler depended on her more than me. I thought it was just because I was an inexperienced new mom. I would try to comfort him when he cried. And when he wouldn't stop, she would hold him. Within minutes he'd be calm. I was so jealous when his first word was 'Mamma'."

Olivia was puzzled. "Why did that bother you?"

"From the start, I always referred to myself as Mommy. 'Mommy loves you. Would you like to ride in the car with Mommy?' Always Mommy. Frank and Liz were Grandma and Granddad. He had trouble with the 'grand' part and called them Mamma and Dadda until he was almost three. I know it shouldn't have bothered me but to have his first word 'Mamma' spoken to his grandmother instead of me..."

"I understand," Olivia said as she thought of the thousands of women whose children's *firsts* were witnessed by their daycare providers. She wondered how Danielle's relationship was now with her in-laws and made a note in her file to talk about that in a later session. She seemed to be comfortable talking about the past and she appreciated her direct style of communicating.

"Danielle, you mentioned that Tyler knows things that are troubling to you. Can you tell me more about that?"

"It came to a head a couple of weeks ago but as I started to think back, there were things in the past that I now think were signs. Maybe I'm just being ridiculous but Tyler is so much like his father, it's uncanny."

"Tell me about the things from the past that seem out of the ordinary to you now," Olivia encouraged.

"Liz spent many nights with us when Tyler was a baby and we both followed the same routine when we put him to bed. At bedtime, seven thirty, I put on his jammies, read him a story and then would say, 'time for night night.' When he started to talk, he would say 'minny mih' meaning Minty milk and we would go up to the nursery."

"Minty milk?" Olivia smiled. "I haven't heard of mint flavored formula before now."

Danielle shook her head and laughed. "No. He had a little mint-green blanket that we named Minty and I would give him Minty to cuddle and a bottle of milk."

"So that was Minty milk?"

"Yes. Except one night he didn't want Minty milk. He wanted 'yammy' and squeezed his fist a couple of times.

'Do you mean Minty?' I asked him. 'No, yammy!' And he squeezed his fist again. I couldn't understand what he was saying and tried to put him to bed with Minty and his bottle. He wasn't having it. He pushed both away and kept screaming 'yammy, yammy'. When I tried to give him his bottle he turned his head away, back and forth over and over again. By then he was crying so hard and screaming at the top of his lungs. I had no idea what to do and finally called Liz.

"There was a long pause on the other end of the line after I explained to her what was happening. She could hear him screaming and Liz said, 'It reminds me of Nicky at that age. He had a little stuffed lamb he called Yammy and I was still breast-feeding him but only at bedtime. Similar to your Minty milk routine, he had Yammy and the fist squeezing meant he wanted to nurse.'"

Danielle continued, "I was at my wits end so when she suggested I look in the box in the closet of Nick's baby things for the little lamb, I didn't think twice. Anything to stop his screaming so he would get some sleep and I could do some writing. Sure enough, there it was. Miraculously, as soon as I gave him the lamb he said 'Yammy' and hugged it close. I was so happy to have him calmed down! I put him in his crib with Yammy, and Minty, just in case, and he took his bottle and fell asleep."

Olivia furrowed her brow and made some notes. "That's really interesting. Were there other incidents like this?"

Danielle poured herself some water and took a sip. "After my husband's death I really felt isolated. I had given up my job at the paper after Tyler was born and totally immersed myself in being a mother. I loved him so much! But I was afraid that if I stayed home too long I would never have the career I had dreamed of. Tyler kept me busy, for sure, but I started to feel restless. I missed being engaged in current events and using my skills. I missed the adult, intellectual conversation and stimulation.

"I started watching the ads for jobs and eventually ran

across a part-time position with the National Wildlife Federation. They were looking for a photojournalist to help in their campaign to preserve the wolf population in Minnesota. I was fascinated to learn that Minnesota's wolf population was second only to Alaska and in some areas of the state the overpopulation was causing a lot of conflict with the livestock farmers. Anyway, the story was interesting to me and had much more appeal than the community news work I was doing before I had the baby."

Olivia smiled and pointed to the photographs on the wall behind her desk. "Those were taken by a good friend of mine who had the opportunity to photograph wolf pups at the Wolf Ridge Environmental Learning Center. So you took the job. Did you enjoy it?"

"I loved it!" Danielle crossed her legs and sat back on the sofa. "It was the perfect mix of writing, photography and for a good, yet controversial, cause. I'd spend several days out in the field and then work from home. Liz stayed with Tyler while I was gone. It was an ideal situation and a satisfying time in my life."

Olivia nodded and made some notes. "You mentioned other incidents?" she said, steering Danielle back to Tyler.

"I know there were many but a few stand out to me now. One night, when he was about two, we were eating supper and Tyler was in his highchair. No matter what I put on his tray, he threw it overboard – small pieces of chicken, potato, even his favorite, avocado." Danielle smiled at Olivia's reaction. "I know. Weird, huh? He loved avocado!

"Tyler kept saying, 'Banolli, banolli' and pointing to the kitchen.

"'Macaroni?' I asked.

"'No. Banolli!'

"'Ravioli?'

"'No! Banolli!'

"I tried everything until we were both so frustrated I felt like throwing a tantrum along with him."

"Did you ever figure out what he wanted?" Olivia asked.

"Not until I mentioned it to Liz a few days later. She told me that when Nick was little he loved baloney and called it 'banolli'. The odd thing was, she told me that she had never fed Tyler baloney. I was glad to hear it. I have this thing about processed foods."

"I know," Olivia agreed. "There are a lot of additives in processed meat. I limit myself to one hotdog…a year! So you have no idea where he learned that word?"

"None."

"Strange. Any other examples?" Olivia said.

"When Tyler was about seven, he came down to the kitchen. I was making his favorite homemade macaroni and cheese for supper. He told me that he couldn't find his Slinky. He had pulled everything out of his toy box, looked under the bed and in the closet. I was confused. I had never bought him a Slinky. The new plastic ones don't work as well as the metal ones my parents had as kids. I told him I didn't know he had a Slinky – thinking maybe Frank, his grandfather, bought one for him while I was out of town. I remember the anguished look on his face.

'Mom, you don't remember? The Slinky Dad gave me for my birthday?'

"'You mean Granddad?' I asked him. Now I was really confused! He shouted that he knew the difference between Dad and Granddad and said if I weren't so busy working all the time maybe I'd remember important stuff – like what he got on his birthday!

"It was the first time he complained about my work and I took it pretty hard. I guess that's why I remember that incident so vividly. I vowed to be more intentional about my time with him. I even started to include him in discussions of what I was working on. I let him help by looking things up on the computer and sometimes brought him along on trips when it worked out. It really bugged me though about the Slinky, so after he was in bed I rummaged through the old boxes that were down in the basement. Know what I found?"

"A Slinky?" Olivia asked.

"Yep. Nick had one of the original metal ones when he was a boy. I wiped it off and put it on the kitchen table. When Tyler saw it the next morning he came bounding up to my room with a huge smile. 'Mom! You found it. Thanks!' He gave me a huge hug and followed the Slinky as it tumbled down the staircase. I didn't know what to make of it. Still don't."

"Is it possible he had seen a picture or perhaps his grandfather had told him about Nick playing with a Slinky as a boy?"

"I asked Frank and Liz if they had ever mentioned the Slinky to Tyler and they didn't recall having done so." Danielle took a long drink of water. "Like I said, the individual incidents didn't alarm me at the time although I was certainly confused by them.

"Once Tyler heard about the old box of toys, he was excited to see what else was in the musty boxes downstairs. The next Saturday we put on our grubby clothes and went down to have a look. I pulled out a marionette – a red-headed freckled boy wearing a plaid cowboy shirt with a kerchief tied around his neck.

"Tyler immediately grabbed it, pulled the string to move it's mouth and mimicked, 'Hey kids, what time is it? It's Howdy Doody time!' and started to sing the song to the tune Ta-ra-ra Boom-de-ay.'

"It was way before my time – Nick was quite a bit older than I – but I had heard of the Howdy Doody TV show. But how did Tyler know the song, all the words and everything? He just shrugged when I asked him. I was still wondering about it when he pulled out an old metal Dick Tracy car. The name was on the car in big letters, even I could see that, but Tyler started talking about Pat and Sam Catchem. He dug out some old comic books from the bottom of the box and sure enough, those characters were in the stories."

"That is odd," Olivia said. "Did Nick's parents maybe tell him about the toys from his father's childhood?"

"They didn't remember doing so but it was the only explanation that made any sense to me. Liz must have been about seventy then and had been showing some signs of forgetfulness."

Olivia thought that was the likely scenario but she was careful to keep her opinion to herself. These incidents clearly bothered the young woman enough to seek counseling. Instead she nodded in affirmation and said, "We have about fifteen more minutes to talk today. I'd like to hear more about the events of the past and then, perhaps next time we can talk more about what's going on now. Would that be okay with you?"

Danielle was not anxious to reveal her most disturbing feelings, but it seemed to help just giving voice to the crazy ideas that had been rolling around in her head. "Sure," she said. "Although I do want to meet again soon. Here in your office it all seems explainable, but more and more my thoughts go crazy when I am around Tyler. I have so much bottled up."

"Let's work together to release that pressure. I will ask my assistant to schedule you in again later this week. Is there anything else you want to share today?"

Danielle's linear thought process served her well in her work as a journalist. Even though she knew the end of the story, she had the patience to take the reader step by step from start to finish. Now she thought she could share the awful reality of her life with Dr. Dunham if she took an objective viewpoint and told the story from start to finish.

"Yes. There is one that I skipped over. It seems so trivial but it has always bothered me. I told you that Tyler's first words were 'Mamma.' I put it out of my mind when soon after he called me 'Mommy'. He quickly learned to say 'wah wah' and a bunch of words that wouldn't mean anything to strangers but were crystal clear to his grandma and me. Frank usually got the obvious ones but Liz and I were completely tuned into his developing speech." Danielle paused and smiled. "Those were such precious times and I loved seeing the dots connect."

Olivia agreed. "It really is amazing how much a helpless baby learns and develops in the first few years, isn't it?"

"Tyler's vocabulary continued to grow and the little sounds he made soon turned into words and phrases that even Frank could understand. But, for some reason, he wouldn't say Grandma and Granddad. No matter what I tried he said 'Hi Mamma' when Liz entered the room and 'Hi Dadda' when Frank came in. At first I thought it was the R sound that was causing the problem. I read that R is a difficult sound for children to make and tried suggested techniques to help him. At some point I realized that he was able to say rabbit and tractor but still he said 'Mamma' and 'Dadda.' Each time he said 'Mamma' I said 'Grandma.' Then he would smile and say 'Mamma.' I said 'Granddad' and he would giggle and say 'Dadda.' I think it became kind of a game. I asked Liz and Frank to reinforce the lessons but I rarely heard them correct him. It wasn't until he was old enough to intellectually understand the difference between a Mamma and a Grandma that he made the change. I remember his Kindergarten teacher calling me in confusion when Tyler drew a picture of his family. He told her it was 'Mommy, Mamma and Dadda.' She knew Tyler's father had died and was puzzled by the names of the two extra parental stick people in his drawing. When I explained the important role his grandparents had played in his daily life since birth, she said the drawing showed that he felt loved and said I shouldn't be concerned about the titles. She told me that the difference between a parent and a grandparent would make sense to him when he was ready and not to worry about it. She encouraged me not to dwell on it that it would come to him in due time.'"

"And did it?"

"Yes, she was right. I don't remember exactly when it happened but he eventually made the transition. After that, the only time I heard him say 'Mamma' and 'Dadda' was in the night when he was having a bad dream. Once he was awake he would call me 'Mommy' and later 'Mom' but in his sleep he always called out for 'Mamma' and 'Dadda.' So I suppose you think I'm making a *mountain out of a molehill*, right?"

Olivia put down her pen and looked directly into Danielle's eyes. "I believe that you have experienced many events that have led you to my door. We know that the accumulation of many small things can be as devastating as one major event and based on your family history and the things we talked about today, I would say you have had your share of both. No matter what, Danielle, I won't judge you. My job is to help you understand why you are feeling what you are feeling and help you work through whatever is troubling you."

"Thank you, Doctor…Olivia. I was really nervous about seeing a psychiatrist. I've always been able to handle whatever came my way. But these feelings – I just didn't know where else to turn."

"Yes. It takes a lot of courage for us to face our troubles and you impress me as a woman of great strength. Be good to yourself and I'll see you in a few days." Olivia stood and Danielle looked at the clock. It was exactly two o'clock.

Wow. An hour right on the nose. She's good! Danielle had plenty of time to stop at the grocery store on the way home. She was glad Tyler had golf and dinner with Frank after school today. It would give her some time alone to ponder her session with Olivia and finish editing the article she was submitting tomorrow.

Knowing she would see Olivia again on Friday was reassuring. She took a deep breath and said, "One day at a time."

CHAPTER 18

"Mom? I'm home," Tyler called out as he plopped his books and gear on the kitchen counter.

"Hi Tyler! I'm out on the porch." Fall was her favorite time of year and tonight after a light supper of squash soup and salad she curled up on the glider with the book she was reading. The evening air was starting to feel cool but with the fireplace burning Danielle could still enjoy the gentle breeze coming through the open windows carrying the musky smell of the fallen leaves.

"Hey, Mom. How's it goin'?"

"Good. I'm just finishing up my book. I have book club Friday night and I have just a couple chapters left."

Tyler plopped down on the antique wicker chair and pulled out his phone. Thumbs flying he was pressing the keys on his phone. Danielle watched him for a little while before speaking.

"How was golf today?"

Without looking up thumbs still tapping he said, "Not too exciting."

"Does that mean you did well?"

"Okay, I guess. I shot eight-eight."

"How was Granddad's game?"

"He shot seventy-nine and complained the whole time," Tyler said without looking up, thumbs still flying.

"Tyler. Would you mind not texting for a minute so we can have a conversation?"

"We are. I can do more than one thing at a time."

Danielle took a deep breath and counted to ten before trying again.

"I know honey but I'd like to see your eyes when we talk."

"My eyes? They're still blue just like my father's as you've pointed out like a million times."

Not wanting to get into a confrontation Danielle tried another tactic. "Have you heard from Alyssa?"

"Yeah. She texted me after History. I haven't wrote back."

"Written back." It popped out of her mouth without thinking. She quickly added, "Is she going to the football game on Friday?"

"Yeah. Her and her friend Julie want to meet me and Joe there."

Hoping to keep the conversation going, Danielle ignored his grammar this time. Julie and Joe each had older brothers on the high school football team and their families went to every game so Danielle encouraged Tyler's friendship with Joe and his family. She had chatted with Joe's father last year several times at the parent teacher conferences and he seemed like a good dad.

Danielle worried more and more about her son not having a male role model especially now in his teen years – someone he could talk *guy talk* with. *That's funny, I believe Tyler would benefit by having a man in the house but why isn't it appealing to me? Maybe I should talk to Olivia about that on Friday.*

She had not dated much since Nick's death, nothing serious anyway and never considered marrying again. Jake remained a good friend but only a friend and he had married a woman from Denver.

"Julie seems like a nice girl."

"She's okay but it's not like she's my girlfriend or nothin'. We just like to hang out. Joe keeps giving me sh...grief about her."

Danielle was glad he caught himself before saying *shit.*

She couldn't stop him from using that kind of language around his friends, and his granddad, but she didn't tolerate it at home. She knew Frank cursed when he had a bad golf shot and with a seventy-nine today, he probably used it more than once. She hoped, at least, that Tyler didn't use the f-word.

"I have book club Friday night but I'll be home by the time the game is over. Just let me know if you guys go out for pizza or something after. Okay?"

"Yeah. Sure."

"Do you have a lot of homework tonight?"

"I have to write a paragraph for English." Tyler looked up from his phone. "Actually, Mom, I could use your help."

Seeing his beautiful eyes and hearing the sweetness in his voice made Danielle's heart skip. His mind was completely tuned to math, science and technology, like Nick's, but Tyler struggled with writing. Writing came so easily to her that at first she was puzzled by his lack of interest and skill with language, but now she was secretly glad there was at least one reason that he needed her.

"What's the assignment?" Danielle said.

"We have to read the first two chapters of *The Scarlet Letter* and then write a paragraph on how Hester's sin of having a kid by some guy that's not her husband compares to our society's values now."

"Have you done the reading?"

"Yeah. The first chapter was pretty boring but then Hester is led from the prison to the square where the people all gather around. They try to make her, like, tell them who the kid's father is but she won't. Everybody is staring at her and hassling her. She's carrying the kid and has a big red 'A' plastered on her chest. So, like, I don't really get it. What's the big deal?"

Danielle thought for a moment her eyes looking up at the ceiling. "Well," she said, "if I remember correctly, the story was set way back in the seventeenth century in the time of the Puritans. Did your teacher tell you about them?"

"I don't remember exactly but seems like they were big on punishing you in front of everybody if you, like, screwed up or somethin'."

"That's right. The Puritans believed that every man is born a sinner because of the fall of Adam and Eve in the Garden of Eden. They felt it was their obligation to point out the sins of others in public to make them an example. Personally, I think they wanted to condemn those who sinned big so they could feel better about themselves. If a man who stole a tool was publicly chastised, someone who told a lie to his wife could think, 'Hey, I'm not so bad compared to him'."

"Okay, I get that now but what did Hester do that was so bad?" Tyler said.

"Well, if I remember correctly, her husband didn't make it over from England. Didn't the townspeople all think he died? Then she shows up pregnant."

"Maybe she got pregnant before he died. You know, like you did."

Danielle was surprised that Tyler made this connection. She had often told him how remarkable his father was and how very much in love they were. When he was old enough to ask more specific questions, she explained *the facts of life* and that she was already pregnant when Nick died. It wasn't exactly the truth, but it was the story she had told everyone from the beginning and now, thirteen years later, it was Tyler's reality. Besides, he *was* Nick's biological son so explaining the details of his conception seemed irrelevant now. "In the story, the author makes it clear that it is not her husband's baby and the townspeople insist that she tell them who the father is. She refuses," Danielle said.

Tyler scratched his head and wrinkled his nose. "So because she is a single mom they punish her? Did people do that to you?"

Danielle uncurled her legs, patted the cushion next to her and motioned to Tyler. "Come sit next to me."

She put her arm around him and said, "I was so happy to

have you, a precious gift from God, I didn't care what people thought. While I was pregnant, I still wore my wedding band and engagement ring. In every way I was still married to your father and having his baby was proof to me that he was still with me. I wasn't ready to let go. I had some complications in the delivery room and they thought I might have to have surgery so they took my rings off. I have been wearing them on my right hand since then."

"But everyone knew what happened right? So they didn't think you like slept around or anything. Man! You could have had to wear a big ole 'A' back in the old days."

"Of course my friends and family knew but it was awkward when I was talking to other new mothers that I didn't know. It's not unusual anymore for single women to have babies and, in general, our society has accepted it, although many religions still condemn it. I usually tried to tell them early on about your father's death. It just made the conversations easier once that was out of the way." Danielle wondered though if they would have been as understanding had they known about the artificial insemination after Nick's death. In fact, some of the women in her book club were adamant that "man shouldn't intervene in God's plan." After that, she decided against confiding in anyone and sharing the truth. "Many people in our country still believe it is a sin to have a baby and not be married to the father. They just don't express it so harshly."

"Mom, do you think it's a sin?" Tyler said.

"I believe that God wants children to be born and cared for by loving parents. But sometimes it's better for the mom to not stay married to the dad – like if he's abusive. Some women never find the love of their life and don't get married. But, they can still be great mothers. You know Robin, the girl in your confirmation class?"

"Yeah? She and I used to talk 'cause she didn't have a dad either."

"Robin's mom adopted her and her younger brother as babies but she had never been married," Danielle said.

"I forgot about that. So adopting sounds okay but what about girls that have sex and have kids without even being married?"

"It's funny that you ask it that way because the boys become fathers without being married too but since the girls get pregnant, they are the ones that wear the scarlet letter."

Tyler leaned over and kissed Danielle's cheek. "It must have been hard for you to have me without a husband. I'm sorry, Mom. I've been kinda mad that I don't have a dad here every day to like hang out with and stuff. I never really thought about how you felt."

Danielle's breath caught as she looked into her son's eyes. The care and concern she saw and felt were overwhelming. "It's okay. I'm just glad you have such a good relationship with Granddad," Danielle said.

"Yeah. He always calls me 'a chip off the ole block'. Today he said, 'your golf swing is just like Nick's – not when he was your age but after he fixed his slice.' I guess when Dad started golf he had a bad slice."

"What's a slice again?"

"It's when the ball goes to the right instead of straight. Granddad said, he could really pound the ball off the tee but it usually ended up in the trees."

"You know your dad and Granddad won a golf tournament or two. He must have fixed the slice."

"Yeah. He took a bunch of lessons from the pro at Southpoint. Granddad said it cost a ton! I don't have that problem though. I just make sure the back of my left hand and the clubface faces the target. Then the ball goes straight."

"Did Granddad teach you that?"

"No. I just know what to do."

"Lucky you! I know you got your beautiful blue eyes from your dad but I didn't realize you could inherit his golf swing! Enough about golf. You'd better go upstairs and get your homework done." She gave Tyler a quick hug.

He hopped up off the glider and at the door to the house

he turned, looked at her and smiled. Danielle was stunned. The glimmer in his eyes and the mischievous little smile was exactly like Nick's.

"Mom? Thanks for your help. Sometime I'd like to read your article in the *Minnesota Daily*. You know, the one about the monkey brains."

Danielle heard him bound up the stairs two at a time and slam his bedroom door. The porch was completely quiet now but her head was buzzing. *I don't remember telling him about the article. Let me think. I know I told him about meeting Nick the night of the A.R.M.S. protest but did I ever say anything about the article? I don't think so. Any of the details? No. Exposed monkey brains? Definitely not. Could he have read the article? I know I have a copy of it in my 'SAVE' box. He wouldn't go through my closet though without my knowing. It was way before everything was online – I'd better check to be sure.*

Danielle went to the kitchen, found her laptop and searched for her name. *Let's see…LinkedIn, articles dating back – about five years or so. Biography.*" Is it referenced there?" she said. *Nothing.* She searched for any hit with her name and the *Minnesota Daily*, 1986, A.R.M.S., Lyons Lab, Sarah Spengler… and found nothing. She knew that Tyler had not stumbled upon it on the Internet. *Where then?*

Okay. Take a deep breath. Maybe he heard it from Frank or Liz. I don't remember telling them about the article but maybe Nick had. After all, he did rescue a young woman that night. But if he did mention it, that would have been thirteen years ago. Why would it come up now?

Danielle's mind kept spinning and she felt that wave of panic coming to the surface again. She was grateful that she had another appointment with the therapist on Friday. Maybe Olivia could shed some light. She picked up her book and forced her mind to follow the author to another world.

CHAPTER 19

"I'm not crazy!" Liz screamed. "I know my own son and I'm telling you, Nicky was here." Liz ran her fingers through her short silver hair until it stood straight up. Her pale blue eyes were wild and frantic. She pushed Frank away with more strength than her frail one hundred pound body should have been capable of.

"Liz. Dear. Be reasonable. Think about what you are saying. Nick died thirteen years ago. You must be thinking about Tyler, our grandson." Frank's voice was calm but firm. "Remember? He and I played golf together yesterday and we stopped here to see you."

"Of course I remember. It was just yesterday. It was Nick. I know it was Nick," she shrieked as she shoved past him. She picked up two scrapbooks and thrust them at him. "It's all in here. I'm not crazy! The proof is here."

Frank's face went white. Both scrapbooks were opened to pages displaying elementary school pictures. There was a black and white photograph of Nick each year from Kindergarten through sixth grade. The other book had full-color school pictures of Tyler. There was no denying it. The boys looked identical. From the day he was born Liz had told everyone how much Tyler reminded her of her Nicky. For years he had been able to convince her that it was normal for Tyler to look like his dad but she had become increasingly obsessed with it. And now he was afraid the situation was getting out of control. Liz had pictorial evidence that anyone would find disconcerting – most of all Tyler and Danielle. As much as he agonized over his wife's state of mind, he couldn't tell her the truth and he couldn't allow her to show these scrapbooks to anyone – he wouldn't risk his reputation or put his family under scrutiny. Sonny would be furious and Frank was afraid of losing his son again. He steeled himself and tried to take her hand. "Yes, Liz. I certainly see the resemblance. Everyone does."

Liz batted his hand away. "Resemblance? Are you blind? They are identical!"

"Yes, dear. Of course. You are right. Tyler is identical to Nick. I'm sorry I didn't believe you. I don't want you to feel upset. Let's get your medication and go to bed."

"Oh Frank. I knew when I showed you the pictures you would agree. Isn't it wonderful? Our Nicky came back!" Liz clung to Frank like a small child her tears drying on her cheeks.

Frank took her hand and led her to their bedroom. He helped her take the pills and gently tucked her into bed. "Get some sleep now, dear," he whispered. "I'll come to bed in a few minutes."

Frank went into the den and made himself a Brandy Manhattan. After gulping it down his hands were still shaking. He made another. He tiptoed to the bedroom and saw that Liz was fast asleep.

"Thank God," he said. He took another long draw from his glass and picked up the phone. "Hello, Sonny? Sorry to call so late but Liz is getting worse. Yes. Lunch tomorrow at the club. See you then." Frank finished his drink and stared out the window not seeing the beautifully lit Minneapolis skyscrapers or the full moon low in the sky over the Mississippi River. He had hoped it wouldn't come to this but he was in too deep. He had to do what he had to do.

The late morning sun was shining and unlike the previous night, today Frank actually noticed the clear blue sky. Aside from signaling the end of the golfing season in Minnesota, he loved the crisp air and the smell of the fallen leaves. When he chaired the golf club's Redesign Committee, he insisted they consult with an arborist to ensure that strategically placed landscaping would ensure that the views from the clubhouse would be magnificent year-round. As he drove through the gates he was welcomed by the bright red sumac at the entrance, the orange maples, yellow birches and tall evergreens that shielded the view of the parking lot from the clubhouse. There were only a few cars in the lot and one of them was Sonny's.

The club's door opened as the membership coordinator came out. "Good morning Mr. Goodman. Beautiful day, isn't it?"

"Hi Emily. Not many like this left I'm afraid. Say, is Dr. Marino inside?"

"Yes. I just saw him going into the dining room. Chef's special today is walleye cheeks."

"Great. Thanks, Emily."

"You're welcome, Mr. Goodman. Have a nice day!"

Frank turned to watch her walk down the sidewalk toward the parking lot. Emily was in her late twenties, he guessed, beautiful long blond hair, cute well-tanned figure and a decent golfer in her own right. *I wouldn't mind letting her take me for a ride around the course!*

The club entryway was traditional and classy and Frank immediately felt at home. His career had been made in this place and while most official business lunches didn't include martinis anymore, he was retired now and often had a noontime cocktail with his buddies at the club. He nodded at Sam and held up his index finger then pointed to the table in the corner as he passed the bar. Sonny was seated discreetly away from the few other diners having an early lunch. Sam nodded without interrupting the conversation he was having with another member. By the time Frank sat down and glanced at the menu, his Brandy Manhattan was delivered to his table. On the rocks with extra cherry juice, just the way he liked it.

He and Sonny clinked glasses and tasted their drinks. "God damn," Frank said. "Sam makes the best Brandy Manhattan."

"Not much skill needed to make Scotch on the rocks. *Salut!*" said Sonny. "So what's going on with Liz? Everything okay, Frank?"

"No, not really but let's wait until we get our food to talk. I don't want to be overheard." No sooner had he said it than the waitress came to take their lunch orders. The two men made small talk until their food arrived and told the waitress they would flag her down if they needed anything else.

"I don't know what to do about Liz," Frank began. "I'm afraid she's gone off the deep end."

"What happened?"

"Last night she freaked out. She insisted Nick had been at the house. Tyler stopped in with me the night of league and now she thinks he is Nick not Tyler. I tried to calm her down but she had scrapbooks of Nick's and Tyler's school pictures as her proof. She believes Nick is alive! I'm afraid her mind has snapped." Frank glanced around aware that he had raised his voice.

"Ah! A consequence we didn't consider." Sonny dabbed his mouth with his napkin and gazed up at the ceiling. "*You* know who Tyler is, so while it's strange, your mind has an explanation. Yes, I can see why Liz is having a hard time especially after seeing the pictures side by side. Danielle didn't know Nick as a boy, so she has no frame of reference for comparison. Has she been asking any questions?"

"Over the years she's asked me about Nick's childhood so Tyler would know about his dad. I've told her bits and pieces about when Nick was a boy but nothing recently. I'm sure she doesn't suspect anything."

"Do you think Liz has shared all the inexplicable similarities with Danielle?" Sonny was now beginning to share Frank's anxiety.

"I hope to God not. Danielle has been traveling a lot lately so she and Liz haven't spent much time together. We need to do something now before this whole thing blows up."

"I'm going to order another Scotch. Do you want another?" Sonny asked as he signaled the waitress.

"Sure."

"As you can imagine, there isn't any precedence for this or at least no one has made it public. I have been forced to record my research in secret hoping that soon the sanctions will be lifted and the world will accept and appreciate the benefits of human cloning – not to mention my brilliance. Dammit, Frank! My work should be published! I have tracked Tyler's growth for thirteen years and he is in every way an exact replica of your son. A normal and healthy thirteen-year-old. I want the world to know of my success."

"I know. Sometimes when we are on the course or eating a pizza I still do a double take. Life is a continuous déjà vu with him. Not just his appearance but his mannerisms are also the same as Nick's! Something I wasn't expecting though are his memories."

Sonny held up his finger to pause the conversation as their second round of drinks was brought over and the dishes cleared. When they were alone again Sonny asked, "What do you mean, memories?"

"Tyler remembers things from his, I mean Nick's childhood."

Sonny sat up straight and leaned forward. "Like what?"

"One time he found a stuffed Mickey Mouse in a box of old toys. He told me that he remembered our trip to Disneyland and asked me to tell him more about it. He was only four or five when Liz and I took him. I was in Los

Angeles on business so we made a little vacation out of it. He remembered 'It's a Small World' and described the teacup ride. Tyler's never been there. How the hell did he have *memories* of that trip?"

"It's not possible," Sonny said. "Our memories are not stored in our DNA. He must have seen some pictures or maybe Liz reminisced with him about the vacation."

"She may have talked to him about it but I doubt Tyler saw any pictures. I was taking slides back then and Liz never could run the slide projector." Frank slowly stirred his drink and picked up the cherry by its stem. "There is something else that's been bugging me."

"What's that?"

"Tyler picked up golf like he has been playing for years."

"He has Nick's natural ability," Sonny said.

"It's more than that. Natural athletes may be able to pound the ball off the tee but it takes years of practice to develop a consistent swing – not to mention the short game. Tyler's swing is just like Nick's." Frank raised his hand to stop Sonny from interrupting. "I don't mean Nick the boy. I mean he has the swing Nick had after years of lessons and twenty years of playing the game. Tyler knows exactly what he needs to do on every damn hole on this course!"

"That's remarkable," Sonny agreed, "but still, it's scientifically impossible for Tyler to have Nick's memories."

"Yeah. Well not so many years ago it was scientifically impossible to create an exact replica of another human being too."

"So it was." Sonny pondered as he finished his drink. "Now back to Liz. I could try a new medication," he hesitated, "but it could have certain side effects."

"Will it help her forget what she discovered?"

"My colleagues have made a lot of progress in the study of Alzheimer's. We now have a better understanding of the cause of the disease and also a possible treatment to stop its progression. There is a new medication in trials. It appears to enhance the brain's ability to store and retrieve memory – or at least stop its deterioration. It took a while to perfect because if the dose isn't exactly right, and of course that varies person to person, it affects the same areas of the brain but in the opposite manner, the effectiveness of the memory center is lessened."

"So you're going to give my wife Alzheimer's?"

"Not exactly. But rather than preventing the progression of memory loss, I think we could actually cause her memories to fade. It shouldn't affect her physical abilities and to the world she will simply continue exhibiting some of the normal signs of aging – forgetfulness, difficulty coming up with a word when speaking..."

"I don't like the thought of using Liz as a guinea pig especially not knowing how it will affect her, but she is so unhappy now – upset and anxious most of the time. She's not sleeping and her mind spins with these crazy ideas of Nick's reincarnation. On some level she knows it's not possible."

"I guarantee she will be more at ease and she'll probably sleep more. If you see that she is not able to function, or has any adverse reaction, we can always alter or stop the medication. It's not a permanent suppression." Sonny paused giving Frank time to consider his proposal. "Frank, you know I appreciate the funding you have provided for my research and I will always be indebted to you. The last thing I wanted was to cause you and Liz any pain."

"I know." As Frank finished his drink, he thought back to the proposal Sonny offered him so many years ago.

"By providing the funding for my research, you will not only help the University of Minnesota stay on the cutting edge," Sonny had argued, *"but you will also provide the opportunity for Nick to make a name for himself."*

Frank had agreed. It was ridiculous that the right wing conservatives influenced public opinion and decision makers to effectively cut off all federal funding for stem cell research. With the money he donated through his private foundation to the University's medical research budget (earmarked for Sonny's projects), Frank had watched his son's accomplishments with great pride. That Nick should die before he witnessed the profound results of his efforts was too much to bear. And although he wouldn't have sought it, Nick deserved at least some of the international recognition that was now bestowed upon Sonny and his team – mostly Sonny.

"Sonny," Frank said. "You know I love my wife. We have been married for over fifty years and her quality of life is important to me. But I also need to think of the future – my legacy and my son's reputation. I turned seventy-five this year and at this age, one realizes that time is getting short."

"Yes. The inevitability of death," Sonny said.

"Liz and I have had a good life. Now I have to protect Tyler's future – the future that belonged to Nick – or, shall I say, the future that is Nick's." Frank paused, then looked directly at Sonny. "How soon can you have the medication ready?"

"I'll begin working on it right away and call you just as soon as it is ready. Hopefully it won't take more than a few days. Meanwhile, give Liz extra doses of the Lorazepam. That should keep her calm." As they left the restaurant, Sonny patted Frank on the back. "Good to see you, Frank. This will all work out. Trust me."

CHAPTER 20

Danielle picked up several magazines from the reception room table and flipped through them all without reading a word. She had arrived fifteen minutes early to her appointment and was fidgety. When the receptionist finally called her name she jumped up from the chair scattering the magazines that had been on her lap.

"Good morning, Danielle," Olivia said as she shook Danielle's hand. "How are you today?" She carefully evaluated the appearance of her client. Danielle stood tense and rigid, fists clenched at her sides. Her wavy brown hair was pulled back from her face in a ponytail but strands had come loose giving her a slightly disheveled look. Her large brown eyes, framed by long dark lashes and smudged by yesterday's mascara, were wide-awake but didn't look rested.

"Hi," Danielle said as she sat down on the edge of the sofa. "I'm fine, I guess."

"Let's talk about the 'I guess' part," Olivia said as she glanced down at her notes. "Last time you told me of some situations with your son that bothered you. Has anything happened since I saw you?"

"Yes. The other night, we were talking about his homework assignment. Tyler had to write a short paragraph about the book he is reading – *The Scarlet Letter*. Writing is not his thing so he actually asked for my help. It's been a long time since we have had such a great conversation."

"That's good," Olivia said. "Was there anything particular about the conversation?"

"He is so insightful for a thirteen year old. We were talking about Hester's public shame around her illegitimate child. Tyler even asked me how I felt when I was pregnant with him without a husband."

"Did that upset you?"

"No, but when he looked at me with his father's amazing blue eyes, I could see and feel his love and concern…not as a child but as a friend…like an adult." Danielle looked up at Olivia trying to read her reaction. Seeing no hint of surprise or judgment she continued. "For a moment he wasn't my little boy anymore. I wanted…," she couldn't continue.

"It's perfectly normal to feel sad when you realize your child is growing up and it's a confusing time for adolescents too. He is struggling with wanting to feel the security of being your little boy but also becoming independent on his way to being a man."

"But I feel different toward him. Sometimes when he looks at me my heart skips a beat. It's as if I am looking into the eyes of my husband Nick…and, I, I feel, um…I want to…" Danielle shook her head as if to shake the thought from her mind.

"Are your thoughts of a sexual nature?" Olivia asked gently. She needed to know if there was a possibility of sexual abuse.

Danielle looked down at her hands. "Yes. I mean, not toward Tyler of course. But I feel the longing and passion – the feelings I had with Nick."

"So because your son is becoming a man and in some ways he resembles your late husband, your feelings for Nick are coming to the surface. Is that correct?"

"Yes. I guess so," Danielle said even though it wasn't.

"And how does that make you feel?"

"It feels wrong. I am ashamed and confused."

"Let's work through those feelings together. Why don't you tell me about Nick?"

For the next fifteen minutes Danielle told how they met, their courtship, the wedding and honeymoon. She described the passionate love they shared and how, after her parents died, Nick became the most important person in her life. When she told Olivia about Nick's sudden death she suddenly could not hold back her tears. Through her sobs she relayed the awful memory of the day she found him dead in his office.

Olivia handed Danielle the box of tissues. "I am sorry that you suffered so much loss and at such a young age. It's never easy to lose a loved one much less the death of both parents followed by your spouse in such a short time period. You have experienced extreme emotional trauma compounded by the sudden and unexpected circumstances surrounding their deaths. We know that there is a physical component as well. Your body experienced a physical shock that I believe is deeply embedded in you and is brought to the surface by certain stimuli."

"But I don't know why I broke down here, now, after all these years. I'm not a crier." Danielle said.

"The body and the mind work together to heal. Perhaps you bottled up your emotions and didn't allow yourself the time to truly grieve your loss. After your parents' death you were caught up in your new relationship with Nick. Those intense feelings of romantic love may have suppressed some of your grief response. Then after Nick's death, you said you kept it together and poured yourself into preparing your home for the baby. Maybe now that your son is growing up and isn't as dependent on you, you are anticipating the loss of your baby to adulthood. This may be bringing your other losses to the forefront."

"I suppose so. I have been self-sufficient for all these years, being alone doesn't scare me. So maybe it's because as Tyler matures, he reminds me more of Nick and that triggers the grief again? I think my mother-in-law is having an even harder time."

"Why is that?"

"I think Tyler reminds her so much of Nick when he was a boy it's hard for her to accept that he is really gone."

"Yes. Perhaps." Olivia made a note, closed her notebook and observed a much calmer Danielle. "I think the feelings you are having are a normal response to the events in your life. Some of the emotional grief responses may have been suppressed and are now surfacing. Your dreams and plans were dramatically altered. I would encourage you to spend some time thinking about you. What do you want out of life? What challenges and fulfills you? What does the future look like in five years? Or ten – after Tyler is on his own? Have you thought about another romantic relationship?"

Danielle smiled. "You mean dating? Honestly, I've been so busy with my work and Tyler I haven't really thought about it. I'm not a kid anymore and the whole dating scene...I don't know. Where would I begin?"

"Sometimes the best way is to just be open to the idea. You are an attractive woman, Danielle. You have probably already met men who were interested in you but you didn't recognize it. Your path forward doesn't have to be about dating. Try setting some personal goals and see where it leads you."

"Thank you. I will try that. Since Nick died and Tyler was born, I haven't really thought much about my own future. Do you think I should set up another appointment with you?" Danielle asked.

"That's up to you. I am certainly here if you want to talk. Clinically, I don't see any mental health concerns that require ongoing therapy or counseling. How about you?"

Danielle thought for a moment. Maybe Olivia was right. It had been too long since she had any male companionship or even had a night out with the girls. She was focusing too much on her son. Already making a mental checklist of action items, she shook her head. "No. I feel much better knowing my reactions are normal and now having a plan... I can always come back if I need to, right?"

"Of course! I'll be happy to see you again anytime. Just

call me." Olivia stood and took Danielle's hand. "Best of luck to you, Danielle. Be good to yourself."

Danielle shook Olivia's hand and left the office. She felt better knowing that she was "normal" and, as before, back in control of her emotions. She had a plan: think about her career goals, stop obsessing about Tyler, have more fun, and go on a date. Although she had no idea how to make the latter happen.

When she got home she noticed the message light blinking on her answering machine. She picked up the phone, pressed star nine nine and entered her passcode – four one zero nine two. It was easy to remember, Tyler's birthday.

"Hey, Danielle. Is that you? It's Jake. It's been a long time and I uh...God, I hate these machines! Anyway I'm in Minneapolis and thought I'd look you up. Call me."

The message ended abruptly. Danielle smiled. Jake. What a surprise! He sounded so nervous and forgot to leave his number. Luckily the next message was from Jake too, this time with his cell phone number. She immediately called him back.

"Jake here."

"Jake, it's me. Danielle."

"Oh my God! It's good to hear your voice. It's been so long. I didn't know if I should call and my message was so lame. How the hell are you?"

"I'm fine. What brings you to Minneapolis?"

"A fluke really. There's weather in Chicago so they put us on a flight to Minneapolis instead. Then we missed the connection to New York and the East Coast is all jammed up because of the hurricane. So, here I am."

Danielle laughed. "I hate when that happens – but I'm glad too. How long will you be in town?"

"I decided to spend the night and take an early flight out in the morning – assuming things are cleared up by then. Any chance you're free for dinner? It would be great to catch up with you."

"I'd like that, but..." Danielle hesitated as she double-checked the calendar. This was the only night this week Tyler would be home for supper and she had planned to make his favorite Chicken Alfredo. But with Olivia's advice fresh in her mind she replied, "Sure! I just have to make a couple of calls."

"I don't want you to cancel your plans."

"No. It's fine. I just have to work it out with Tyler."

"If you're sure," Jake said.

"I'm sure!"

"Can you meet me in the bar at the Airport Suites? Say seven o'clock?"

"I'll be there. See you soon Jake."

Danielle immediately dialed Liz and Frank's number. After four rings, Frank answered. He sounded out of breath.

"Hi, Frank. Am I interrupting?"

"Ah, Danielle! No, it's fine. I was just helping Liz get changed."

"Is she okay?" Danielle felt guilty for not checking in with them more often. She knew Liz was not doing very well these days.

"She's fine. She just doesn't have much energy. Some days are better than others. Today I went in to check on her and she was just sitting on the end of the bed staring at the clothes I put out for her. I figured it was easier to just let her spend the day in her pajamas."

"Oh dear."

"But then this afternoon she perked up and I thought we could walk across the street to the *bistro* and have something to eat. We just finished getting her dressed. How are you?"

Danielle hesitated. *Frank has his hands full with Liz and, after all, Tyler is thirteen. He can stay home alone for an evening can't he? I can make supper for him before I leave and get him started on his homework. He can always reach me on my cell phone if he needs anything. I'll only be twenty minutes away.*

"Yes, Frank. Fine. I was just checking in to see how you are doing. Let's find a time soon when you and Liz can come for dinner."

"I'm coming, dear." Frank called out to Liz. "That sounds great. Thanks for calling, Danielle. See you soon."

The phone went dead. Another wave of guilt hit her. She admitted that being around Liz had become increasingly stressful. She often called Tyler "Nicky" and talked to him as if he were her little boy. Danielle hadn't intended to drift away from the relationship she had with her mother-in-law but now she realized, that is exactly what had happened. *I really should spend more time with Liz. I'm sure Frank could use a break. But what about tonight? I promised to think about my own needs and out of the blue, Jake calls. Coincidence? Maybe. Okay. Decided. Tyler will be fine at home alone tonight. Sheesh! Not a big deal!*

She had supper on the stove when Tyler got home. "Hi, Tyler. How was your day?"

"Hi, Mom. What's for supper?" Tyler plopped his stuff down next to the door and took off his shoes.

"Guess."

"Chicken Alfredo? Yes! My favorite," he said as he gave his mom a quick hug. "Hey Mom? How come you're dressed up?"

"I'm not really."

"Yes you are. You look nice."

"Should I take that as a compliment? Like I normally don't look nice?"

"I didn't mean that."

"I know. I was just teasing you. As a matter of fact, I'm going to dinner tonight with an old friend."

"Really? Who is it?"

"Do you remember me telling you about Jake? We went to college together and were good friends. He is a professional photographer."

"Oh yeah. The guy that took some awesome pictures of a dead gorilla in Africa, I think it was?"

"Yep. That's him. He was working on a story about the poachers that kill the gorillas just to take their hands, feet and heads. I would say awful, not awesome."

"Yeah. I guess," Tyler said.

"Anyway, I haven't seen him in years and he happens to be in town tonight. If you're okay, I'll sit with you while you have your supper and then leave about six thirty. Will you be okay staying home alone?"

"Duh, Mom. I'm thirteen years old. I don't need a babysitter."

"I know you don't. We've always had Grandma and Granddad to keep you company but Grandma isn't feeling well today so I thought you could handle it alone tonight. Do you have a lot of homework?"

"I have to read three more chapters of *The Scarlet Letter* and solve a page of algebra problems. That should keep me out of trouble for a while."

Danielle laughed and gave her son a kiss on the cheek. "Maybe I'm oblivious but I never worry about you getting into trouble. Should I?"

"Not unless you consider curing the common cold trouble."

"Ever the budding doctor. What's your secret?"

"I can't tell you yet. I think I have it figured out but I am still testing it. When kids at school start sneezing, I give them my recipe. Then I ask them to fill out a survey to let me know if it worked."

"Wow. How come I didn't know about this?"

"I wanted to surprise you after I get the results."

"I'm so proud of you. Can I try it?"

"Sure. But you have to get a cold first."

CHAPTER 21

Danielle took one last look in the mirror. Her hair hung loose to her shoulders instead of pulled back as usual. A bit of eyeliner and mascara accented her big brown eyes. *Not too many smile lines yet.* A touch of powder and blush for good measure and her favorite shade of lipstick, Vivid Rose, and she was satisfied. She had chosen her skinny black leggings and a bold printed tunic. Her legs were her best feature and the tunic hid the tummy bulge she just couldn't get rid of. She grabbed her black ballerina flats and her purse and popped her head into Tyler's room.

"I'm leaving now. Are you sure you'll be okay?"

"For the hundredth time, yes. Have a good time Mom!"

"I will. Call me if you need anything okay? I'll lock the door and set the alarm. Don't open the door while I'm gone."

"Okay. Okay. I'm not a baby ya' know."

"I know. I won't be late. Love you."

Danielle closed his bedroom door and took a deep breath to try to calm herself. Even though this wasn't a date, she was nervous about seeing Jake after all these years. He had had a crush on her in college and she knew that his photographer's eye would notice every change in her.

The worst of the rush hour traffic was over and she arrived at the hotel at ten minutes to seven. Not wanting to be alone in the bar, she stayed in the car and checked her e-mail. Nothing important. She resisted the urge to call Tyler.

"Just go," she said. "It's time to step back into the world."

Thankfully, Jake was already at the bar when she walked in. She noticed his hair was thinning and the back of his neck was weathered from years out in the sun. She tapped him on the shoulder and said, "Buy you a drink?"

Jake leapt from his stool and gave her a giant bear hug. "Danielle! My God. You are a sight for sore eyes."

"You always had a way with words," she laughed. "It's good to see you." Other than a little grey at the temples, Jake looked the same. He was lean, a little too thin actually, dressed in faded blue jeans, a black long sleeved t-shirt and heavy leather sandals.

"Let's get a table where we can talk. I don't know if the food is any good but it's convenient," Jake said as he led her to a quiet table by the window.

As soon as they were seated the waitress came and took their drink orders – a Guinness for Jake and a glass of Merlot for Danielle.

"Man! It's so good to see you," Jake said. "It's been way too long. There is so much to catch up on. Where to start?"

"I've followed your career, Jake. Your work is amazing and to think, I knew you when. How did you get into photographing disasters?"

"I've often wondered that myself. I was in New York on 9/11 and saw first-hand the absolute devastation. The thing that haunted me was the anguish in the eyes of family members as they searched for their loved ones. I literally roamed the streets obsessed by the frantic search for the survivors and by the survivors trying to reunite with their families. Anyway, some of my photographs caught the attention of Meredith Portenzia. I guess you could call her a scout for a company called Freelance International."

"I haven't heard of it. What do they do?"

"Its harder than I thought to make a living as a photographer. You have to sell your work and I'm not much of a salesman. So, you either get a job with a publisher that sends you out on assignments or you do freelance. The problem with freelance is that much of your time is spent marketing yourself and your work. I suck at that! Freelance International makes the connections and handles the contracts and payments."

"So it's kind of like a talent agency but for photographers?"

"Photographers and writers use it. There's a pretty intensive screening process so only top-notch content is brokered. Kind of like today's online stock photo market but super high end. Instead of getting fifty cents for a photo, payment can be in the thousands. Anyway, I was in the right place at the right time and established myself to the point where I was getting more requests and assignments than I could handle alone."

"Wow. That's great! I saw your work on the gorilla poachers and it was amazing. What else have you done?"

"Thanks. Lets' see…the heat wave in France and last year it was the earthquake and tsunami in Indonesia. Now I'm working on the devastation of Hurricane Katrina. You know. You watch the news."

"Isn't it kind of depressing? It seems like there are more events now than ever before. Or, maybe I'm just more aware."

"I think there are more. You'd be surprised at the number of big events that don't even hit our mainstream media." Jake shook his head and picked up the menu. "I'm sorry, Danielle. I'm blabbing on and on and you're probably starving. Let's order and then I want to hear about you."

"Good idea," Danielle said. "The salmon sounds really good but you never know in Minnesota. May be risky."

Jake signaled for the waitress. "How is the salmon?" he asked.

"It's very good. It's prepared with a citrus glaze and served with brown and wild rice pilaf flavored with pine nuts and dried cherries." The waitress smiled sweetly at Jake.

"That sounds wonderful," Danielle said. "I'll have that but please be sure it's not overcooked."

"Yes of course. And for you, sir?"

"The bleu cheese burger with a cup of the tomato basil soup." Jake handed his menu to the waitress.

"May I bring you another round of drinks?"

"Sure." Jake answered without waiting for Danielle to respond. "So, Danielle. Tell me about you."

"There's not really much to tell. The past thirteen years have been centered around Tyler. Gosh! The time has flown by. It seems like just yesterday he was a toddler. I love being a mom and have done some writing over the years. Nothing as exciting as your work, though."

"Maybe not but exciting takes it toll," Jake looked down unwilling to meet Danielle's inquiring eyes.

Danielle hesitated a moment before asking. "You are not wearing a ring. Are you still married?"

"Unfortunately, no," Jake said. "It lasted seven years. Melissa is a great gal. We just couldn't keep it together. You know, all the travel and crazy schedules. Even though that's how we met, on a flight to Tokyo."

"That must be a really long flight," Danielle said.

"It is. By the time we got there we had shared our entire life stories and had, you know, really connected."

"So what happened?"

"We both traveled a lot – sometimes together but often not. At first I think being apart made everything exciting. You know. Meeting in Paris or Mumbai – passionate reunions followed by teary goodbyes. But then our schedules got out of sync and we both resented it when the other had to leave. We talked about finding a place to settle down – she wanted to have kids – but neither of us wanted to give up our careers. Eventually we had drifted too far apart to keep it together so we split."

"I'm sorry, Jake. That must have been very hard."

"Yeah, it sucked. The funny thing is that now, five years later, I'm getting a little tired of being on the road so much. Hotels and restaurant food get tiring after a while, not to mention lonely."

As their meals were served and enjoyed, Jake and Danielle reminisced and laughed about their college days. At exactly nine o'clock, Danielle's phone rang. Still laughing, she answered, "Hi honey."

"Mom?"

"Hi, Tyler, is everything okay?"

"Yeah, fine. It's nine o'clock and I just wondered if I could stay up 'til ten instead of nine thirty. My homework is done and I'd like to watch *Grey's Anatomy*. They are going to do neurosurgery on this guy and I'd really like to see it."

"Okay. This one time. I'll be home by ten, okay?"

"Yeah, Mom. Are you having fun?"

"I am. I'll be home soon. 'Bye. That was Tyler," she said to Jake. "He called to ask if he could stay up and watch *Grey's Anatomy*. I guess they're doing neurosurgery on tonight's episode. Who knew?"

"Not me. I don't watch much T.V. He must be a great kid! When I was his age I would have just done it and then dove under the covers as soon as I heard my parents come home."

"Yes. He's pretty great. Believe it or not, this is the first time he's been home alone at night. I don't get out much."

"No way! Are you saying you haven't been on a date in thirteen years?"

"Not exactly. Well, ah, actually – yes. I mean..." Danielle stammered and stuttered. "Nick's parents, you remember Liz and Frank, have been wonderful all these years. Tyler spends a lot of time with them and if I had to be away, they were thrilled to take care of him. Liz isn't well and I didn't want to ask them at the last minute and, well, I haven't seriously dated anyone since Nick..."

"Hey, Danielle. It's okay. I didn't mean to pry. I just thought a beautiful woman like you would have been snatched up by now."

"Thanks for the compliment – I think."

"So what do you want to do now that Tyler's older? Any plans to do some serious writing again?"

"I don't know. I've been so focused on raising Tyler on my own I haven't really thought about what I want. But, as a matter of fact, I've been thinking more about this lately. Any ideas?"

"I've always got ideas," Jake said. "Whether or not they are any good is always the question. You know, I could refer you to Meredith. There are lots of writers pounding on her door but I've known her for years and she would give you a shot...if you want."

"What's the process?"

"I'll talk to her and then she'll want to see some of your recent work."

"I appreciate it, Jake. Let me think about it."

"Sure, Danielle. No pressure. I just thought you might like to get back into the business. You are one of the best writers I know and selfishly, I'd love to work with you again. I'm looking for a new angle myself – you know, maybe closer to home. Let me talk to her and we can see what happens. Okay?"

Danielle reached out and put her hand over Jake's. "Thanks, Jake. It's so good of you. I can't believe after all this time you still have so much confidence in me."

"No problem, Danielle. Hey, I should let you go. You've got someone waiting for you. *Grey's Anatomy*, huh? He sounds like a chip off the ole block."

"That's exactly what his grandfather says. I keep trying to see some of my wonderful traits in him but all I can see is Nick."

Jake smiled warmly as he pushed back from the table. "He is lucky to have such a great mom. I hope he knows that."

Danielle gave Jake a hug and smiled as he kissed her cheek. "Thanks for calling me. This was great."

"Let's stay in touch, okay?" Jake said.

"Okay. Good night, Jake. And thanks again for a great evening. It was just what the doctor ordered."

Before he could ask, Danielle was out the door. *Ah*

Danielle. If only you could have loved me the way I loved you. Jake lingered and watched Danielle walk through the hotel lobby and out the sliding glass doors to the parking lot.

Danielle lifted her head into the cool night breeze. Soon it would be cold in Minnesota but tonight the temperature was just right. The gauge on her dashboard read sixty-one degrees. *Almost jacket weather,* she thought as she maneuvered through the parking lot and out onto 494 West. Traffic was light until she approached the 35W exit. *Accident or construction?* Up ahead was a truck with a lighted arrow pointed to the left. *Darn! The right lane is closed.* She only had a second to decide whether to stay on the freeway or take the Lyndale exit. Off she went glancing at the clock. *I won't quite make it by ten but it will be close.*

As she drove through Richfield into South Minneapolis she was struck by the number of Somali and Mexican businesses operating side by side. She read the names aloud as she passed them. "The Hamdi Restaurant, Dallo Grill, Mercado Market, El Lorro, Suug Caramel, Pecitos, Safari Grocery."

It is amazing that Minnesota has the largest Somali population in the world outside of Africa. I wonder why. And so many Hmong immigrants. I can't imagine the shock of the first winter on those poor people. I wonder why they didn't settle in Florida or Louisiana. There are so many hot and humid places in the country. Why Minnesota?

By the time she pulled into her driveway, her mind was already forming the story. "Minnesota Ice or Minnesota Nice? A New Life for Immigrants."

It looked like every light in the house was on and the drapes were wide open. She'd have to remember to close them next time. *Next time. That's a pleasant thought.*

She quietly opened Tyler's bedroom door. The clock by his bed said ten fifteen and he appeared to be sleeping. She pulled his covers up to his chin and when she leaned over to kiss him his eyes blinked open.

"Hi Mom."

"Hi honey. I'm sorry I woke you."

"That's okay. I was having a dream about you and Jake."

"Really? What was it about?"

"It was kind of mixed up but you were wearing a red hoodie and something about animals in cages. It was like you were trying to rescue them or something. It wasn't a zoo though. More like a lab but really dark. Then you fell and bumped your head and I rescued you. Funny huh?"

"Yeah, funny. Everything is fine. Go to sleep now, it's late. I love you."

"Love you too," Tyler said as he closed his eyes.

Danielle closed his door and walked down the hall to her bedroom. Her mind was going a mile a minute thinking about her evening with Jake, the excitement of writing the immigrant story and Tyler's amazing knack for remembering details. She had told him the story of meeting his dad many times but didn't remember ever mentioning her red hooded sweatshirt. Well he remembered it in living color.

"He has a mind like a steel trap. I'd better be careful what I tell him."

Jake's alarm rang at six thirty a.m. He took a quick shower, didn't bother to shave and threw on the same jeans and shirt he had worn last night. Grabbing his backpack and his camera gear, he waited impatiently for the elevator to take him down to the ground floor. He dropped his key into the express checkout box and grabbed a cup of complimentary coffee and a pastry. He had the routine down to a science and was licking the frosting off his fingers when the airport shuttle pulled up.

"Good morning," the driver said. "Need help with your bags?"

"No thanks." Jake never let anyone else handle his gear

and the backpack contained his personal stuff, little that there was. "I got it."

"Which airline are you flying today?"

"Delta."

"Got it," the driver said. "That's terminal one. Most folks still call them the Main or the Humphrey. As long as I know the airline, I can get you to the right place."

"Appreciate it. Thanks."

Jake's work often got him out of bed before dawn – best light at dawn and dusk – but he wasn't talkative this time of day – not by any means. And this morning he wanted to reflect on his dinner with Danielle. He didn't know exactly why he called her. Maybe it was just being in Minnesota in the fall or maybe it was his loneliness. Whatever the reason, he was glad he did. Seeing her again brought back a flood of memories – and a twinge of pain of love lost for both of them.

As soon as Jake was settled in New York, he sent an e-mail to Meredith introducing Danielle. He should have waited for Danielle's response but he figured it wouldn't hurt to inquire. Meredith was just politely interested and only because of their personal and professional relationship. As expected, she asked him to send her a recent article.

"Damn! I didn't even ask about her work last night," he said to his empty hotel room. He did a quick Google search and found several articles on the grey wolf. "Hmmm. Two years ago. That's probably not going to fly."

He thought about calling her but time was short and he had to be at Ground Zero by four o'clock. He had arranged to meet a group of family members at the site for a follow-up story on 9/11. He had been out of the country on the actual anniversary this year but a few of the first responders' families were gathering privately to remember their loved ones. While the country vowed to never forget the awful tragedy of that day, these families preferred to stay out of the media frenzy that occurred each year on 9/11. Jake had chronicled their recovery through photos of funerals held, children born, and weddings celebrated. They let him share in their deeply personal journey from the rubble to the reality of a forever altered future without the presence of their loved one.

Jake had seen that same life filter in Danielle's eyes last night. The tragic loss of her husband was still there, it probably always would be, but she was able to live through it and find joy in the now. Yet, she hadn't fallen in love again. Could she? Or would her heart always belong to Nick? He thought back to her wedding day and remembered her radiance pouring in through his camera lens.

By the time he got back to the hotel, it was too late to call Danielle, even with the one hour time difference. He'd try her in the morning. When Jake got out of the shower he grabbed his cell phone to plug it in. One missed call and one voice message. It was Danielle.

"Hi Jake. Hope it's not too late to call. I'll be up for a while so if you get this before midnight your time, call me."

With a towel around his waist and hair still wet, he pressed her number to return the call.

"Hi, Jake! How was your flight?"

"Good. Uneventful. Just the way I like it."

"I just wanted to let you know how great it was to see you last night. I can't remember the last time I laughed so hard."

"Me too. I loved seeing you smile."

"On the way home I had an idea for a story I want to run by you."

"Yeah?"

CHAPTER 22

Danielle could no longer deny her feelings. There was no doubt in her mind that she was passionate for this man. She had no way of knowing that selling her first story through Freelance International would change her life so dramatically. In the early years she mostly stayed local and only travelled internationally when Tyler was on spring and summer breaks – so he could go with her. She was amazed and so proud of him. He had graduated a year early from high school at age sixteen with honors and with college level credits in biology, chemistry and math. Dr. Marino had written a powerful letter of recommendation and with his MCAT scores in the ninety-fifth percentile, Tyler had been accepted into the six-year medical school program and finished it in five. He was mature beyond his age and like his golf game, the world of medicine came naturally to him.

Since high school, Tyler had been extremely interested in his mom's work. When she did a story with Jake on the cholera epidemic in Haiti, Tyler worked it out with his instructors to go along and get credit for participating in the efforts to evaluate and contain the outbreak. It was a grueling trip for the three of them and she had to laugh when she thought about both Jake and Tyler competing to make sure she was safe and as comfortable as possible in the extreme conditions. It was during this trip that Tyler started calling her Mrs. Goodman or Danny instead of Mom.

She was so proud of the work he was doing and the

respect he got at his young age from the other medical personnel, she understood why he didn't want to be perceived as a kid tagging along with his mom. It was weird at first, especially since no one other than the Myers' family called her Danny, but there was so much to deal with in Haiti, it was the least of her worries. He was a vital resource to her as he explained the suspected connection between the United Nations' response to the earthquake that had killed and injured thousands to the hundreds of thousands now sickened and killed by cholera. His medical knowledge and scientific insight had been as valuable to her as Jake's stunning photographs were in creating the photo essay that garnered widespread publication and recognition.

Jake and Tyler got along okay although there was some tension when the three of them were together for extended periods of time. She recognized their competitive natures and little jealousies and made a concerted effort to give them each her undivided attention one-on-one.

This vacation in Hawaii was exactly that. Just the two of them for ten glorious days in paradise. Today was just like yesterday and the day before with a beautiful blue sky, the warm ocean breeze and the sweet scent of plumeria filling her spirit as she breathed deeply. Danielle had just come out of the pool and was lying on the lounge chair enjoying the feeling of the cool water evaporating from her skin. As it dried and the hot sun warmed her, she felt her stomach muscles contract. It was a pleasant almost sensual feeling and she allowed the feeling to wash over her. They had already had two Mai Tais and for once she didn't think about the calories when he offered to go to the Tiki bar for another round.

She took off her sunglasses and rolled over onto her stomach feeling the full warmth of the sun on her body. Eyelids heavy, the Hawaiian music faintly lulling her into a state of other-worldliness, she was barely aware of his hands on her back.

"Hey there," his soft voice entered her consciousness. "Your beautiful skin needs sunscreen."

She felt the tug of her bikini top as he untied it. The lotion was warm from being in the sun and smelled of coconut oil. His strong hands massaged the oil into her back, shoulders and neck eliminating any trace of stress and tension. She shivered as his fingertips traced the soft breast tissue at her sides. The gentle motion lulled her into a deeper sense of relaxation and she fantasized turning over so she could feel his touch on her nipples. She thought of being here before – in another time – on her honeymoon. She felt the oil being rubbed into her arms and hands. A slight tug and the ring on her right hand was removed. Each finger attended to and then his thumbs pressed firmly into her palms. Her mind floated enjoying the warmth, the touch, the smell and the warm sun. She felt the ring being placed back on her finger but on her left hand. She remembered the day Nick did the same, the day they pledged their love to each other for all time.

His fingers traced her spine from her neck to her waist, skimmed over her bottom and down the back of her legs to her feet. The lightness of his touch sent a wave of pleasure that she didn't attempt to suppress. Her feet, sore and tired from yesterday's hike, responded with a pleasant ache as he massaged her instep, first the right foot then the left. He stretched and bent back each toe, slowly, one at a time before moving up to her calves. With a hand on each he alternated between a brisk rubbing motion to circulate the blood and a slow deep massage. She almost cried out when he stopped but almost immediately felt the warm oil being poured onto the back of her legs, her thighs. His hands stroked her delicate skin and with each stroke his fingers moving closer and closer to the center of her passion and she wanted to be touched. She wanted to be completed as she had been so many years ago.

He leaned over and kissed the back of her neck. "There

you are, Danny," he whispered. "Oiled and protected. Your Mai Tai is here when you get thirsty."

"Mmmmmm. Thanks." It was all she could manage to say before drifting off.

The next sensation she had was of cold water on the bottom of her feet. She almost popped up before realizing her top was untied. Making sure everything was covered she rolled over and sat up. Tyler was in the pool swimming laps and as he turned in front of her the slight splash reached her feet. She reached for her drink and sipped the cool sweet nectar thirstily.

"Hey sleepyhead. Come on in," he called out from the other side of the pool.

She was hot but not quite ready to give up the lingering warmth of her dream. She held up her finger.

"In a minute."

"That's what you always say. Are you a fish or a sand crab?" He swam up to the edge of the pool and playfully splashed water at her feet.

"You'd better be careful," she scolded. Then she surprised him by hopping up and doing a cannon ball right next to him. The cool water felt heavenly and she surfaced right up into his arms. She didn't know if it was the dream, the Mai Tais or simply impulse but whatever it was it happened so fast. She looked into his beautiful blue eyes and kissed him on the lips. It only lasted a moment before they both pulled away, but it was a heavenly moment.

Tyler spoke first. "We need to talk."

"I know. Want to take a walk down the beach?"

"Yeah. A walk would be good."

They toweled off. Tyler put on his T-shirt and sandals and Danielle slipped on her cover-up and flip flops. A group had gathered on the beach to watch a mother whale and her baby playing in the warm coastal waters.

"Amazing aren't they?" Danielle said. "The last time I was here we..."

"Took a whale watching boat trip. A baby swam right up

to the boat. You were afraid the boat was going to hit it. Then it swam out and jumped high enough for you to see its tail fin. The guide said it was rare for them to come so close without their mothers and then she appeared." Tyler stopped. "I know. I remember everything."

"What do you mean you remember?"

"I don't know. It's hard to explain. I can see you in your black and white polka dot swimsuit and the big red floppy hat. I can see you wearing a snorkel mask and flippers trying to walk into the water when a wave knocks you down filling your suit with sand. I remember being underwater looking at the fish along the coral reef. I was pointing like crazy and you finally turned yourself around to see the huge sea turtle."

"But, how can this be?"

"I don't know. It's like watching a movie in my mind. I see the memories and when I think about them rationally, they don't seem real. My conscious mind explains them away. But when I allow myself to just feel and not think, somehow they are more real than reality itself. Does that make sense?"

"Kind of," Danielle said. "Like déjà vu?"

"Sort of. I read up on the déjà vu phenomenon and they say it's caused by having a brief glimpse of something before the brain has completely grasped a fully conscious perception of the situation. So when it is fully constructed it seems already familiar. But most people don't remember details about the 'past' experience and I do – vivid details including sounds and smells. It's not new to me. This has been happening my whole life but being here in Hawaii has brought forward disturbing thoughts and feelings. I want to get this out but I don't want to hurt you."

"It's okay. You know you can tell me anything."

"From the time back as far as I can remember, I thought of Grandma as my mother." Tyler paused waiting for Danielle's reaction before going on. Seeing the slight nod, he continued. "I mean, you were my mom too. You fed me and took care of me. You taught me more than you realize and I knew you loved me more than anything. But in my room at night the streetlight shone in my window and I could feel Grandma sitting in the rocking chair knitting. She waited until I went to sleep humming softly. When I was older and I mentioned it to her she said she had done that with Nicky but that she hadn't been able to knit in years because of her arthritis. She said I must have been dreaming. She would do things exactly the way I liked them without me saying anything. Like putting cinnamon on my peanut butter sandwich and folding over the bread instead of cutting it in half. It felt so normal.

"But then she started to call me Nicky – not just a slip once in a while but with this faraway look in her eye – like her mind was somewhere else. When we were at the store or doing errands she would call me her son. I didn't really understand it but it never felt odd to me. It was kind of like I had two moms.

"I knew that it upset you when I talked about my old toys and stuff so I tried really hard to separate my Grandma memories from my memories with you. I messed up once in a while but if I thought really hard about something that happened in the past, I could see your face or Grandma's face and then I knew who I should share the memory with."

"Oh Tyler. I had no idea! I felt so bad when you said Mamma before you said Mommy. And there were times when you cried and screamed and I couldn't figure out what you needed but Liz always knew. I chalked it up to my being a new mom and her spending so much time with us."

"Being with Granddad was easier. He always seemed to know what to expect from me and I didn't have to worry about what to say. In fact, he liked to talk about the past and sometimes filled in the blanks to help me make sense of the fuzzy memories I had of my childhood. He was amazed that I could play golf so well even before having any lessons. He encouraged me to work hard and to become a doctor. He told me I was just like my dad and I liked that. It made me feel like I had a dad."

"Yes. Frank is a good man. I've been so thankful that he has been there for you as a father figure – a great role model."

Tyler stopped walking and stared out at the vast sea. Danielle could feel his inner struggle as surely as she felt the power of the waves crashing against the rocky pier.

"I told you how I compartmentalized my thoughts," Tyler continued. "I thought I had things pretty much under control. Until I got here. It's like my mind has completely snapped."

Danielle heard the anger and the angst in his voice. Not knowing what to say, she just waited.

"I can see you so clearly in your wedding gown the light absolutely radiating from your eyes. You were so happy. I often let my thoughts go to that day. But being here is torture. My heart is bursting with love for you – not the kind of love a son should be feeling for his mother but a passionate love. I know it's wrong and my soul may be damned but I can't control it. Worse yet, I don't want to."

Tyler turned to look at Danielle searching for her reaction. He had risked a lot by finally telling her but hadn't she kissed him in the pool?

"I never believed in reincarnation," Danielle said, "but when I look at you, I see Nick. When I close my eyes and listen to you speak, I hear his voice. Your mannerisms, the way you walk, the food you enjoy and now the profound physical attraction I have...I'm afraid I have projected my feelings for him so strongly on you that..."

Tyler pulled her to him and held her face in his hands. "No, please don't. This is not your fault. Maybe it is reincarnation or some other force of nature, I don't know how or why, but I can't separate my dreams from reality any longer. If I try to deny my love for you, I fear it will..." Tyler couldn't go on. Seeing the tears slowly roll down her cheeks was too much to bear. He gently wiped them away and held her close – so close that he could feel her heart pounding against his chest. He backed away enough to see the longing in her eyes and he kissed her. And in that moment, with the sound of the surf crashing around them he let down his defenses and let his passion go as their lips and tongues melted into one. When he finally released her he knew two things. There was no going back and his soul was damned to hell.

Before either of them could speak, Tyler's cell phone rang. He looked at the number, saw that it was from Minnesota, but not one he recognized.

"I'm not going to answer it," he said. "If it's important they'll leave a message." He let it ring then waited until the screen reported one missed call. "Must not have been important. No messages."

No sooner than he had put his phone back into his pocket, Danielle's phone buzzed.

"It looks like the same number. Maybe I should answer it."

Tyler nodded.

"Hello? Yes. This is Mrs. Goodman. Who's calling?"

She handed the phone to Tyler. "It's a Doctor Benson from the University. He wants to talk to you."

"Benson? Yes. I can barely hear you. I'm standing on the beach on Maui and the reception isn't great. Hold on while I go to a quieter place." He motioned to Danielle that he'd be right back as he walked away from the beach over the berm toward the resort. "There. That's better. Can you hear me now?"

"Yes. Tyler. I'm so sorry to tell you but there's been an accident. Your grandparents were brought in a couple of hours ago."

"A car accident? Are they okay?"

"Yes. I mean yes, a car accident but no, it's not good. I'm sorry. Your grandmother didn't make it and your grandfather is in the ICU. From what we've been able to piece together, it looks like he suffered a stroke while driving causing the car to cross the center line into oncoming traffic. Several vehicles were involved and unfortunately your grandmother didn't survive the crash."

"Oh God, no! What is my father's condition?" Tyler didn't realize he had referred to him as his father.

"Your grandfather Frank is stable now. That's the main thing. It will take time to determine the extent of his injuries. It's complicated by the stroke. We don't really know much yet. I'm so sorry."

"Thanks Ben. Tell him to hang in there. I'll be back just as soon as I can get a flight."

"Okay. I'll give the team your cell phone number and we'll call you if there is anything significant to report."

"Thanks. Will you call my number again and leave a message with the phone number and access code? I'd like to call the station periodically and check in on him."

"Sure. No problem. Let me know if there is anything else I can do," Doctor Benson said.

It seemed like forever before the twelve-hour flight landed at Minneapolis International Airport. It was seven a.m. and with little sleep, he felt like crap. Danielle looked bleary eyed as they stood at baggage claim silently waiting for their luggage. He had played out all the scenarios based on the limited information he had but Benson was right. There was no way of knowing what to expect. He had called the hospital right before takeoff and again when they landed. There was no change.

Tyler was annoyed at the hassle it took to get a cab. They had to wheel their luggage from the baggage claim area through the concourse, up the escalator, walk across the bridge and take the escalator down on the other side. By the time they were on the highway it was rush hour and his impatience grew by the minute. The cabbie didn't speak much English and was not willing to exit onto the side roads Danielle suggested he take.

He said, "Stay on highway – fastest way."

They finally arrived at the University of Minnesota Hospital and lugged their bags up to the ICU waiting room.

"I'll stay with our stuff, Tyler. Go see Granddad," Danielle said. She watched him as he spoke to the nurse at the station and then quickly walked into one of the curtained patient care areas. Soon a volunteer aide came into the waiting room.

"Mrs. Goodman?" she asked.

Danielle nodded.

"Your husband asked me to send you in. I'll stay with your belongings, if that's okay with you. Mr. Goodman is in bed five just to the left of the nurses station."

Danielle was startled by the reference to her husband but gave the aide a grateful smile and headed into the ICU. The unit was arranged in a circle of beds separated only by a thin blue curtain. Most of the curtains were open to the center – a hub of monitors, alarms, charts, paperwork and nurses. She followed the circle around half way to bed five. She brushed aside the curtain that was partially drawn and saw Frank lying on his back hooked up to an IV and various monitors. Tyler was at his side holding his hand and talking softly to him.

"Hey Granddad," Tyler said. "Look who's here. It's Danny."

There was no response of any kind from Frank. Danielle looked at Tyler and raised her eyebrows.

"Can he hear us?" she asked.

"He hasn't been responsive but one never knows. We can't stay too long but I wanted you to see him before we meet with the attending. He is due to make rounds in a few minutes and will meet us in the family lounge for an update."

Danielle moved to the other side of the bed and took

Frank's hand. It felt cool to the touch. As she stroked his hand she thought his eyes fluttered slightly.

"Hi Dad. It's Danielle. Tyler and I are here. It looks like you got a little banged up. Don't worry, they'll get you all patched up and as good as new. Get some rest now and I'll be back to see you a little later. I love you." She squeezed his hand and looked over at Tyler. He needed a shave and his normally bright eyes were dark and dull.

"Let's go get some coffee while we wait for the doctor," she urged. "He is going to make it. He's a strong man."

They walked single file past the beds of the most seriously ill patients in the hospital. Danielle wondered how the nurses could stay positive working in this environment day after day. They were truly remarkable people and she made a mental note to remember to express her appreciation for their care.

The aide was in the lounge and pointed out the family restrooms, coffee, water, blankets and pillows. A television was tuned to CNN as the rest of the world continued to turn without regard to their pain and grief. The coffee was hot and black and as they sipped their second cup Doctor Townsandt came into the room. He grabbed a chair and pulled it up in front of the sofa where Danielle and Tyler were sitting.

"Hi folks. I'm Dr. Townsandt. I understand you are Frank Goodman's family."

Tyler extended his hand. "I'm Tyler Goodman, his grandson and this is Danielle Goodman, his daughter-in-law. We are his most immediate family now. We got the call yesterday about the accident and just arrived less than an hour ago on a flight from Maui."

Danielle shook the doctor's hand and looked into his eyes for some sign of hope. "What can you tell us about Frank's condition?"

"He's stable. Pulse, blood pressure and blood oxygen readings are within normal range. Can you tell me if he has a history of heart disease or TIA?"

"Not that we are aware of," Tyler said. "I just saw him a week ago and he was the picture of health. I just graduated from the U's med school program so I'm pretty sure he would have talked to me if he was having any health issues."

"Thank you. That's good to know. We have been watching his heart through a continuous EKG monitor. His pulse was thready and erratic when he came up from the ER but as I said, it's stable now. Our main concern is damage to the brain. The CT scan showed cerebral contusions in the left front hemisphere and a subdural hematoma. These injuries are consistent with the vehicle accident. Our physical exam noted drooping of the mouth and eyelid on the left side indicating stroke."

"Was this a result of the accident?" Danielle asked.

"It's possible or he could have suffered the stroke which led to the accident. I have ordered a cranial MRI to give us a better idea of what's going on now."

"Doctor Townsandt," Tyler said, "are you aware that his wife was fatally injured in the crash?"

"Yes. That was noted on his chart. I am so sorry for your loss."

"Do you know where she was taken? We'd like to see her," Danielle said choking back the tears.

"I will let them know that you are here and someone will come up and talk with you. You have a lot to deal with right now. Our family services resources are available to help you in any way possible. Again, I am very sorry. We will continue to carefully monitor Mr. Goodman and you can check in with the nurse's station any time day or night." He shook their hands and left the room.

Tyler closed his eyes and put his head down in his hands. "I can't believe this is happening. Just yesterday..." his voice trailed off.

Danielle stared at the television without seeing it. Liz was gone without warning, without time for goodbyes, just gone. And Frank. What if he doesn't recover? They had been parents to her and now they had been taken too. She shook away the thought. *No, Frank is not gone. Please, God. Let him come back to us.*

She was exhausted but nervous and jumpy from the coffee. She stood up and paced around the small room. Outside in the long corridor she saw gurneys transporting patients in and out of the intensive care unit. Technicians wheeled medical equipment and aides brought trays of juice and broth to patients who were well enough to eat. For many, the food would remain untouched. The coffee gurgled in her stomach making her nauseous. She knew she should eat something and Tyler too. Their last meal had been a turkey sandwich in the airport. She sat down next to Tyler and put her hand on his arm.

"I'm feeling a little queasy. Do you feel like eating something?"

"Not really. Are you hungry?"

"I wouldn't call it hunger but I feel like I should eat something."

"There is a cafeteria on the second floor," Tyler said. "Do you want me to go get something for you?"

"That's okay. I'll go. Do you want me to bring something back?"

"Anything is fine. Nothing sounds good at the moment."

"I hear you. Text me if you need me."

"Will do. Hurry back." Tyler managed a weak smile and got one in return.

Tyler felt like he should do something or call someone but there was nothing to do and no one to call. His entire family was in this building and there wasn't a damn thing he could do for any of them. Until they knew the results of the MRI there was nothing to do but wait. He could call the club and get the word out to the members. Frank and Liz were well liked and he knew there would be an outpouring of support. But he wasn't ready for that yet. There would be a time for that but not now.

He closed his eyes and tried to focus on the sound of the

newscaster's voice. *The Dow Jones is up fifty-three points on news of improvement in the housing market. In almost all areas of the country, home values are up an average of ten percent. The Department of Labor reported a net gain of one hundred thousand jobs in September. Today in international news...*

"Hey there," Danielle said softly. "Are you sleeping?"

Tyler opened his eyes and saw Danielle holding a tray. "No, just resting my eyes."

"I brought grilled cheese sandwiches and tomato soup. Sound good?"

"I didn't think I could eat but it smells good. Thanks for getting it."

"Sure. Any word from the ICU?"

"No but I wasn't expecting to hear anything. Granddad is stable so now it's just waiting for him to regain consciousness. Could be hours or could be days or even longer."

"I know but I keep hoping for a miracle." Danielle put the tray down on the table. "I called Jake. I let him know about the accident and asked him to let our team know that that I would be out of touch for while. He sends his best wishes. Here, have something to eat."

They ate their lunch in silence, both absorbed in their own thoughts and trying not to think the worst.

"He didn't take long, did he?" Tyler said.

"Who? What do you mean?"

"God. He didn't take long to punish me for – you know."

"For Hawaii? Oh Tyler, I don't believe God is punishing us. Bad things happen, that's all."

"Well, I knew as soon as I admitted my feelings for you that I would be damned."

Danielle took Tyler's hand. "Stop it," she said fiercely. "What happened to your grandparents is not your fault! Believe me, I know. After my parents were killed in the plane crash and again after Nick died, I went through periods of wondering what I had done to deserve such loss. I searched my soul, went back to church and prayed for forgiveness. I'm sorry I didn't take you to Sunday School or bring you to church more often. That I do regret. But believe me when I tell you that God doesn't send us hardship to punish us for what we do wrong. If that were the case we would be experiencing bad stuff each and every day."

"Well, maybe he just focuses on the really bad things we do," Tyler said as he pulled his hand away.

"I don't believe that. What did all the people do to deserve dying in the plane crash, or the epidemic in Haiti or all of the innocent children that suffer child abuse? They are not being punished. They are victims of an imperfect world."

"Sorry, I'm not buying it. In this case, there is a direct cause and effect," Tyler said.

"Okay. Then think about it logically. We got the call in Hawaii just after 'it' happened. But the accident happened hours before that. It's just the timing of the phone call that is causing you to connect the two. Please, Tyler. Don't blame yourself. We need each other right now and Frank needs our love and support to help him pull through this."

"I suppose you're right. I have so many feelings and thoughts racing through me. It's hard to sort it all out."

"I know. I do too. Let's just take one day at a time and work through it together." Danielle looked straight into his eyes and said, "I love you, Tyler, more than ever."

"I love you too," Tyler said.

"Ahem. I'm sorry to barge in on you."

Tyler and Danielle were startled to see Sonny Marino standing in the doorway.

"I came as soon as I heard and the ICU nurse told me you were here."

"Not at all," Danielle said as she stood to greet him. "It's been a long time. Tyler, you remember Dr. Marino."

"Of course. We've met at Southpoint. Granddad introduced us. Good to see you," Tyler said. As he shook his hand a flood of images filled his head. Pushing them aside, he struggled back to normalcy. "You and my father worked together."

"Indeed," Sonny said. He was stunned by the resemblance to his former partner, Nick Goodman. Nick was older when they first met but it didn't take much imagination to add a few years and see Nick standing before him. "Your father was a brilliant doctor and a top-notch research scientist. From what your grandfather has told me, you are following in his footsteps."

"You've spoken with Frank?" Danielle asked. "Recently?"

Sonny was surprised by the question but then realized that Danielle would have no reason to be aware of his alliance with Frank. "I ran into him at the country club a few months ago. He couldn't stop talking about his grandson."

"We have never golfed together. Are you a member?" Tyler asked.

"No," Sonny lied, "and I'm a terrible golfer. I have lunch there occasionally with a colleague of mine. The food is great and he's kind enough to invite me as his guest."

"And who is that? I know most of the active members," Tyler said.

Sonny was taken off guard by Tyler's pointed question and intense look. Luckily before he had to answer a woman approached them.

"The Goodman family?" she asked.

"Yes," Tyler and Danielle said in unison.

"I'm Dr. Marino, a friend of the family. I just stopped by when I heard the news." Sonny turned to Tyler and Danielle and said, "Please let me know if there is anything I can do." Then he quickly left the room.

"Hello, my name is Patricia. I'm one of the Family Services volunteers here at the hospital. I will be taking you to see Mrs. Goodman and to assist you in any way I can through this difficult time."

CHAPTER 23

Death and grief were no strangers to Danielle. It's not that she embraced them, more like she understood them and they felt familiar to her – more familiar than the feelings of love and passion that were so fleeting during her lifetime. She felt comfortable as she sat by his bedside, guided Frank through the funeral arrangements and graciously managed the outpouring of support from the Goodmans' friends. Now, two months after the accident, there were two things troubling her. Would Frank ever have a firm grasp of reality and why was Sonny Marino hanging around so much?

When Frank regained consciousness the doctors assured them that his confusion was normal given the damage done by the stroke and the trauma of the accident. It was a miracle really that he was strong enough to be transferred to a nursing care facility so soon and his rehabilitation therapy was going very well. Frank still had partial loss of function on his left side and couldn't walk yet but he was slowly regaining the use of his left arm and leg and the only sign of the stroke in his facial features was his Mona Lisa like smile. His cognitive recovery was slower but the doctors, including Tyler, reminded her that the brain is so much more complex and it's impossible to predict how any given patient will recover. While Frank didn't remember the accident, he understood that Liz was gone and grieved for her in his stoic, controlled manner – like before. Still, it puzzled her as to why Frank seemed to know exactly who Danielle was, remembered details about her wedding to Nick and yet insisted on calling Tyler 'Nick' every time he saw him.

Before the accident, Frank had sometimes slipped and called him Nick so Tyler was not surprised or too concerned. He told her that Frank's recollection of current events along with memories of the past were good signs – just that sometimes the two intermingled and were slightly reorganized. Tyler was grateful that Frank was continuing to improve and predicted that within three months he would be able to leave the care facility. Danielle shared in his thankfulness and knew that they should begin making plans for Frank's next step. She couldn't see him going home to the condo – at least not initially and certainly not alone. Would he ever return there? Would the familiar surroundings help him heal or cause a setback? At the least, it was time to talk to Tyler about Liz's things and make some decisions about Frank's future living arrangements.

With a plan in place, Danielle's thoughts moved on to Sonny. At first she accepted his support. After all, he had worked closely with Nick and made it possible for her to have his child. But those were essentially professional relationships and many, many years ago. Why was he suddenly so involved with Frank? She didn't think Sonny would divulge how Tyler was conceived. Why would he now after all these years? If he did, she didn't think Frank would care. Not about the artificial insemination anyway. It was such a common practice these days that there was no stigma at all attached to conceptions resulting from fertility treatments of all kinds. But he may resent the fact that she wasn't honest with him. It's not like Nick wasn't Tyler's real father so what difference does it make? Well, if Sonny did tell Frank, she would have to deal with it then.

But now Sonny seemed to be latching onto Tyler. She could understand how in Tyler's desire to learn more about his father he would be receptive to Sonny. That would seem reasonable since he just lost his grandma and almost his granddad, the only family he's ever had – besides Danielle of course and Sonny could fill in the blanks about Nick's career. Surely there was no harm in that.

So what was troubling her? Since he was born, Tyler had been the center of her life – her reason for living. Maybe she was jealous of the time he was spending with Frank and Sonny. Between his work and his dedicated visits to the Greenhaven care center, she hardly saw him. But that in itself wasn't new. She didn't feel anxious or resentful when he was away at school or working round-the-clock at the hospital. If she were really honest, her troubling thoughts originated in Hawaii…no, before that. She tried to remember the last time she truly felt like Tyler's mother and nothing else. Little by little her maternal feelings had been overshadowed by the other – the unwanted and unwelcome thoughts of Tyler as a man and now she couldn't separate them at all. Frank's confusion was understandable. He had a medical reason for mixing up Tyler and Nick. What was her excuse? Had she really ever dealt with the death of her parents and her husband as her therapist Olivia had surmised? Had Liz's death driven her into a state of emotional chaos that caused her to project her feelings for her husband onto her son? Self-preservation and survival are at the core of the human condition. Was her mind simply trying to survive another loss or was there a darker force at work in her?

Danielle was so deep in thought that she didn't hear the phone until its fourth ring.

"Oh. Hi! I was just going to leave a message. Where were you?" Tyler asked.

"Right here. Why?"

"The phone rang four times."

"Oh…I uh…didn't hear it," Danielle stammered.

"Hey. Are you okay? You don't sound like yourself."

"I'm fine. Just a lot going on, I guess. How are you?"

"I'm good," Tyler said. "I was just thinking that we haven't had dinner together for a long time and, well, I miss that."

Danielle smiled. "Me too. How is Granddad doing today?"

"He's good. I was there while he was in PT so I got to see for myself how he is progressing. His left side is getting stronger and he can actually put some weight on his left leg."

"That's amazing! Do you think he will be walking soon?" Danielle asked.

"I don't know how soon but yes, I spoke with the therapist and he was very encouraging. Granddad has a lot of determination and he is determined to get out of that place."

"That's great news. I was just thinking this morning, we should talk about next steps – I mean about his living arrangements." Danielle smiled at her unintended pun.

"You're funny, ha, ha," Nick said. "Seriously though, we do need to talk."

"About Granddad?"

"Yeah. You know he calls me 'Nick' all the time now," Tyler said. "It hasn't bothered me but today he kind of went over the edge."

"Why? What did he say?"

"Well, instead of *a chip off the ole' block*, he said that I was a 'clone of my dad.' You know, he always tells me how much I am like Dad so calling me his 'twin' or his 'clone' or whatever, same difference, right?"

"I guess."

"But when I laughed it off, he grabbed my arm and told me he was serious. He looked me in the eye and said, 'Son, I might not make it out of here and, if I don't, I want you to know the truth.' Just then Sonny walked in and asked, 'What truth, Frank?'"

"Sonny was there today?" Danielle said.

"Yeah. He seems to turn up when you least expect him."

"So what happened?"

"I winked at Sonny and said that Granddad was just telling me how much I remind him of my dad and it's like

I'm a clone of him or something – wink, wink. You should have seen the look on Sonny's face. If looks could kill."

"Sonny was angry?" Danielle asked.

"For a minute he looked like he would explode. Then, just like that, he smiled and slapped me on the back. 'Just a chip off the ole block right, Frank?' I looked at Granddad he...he looked scared. He didn't say anything but squeezed his eyes shut. It was the strangest thing."

"I don't know what to make of it," Danielle said.

"I don't either. You know how sometimes you just feel like something is wrong but you can't put your finger on? It was like that. The conversation was benign but the undercurrents were palpable."

"Tyler, your dad didn't talk much about his work but around the time we were married there was a lot of buzz about cloning. They had just cloned a sheep and people around the world were afraid that the discovery would lead to human cloning. Sonny and your father worked on genetic research so maybe the topic came up between the three of them. You know, like at a dinner party or something. It sounds far-fetched but there must be some history between them to cause such tension just at the mentioning of the word clone. Was anything else said?"

"Not while I was there. I'm on my way back to the hospital now – I didn't stick around. When I said goodbye to Granddad though, he squeezed my hand tight and it almost looked like he was crying."

"Oh dear! I'm sorry the whole thing was upsetting to him. Hopefully he'll have a restful afternoon. He's been making such good progress, Danielle said.

"He has, but I don't know if he can handle going back to the condo – not alone anyway and I worry about his reaction to going back there without Grandma. I suppose we could hire a home health aide. I don't know. The options just keep circling around in my head without landing anywhere. What do you think?"

"If he could handle an assisted living arrangement, that

might be a good transition. I could look around and see if there is a good one nearby with an opening."

"Good idea. Then at least we'll have more information when the time comes," Tyler said.

"Sounds like a plan," Danielle said. "Is everything else okay?"

"I feel like it is until I think about you and, well you know. We need to talk about it but now is not the right time," Tyler said. "Let's get through one family crisis before we delve into another."

His words stung. "Is that how you think of me – as a crisis?" Danielle said.

"Of course not. I didn't mean it that way. I just mean that what is or isn't going on between us is deep and complicated and I'm not ready to go there right now. Please understand."

"I do, Tyler. Believe me, I do. Just know that I love you with all my heart and whatever that means, we'll work it out."

"Me too. I have to go now. I'm just pulling into the ramp. I have rounds and then office visits. Busy afternoon," Tyler said. "We'll talk soon."

"Okay. Talk to you later."

Frank's eyes blinked rapidly as Sonny approached his bedside. Sonny's dark eyes were now a pool of blackness. The forced smile he had given Tyler as he left was long gone – his mouth set in an expressionless straight line. How much had he heard? Frank had told Tyler he was a clone of his dad but of course he didn't take it literally. With Sonny's untimely arrival, Frank didn't have time to explain and now he was terrified that Sonny overheard more than just the end of their conversation.

Sonny broke the tension. "Hello, Frank."

Frank choked out a strangled, "Sonny."

"Did you have a nice visit with your *son*?" he sneered.

Frank was afraid. Sonny had never openly referred to Tyler in this way before and now there was no mistaking his anger. Had he heard? Frank glanced up at the clock. It would be at least forty-five minutes before the nurse would be in to give him his medication. He strained to reach the call button with his right hand as he stretched his weaker left hand toward the water glass on the bedside table.

"Damn. Why don't they put my water on the right so it's easier to get? Mind giving me a hand?" Frank said.

Sonny moved in closer and handed Frank the glass. "Looks like your mobility continues to improve," he said noticing Frank could now grasp the glass in his left hand.

"Thanks. Yeah, think I'll be going home soon," Frank said as he sipped the cool water and pulled the call button toward him under the blanket. "I was just telling Tyler that I'm nervous about going home to the condo – you know, without Liz."

Sonny stared intently at Frank. "So this was the *truth* you were sharing when I came in?"

Frank nodded. "You know I can't admit any weak...weakness. Now I...uh...need so much help. Can't do anything on my own. I want to get out of here but I don't know how I can go home..."

Sonny took the water glass from Frank and looked at his friend. He saw an old man with grey stubble on his chin, a tired resignation in his eyes and trembling in his left hand as the weight of the glass was lifted. Sonny relaxed as he discerned that Frank was not a threat. When Nick challenged him and threatened to undermine his research, Nick had been a young man with his whole life in front of him – a beautiful new wife, a bright future – ideals worth protecting. Frank had lost his son, his wife and now his independence. Sonny couldn't imagine him doing anything so stupid as to lose Tyler now. Besides, on the heels of a stroke and brain injury, who would believe him anyway? Sonny smiled, confident that his secret was safe.

"That's understandable," Sonny said. "You've been through a lot. Hang in there and I'm sure things will work out. They always do. Looks like you could use some rest so I'll be going. I just stopped by on my way to the club. Tonight is the new member banquet and I've been asked to meet and greet. You know the drill."

"Yeah. Wish I could be there. Say hi to the guys for me."

"Will do. See you soon, Frank," Sonny said as he left Frank alone in his room.

Tears of relief and deep regret sprang to Frank's eyes. He tried to think but everything was so confusing. Earlier he had been sure that telling Tyler was the right thing to do but now? The loss of his only son Nick, and Liz – gone – he couldn't bear what was certain to be Tyler's rejection if he knew the truth. His head was spinning. Sonny was brilliant but he had a dark side. What if Tyler confronted him? He could be in danger. Sonny wouldn't hurt his family, would he? It was because of Sonny that he had his son back. Nick. Nick. There was a thought trying to surface but the harder he tried the more elusive it became.

"Damn it!" Frank cried out. He swung at the table and knocked the bedside tray over. Now with clarity he knew he had to warn Tyler.

"Tyler is not safe!" He swung his legs out of bed and put his weight on his right foot. "Tyler!" he cried as the glass cut into his foot and he crashed to the floor. "What have I done?"

CHAPTER 24

Tyler felt his pager buzz just as the nurse entered the ICU.

"Dr. Goodman?" she said softly. "You've had several calls from Greenhaven. They asked that you call as soon as you are can."

"Thank you. I'm just finishing up here." By the time Tyler removed his gloves and mask, scrubbed and exited the area, his pager had rung again. Danielle's number this time. Expecting the worst, he called her first.

"Danny, hey. It's me."

"Tyler! I'm sorry. They told me you were with a patient but I had to call."

"It's okay. I was just finishing up. There was a page from Greenhaven too. What's going on?"

"When they couldn't reach you they called me. Your granddad fell trying to get out of bed."

"Is he all right?"

"He's hurt that's all I know."

"I'm on my way," Tyler said.

"Me too. I'll meet you there."

Tyler flew down the corridor as he called the desk to let them know he was on his way to a family emergency. He felt a moment of guilt for leaving his patients but Granddad was the only family he had left and he had almost lost him once already. His tires squealed as he maneuvered through the parking garage faster than he should have. His adrenaline was high. Practicing medicine always affected him that way – the extreme concentration, the life and death ramification of every movement, the rush that came when he had to react to the unexpected. He thought it prepared him for life but in the end, he had to admit that there was so much out of his control. He couldn't save Grandma and now Granddad.

"Please, God! Let him live," he pleaded though he was convinced God was against him.

Danielle was waiting for him in the entryway when he arrived.

"I just got here and saw you drive in," she said.

They shared a quick hug and rushed up to the fourth floor nursing station.

"Dr. Goodman, Mrs. Goodman, I'm Kate Anderson," she smiled warmly as she extended her hand. "I'm so sorry to have to meet you under these circumstances."

Tyler's heart dropped. He was sure Granddad was gone.

"It seems Mr. Goodman was trying to get out of bed. I'm not sure why he didn't ring the call button." She shook her head sadly and looked into their eyes to dispel any hint of wrongdoing on the part of the facility. "Unfortunately, he fell and sustained a few cuts to his hand and foot. Nothing serious there."

Tyler took a relieved breath and looked at Danielle. Her face was pale and her eyes still intent on the nurse.

"However, I'm afraid he also bumped his head. We don't know if he hit it on the floor or on the bed frame as he fell – or both."

"Is he okay?" they said in unison.

"I'm afraid it's serious. It's not uncommon for a trauma like this to dislodge a blood clot. He had another stroke – a severe one. I'm so sorry. He is completely paralyzed."

Danielle gasped and reached out for Tyler's hand. She gripped it tightly and said, "Why wasn't he taken to the hospital?"

"A few days ago, Mr. Goodman completed a healthcare directive indicating that if he had another stroke or a heart attack – an event that would permanently incapacitate him – he didn't want extraordinary medical treatment. He was explicit in his desire to not be put on life support and to let nature take its course." She looked kindly into the eyes of her patient's loved ones. "You didn't know?"

Tyler and Danielle looked at one another. Each shook their head no.

"Mr. Goodman also wrote that he would endure a moderate amount of pain in order to remain alert enough to talk to the two of you one last time. Then he wants whatever treatment necessary to be kept comfortable until his death. I am so sorry to be the one to tell you this."

Tyler let go of Danielle's hand. "So are you saying he is able to communicate?"

"We are not exactly sure of his mental capacity at this point. We have given him Lorazepam to calm him and he is drifting in and out. He had made some sounds but nothing intelligible yet. I'll take you into his room now. I just wanted you to be prepared."

She led the way down the corridor past the other residents.

Danielle couldn't help but see the blank stares of the elderly sitting alone or lying in their beds, waiting to die. Frank was right. Sometimes life is not worth living.

Tyler's mind was racing. He thought of the oath he took as a doctor, *I will prescribe regimens for the good of my patients according to my ability and my judgment and never do harm to anyone.* How could he stand by and not do everything possible to save his granddad? It was entirely possible that the effects of this stroke were reversible too. Granddad had improved immensely since the last one. Earlier today they had been talking about bringing him home.

Kate entered the room first and raised the head of Frank's bed slightly. "Mr. Goodman?" she called. "You have visitors. Can you wake up?" She motioned Tyler and Danielle in. "I'll leave you alone. Please just press the call button if there is anything I can do."

"Granddad? It's Tyler and Danny. Can you hear me?" he said as he reached out to touch the unbandaged hand. Frank's hand was cool and without thinking his fingers moved into position to feel the rapid, thready pulse. "Granddad?"

"Tyler look. He is trying to open his eyes," Danielle said. "It's okay, Frank. We are here. We love you."

Frank's eyes fluttered and his lower lip twitched ever so slightly. All at once his eyes opened. "Fuh fuh fuh," Frank struggled to speak. "Fuh, fuh fuh."

"It's okay, Granddad. I'm here," Tyler said. "Don't try to talk. Just rest."

Frank's eyes were wide with determination. "Fuh, fuh, fuh," he gasped.

"I'm here," Tyler said. "If you can hear me blink once."

Frank squeezed his eyes closed and opened them again.

"That's good. You had a nasty fall but you are safe in bed now."

"Say – ow," Frank said.

"Yes," Tyler said, "you are safe now. I need to ask you some questions but I don't want you to strain to talk. Can you blink once for yes and two times for no?"

Frank blinked once.

"Are you in any pain?"

Frank blinked twice.

"That's good. The nurse told us of your wishes and we want to make sure you are comfortable."

Frank blinked twice.

"No? You don't want pain medication?"

Frank blinked twice. "Fuh, fuh, fuh. Say, say, say."

"It's okay, Granddad. It's Tyler and you are going to be okay."

Frank blinked twice.

Tyler looked at Danielle. "What does he mean, no?"

"I don't know. Maybe we should let him rest."

Frank blinked twice and then twice again. "No, no ress. Teh you. Teh you."

"Tell me?" Tyler said.

Frank blinked once.

"Okay, Granddad. You want to tell me something?"

Frank blinked once.

"I love you Granddad," Tyler choked.

Frank blinked once and a tear trickled down his cheek.

"I know. You love me too."

This time Frank closed his eyes and his face was still.

"Tyler?" Danielle said. "Is he...?"

Tyler checked his granddad's pulse. "He is weak but still with us."

"Frank, it's Danielle. I don't know if you can hear me but I want you to know how much you mean to me. You have been like a father to me and..." Danielle's eyes filled with tears. She struggled to maintain control fearing that there wasn't much time to say what she needed to say. "You and Liz were always there for me and I want you to know how much I love you. I don't think I could have survived after Nick..."

Frank's eyes opened slowly then he blinked once. He shifted his eyes slightly to look at Tyler and then back to Danielle. His lips moved. "Wah," he whispered.

Danielle found a small blue sponge swab, dipped it in the water cup and dabbed his lips. Frank opened his lips and allowed the cool water into his mouth.

"Would you like more?" Danielle asked.

Frank blinked once.

Frank's eyes closed again as Danielle dripped cool water into his mouth and moistened his lips with the sponge.

"Nick," he whispered.

Tyler leaned closer to hear. "It sounded like he said Nick."

Frank's eyes opened and while they seemed clear he did not focus on either Tyler or Danielle. "Luh ooo. Suh. Suh."

Frank strained to say the words. Then he looked directly at Tyler. "Safe."

"Granddad? Did you say safe?"

Frank blinked once.

"Yes, you are safe here."

Frank blinked twice. "Safe. Ih safe."

It sounds like he is saying in safe," Danielle said.

Frank shifted his eyes to Danielle and then blinked once.

"Something about safe and home. Does he have a safe at the condo?" Danielle asked.

"I haven't ever seen a safe but I know he had a few rare coins. Maybe he kept them in a small safe? I don't know."

Frank blinked once. "Safe," he whispered.

"Okay, Granddad, I remember you told me the coins would be mine," Tyler choked on the words.

"How will we open it?" Danielle wondered aloud.

Frank looked at Danielle, then Tyler. "Buth...ay."

Danielle said the words over and over in her mind. Then it came to her. "Birthday? Tyler's birthday? Is that what you are trying to say?"

Frank blinked once.

Exhausted from struggling to communicate Frank closed his eyes. Tyler and Danielle sat quietly for a long time deep in their own thoughts but alert to any sound or movement from Frank. There was none.

"Tyler?" Danielle whispered. "Are you awake?"

Tyler opened his eyes. It took him a moment to register where he was. "I must have nodded off," he said softly.

"You must be exhausted," Danielle said. "The nurse just stopped by to see if Frank needed medication. He hasn't stirred so I assume that means he is comfortable. What do you think?"

"What time is it?"

"It's seven o'clock. It's been about an hour since he went to sleep."

Tyler stood up and rubbed his neck. He took his sleeping Granddad's wrist and checked his pulse. "Pulse is 40. That's good under the circumstances. I'm going to review his health care directive. I'll be right back."

Alone in the room Danielle thought back to the losses she had suffered. All had been sudden, unexpected and unencumbered by decisions to be made. Was she ready to confront yet another death? Maybe Tyler would find a way to honor Frank's wishes and still prevent Frank's death. The nurse had said he didn't want – what was the term – extraordinary medical treatment? But certainly if he could talk and take water, there might be hope that he would recover. On her way to his room she had thought that the residents had nothing to live for but now she realized that they were strangers to her. How much harder to let go of someone you loved. It took great strength to survive the loss of a loved one but how much harder it was to sit by and do nothing knowing that the lack of action would eventually lead to his death.

"God," she prayed. "You alone know what is best. Give us the strength and wisdom to do the right thing."

Tyler returned to the room carrying the manila folder that contained Frank's healthcare directive documents. He looked at Danielle's closed eyes and folded hands as he gently put his hand on her shoulder touching her soft hair. "Danny."

"Hey. How are you doing?"

"I'm okay. Any change?"

"No. Still asleep."

"That's good," Tyler said. "Let's go out to the lounge. We can talk there."

"Oh. It feels good to get up and walk. I didn't realize how long I had been sitting in the same position."

"The night shift just came on and they brought in a tray for us – hot soup and a sandwich," Tyler said as they entered the lounge.

"The coffee smells good," Danielle said as she poured two cups and picked up half a sandwich. "So tell me. What do the papers say?"

"I've read the documents and everything seems to be in order. After recovering from the car accident he must have realized that another stroke was possible and he was worried that he would be kept alive in a vegetative state. As much as it hurts, I think the staff here did the right thing by not taking him to the hospital. He did not want to be a burden to us and definitely did not want to be kept alive with tubes and machines if there was no hope of recovery. It's funny. He always said if he had a choice he would like to die on the golf course. Then he would laugh and say, 'but only if I am having a good round.' He wanted to die with a smile on his face."

Danielle looked up at Tyler and smiled. "That sounds like your granddad. I was just praying for help in deciding what to do but it looks like Frank made the tough choices for us."

"I'd say he did. It doesn't make it any easier though, does it?" Tyler said.

"No. I've been thinking about how hard it was for him to communicate with us. It must have taken every ounce of strength he had and the frustration. I can't imagine it!"

"I know. I've been thinking about that too and after reading his wishes, I don't want him to suffer any more than he already has. If you agree, I'd like to talk to his nurse and make sure he gets the best palliative care."

"What does that mean?" Danielle said.

"He will receive regular medications to ensure he does not have pain or anxiety. If he can eat or drink on his own, they will feed him but only if he wants to."

"Do you think he will wake up again?"

"He may drift in and out but the medication will help keep him calm; he'll sleep a lot. It may mean that he won't be able to talk to us again but he may be aware that we are here. We don't know for sure but there is some evidence that a person's sense of hearing may be the last to be lost. It's important that we continue to talk to him in comforting ways and not to say anything that might be upsetting."

"I'm so glad you know about these things, Tyler."

"My training helps me understand what is happening on the physical level. Emotionally though? When I really let it sink in, I'm a wreck."

"I know. Losing your grandma was hard but she had been drifting away from us for a while. You know what I mean?"

Tyler nodded.

Danielle continued, "I really thought Frank would be coming home soon. I can't believe how quickly things have changed. Here," she said as she handed him the tray. "You need to eat something too, then we can take the next step together."

Tyler sat at the small table while Danielle stood next to the counter nibbling at her sandwich. He opened the file folder again and as he removed the health care directive document a small piece of paper fluttered to the floor. It was a piece of notepaper folded in half and stapled shut. Danielle's name was written on it.

"Danny? Look at this. It was in Granddad's papers. It looks like a note to you," Tyler said as he stood and handed the paper to her.

Danielle opened the note. Like her name on the front, the handwriting was neat and feminine. It said, "Follow your heart." Beneath the message was Frank's distinguishable signature.

She looked up and saw Tyler looking expectantly at her trying to read her face. Not knowing what it meant or why it was in the folder she said nothing.

Tyler finally spoke, "What does it say?"

"Follow your heart."

"That's it?"

"Yes. Just follow your heart."

"That's strange. Who is it from? The handwriting on the front looks like a woman's," Tyler said.

"It's from your granddad."

CHAPTER 25

Danielle leaned back in the hot water and concentrated on each of her muscles starting with her toes. She flexed each foot as tightly as she could and then enjoyed the sensation as she released and relaxed – first the left, then the right. She tightened her stomach muscles, held them tight for a count of ten and then exhaled as she relaxed them. The hot water soothed her lower back.

Thoughts of the day crowded in - Frank's condition, his mysterious note: 'Follow your heart.' Tyler had insisted that she go home and get some rest. There was nothing more they could do tonight. Tomorrow they would meet with the hospice team and then? She didn't want to think about preparing for another loss, another funeral and yet, it was inevitable.

She clenched each fist then released it willing herself to relax. She closed her eyes and forced her mind to think about something else. *Two doubled is four. Four doubled is eight. Eight doubled is sixteen...eight thousand, one hundred and ninety two...*

Danielle felt the warmth of the sun on her face as she shielded her eyes from its brightness. She listened to the gentle swoosh of the waves as the surf swelled toward the beach and receded again. The vivid blue sky was a perfect backdrop for the three white puffy clouds positioned in symmetry between the palm trees. It was almost as if the scene had been drawn by a child.

Danielle sat up as she heard the familiar whistle, "fee-fee-bee-bee. Fee-fee-bee-bee." When she turned around toward the sound the beach had vanished and she found herself in a clearing with tall pine trees all around her. The abrupt change of venue did not frighten her. She listened for the call and knew her father was nearby. Soon she heard the whistle again and leaves rustling as two men walked into the clearing. Though she was having trouble seeing – it was as if her eyes wouldn't open – she recognized them immediately. Her father, wearing blue jeans and a red paid shirt was walking arm in arm with Nick who was dressed in light blue scrubs, wearing a paper cap and a mask over his mouth and nose.

"Dad! Nick!" she cried out as she ran to meet them. Nick took her left hand and her father held her right as the three of them walked to the other side of the clearing. There was no need for words. She knew without question of their love for her and her father responded to her thoughts with a nod, a smile or a squeeze of her hand. Nick looked straight ahead but she felt the constant comfort of his hand holding hers. As they approached the edge of the trees her father let go of her hand and stopped. She sensed something was wrong and although Nick tried to lead her on, she pulled away and turned toward her father.

"Dad? Why did you stop?"

Tears were in his eyes as he gave her a small, sad smile and said, "It's okay, Danny. Follow your heart."

She hesitated for a moment looking at Nick's outstretched hand. When she turned back, her father had vanished. Still wearing the mask, Nick gently took Danielle's hand. She looked into his beautiful blue eyes and knew that she would be okay. They entered the peaceful pine forest and the scent of pine needles surrounded her. Her feet were bare but the forest floor was covered in surprisingly soft pine needles and she felt them between her toes. They hadn't gone far when Nick stopped, held both of her hands and slowly rotated, pulling her around so that she was facing the clearing as he faced the forest. She heard the sound of the chickadee far off in the distance.

She looked into his eyes, nodded her understanding and said, "I will always love you, Nick."

Nick smiled and Danielle knew that his love for her was real and everlasting. He let go of her hands, took off his cap and untied his surgical mask. As he did so he spoke to her for the first time, "Danny, promise me. Follow your heart."

Now that the mask and cap were off Danielle became confused. She knew with all her heart and soul this was Nick but he looked younger. His hair was thicker on top and longer in the back. The ends curled up slightly. But there was no mistaking his eyes, the bone structure of his face and the shape of his mouth. He leaned down and kissed her. Danielle closed her eyes and responded with the longing and passion that had been pent up inside her for so long. As the kiss ended, Nick once again took both of her hands in his. When she looked up at him she realized that the man standing in front of her was not Nick. It was Tyler. She felt that it was Nick but somehow she knew it was Tyler. It was so confusing! She looked beyond him to the clearing and knew that her father was gone. Should she go back and try to find him? Perhaps if she whistled the chickadee's call, Dad would come to her.

Tyler stood patiently looking ahead into the forest understanding her confusion and hesitation. Danielle felt that what lay ahead in the forest was unknown and frightening. The sun was low in the sky now and she shivered as the soft pine-scented wind blew across her body. In the wind she heard voices whispering, "Follow your heart." Unable to walk toward the clearing nor turn toward the forest, Danielle was stuck. The wind grew strong and cold, the blowing pine needles pricked her skin. She called out and the sound of her anguished cry awoke her.

CHAPTER 26

Tyler felt better having showered and shaved. He was used to getting by on catnaps and functioning on little sleep. After an extra large cup of coffee and the brisk walk from his car to the Greenhaven family conference room, he felt ready to tackle the day. He felt ready until he saw Danielle. She was sitting in the waiting room outside the conference room and hadn't seen him walk in. Her head was bowed and he saw her shaking slightly and dabbing her eyes. Fearing the worst he touched her shoulder and said, "Danny?"

Her head jerked up in surprise and when she realized it was him she pasted on a smile. "Good morning," she said softly.

"Hi, are you okay?"

"I'm fine. I didn't sleep very well and it's, it's j-just so hard," she stammered as her voice broke and tears rolled down her cheeks.

"Come here," Tyler said as helped her up from the chair into his warm embrace.

She cried quietly for a few moments taking comfort in his strength. "Thanks. I'm okay now."

"Let's sit for a few minutes," Tyler said as he guided her back down into her chair and kissed the top of her head. "We have some time before our appointment and...well...I did a lot of thinking last night."

"Me too. I couldn't sleep."

"I was thinking about Granddad and his wishes. At first I

was resentful and angry that by following his directive I won't have the chance to help him recover. But then, I realized that it would take a miracle to change his prognosis."

"I believe in miracles," Danielle said as she thought back to the miracle of Tyler's birth.

"I'm not saying they don't happen, I just think that Granddad was wise to allow nature or God to call the shots from here. Hooking him up to a feeding tube and eventually a respirator will prolong his life but all we would really be doing is prolonging his death. Granddad had a good life and lived it to the fullest. Much as I don't want to say goodbye, I think I can accept his wishes to die with dignity."

Danielle looked over at Tyler sitting quietly with his hands folded in his lap. He did seem to be at peace and she wished for the same clarity. She wondered if Frank had written the note to her to encourage her to allow love to help her through. He knew how many times loved ones had been taken from her without warning and maybe he anticipated that it would be hard for her to let go this time willingly – without a fight.

Before she could comment, the hospice nurse Nancy Finseth and the social worker Sandy Langsten arrived and ushered Danielle and Tyler into the family conference room. The room was appointed with a small table and four dining chairs, a sofa, coffee table and two arm chairs and a long counter set with coffee and water.

Danielle and Tyler sat down next to each other on the sofa as Sandy warmly greeted them and offered them something to drink. Nancy gave them each a folder and sat down across from them.

"We are so sorry for your pain," Sandy began. "It's always difficult to manage a loved one's care in this very emotional time and it may be difficult for you to make decisions. This is a normal part of the process and we are here to help you as much as we can. Your grandfather," she said, looking at Tyler, "and Mrs. Goodman, your father-in-law," addressing Danielle, "prepared for this day in advance – in the event he would not be able to make his own decisions. In a way, it relieves some of the burden of the family to make tough choices and especially when family members may have differing thoughts as to what course of action to take. End of life decisions are very personal and we are so grateful to have these tools available to help guide us all in caring for Mr. Goodman according to his wishes and to the best of our ability. I have made copies of his executed documents naming Tyler durable Power of Attorney for heath care decisions and you, Danielle, authority to handle his finances. It's a bit unusual to separate these duties between two family members but Mr. Goodman was very clear that these were his wishes."

Tyler couldn't help but smile. "I'm not surprised. He always said I was bad at managing my money – an opinion I contested every chance I had – but he is right, Danny should handle the finances."

Sandy smiled warmly at Tyler. "You also have a copy of his health care directive, the DNR and DNI orders. These provide specific instructions on his treatment and care. You may want to share this with Mrs. Goodman so that the two of you can coordinate the medical and financial aspects of his care but that is up to you."

"I will. I am very familiar with these and don't see any reason to withhold any information from her," Tyler said.

"And I feel the same about the finances," Danielle added.

"Our role today is to explain the hospice care philosophy to you, answer any questions you may have and provide assistance to you as you help Mr. Goodman in his journey," Nancy said.

Listening and talking with the hospice team relieved any remaining hesitations Danielle had about the care Frank would receive. Having been through the end of life journey with many families and their loved ones, Nancy explained what to expect and how hospice care differed from other medical treatment. She assured Danielle and Tyler that every effort would be made to keep Frank free from pain and anxiety and to allow him to die in peace, comfort and with dignity.

"So how is this different from the care he would receive if not in hospice?" Danielle asked as she looked at Tyler.

"My understanding is that he will not receive medical treatment to prolong his life or treat another condition. For example, if his heart stops he will not receive CPR or defibrillation. If he develops pneumonia, he will not be treated with antibiotics," Tyler said. "Nancy, is this correct?"

"Yes, those are good examples. I understand that you are a physician and not responding to medical events like these may be particularly difficult for you," Nancy said to Tyler. "There will be a physician involved who will review and monitor your grandfather's condition and his treatment day by day and I can arrange for you to talk with him or her directly along the way if you need to."

"Thank you. I may take you up on that at some point. For now, I am at peace with Granddad's wishes and believe that palliative care is appropriate given the circumstances," Tyler said as he reached over and put his hand over Danielle's.

"I'm glad you feel that way," Nancy said. "I will be your main medical contact and will check in on Mr. Goodman regularly. But you should know that there is also a hospice service center available to you both by phone any time day or night – twenty-four seven. You can call any time to ask questions or report any changes you see. And, of course, Sandy will talk with you in a moment about other services we offer to help support your emotional and spiritual needs. Do you have any questions, Tyler? Mrs. Goodman?"

"Please, call me Danielle. I was wondering. How long will he be expected to live this way?"

"We never know for sure," Nancy said. "Barring other medical complications related to his latest stroke, it depends on whether or not he takes food or water. We will bring him food and drink and will offer it to him regularly. If he does not eat or drink, he will likely pass within the next ten days or so."

"Oh dear," Danielle said. "I had no idea it would be so soon."

"Like I said, we don't know what his journey will look like. The main thing is that we are here for you and for him to help you through this. There are a few documents to sign to formalize your authorization of hospice care. Would you like some time alone to talk it over?"

"I'm fine going forward," Tyler said. "How about you, Danny? Do you want to think about it?" He squeezed her hand.

"It is all happening so fast. I don't know," Danielle said as tears welled up in her eyes.

"Why don't you give us a few minutes?" Tyler said.

After Nancy and Sandy left the room, Tyler brought Danielle a fresh glass of water. "Talk to me, Danny. What are you thinking?"

"I'm not sure," Danielle said. "I don't know how I feel."

"Are you concerned about authorizing the hospice care instead of taking him to the hospital?"

"No, not really. Everything they told us seems so compassionate and caring. The last thing I would want is to put your granddad through any undue pain or suffering."

"I know. I agree. What is it then? What's bothering you?"

"When my parents died, it was completely unexpected. I couldn't bear to think about how they died, how they suffered...all I knew was that they were gone. Then your father. I never knew exactly what caused his death. He was all alone. Did he have pain? Was he afraid? At the time, the shock and grief were almost too much to bear. Over the years I have tried to understand and place myself by his side but it's impossible. I will never know what he experienced in his last moments." The tears were now streaming down her cheeks. Tyler moved closer and silently held her until she continued. "Until now I have only experienced the shock of learning they were gone. Everything changed in an instant – a blink of the eye. All I could do was try to deal with the reality of their deaths and the overwhelming sense of loss I felt. With your grandmother, I knew she was declining mentally and I didn't spend as much time with her as I should have. And then to suddenly lose her in the accident. I have so many regrets!"

"Please, Danny. Don't. Grandma was not herself. She was difficult to be around. There were times when I lost patience with her too. It was best for her to be alone with Granddad. Her daily routine kept her calm and usually when I stopped by she was sleeping anyway."

"I know. But I still feel like I should have done more to help your granddad."

"Maybe now is our chance. I have seen patients dying but have never experienced it personally like this. I don't know how to go through this end of life process with Granddad either but my medical training has prepared me some. Let me help you through this."

"I want to but I feel like I should be the strong one, the adult the…" Danielle couldn't finish.

"The parent?" Tyler asked.

Danielle looked up at Tyler and saw the same strength and maturity she had relied upon in Nick. Remembering her dream and Frank's note, she let go of what she thought she should do and gave in to her heart.

"Your granddad told me to follow my heart and right now, my heart is telling me to lean on you. I agree that the hospice program sounds best and if you think there is no hope for recovery, I agree. I want to make Frank's last days as easy as possible – with you by my side."

Tyler went out into the hallway, spoke briefly with Nancy and Sandy and the three of them came back into the conference room.

"Tyler has told us that you both agree with Mr. Goodman's directive and that hospice care is best for him. Let's sit down at the table and go over the forms that need to be signed," Sandy said.

When the paperwork had been completed she said, "We also want you to know that now that he is in hospice care, you have the option of moving Mr. Goodman to one of the respite care suites up on the third floor. The patient's rooms look more like bedrooms and less like hospital rooms and the wing tends to be quieter than the extended care areas of our facility. He will be in a hospital bed so we can care for him and keep him comfortable but, other than that, the surroundings are very much like home. You are welcome to being in pictures and any other personal items that may be meaningful to Frank and to your family. There is a family living area, kitchenette and sleeping accommodations connected to his room but separated from the other patients in the wing."

"Is there an additional charge for this?" Danielle asked.

"Yes but I believe Mr. Goodman made financial arrangements. He paid for a period of care in advance. We will check into that for you and let you know later today if there is a respite suite available at this time and what the cost difference will be. Since Medicare pays for all of the hospice expenses, the additional cost may be minimal," Sandy said. "I meant to ask you. Is there a pastor or religious organization that you would like us to contact?"

"Not really," said Tyler. He turned to look at Danielle. The last conversation they had about God was after the accident. Tyler was convinced it was God's punishment for acting on his feelings for her in Hawaii.

Until this morning, Danielle's last conversation with God was at Liz's funeral. It was ironic that the choir sang Brahms' "How Lovely is Thy Dwelling Place" – the same music she had listened to after Nick's death. She still had Liz's funeral service bulletin in her purse and had just reread the words of Psalm 84:1-4, the basis for Brahms' beautiful chorus, this morning while waiting for Tyler.

Tyler saw that Danielle was deep in thought. "Danny?" Tyler said softly. "Is there anyone you would like to come?"

"Yes. I was just thinking about Pastor Gunderson – he

conducted Nick's funeral and was kind enough to preside over Liz's service. He's retired now but has known our family for years. I'm sure he would appreciate knowing of Frank's condition and would come if he is able."

"Thank you," Sandy said. "If you send me his contact information, I'll reach out to him. That is, unless you want to call him."

"If you could contact him, I would appreciate it. Frank handled all the arrangements so I don't have any details other than he served at Beautiful Savior Lutheran Church in Edina for years. I'm sure the church office will know how to reach him."

"Okay," Sandy said. "I will contact him. We will also check into the respite care suite availability, finances etcetera and get back to you hopefully by tomorrow. If there aren't any other questions I'd like to go over the other information in your folders. There are brochures and a helpful Q&A about hospice services. You each have copies of those along with our contact information, the 24-hour phone number and a brief explanation of the Medicare benefits. Tyler, your grandfather listed you as the Power of Attorney for his Health Care so you have a copy of that along with his Advanced Health Care Directive in your folder. Danielle, you have a copy of the financial authorization paperwork along with a handwritten note of instruction on where to find things at Mr. Goodman's home."

Danielle nodded.

"You have had a lot to absorb today," Nancy said. "Just know that we are here to support you every step of the way. If you would like, I can take you to his room now. I'd like to check in on him and I can update you on his condition."

"Thank you," Tyler said. He stood up from the table and shook Nancy's hand and then Sandy's. "We are grateful for everything you have done."

CHAPTER 27

Danielle and Tyler let themselves into the Goodmans' condo a little before six. Tyler dropped the take-out food containers on the dining table and opened the refrigerator. "Oh man! There is something growing serious penicillin in here. Guess I should have emptied the refrigerator, huh? Later. I'm going to have a beer," he said. "Do you want one?"

"No thanks," Danielle replied. "I'd like a glass of wine though if there is a bottle handy. Do you mind if I turn on the T.V.? I feel like I've been out of touch with the rest of the world for so long. At least we can catch the local news."

"Fine with me. After we eat I need to check in again at the hospital. I see a bottle of Merlot. Is that okay?"

"Perfect." Danielle glanced around the condo. It had been almost two months since she had been here with Tyler to pick up a dress and some jewelry for Liz's funeral. Tyler had Frank's mail forwarded to Greenhaven and, with his laptop computer and some files from home, Frank had managed his affairs from his room with the assistance of the volunteers at the care facility. She knew that Frank occasionally had asked Tyler to pick up personal items, additional papers and files. She was struck again with a pang of guilt for not making a point to come over here. Besides the refrigerator, the condo was in need of a good cleaning. They hadn't done anything with Liz's clothes and personal items. With Frank at Greenhaven it hadn't been necessary and as of today, the job had doubled in scope. "Time. It will all be done in due time."

"Hmmm? Did you say something?" Tyler asked.

"Oh. I was just looking around and thinking about how much there is to do. And the finances. Where do I begin?"

"Try not to worry. It will all work out. I have a call in to our chief of staff and the HR representative. I've been thinking about taking a leave of absence from the hospital. I want to spend as much time as I can with Granddad and honestly, I'm not sure I'll be at my best given the circumstances. I've been there long enough to take what they call FMLA leave. After I use up my vacation and sick time I won't be paid but they will hold my job for me. When we were talking about bringing Granddad home I actually looked into it then. Now that we know his time is short, I really want to take the leave."

"I wasn't aware you were thinking about all of this," Danielle said. "I keep underestimating you."

"There is a lot I have been thinking about," Tyler said. "But, let's not get deep tonight. It's been a long day and I think we're both shot. How about I find a movie and we vegg out in front of the tube?"

"Sounds wonderful. Nothing heavy though. How about *Mary Poppins*?"

"Seriously?"

"No," Danielle laughed. "But something light and funny."

After realizing they had different ideas of what constituted light and funny – he suggested *Airplane*, she liked *When Harry met Sally* – they settled on *The Full Monty*. It didn't matter much because within fifteen minutes Tyler was sound asleep in Frank's recliner. Danielle covered him with an afghan and turned the volume down. Finding it hard to focus on the movie, she took out the folder from Greenhaven. She quickly read the boilerplate financial Power of Attorney and then opened the handwritten note.

Like the other note from Frank, it was written by someone else and signed by him. Danielle assumed that the volunteer that had been helping him with his finances also wrote the notes that he dictated to her. The handwriting was neat and cursive so she assumed it was a woman. Probably an older woman. *Young people these days aren't even learning to write in cursive. Why should they? All of their communication is done by computer or text message. A keyboard and a couple of thumbs is all you need these days.*

The note was clearly penned but somewhat cryptic. Danielle wondered if Frank was hesitant to reveal too much to the volunteer for fear of...fear of what exactly? What would Frank have to be afraid of? Danielle was not aware of any skeletons in the Goodman family closets.

The note directed Danielle to a folder at the back of Frank's lower desk drawer. It was not labeled therefore it was hard for Frank to describe in the note which folder to look for without sounding mysterious. The note directed her to the file folder just behind the one labeled "Retirement Statements." The note said this folder would contain everything she would need to manage his affairs. The note also requested that she carefully review all of the documents in the file and do so without anyone else present. Just above his signature were the words, "I love you like a daughter. Follow your heart."

"How odd," Danielle said. She checked to be sure Tyler was still sleeping before going into Frank's den. There were papers scattered on the desk and she imagined Tyler's frustration as he searched for the particular documents Frank had requested. The bottom desk drawer was packed tight with neatly labeled folders containing past years' taxes, bank statements, insurance documents and medical records for Frank and Liz. She pulled out the folder labeled "Tyler". In it were pictures, crayon drawings, newspaper clippings and articles chronicling Tyler's life. She smiled at his baby and childhood pictures taken with Granddad and Grandma. It was clear that this folder held the precious mementos of Tyler's proud grandfather.

The folder directly behind it was labeled "Nick". In it was

a similar assortment of keepsakes but she was surprised to also find Nick's baby book in the file. Something about seeing the blue book in Frank's desk bothered her but she couldn't put her finger on it. As she flipped through the first few pages she saw Liz's entries of her due date, the date she first felt the baby kick, foods she craved and details about the showers given her by her family and friends. The next page had details of Nick's birth: date, time, weight, length, full name, hair color, eye color and a tiny footprint. A sticky note was stuck to the page. At the top was written "Tyler" along with his birth weight and length. The handwriting was not Frank's and definitely not Liz's. It was remarkable! Tyler's weight and length were exactly the same as Nick's when he was born.

The next pages noted baby milestones: first sounds, first tooth, first birthday, and first step. Slipped in next to the picture of Nick on his first birthday was a picture of Tyler. They looked identical! She quickly turned to the next page. Age two, three and four. Each picture of Nick was accompanied by a picture of Tyler at the same age. They could have been twins. It was kind of creepy when she saw each of them in their bedroom. It was, after all, the same room, in the same house, decorated the same way. It was like looking through an hourglass or a time machine. Most disturbing though were the sticky notes that documented details about Tyler as he grew up. They were almost clinical in nature. She felt like she was reading a cross between a diary, a scrapbook and a medical chart.

Why would Frank keep such a detailed account of the similarities between Nick and Tyler? It was almost as if he were obsessed by it. No wonder Tyler had been uncomfortable with Frank's recent talk of being "a clone of his father." Liz had always openly compared Tyler to Nick and then, after her illness set in, she became quite confused to the point of believing Tyler was Nick. But the notes were clearly not hers and not Frank's either.

Danielle put the book back into the file and scanned the

file tabs in the rest of the drawer. Nothing struck her as odd and she easily found the thin file labeled "Retirement Statements". She was shaken by what she had seen in Nick's baby book and her hands trembled as she lifted the file from the drawer. She hoped that there wasn't anything unusual in this file.

Sitting forward in the desk chair, she set the folder on top of the scattered papers on the desk and opened it. The first few pages were clipped together and contained a neatly typed list of bank and brokerage accounts and insurance policy numbers. At the bottom were the names of Frank and Liz's attorney and accountant with their contact information. She recognized the attorney's name from the Power of Attorney document she received at Greenhaven.

That's good, I'll start by contacting them and rely on the help of the professionals to help me through this.

Next were statements from each of the listed accounts. They were dated six months ago so Danielle guessed that that was the last time Frank had updated this file. She scanned the balances and was shocked to see that as of six months ago, the cash and investment assets totaled over five million dollars!

"Wow!" she said aloud as her mind tried to wrap around the wealth that was laid out in black and white in front of her. She flipped back to the summary page and saw that Frank and Liz also each had life insurance policies for another five hundred thousand each. With the condo, club membership, jewelry, art and personal property, the number kept climbing.

The next document was a cover letter from the attorney stating that the fully executed revocable trust and will documents were enclosed. There were only a few pages behind the letter and she didn't see the thick legal documents she had expected to find in the file.

Next was a folded piece of paper with her name on the front. Inside was a handwritten letter from Frank.

Dear Danielle,

If you are reading this I am either gone or no longer cognizant and incapable of making decisions about my future. I trust that you and Tyler will honor my wishes to slip away to the next life without machines and hopefully without drama. I admit that this last wish is a cowardly act on my part for I can't face the thought of losing your and Tyler's respect and love. I am also sorry for burdening you with the truth and the decision whether or not to share it with Tyler. I fear that Tyler's reaction to the truth may put his life in danger just as I am sure keeping the truth from Liz caused her mental collapse. Do not speak to anyone of this letter and specifically be careful of Dr. Sonny Marino. He is a very dangerous man and you must believe me when I say he would have destroyed our family had I betrayed his secret. I don't believe his are idle threats and suspect that he may have been responsible for Nick's death.

Please know that all I have done was out of love for my family. I beg your forgiveness for mistakes I have made. Having witnessed the love you have for our son has brought me the greatest joy and I hope that you will both find peace and happiness in each other.

Please be careful, be diligent and <u>follow your heart</u>. There is a safe in the back of the guestroom closet. Do not open it if you are with Tyler. The combination is Tyler's birthday. All will be made clear.

With love for you and Tyler,

Frank

Danielle heard footsteps and quickly put the note back into the file and closed it. She spun around in the desk chair just as Tyler entered the den. "Hey sleepyhead," she managed to say.

"Hey yourself," Tyler replied. Then he saw Danielle's face. "What's wrong? You look like you've seen a ghost!"

"No, I'm fine," she tried to cover.

"No you're not. Tell me what's wrong."

"I was just going through your granddad's papers and the reality of losing him is sinking in. That's all."

Tyler moved closer and put his hands on her shoulders. "I know what you mean. I haven't really accepted it yet either."

"It will take time," she said. "I have to admit I'm also a bit in shock. I had no idea that your grandparents were such wealthy people. Did you?"

"Well sort of. I mean, money was never any object when it came to lifestyle. They traveled the world, enjoyed the arts and paid all of my college expenses. Why?"

"I saw the file of investment statements. Of course things may have changed in the past six months, but it looks like their net worth could be almost ten million dollars."

"My God! Really?"

"I know. It's unreal. Course we don't know what provisions were made in their wills but I have to assume you are the sole beneficiary."

"I didn't expect their net worth to be half that!"

"It seems to be. Frank left me the contact information for his attorney and accountant. I'll call them in the morning and try to get an appointment right away. At least we know that if a hospice care suite is available, we can move Granddad there without worrying about the cost. Do you agree?"

"Absolutely. I'll know more tomorrow about my work situation. Assuming everything works out, I'm considering moving into the suite temporarily. It's important for me to be there with him to the end. I don't know why but I have such a strong feeling about this."

"I understand, Tyler," she said as she got up from the desk. "I don't know how you feel after your nap but I'm beat. How about we get some sleep? There is a lot to do tomorrow."

"Yeah. Why don't you sleep in the bedroom and I'll crash on the hide-a-bed in the guestroom? I'm used to sleeping on worse in the doctor's lounge and I'll probably be awake for a little while yet anyway."

"Okay, I will. Thanks. I'll see you in the morning."

"Good night."

Danielle took the file with her to the bedroom. Her curiosity about the contents of the safe was overwhelming but with Tyler in the guestroom, she couldn't be tempted to open it.

CHAPTER 28

The next morning after a quick cup of coffee, Danielle offered to stay behind and empty the refrigerator of the offending food items. They each had their own cars and Danielle wanted to try to get an appointment to see Frank's attorney today, if possible. Tyler was grateful that he didn't have to deal with the mess in the refrigerator and rushed out the door before she had a chance to change her mind. He was anxious to meet with the HR representative at the hospital, clear out his locker and wrap up any other loose ends at work.

Danielle had a bad feeling about the contents of the safe so she tackled the refrigerator first. After making several trips to the garbage chute at the end of the hall, she cleaned up a bit and went into the guestroom.

Behind the hanging clothes, she found the safe and spun the dial to Tyler's birth date. Inside was a single thick envelope which she brought out to the small desk and opened it. It contained the lengthy trust and will documents. She had assumed the lawyer would have copies but it was nice to have them in front of her now. Then she saw copies of cancelled checks made out to the Goodman Foundation. Most checks were for ten thousand dollars and by the looks of it, Frank had donated over a million dollars beginning more than twenty years ago. After getting a glimpse of Frank's net worth yesterday, this didn't completely surprise her but she wondered why the cancelled checks were kept locked in the safe with Frank's other important papers.

The only other item in the envelope was a small black hard-covered book. It was about half the size of a standard sheet of paper, each page was lined but had no other pre-printed information. Danielle immediately recognized Frank's handwriting and flipping through the pages saw that each began with a date – month and day only, no year. If it had been a woman's book she would have thought it a diary but being it was Frank's, she dubbed it his journal. His handwriting was difficult to read but she was sure that this small book held the information Frank was desperate for her to read in private. She took a deep breath and opened the small book.

The first twenty entries looked like they had all been written at the same time. The ink color was the same and the handwriting was mostly legible once Danielle understood the shorthand. Frank met SM (Frank's shorthand for Sonny Marino) on July 4th at a members' event at Southpoint Country Club. N (Nick) had just finished his graduate work at the U and was interested in medical research. Introductions were made and in August, N got the job working on SM's prestigious genetic research team.

This was a surprise. Danielle had assumed that Frank met Sonny through Nick's work. In fact, it was the other way around.

Soon after N went to work for SM, SM asked F for money. The U lost a large Federal research grant and SM's research would be shut down without private funding. F agreed to help but did not want N to be aware of his support. F believed that SM was on the cusp of a major discovery and with his financial help, N was sure to gain status and recognition when the findings were published.

Danielle made a mental note to compare this entry with the check copies and continued on. Next there was a record of when Frank learned of N and D's meeting followed by entries marking significant events in their courtship –

meeting Liz and Frank, the engagement and wedding showers and preparation. Considering Frank was not an outwardly demonstrative man, Danielle smiled as she read these pages. He described her as beautiful, smart and spunky and mentioned in several entries how happy N was. L was also thrilled with her future daughter-in-law. The only wet blanket was SM. F didn't understand why SM was concerned by the quick engagement and upcoming wedding. F thought maybe SM was jealous of N's attention to D. N was still dedicated to his work but not spending as much time at the lab as he had been.

Interspersed were entries of lunches with SM at the club, golf outings with N – including an incident where Frank ended up in the pond after trying to make a shot from its edge. And then on May 4, the word *clone* jumped off the page at her. Frank and SM had a spirited discussion about the ethics of human cloning. Without SM saying so directly, Frank had the impression that SM's work was going way beyond what he included in his official reports. Several entries later Frank mentioned he and N played golf. They discussed N & D's excitement for their wedding. Frank brought up SM's research. N assured Frank that SM was going by the book – N would surely know if SM was delving into the forbidden science of human cloning. Frank told N that he was proud of him and cautioned him to keep his eyes open. Frank told N that he wanted to pay for their honeymoon in HI – a wedding gift just between Frank & N.

Several entries in June referenced Frank's growing concern and suspicions. SM denied working on human cloning. Frank considers ending his funding for SM's research. Frank feels threatened by SM. SM will cut N out of his research. June 15 N & D's wedding. Happiness until the reception. SM was drunk and hints at N's future. SM Asks Frank, "Are you on board?"

July 3, Italian professor announces plans to implant cloned human embryo...story mentions unnamed American partner. SM???

Danielle rubbed her temples. She tried to remember anything unusual with Nick or his work around the time of their wedding. She had been on cloud nine. Nothing seemed out of place. The journal was so strange! Danielle got up from the table and stretched. She needed a bathroom break and only had about an hour before she would have to shower and get ready to go to Greenhaven. She could make her phone calls later from there.

When she returned to the journal and read Frank's entries when N died, she almost couldn't continue. There were few words but filled with such pain. Notes about D and L and his concern for both. L's loss of her beloved son. D has lost so much in her young life. Then SM popped up again along with her pregnancy.

Frank knew about the artificial insemination? Danielle was stunned. She skimmed the next pages chronicling T's (Tyler's) birth and childhood. Frank's mood was lighter now and the pages brimmed with joy and pride. Frequent lunch invitations to the club with SM. Frank misses N. SM is really interested in T. Asks for pictures. Since N is gone, Frank hints at stopping the funding. SM is furious. Storms out. SM asks for meeting. Thrusts N's blue baby book at him. "Open your eyes, Frank. Even L can see it. I have the medical proof. T is N's clone!"

"Oh my God!" Danielle dropped the book as the world went black. The next thing she heard was the ringing of her cell phone. Dazed and confused she looked around the kitchen but by the time she found it the ringing had stopped. She struggled to focus on the screen. Tyler – four missed calls. She touched her forehead and felt the lump – one source of pain. Her mind was trying to stay black to spare her the shock of what she had just read but soon she jolted to full consciousness. Tyler was Nick's clone! She felt as if she had been kicked in the stomach. Grabbing the counter she steadied herself. Not knowing what to think, she did what she'd always done in the past. She blocked out all thoughts of the journal and got busy.

First, not trusting her voice, she sent a text message to Tyler explaining that she had been in the shower and missed his calls. She told him that she had to take care of some business for Frank and would meet him at Greenhaven later.

Next, she stripped off her clothes and took a long hot shower. The heat made her head throb but the hot water steadied her senses. When she felt the water start to cool she turned it off and grabbed a towel. Without thinking, she went through the mechanics of drying her hair, bangs down today, applying her makeup and getting dressed. Only then did she return to the kitchen steeled to face what lie before her.

Her first call was to the attorney and upon her insistence, the receptionist agreed to squeeze her in if she could be there by twelve thirty. The clock only allowed her time to throw everything into a bag and run out to the car. She punched the address into her GPS and took off. Without having read the will or the trust documents, she was going to this meeting blind but maybe it was better this way. She would alert Mr. Johnson to Frank's condition and ask him to explain the basics of the arrangements Frank had made. They could go into more detail later.

Her head was still throbbing as she sat in the reception area. No sooner had she washed down two pain relievers with the water that had been offered her than Mr. Johnson, Ted, appeared. Seated in the comfortable conference room, she quickly updated him about Frank and their decision to move him into hospice care. It was clear that Frank and Ted had been friends as well as business associates and he expressed his sadness when he heard of Frank's condition – and so soon after Liz's passing. Ted had another appointment at one o'clock so he apologized for not being able to spend more time as he quickly explained the workings of the trust and pour-over will.

"One of the greatest benefits is that the estate will not get tied up in probate. As Power of Attorney and after Frank passes, successor trustee, you have full and immediate access to the entire estate. I'm not sure if you are aware, but the last time Frank and I met, the estate was estimated at around ten million dollars. Of course some of those assets are tied up in real estate and other assets that will take time to liquidate, if you choose to do so. However, there will be more than enough readily available to take care of Frank at Greenhaven and provide for your and Tyler's short term needs. Frank spoke very highly of you and was certain that you would be more than capable of handling his affairs. Please know that I am here to help you in any way I can. Why don't we set a time to meet again next week after you have had a chance to read through the documents? My secretary can set it up on your way out." Ted stood up and shook her hand. "Danielle, I am so sorry to hear about Frank. He is a good man and a good friend. Please let Tyler know that my thoughts and prayers are with you all."

"Thank you," Danielle said. "You have been most helpful. I will see you next week and will keep you informed on Frank's condition."

It was one fifteen by the time she got to her car so she decided to wait to call the accountant. There didn't seem to be any immediate sense of urgency to talk with him. She made a mental note to talk to the business manager at Greenhaven to see what financial arrangements had been made. Based on Sandy's comment yesterday (was it really only yesterday?) it sounded like Frank had prepaid some of his expenses. She gently touched her forehead and glanced in the mirror. The swelling had gone down some and her bangs covered the bump. She took a very deep breath and put the car in reverse.

CHAPTER 29

After meeting with the business manager, Danielle went up to the third floor. She was told that a hospice suite had been available and Tyler had already arranged for Frank to be moved. As she stepped off the elevator she felt like she had left a health care facility and entered a hotel corridor. The walls, floors and furnishings were warm and homey – the kind of décor one would find in a four star hotel. Suite 304 was to the left and she tapped softly on the door before going in. The main room served as a gathering/living area with a kitchenette along one wall. Toward the back of the room to the right was a doorway into Frank's room. The head of his hospital bed was raised and positioned so that it faced a full wall of windows. He was clean-shaven and wearing his light blue pajamas instead of the hospital gown she had last seen him in. Tyler was sitting in the recliner next to the bed reading aloud from *Golf Digest Magazine*. The cover advertised "America's 100 Greatest Golf Courses" and Tyler was reading the description of number seven – Pebble Beach. He stopped when Danielle entered the room.

"Hi," she said to Tyler. "Wow! The room is beautiful. Don't you think so, Frank?" she said as she leaned down to kiss his forehead. "I see you and Tyler are walking the best golf courses. I'm not sure they will let you play wearing your pajamas – dashing as you are." She looked at Tyler. "Has he been awake at all?"

"Not since I've been here. The nurse said he was a little

restless last night but they are giving him medication every two hours to keep him comfortable."

"Frank, can you wake up?" Danielle said softly. "It's me, Danielle." Frank's eyelids fluttered slightly. "Tyler is here too and we want to talk to you." Danielle nodded to Tyler.

"Granddad? It's me, Tyler. I'm here, Granddad."

Frank's eyes fluttered again and opened ever so slightly. Danielle smiled and took his hand. "Hi there good lookin'. How's my favorite father-in-law? You don't have to try to talk. I just wanted you to know that we are here and we love you very much. There is nothing for you to worry about. Tyler and I are fine and will take good care of each other."

"I love you, Granddad," Tyler said with tears in his eyes. Frank's eyes fluttered.

"Liz and Nick are waiting in heaven to greet you. You know that, don't you?" Danielle said as she softly stroked his hair. "Whenever you are ready, it's okay for you to go to heaven. Jesus has forgiven all your sins and has prepared a special place for you. Who knows, maybe heaven has a golf course better than Pebble Beach."

Frank's eyes closed completely and he seemed to relax. "Do you want to read for a while longer?" she asked.

"Actually, I could use a break. Let's go into the living room. I'm going to get a glass of ice water. Can I get you one?" Tyler asked.

"Yes, thanks. This suite really is beautiful. I'm so glad they had space and that you had him moved up here. The whole atmosphere is different – so peaceful."

"I think so too. Thank you," Tyler said.

"For what?"

"For talking to Granddad like that. I've had a hard time knowing what to say and you were just perfect. I believe he heard us and knows how much we love him."

Danielle said, "I don't know where those words came from. They just sort of spilled out. So, how did it go at work?"

"No problems. They had anticipated my absence and

brought in another doc to cover for me. I can take as much time as I need – well, at least up to twelve weeks and we both know it won't be that long," Tyler said. "Now tell me about your morning."

Danielle quickly recounted the events of the morning leaving out the journal, the shocking secret and the bump on her head. Tyler seemed pleased that she had gotten in to see the attorney so quickly and they both poured over the trust and will documents.

"Wow!" Tyler said. "Granddad took care of everything, didn't he?"

"It sure looks like it. Now that I've read the documents I have some questions and I know you do too. Will you go with me when I meet with Mr. Johnson, Granddad's lawyer next week?"

"That sounds good. I know Granddad appointed you to handle his finances but I'd like to help, if I can."

Danielle felt a jolt as she looked at Tyler. Her heart told her those were Nick's eyes but her mind would not accept it.

"Hey, you okay?"

"Fine," Danielle said with a small smile. "I'm just brain dead from dealing with so much heavy stuff. How about we pick one of the games over there and play it in his room? It will be a good distraction for all of us."

They passed the afternoon playing board games, watching a golf tournament on T.V. and reliving happy family times. Many of the stories were Tyler's about Granddad on the golf course. Tyler had a knack for portraying his grandfather to a tee (no pun intended). Frank did not stir again. After a light supper in Greenhaven's dining room, Danielle said her goodbyes and went home. Tyler was spending the night and assured her he would let her know if there was any change.

Danielle ran a hot bath and poured a large glass of Merlot. She wanted to read the rest of the journal but needed to decompress first. While she was relaxing, she thought back to the stories Tyler told. She didn't realize he and Frank had been so jovial together. She smiled as she remembered Tyler's telling the story of Frank falling into the pond. He was always so dignified, so put together – it must have been hilarious. The more she thought about it the more certain she was that she had read about that incident in Frank's journal. She was too comfortable to get out of the tub just yet so she tried to picture the pages and the order of things. She couldn't be certain but she thought the event was toward the beginning – wait! That was Nick! He was with Frank when he fell into the pond!

Her mind wound backward and incongruencies from the past rearranged themselves into an impossible but now logical order. If she allowed herself the possibility that Tyler was really Nick, things made sense – if believing her son was a clone of her husband could make any kind of sense at all! Not only did Tyler look identical to Nick – the baby book had laid that evidence out to her – he had his mind as well. His natural grasp of golf, his talent and love for medicine and, is it possible? He seemed to have Nick's memories. In Hawaii he had recounted perfectly the whale-watching trip she and Nick had taken on their honeymoon. He even described her bathing suit and the snorkel incident with the sea turtle. What had he said?

"It was like watching a movie in my mind."

Tyler had told her that he had those *movie memory* experiences as far back as he could remember. As a baby, Liz could understand his baby talk because he used the words she had taught him – that is, she had taught Nick. And Tyler was an exact physical copy. No wonder Liz had become so distraught. It must have driven her crazy! But not Frank because he knew the truth.

So, is it possible? Is Tyler a clone? Could Tyler not only have Nick's body, his aptitude and interests but also his memories? Danielle finished her wine, added hot water to the tub, leaned back and squeezed her eyes shut.

Frank had implored her twice to "follow her heart."

It hadn't even been a week since she and Tyler had been in Hawaii. She tried to listen to her heart and to focus just on the feelings – the warmth of his familiar touch as he massaged oil into her skin. He had removed her ring. Her eyes snapped open. She hadn't even noticed that he had put it back on – but on her left hand! On the beach he had told her of his conflicted love for her – love not as a mother. They had kissed. Then they got the call about Frank. She had many reasons for pushing down what happened in Hawaii and as she allowed herself to think about it now, the confusion and guilt resurfaced.

Frank must have recognized Tyler's growing love for her and had been helpless to stop it. Yet he would never have told Tyler the truth for fear of destroying their relationship. Frank must have thought his only option was to reveal it to her and trust that her heart would lead her to understanding, forgiveness and acceptance. Danielle got out of the tub and put on her robe and slippers. She took the journal to her bedroom and reread it in its entirety. Like a novel, knowing the ending made reading the early entries more compelling. Exhausted, she closed her eyes and slept a deep and dreamless sleep.

CHAPTER 30

It was impossible to look at Tyler in the same way. Danielle's life was now distinctly divided into B.K. (before knowing) and A.K. (after knowing.) During the immediate A.K. days, her mind refused to accept the new reality but when she closed her eyes and listened to her heart, she saw Tyler for who he really was. Unbelievably, he was Nick! She took delight in hearing his voice, watching him walk and feeling his strong arms around her. They talked quietly at Frank's bedside and found comfort in one another during his last days. Sonny only stopped in once and the Greenhaven staff told him that the family had requested no visitors. Danielle hid her nervousness when she met him in the lobby and dropped enough hints to assure Dr. Marino that Frank had been unable to communicate since his second stroke. She lied and said they had been too preoccupied with Frank's care to spend any time looking into his financial records or papers. She was sure that Sonny had no idea that she knew his secret and, for now, he posed no threat. Seeing him though gave her a chill. Frank's note had warned her that Sonny was dangerous. It sickened her to think that Sonny had been responsible for Nick's mysterious death.

The days passed as Danielle and Tyler faithfully watched and waited by Frank's bedside. The hospice staff was so kind and helpful and when the end was near, Danielle and

Tyler were told what to expect. At last, Frank's breathing slowed and he peacefully slipped from this life to the next.

Frank's life was remembered and honored by the many friends and colleagues that attended his memorial service and the reception at Southpoint that followed. Danielle recognized some of the stories and anecdotes from Frank's journal and enjoyed hearing them told by his friends in a variety of versions and amplifications. Tyler gave a poignant eulogy as he spoke of his granddad's importance in his life and in the lives of so many that knew his kind and generous spirit.

The only tense moment was when Sonny cornered Danielle in the hallway leading to the club's offices. She was on her way out after taking care of the catering bill and practically ran into him as she rounded the corner.

"Sonny!" she said. "I'm sorry. I didn't see you."

"My fault entirely. Someone told me you were headed this way and I wanted to catch you before I left."

"I'm headed back now. But since you are here, I want to thank you for coming. I know now how important your work was to not just Nick but to Frank as well."

Sonny stiffened.

"I have had a chance to go through all of Frank's papers and know about his donations to the foundation. He clearly respected you and your work and was grateful for the many opportunities you provided Nick while working with you."

Sonny relaxed and smiled. "Danielle, I am privileged to have known Frank and to have worked with Nick."

"And, I should add, I am forever grateful to you for making it possible to have my wonderful son Tyler."

"Does Tyler know about his conception?" Sonny asked. He hoped that the question might reveal whether or not Frank had told Danielle the truth.

"No and I don't think there is any reason to. He knows that his father and I loved each other very much and he is a result of that love. That's enough, don't you think?"

"Yes, quite enough," Sonny said. "Well, I must be going.

It was good to see so many here today. Frank would have been pleased."

"Goodbye, Sonny," Danielle said as she shook his hand. "Thanks again for coming," she said as they entered the main lobby with the other guests.

The next morning, Danielle and Tyler boarded a plane to the Cayman Islands. It had taken some convincing, but since the tickets were non-refundable and the all-inclusive resort fees were pre-paid, Tyler went along with her unexpected gift to finish their vacation, rest and share their grief in privacy before tackling all of the estate and business details that had to be handled.

Tired from the stress and strain of the past two weeks, Danielle and Tyler spent the first two days relaxing at the pool and walking on the beach. They talked about the experience of being with Frank when he died and relived many of the sweet moments of the past weeks. Danielle gave Tyler the comfort and support he needed to express his grief and mostly just listened.

"I feel as though I just lost my father," Tyler said.

"That's understandable," she said. "You and Granddad were so close."

"But, it's more than that. I haven't said anything, but I've had so many *movie memories* lately. As I was sharing stories of the past in Granddad's room, and with his friends, I realized that the time frames don't make sense."

"How so?"

"The best example I have is when I was talking to Granddad about my high school graduation. You remember? We wore those hideous maroon robes that were paper thin – in fact, I swear they were paper. When we paraded into the gymnasium the sound was like thousands of cheap paper napkins being crumpled up. Most of the kids just threw them away after pictures had been taken.

But as I was reliving it by Granddad's bedside, my mind flipped and I saw hundreds of students in blue robes and I was wearing one. I remember Grandma telling me that the color matched my eyes perfectly. They were heavy and really hot! Grandma told me not to throw my cap because we had to return it the next day and she didn't want to lose the rental deposit. I clearly remember throwing my cap."

"When you were wearing the blue robe, it was the graduating class of what year?" Danielle asked.

Without hesitation Tyler answered, "1970."

"Tyler, we need to talk."

CHAPTER 31

Danielle's head felt like it would burst from the force of her conflicted thoughts. Had she done the right thing? Should she have told Tyler of his identity?

She had agonized over the decision. How could she tell him? How could she not tell him? She knew that either course would damage him and she couldn't bear the thought of causing her son so much pain.

Yes, she had loved him as a son. She had carried him in her womb, nursed him at her breast and cared for him as only a mother could. Watching him grow and learn was a profound joy in her life, truly a gift from God. She had cherished her son and held tightly to the connection he provided to her beloved Nick.

As soon as her thoughts went to Nick her heart raced and her body shuddered violently. It was no longer possible to think about Nick without seeing Tyler.

"God, why? Why did you lead me to Nick only to take him away? And now Tyler? I can't bear it!"

Danielle cried bitter, angry tears over the loss of her parents, her husband and now, Tyler. Seeing his reaction, the look of horror and disgust on his face as he pushed her away and fled. She knew that she had lost him too.

But telling Tyler the truth had been the right thing to do. She had seen how Liz had crumbled under the conflict, knowing in her heart that Tyler was Nick but fighting the impossibility of it with her mind and her very soul. Frank had made what he thought was the right decision – to withhold the truth – and now she had to live with hers. She had to do what was best for Tyler even if it meant never seeing him again.

And her anger toward Sonny was visceral. If he had walked into the room, she would have killed him. How dare he use her this way? She had no proof but knew with her entire being that Sonny had killed Nick. He would have fought Sonny over the experimentation of human cloning and in the end had died for his principles. Frank had warned her that Sonny was dangerous and that truth could not be denied.

"Oh my God! What if Tyler remembers?" She picked up her phone and called his cell. It immediately went to voicemail.

Tyler sat for a long time watching the sand crab crawl up the rock only to be washed back by the waves. The air was beginning to cool following the fiery sunset. After Danielle had told him the whole story his emotions had erupted. First running, then walking down the beach he was now beyond the line of hotels by the shore. The coastline was rugged here making it more difficult to walk. He was alone. He closed his eyes and listened to the sound of the surf allowing its constant rhythm to calm him. While the news that he was his father's clone seemed impossible, it also provided a crazy explanation for the thoughts and feelings that had first confused and then tormented him. The *movie memories*, the inexplicable sense from childhood that Frank and Liz were his parents not his grandparents and most of all, the passion he felt for Danielle all made sense if, and that was a big if, he could accept the unacceptable. He was a clone. He *was* Nick Goodman and Sonny Marino was one crazy son of a bitch. For all he knew, there could be more clones just like him running around the world.

Danielle had shared Frank's warnings about Sonny and he now understood her decision to leave town at least until they sorted things out. Would their hasty departure raise a red flag? Did Frank's death eliminate or heighten the danger? Tyler thought about returning home to confront Sonny. If he could access his father's DNA, the proof would be irrefutable and Sonny would be prosecuted or at least ostracized. But if he went public, his mother would surely wear the scarlet letter. Who would believe that she was an innocent victim in all of this?

The shock of the memory exploded in his head. He had returned home from Hawaii with Danielle. It was their honeymoon. Back at the lab he had argued with Sonny – confronted him about his work to make a human clone. He could picture Sonny towering over him, his face dark and angry. And then, he felt Sonny stab him with a syringe.

"Oh my God!" Tyler cried. "Sonny killed my father! Sonny killed Nick. No, Sonny killed me!"

Distraught and overcome with grief and anger, Tyler broke down. He cried for the loss of his father, Nick. He mourned the loss of his grandparents – no, his parents, Liz and Frank. He cried for his own lost identity – Tyler wasn't real. No, Tyler, Nick and Danielle's son wasn't real, but *he* was and he was Nick. He felt it in every fiber of his being. And he cried for Danielle. She had lost so much and now she had lost Tyler, her son. He loved her desperately and as the reality of who he really was seeped into his consciousness he allowed himself at last to feel the deep love he had in his heart for her – for Danny – for his wife!

But there was no way she could love him now. Not as a son, not as a husband. What could he be to her now? He was a freak!

Cold to the bone with shock and shaking in the dark he felt his cell phone vibrating in his pocket. The screen displayed Danielle's beautiful, smiling face. He answered.

"Hi," she said. "Are you okay?"

"I don't think so."

"Please come back," Danielle said.

"I don't think I should."

"Of course you should. I need you," Danielle said.

"What for? I'm a frickin' freak."

"Please don't say that. Just come back. You sound cold."

"Incredibly," Tyler said as his body shook violently.

"Please come back. You can warm up in the hot tub. You can be alone or we can talk or not talk. Whatever you need."

"I don't know what to say."

"I don't either but we can figure this out together. Please come back."

"Okay," Tyler said reluctantly as he stood and picked his way over the rocks down to the sand below. The shoreline was dark now but the moon was bright and the lights from the hotels flickered in the distance. He walked slowly – careful to avoid the water but close to the tide where the sand was firm. He no longer had any concept of time. As his *movie memories* became part of him and melded with Tyler's past, the days, months and years became a jumbled mess. His biological age didn't fit with his mental age but then, it never really had. He had always felt older than his years and now with the recognition of the memories that were much older than his body, he felt a sense of vertigo. Stumbling toward the lights he focused on the sound of her words, "I need you."

Danielle was worried. She left the pool area and made her way down to the beach. It was dark and the evening breeze felt cool. Not knowing which direction Tyler had gone, she was afraid to move. She strained her eyes in both directions willing him to come into view. At last she saw a lone figure in the distance. Sure that it was Tyler, she ran toward him.

"Tyler? Tyler!" she called.

The figure raised his hand in acknowledgement and she could see him stumbling now. At last she reached him. Not knowing his state of mind she held out the large beach towel and said, "Here, put this on."

Tyler wrapped the towel around his shoulders and then allowed Danielle to wrap her arms around him. He cried from the depths of his soul until there were no more tears left within him.

Danielle and Tyler spent the rest of the night talking, crying and rearranging the pieces of their lives into a new order. They started with the rationality of the facts - impossible as they were. Since Tyler was Nick's clone, his DNA originated with Frank and Liz. That meant there was no biological relationship between Tyler and Danielle. Though she had carried him in her womb, they were not related in any way. She was not his biological mother and he was not her son. For the first time, they acknowledged how their relationship had changed as Tyler had grown into manhood. He rarely referred to her as Mom and had called her Danny for years.

Danielle told Tyler of her struggle in the past weeks after she learned the truth. She had tried to stop thinking of him as her son. But how could she? She had given birth to him and raised him. She had tried to imagine herself a surrogate mother and wondered how those women felt after going through the pregnancy and then giving back the baby to the parents. Is that what she was, a surrogate mother? No wonder Liz couldn't handle the situation. In her gut, she must have known somehow that Tyler was really Nick – reincarnated. Yet with the impossibility of it and everyone denying her reality, it had torn her apart. Danielle wished she could talk with Liz now. Maybe by giving Tyler/Nick back to his mother, Danielle could shed the maternal feelings she had for him. No, with Liz and Frank gone, there wasn't anyone left who could help them make sense of all of this – except Sonny Marino, that is.

When Danielle mentioned his name, Tyler shook his head violently and described his *movie memory* of Nick's death. Danielle relived the horror of that day and now experienced it along with new emotions, anger and fear. Frank had suspected Sonny's involvement and now she understood just how dangerous Sonny was. If he killed his partner to protect his cloning research, what might he do to Danielle or to Tyler?

After hours of talking, Danielle and Tyler were mentally and emotionally exhausted, their feelings and identities lay open, raw and wounded. So distraught, vulnerable and fragile, and unable to help each other, they went to their separate rooms to rest.

Danielle woke up to the smell of coffee and the sun shining brightly through the crack in the heavy draperies. There was a soft knock on the door.

"Danny. Can I come in?" Tyler said.

"Sure. I'm awake."

Tyler came in carrying a tray with hot coffee, a bowl of fresh strawberries and a basket of toast and pastries. "It's almost noon," he said. "I thought you might be hungry."

"I guess I am," Danielle said sleepily. "I had no idea it was so late. How long have you been up?"

"I got up around nine. I didn't shut my drapes last night and the morning sun woke me up. I had some coffee, took a walk on the beach and stopped at the café for breakfast. How did you sleep?"

"I don't feel like I did at all. I was so restless and I couldn't get to sleep. But I must have conked out at some point. I kept seeing your granddad – I mean dad – oh, Tyler! Everything is turned upside down. During the night I had myself convinced that it would be best if I moved away somewhere. You know, less complicated for you. But now, when I see you in the morning light, I see you – I see Nick – and I can't bear the thought of losing you again. Is that wrong?"

Tyler shook his head and sat down on the bed beside her. "I know what you mean. I've had those same thoughts for a long time. I knew I should leave. It was so painful and so confusing to be around you. But I couldn't make myself do it and I hated myself for being so weak. Dad said in his note to *follow your heart*. What is your heart telling you?"

"My heart tells me to hold on to you, to love you and never let you go."

"Then, maybe we should go with that," Tyler said.

"You know it's not that easy."

"Isn't it?"

"I don't know. My mind is still spinning. I'll be right back," she said as she got out of bed. "I need to use the bathroom." Alone in the bathroom, she splashed cool water on her face, ran a brush through her hair and brushed her teeth. She slipped on the brightly colored cotton robe she had bought in Hawaii and looked in the mirror. Her eyes were puffy and red. She noticed the fine lines at the corners.

Can this work? Our ages are about the same as when Nick and I married – only reversed. It's not safe to go home, not while Sonny is still there. I could contact the attorney and have him take care of everything for us. Money is not an issue. Thinking about being happy and living the rest of my life with Tyler — Nick, doesn't seem possible. But could it work? No one would know. We could live as husband and wife anywhere in the world. It feels weird but in a way it feels more right than living as mother and son. Is this what Frank meant when he said to follow my heart?

She took a deep breath and walked back to the bedroom. Through the open door she saw him standing out on the veranda. She shivered as she felt the cool tile on her bare feet – or was it from nervousness? Danielle took his hand in hers and as he slowly turned toward her, his face had a look of hope and expectation. She smiled and said, "I love you, Nick," as he leaned down to kiss Danny, his wife.

ABOUT THE AUTHOR

Laurie Ann Rossin (Swonger) was born in July, 1953 and spent most of her childhood with parents and two brothers in the Saint Paul suburb of Maplewood, Minnesota. When she was about nine years' old, she found a book of Alfred Hitchcock stories on her Aunt Jeanette's bookshelf (she was supposed to be napping) and was hooked. She loved to watch "The Twilight Zone" on TV, read stories by Edgar Allen Poe, Stephen King and other spooky authors and was thrillingly scared to death by the movie "Wait Until Dark." Her favorite scary stories contained enough reality to be plausible but stretched her imagination to wonder "what if?"

Her teen years were spent in Golden Valley and she graduated in 1971 from Armstrong High School in Plymouth. In the early seventies, she attended Concordia University in Saint Paul as a liberal arts student with a concentration in music and English literature. She learned that she didn't want to teach and didn't think she could make a living in either music or literature so at age 19 she quit college to work in business. Later in life, as an adult student in Augsburg's Weekend College program, she earned a bachelor's degree in Business Administration followed by a challenging and rewarding career in the 401(k) retirement plan industry.

In 1996, as moral and legal controversies swirled around the news of Dolly the first cloned sheep, Laurie wondered what a human clone would experience in family and social life. She began writing *Danny's Boy* and as the story developed found that it wasn't a spooky or sci-fi story, but one that challenged her once again to explore "what if?"

Danny's story waited patiently while the author's professional life, new marriage to conductor Dr. Thomas Rossin and love for her step-children and grandchildren took priority. In 2013 she found the original printed manuscript and floppy disc in a box and after reading it wondered, "Whatever happened to Danielle?"

Published in 2016, *Danny's Boy* is only the beginning of Danielle's story. We hope you enjoy the journey!

www.ingramcontent.com/pod-product-compliance
Lightning Source LLC
Chambersburg PA
CBHW060942120726
47910CB00002B/458